DOES SHE
LOVE YOU?

What Reviewers Say
About Rachel Spangler's Work

Trails Merge

"Spangler has done her homework and she does a great job describing the day to day workings of a small ski resort. She tells her story with wonderful humor, and gives an accurate voice to each of her characters. Parker Riley's best friend Alexis is as true to the sophisticated 'City' girl as Campbell's father is to the country. *Trails Merge* is a great read that may have you driving to the nearest mountain resort."—*Just About Write*

"Sparks fly and denial runs deep in this excellent second novel by Spangler. The author's love of the subject shines through as skiing, family values and romance fill the pages of this heartwarming story. The setting is stunning, making this reviewer nostalgic for her childhood days spent skiing the bunny hills of Wisconsin."—*Curve* magazine

Learning Curve

"Spangler's title, *Learning Curve*, refers to the growth both of these women make, as they deal with attraction and avoidance. They share a mutual lust, but can lust alone surpass their differences? The answer to that question is told with humor, adventure, and heat."
—*Just About Write*

"[Spangler's] potential shines through, particularly her ability to tap into the angst that accompanies any attempt to alter the perceptions of others…Your homework assignment, read on."—*Curve*

Visit us at www.boldstrokesbooks.com

By the Author

Learning Curve

Trails Merge

The Long Way Home

LoveLife

Spanish Heart

Does She Love You?

DOES SHE LOVE YOU?

by
Rachel Spangler

2013

ISBN 10: 1-60282-886-5
ISBN 13: 978-1-60282-886-5

THIS TRADE PAPERBACK ORIGINAL IS PUBLISHED BY
BOLD STROKES BOOKS, INC.
P.O. BOX 249
VALLEY FALLS, NY 12185

FIRST EDITION: JULY 2013

CREDITS
EDITORS: LYNDA SANDOVAL AND SHELLEY THRASHER
PRODUCTION DESIGN: SUSAN RAMUNDO
COVER DESIGN BY SHERI (GRAPHICARTIST2020@HOTMAIL.COM)

Acknowledgments

The first person I need to thank when thinking about this book is Reba McEntire. I've long been a big fan of hers, and the initial idea for this book came from her duet with Linda Davis called *Does He Love You*. I had a lot of fun playing with various scenarios for women confronting their spouse's mistress. However, that's where the pure fun of this project ended. The subject is ultimately a heavy one that interweaves deep questions about our ability to trust and love in the wake of a crushing betrayal. It was a challenge that offered many rewards, but also a lot of hard emotional work along the way. Thankfully, I've never been in a situation similar to the one my characters find themselves in, but unfortunately, it's not uncommon. I pulled heavily from my best friend and God-baby mama, Heather Lohnes-Kanllakan, whose fortitude, faith, and ability to love again very much inspired the character of Annabelle. Thank you, Heather, both for sharing your experiences and for demonstrating the ability to work through them to something beautiful. I hope the power of love to not just overcome, but to grow, evolve, and ultimately thrive is what readers take away from this story.

I also want to thank Len Barot and the wonderful staff at Bold Strokes Books for taking this story of mine and turning it into the book you're reading now. My editor, Lynda Sandoval, is more than a colleague. She is a friend. She takes the time to understand my vision for every single character, then she makes sure that vision comes across on the page, even if it involves endless phone calls. She edits with a great attention to detail and a wicked sense of humor. Every part of this book is stronger because of her. Sheri worked through several great covers to find the one that best captures the tone we wanted to convey, and as always, she did so perfectly. Thank you to Shelley Thrasher, who did an eagle-eyed copy edit. It was fun to work with her again. Toni Whitaker brilliantly does all things eBooks, and

I love her for it. Thank you to Lori Anderson and Ruth Sternglantz, who do the important work of making sure you can find these books online, and Cindy Cresap, who makes sure the whole process runs smoothly. Finally, thank you to all the other associates and authors who make my job so fun.

Beta readers Toni and Barb continue to work with me as I grow as a writer. They offer encouragement, support, and the best questions to push me and the work forward. I couldn't have turned out this book without them. My students in the Introduction to Romance Writing course I taught also offered tons of suggestions, and more importantly, shared my enthusiasm for telling this story. They were a wonderful bunch of young storytellers who filled me with energy and reminded me what a blessing it is to do this kind of work. I also want to thank all the people who have read my books and taken the time to get in touch with me on my webpage, e-mail, or Facebook. This is a lonely business with little chance to really see your work come to life. Each and every one of you who's taken the time to tell me you read and enjoyed my work has helped keep me going through the hard days of writing this novel.

Finally, thank you to my family, both extended and nuclear, blood and choice, who continue to shower me in love. My son, Jackson, is my light and my reason. I am grateful every day for the fullness of love he brings to my life. My wife, Susan, is both my roots and my wings. If I've written convincingly about trust, faith, and love in this novel, it is only because she has taught me the true meaning of those words. I know I have done nothing so grand as to warrant this abundance of blessings, but have been given them through the grace of God. Soli Deo Gloria.

Dedication

To Heather, who was strong enough to love again.
And for Susie because my career is all your fault.

CHAPTER ONE

February

Annabelle ran through her internal to-do list for the morning. She'd brewed Nic's coffee and packed her suitcase, with the exception of her toothbrush. Nic's suit was freshly pressed in a garment bag hanging in the hall closet, and her travel clothes were folded neatly in the bathroom. She loved these moments when everything was exactly how it should be, and she took pride in knowing the work she'd done helped provide a sanctuary for the woman she loved. She'd put off her next step long enough, but she wanted to let Nic sleep as long as possible, partly because, after thirteen years, she knew how grumpy she was first thing in the morning, but mostly because she wanted to keep her close for as long as possible. She finally pushed open their bedroom door and was struck once again by the blessing of still being in love with the woman in her bed after all these years.

Nic sprawled, one leg and one arm thrown over the pillow Annabelle had tucked beside her when she'd gotten up an hour earlier. Her lips parted slightly and her dark hair was pushed into a makeshift fauxhawk. Nic's dark eyelashes fluttered slightly when Annabelle sat down lightly on the side of the bed, but she didn't actually stir until Annabelle placed a gentle kiss on her temple. Nic snuggled closer to the pillow. The corners of her mouth twitched as if trying to hide a smile.

"Wake up, sleepyhead." Annabelle kissed the dimple in her cheek. Nic closed her eyes tighter as she burrowed into their down comforter. Annabelle had to scoot farther onto the bed to kiss the only bit of skin still exposed, the top of Nic's ear.

Suddenly, Nic sprang to life, wrapping one arm around Annabelle's waist and the other around her shoulders. She quickly pulled her down onto the bed and placed little kisses along her cheek and neck.

Annabelle shrieked and tried to push her off. "You're going to wrinkle my clothes."

"Good, maybe you'll take them off."

"You're so bad."

"You love that about me."

Annabelle rolled her eyes. "And modest, too."

Nic zoomed in on the ticklish spot on Annabelle's side and pressed, eliciting a giggle. "Say you love me."

"You know I do."

She tickled more vigorously. "Say it, Belle. Tell me you love me."

Annabelle laughed and tried to sit up, but Nic quickly straddled her, tickling her all over now.

She could hardly speak through her laughter but managed to squeak out, "I love you."

"What was that?"

Annabelle wrapped her arms about Nic's neck and pulled her down until her lips brushed the ear she'd kissed minutes earlier. "I love you."

Cupping her face, Nic kissed her in earnest. Annabelle sank into the mattress, unable and unwilling to resist. She surrendered to the familiar feel of soft lips against her own. Nic had always been able to shatter her resolve with a kiss, and she hoped that would never change.

They lay intertwined for too long, and yet not long enough, before Nic said, "I hate to go."

"Then don't."

The mood in the room shifted. Annabelle regretted the words immediately.

Nic kissed her curtly on the cheek and got out of bed.

"I'm sorry."

"It's fine." Nic padded into the bathroom, but she left the door open as she started to brush her teeth.

Annabelle stared at the ceiling until she heard the water running to rinse the sink.

"I know you work hard for us. I appreciate it. You know I do. I just miss you."

"We've got a good life, don't we, Belle?"

"Of course we do."

"I hope you think so. I try to make sure you don't want for anything."

That was true. She had everything a woman could ask for: a four-bedroom house, a new Mercedes, a country-club membership, and any little bauble that caught her eye. Nic took so much pride in providing for her that she hardly had the heart to say she didn't really care about any of it. She'd gladly trade everything for a two-bedroom apartment and a partner at home every night.

Nic came back into the room wearing her tailored black slacks and a sky-blue oxford shirt. "I know you get lonely. Why don't you call your sister and go play some tennis at the club today?"

"Maybe I will, but you know I'd rather play with you."

"Reserve us a court for Friday when I get home, and then I'll take you out to dinner anywhere you want. But, if I'm going to be able to afford to keep you in the lifestyle to which we've both grown accustomed, I have to go."

Annabelle got up and followed Nic downstairs. "You know you don't have to do this for me. All I want is you."

Nic looked momentarily frustrated but covered it quickly with a smile. "That's not true, darling. You want a baby, and those little bundles of joy get expensive."

"Oh, Nic, we've got more money in the bank than any of our friends." She didn't want to nag, but she was tired of petty excuses. She gestured as they passed through their expansive foyer to the large, open kitchen. "And we're not lacking for space. How much more do we need?"

"I've actually thought a lot about that."

Annabelle stopped in mid-reach for the coffee pot. She was always the one who broached these particular conversations, not Nic. "What have you been thinking?"

"Just that a senior vice-president of sales would be able to give her wife and child a pretty nice life."

"Nic?"

"And I just so happen to be up for a promotion to senior VP this summer."

"Oh, please, don't joke."

"I'd never joke about our future, Belle. You know I take my responsibilities seriously. I want a family as much as you do. If I put in the hours I need to now, we could turn the spare room into a nursery by next fall."

Annabelle threw her arms around Nic's neck and hugged her tight. "Really?"

"Really."

She kissed Nic fully on the mouth, joy and love pouring out of her.

"Whew, woman. You kiss so well, you make me forget where I'm going today."

She took a hint of pleasure in the lust-filled gaze that clouded Nic's sharp blue eyes, and her desire to drag her back to bed warred with her inner secretary. "You're headed to Atlanta today, then Boston tomorrow."

"Ugh, Boston will be wretchedly cold this time of year."

She handed Nic her garment bag and a travel mug of coffee, sad the moment had passed but proud of her ability to keep things running smoothly. "When whoever's in New England's through with you, I'll make sure you get warmed up properly, but you'd better get going or you'll be late."

"I see how it is. I just mention a baby and you're ready to push me out the door."

"No." Annabelle shook her head and hoped Nic knew that wasn't true. "I miss you so much when you're gone, but the sooner you go, the sooner you come home to me."

"Fair enough, Belle." Nic smiled and kissed her one more time, then grabbed her suitcase and headed out the door.

Annabelle waited until her taillights faded from view before wandering back upstairs.

She needed to change her wrinkled shirt and make their bed, but instead she entered the room across from hers. She'd secretly considered this room the nursery ever since she and Nic had moved in five years earlier. The space currently held a four-poster, queen-sized bed with a matching oak dresser and nightstand, but Annabelle saw the space differently. In her mind, a crib stood against the other wall with a rocking chair instead of a nightstand. They'd put a changing table by the window and fill the dresser with clothes so tiny they'd make the drawers seem enormous in comparison.

Could her dreams really be so close to coming true? Despite her frequent assurances that she wanted kids as badly as Annabelle did, Nic had been hesitant to talk about the particulars of having a family. Responsibility weighed so heavily on her that surely she wouldn't have broached the subject at all this morning unless she felt ready.

She closed the door as softly as if a sleeping baby was actually there. She had work to do around the house and errands to run, but they'd all be a little easier now with the knowledge that she and Nic were equally committed to the idea of family.

"I want to go home," Davis Chandler said over the music that wasn't loud enough to be obnoxious but still grated on her nerves. Blake's was little more than a neighborhood bar on a weeknight. Aside from the mostly male clientele, its brick walls, cheeky waiters, and eight-dollar burgers made it pretty standard fare for Midtown Atlanta. "Nothing's happening here anyway."

"That's because we're at a men's bar, dear, and you're the one who chose it. Let's go to My Sister's Room."

"No. I don't want to go all the way out to Decatur this late."

"It's only nine o'clock, Davis. You promised to go out with me tonight."

"I did. I came, I saw, I got tired. And you're not having fun either. Other than one diesel dyke playing pool in the corner, we haven't seen another woman in an hour. Even you like more options than that."

"Oh, I wouldn't go that far," Cass said, giving the denim-and-leather-clad woman another once-over. "But there's no one here for you, and I think you planned it that way. Why else choose a men's bar on a Tuesday night?"

"It's right around the corner from my house, I'm on a deadline for work, I wanted someplace that serves food, and—"

"You've given up on ever having sex again."

"I haven't given up on sex. I'm just tired of all the other crap that comes with it." Ten years ago she probably couldn't have imagined saying that phrase, but at thirty-one she was a little more level-headed, or maybe she just wasn't having any sex good enough to put up with the awkwardness, disappointment, or heartbreak that usually followed.

"I don't put up with any crap, and I have plenty of sex."

"You told me the last woman you took home wore yellow dishwashing gloves the whole time."

Cass smirked. "I didn't say that didn't have its charms."

"Well, good for your open-mindedness, but I don't want to wake up to lover-Rubbermaid every morning."

"I didn't wake up with her." Cass seemed appalled at the idea. "And that's your problem. You go into everything looking for the U-Haul."

Davis sighed. "I don't need a U-Haul, but all I've found lately are liars, cheats, and skeezeballs."

"Maybe your standards are a bit high."

"Possibly, but I'm done, Cass. No more spending the night with someone I don't want to spend the next morning with, too."

"What about that one?" Cass asked, nodding to someone who'd just come through the front door. "I wouldn't mind having her for dinner, breakfast, and brunch."

Davis intended only to glance over her shoulder, but a glance turned into a second look that edged close to a stare. The woman looked like a lesbian Prince Charming with her dark hair, high cheekbones, and sculpted jaw. Her black slacks and blue oxford were disheveled just enough to add a rakish edge to her business professional vibe, and the dimples encasing her smile when she caught Davis gawking almost did her in.

"So much for sleeping alone." Cass's voice brought Davis back to their conversation.

"What?" She turned back toward the bar and tried to sip her amaretto and Coke casually.

"Don't pretend you don't want to suck on that eye candy."

"Geeze, Cass, why do you have to go there right away? Why can't I just say I'd like to get to know her?"

"You can, so long as we both understand you want to know her in the Biblical sense."

"No," Davis said emphatically. "She's attractive, but that's not enough for me anymore. She could be a pervert or a drug addict or married. I mean, really, why's a woman who looks like her in a gay men's bar on a Tuesday night?"

"I could ask you the same thing," came the sound of a woman's voice over her shoulder.

Davis turned around slowly. "I'm sorry. Do you make a habit of eavesdropping on other people's conversations?"

"I do, actually," the woman said with a maddeningly confident smile. "It's rude, I know, but really it's the least of my faults, what with being a drug-addicted pervert and all."

Cass snorted and raised her glass. "Well-played."

The woman turned to the bartender. "I called in an order to go. The last name's McCoy."

"It'll be a few more minutes. Want a drink?"

"Sure, I'll take an amaretto and Coke."

"You two have the same drink order," Cass said. "I think it's a sign."

"Maybe, maybe not," the woman said. "The true test would come if the bartender says, 'We just have Pepsi.'"

"Shut your mouth," Davis replied forcefully.

Prince Charming laughed. "Well, then, I think this could be the start of a beautiful friendship."

"No so fast," Davis cut in. She wasn't about to get swept away in another pretty face, even one with dimples. "You never answered my first question. Why are you in a gay bar at nine on a Tuesday?"

"You mean aside from jonesing for an 8-ball?"

"Obviously."

"Sorry to disappoint you, but I'm staying at the Wyndham down the road, and I'm sick of eating in a hotel room."

That she could understand. She ate her fair share of bad food in lonely rooms, but that didn't mean she was softening. "Why order the food to go?"

The woman crooked an amused smile. "Now you've caught me in my big perversion. I intend to take my sandwich and eat it in Piedmont Park because I like the way the skyline lights up the darkness from there."

Davis frowned as she thought of a little grassy knoll where she liked to watch the sunset behind the high-rises. The idea of this woman she wanted to be suspicious of enjoying the same view made it much harder to keep her resolve.

"Order for McCoy," the bartender called from the other end of the bar.

"Well, ladies, it's been fun being interrogated by you. I hope you have a lovely night."

"Sure, and any time you need someone to sass you into submission, come on back," Davis quipped with the last of her resolve not to be any easy mark.

"I'll keep that in mind," she said with another beautiful smile, and walked away.

Davis watched her go, wishing she'd made her invitation a little nicer. She'd just finished telling Cass she wanted to meet a woman she was actually interested in getting to know better, and yet she'd spent the last ten minutes pushing one away. Maybe her standards *were* too high, or her trust issues too deep. Was it so unreasonable to think single, attractive, socially adept lesbians still existed in Atlanta? There was really only one way to find out.

Davis slapped a twenty on the bar and faked a yawn. "I'm calling it a night, too."

"Fine. Go. Both of you lonely bastards," Cass said theatrically. "The night is young and so am I. I'm going to cuddle up to Diesel Dyke across the room and see how I like the smell of motor oil in bed."

"You have fun with that, and be careful."

"Me be careful? You're the one about to go to the park at night with an admitted pervert."

Davis feigned shock.

"Don't deny it. Just go before she gets away."

Davis kissed Cass on the cheek and headed out the door.

Prince Charming was only half a block ahead, walking slowly, and Davis took a second to enjoy the view before she caught up and fell into step beside her.

"All right. Well, if I'm about to go to the park with a pervert at night, we should at least know each other's names."

"Sounds reasonable, assuming I can trust you to give me your real name."

Davis grinned. "I suppose that's a chance you'll have to take. I'm Davis."

"Nice to meet you, Davis. I'm Nic McCoy."

❖

Nic could stop right now.

She could tell Davis she was tired and had an early flight, or, better yet, she could tell her she had a wife of thirteen years at home. Women hit on her all the time, and she always said no.

Well, she almost always said no.

Davis struck her as one of those women she should definitely say no to. She seemed too smart, too together to settle for any half-worked excuses or easy outs. Even after a few minutes, she could tell Davis wasn't like anyone else in her life, and while that excited her, it was a complication she didn't need. She should end their little flirtation before it became something more. Instead, she took a seat on a park bench and pulled a double cheeseburger out of a paper bag. "Here, split this with me."

"Don't offer me something to be polite," Davis said. "I will not hesitate to eat your dinner. I'm not one of those girls who watches her figure."

"Well, I am, or at least I should be. Please, you'll save me from just injecting the fat right into my love handles."

"When you put it that way, how could I resist? The first thing I thought when I saw you was, 'She's cute but a little pudgy.'"

Nic laughed. Women didn't usually talk to her like that, not at work and not at home. Annabelle certainly didn't.

Belle. Good. Think of Belle.

Think of her blue eyes and her shy smile. Think about how lost you'd be without her, how much you depend on her to keep you steady. Think of her at home all soft and sexy in your bed. Think of her cooking breakfast and talking about a baby...and putting so much freaking pressure on you to live a perfectly orchestrated life.

God, what's the matter with me?

"Hey, space cadet, you going to pass me that burger or not?"

"Sure." Nic tore the burger in half and handed part of it to Davis.

"I like to come watch the sunset here sometimes, but I've never stayed past dark, you know, because only perverts go to the park at night," Davis said, then looked around and softened slightly. "It's really beautiful, though."

"Yes, it is." Nic agreed, but she wasn't looking at the city. She was captivated by the unexpectedly sassy redhead sitting next to her. Why did she have to be a redhead? That, combined with her hypnotic green eyes, made Davis even harder to resist. Still, she had to try. "Hey, Davis, there's something you should know before we go any further."

"Oh, here it comes," Davis said ominously, taking a big bite of the burger and swallowing, having barely chewed. "Let me guess, genital warts?"

Nic coughed and sputtered part of her burger onto her lap. "What?"

"You've got genital warts?"

"No."

"You're on a prison work release?"

"I've never been in prison."

"You're really a man who's transitioning?" Davis kept eating her burger as if having a completely normal conversation. "Actually that's not a total deal-breaker, but I'd have questions."

Nic chuckled. "Good to know, but no, all my plumbing is original."

"Are you carrying a concealed firearm?"

"No, Davis, it's just—"

"You want to play blood sports?"

"I don't even know what that means."

Davis stood up. "Oh, shit, you really did bring me here to rape me."

"Jesus, no." Nic rubbed her face. "Man, who screwed you up so bad your mind goes there so quickly?"

"Ugh, you could fill a small phone book with the names on that list." Davis sighed and flopped back onto the bench. "There's no one person to blame, unless of course you want to blame me."

"Blame you?"

"For believing them."

"Ah." Nic rushed to tell this witty, beautiful, and funny woman that any woman who hurt her wasn't worth her, and then she remembered she'd probably be one more name on the list of disappointments.

"It's a fairy tale anyway," Davis said. "No one ever really has everything."

"Maybe that's true." *I certainly seem to have it all, and yet here I am reaching for more.* "But that doesn't mean we don't keep chasing it."

Davis polished off her half of the hamburger and drew her knees to her chest. "I don't know. I've got a dream job, a great place to live, a little money in savings, and wonderful friends. Maybe that needs to be enough."

She was right. Nic should tell her so. They were both blessed beyond what the majority of the world could even wish for, and yet here they were both yearning for more, some intangible they both missed amid the seeming perfection. Were they greedy? Unrealistic? Or were they meant to meet tonight? They were clearly searching for something or someone to fill some unnamed need. And Davis looked like she knew how to fill a need with her sexy lips, tight blue jeans, and those green eyes. It really was her eyes that Nic couldn't pull away from. Something deep and mischievous filled them, something that made her feel challenged, excited, alive. Or maybe the thrill of the chase stirred her emotions, but either way she couldn't remember the last time she'd felt like this.

"I'm not demanding a forever kind of let's-go-pick-out-china-patterns relationship," Davis whispered. "I'm just looking for a little passion."

"Passion." Nic jumped up. "That's it."

"What?"

"I was sitting here trying to decide what you're stirring in me. It's passion."

"Me?"

"Yes, you." Nic reached for her hand. "I feel loyalty and duty and caring and responsibility, and even love, all the time, but I can't remember the last time I felt passionate enough to do something against my better judgment."

Davis cautiously took Nic's outstretched hand. "What's that?"

Instead of answering, Nic pulled Davis into her arms. Their lips met in an explosion of heat and need. It didn't take coaxing. Davis opened up willingly, eagerly, her lips parting to welcome Nic's tongue. Refusing to be a passive passenger, Nic returned the kiss with ferocity. There was no going back. Nic felt weak, and she didn't care. How could something so wrong feel so damn perfect?

She'd never been one to think clearly with a woman in her arms, so she chose to not think at all. She didn't think about what she'd do in the morning. She didn't think when they raced back to her hotel and fell into bed. All she let herself do was feel. She reveled in the softness of bare skin as she stripped off Davis's tight shirt and thrilled at the hum of her own pulse as she peeled away Davis's blue jeans. Aching to release the pressure building in her coiled muscles, she positioned herself over Davis's body. She got lost in the realm of the physical, soaking up the sight of Davis's lithe body arching up to meet hers. The subtle taste of sweat as she licked her way from one nipple to the other and the mingled scent of their growing arousal burned away her ability to feel anything other than lust.

They panted, kissed, nipped, and sucked as Nic worked her hand between Davis's legs until she was positioned perfectly to push inside her. Davis wrapped her strong thighs around Nic, trying to pull her in, but Nic summoned all her fortitude to hold off. She was able to assert some semblance of self-control as she teased around the edges of where she really wanted to be, intending to draw the encounter out as long as she could, but Davis dug her fingernails into Nic's back and, thrusting up, panted, "Fuck me now."

Being wanted was a drug to Nic. She lunged forward and crashed into Davis. Hammering into her, their bodies rocked in a primal rhythm. She flicked her thumb across Davis's clit and attempted to keep it there as they continued fucking. Thankfully they were so turned on by that point it didn't take any great coordination to send Davis over the edge. She came loudly, clutching tightly and trying to muffle a shout with her mouth against Nic's neck.

She shuddered and contracted around Nic's fingers, pulling every last bit of pleasure she could from the body against hers, but even as the tremors subsided, she started to kiss and suck her way up to Nic's ear. "Let's see if you receive as good as you give."

Nic's clit begged to answer that question, but she generally basked in the afterglow as a courtesy to her lover. "Don't you want some time to catch your breath?"

"My, someone has a high opinion of herself." Davis laughed and pushed Nic onto her back. "Or are you one of those dykes whose ego is going to crumble if I flip your script?"

"Flip my script?"

Davis straddled Nic's hips, her naked body looming firm and deliciously touchable. "You know, if I top you, rock your world, fuck you like a piston, and turn you into a big ol' pillow queen."

"Considering how turned on I got at that explanation, I'm pretty sure I don't have a problem with it."

Nic sat up and took a nipple between her lips, giving it a playful suck, but Davis pushed her back at arm's length. "Good, then turn around."

"Why?"

"You ask too many questions."

Nic bit her tongue. She wasn't used to being bossed around in any area of her life, especially in bed, but she did as she was told and rolled onto her stomach, then pushed up on her knees facing the hotel-style headboard. Davis pressed up behind her, nipples hard against Nic's back as she snaked one arm around her shoulder and the other around her waist. With the upper hand she went to work squeezing and caressing Nic's breasts, and with the other she began to draw delicate circles around her clit, getting a little firmer with each pass.

Nic groaned and leaned forward, bracing herself with one arm against the headboard. A flush spread across Nic's face and chest as a by-product of her arousal and the heat of their bodies pressed together. A sheen of sweat covered them both from the exertion of increasingly erratic movements, and Nic's focus blurred. She lolled her head back onto Davis's shoulder and gave in to the sensations building between her legs. Davis's breath pulsed heavy and heated against her neck as she continued to stroke. When Nic's legs shook with her impending orgasm, Davis held her up and whispered, "Come on, let go, come for me."

Nic tipped into oblivion, the release rattling through her core and radiating through her limbs until they both collapsed onto the bed. "Wow," Nic said, after a few stunned moments, "you're very good at that."

"You're not bad yourself," Davis said with a little grin, then rolling onto her back added a little bit more seriously, "so much for being careful and taking it slow."

"Yeah." Nic rubbed her eyes. This had been an epic failure of restraint on both their parts. The regret would seep in soon enough, but she tried to shut it out for a few more minutes.

"What were you going to tell me back at the park? You know, the thing I should know before we did what we just did."

So much for holding off the guilt. "Oh, yeah, about that."

"The room is filled with webcams, and you broadcast the big event all over the Internet?"

"Geeze." Nic rolled onto her side. "Why do you assume I had something awful to tell you?"

"Because I make bad decisions quickly and always get the awful news too late. Go ahead and lay yours on me."

Nic sighed. She should just say she had a wife, rip off the Band-Aid, go ahead and be a disappointment to Davis and Belle, and to herself. Davis expected it from her. Why couldn't she say the words? They could have a big scene and never see each other again, or was that why she couldn't bring herself to confess? She wanted to see her again.

"Tell me, Nic."

"I have to catch a flight to Boston at five thirty in the morning." She glanced at the clock. "I have to leave in a few hours."

Davis sat up and swung her legs over the edge of the bed. "Oh, well, that's convenient. I guess it could be worse. I mean, really, you're staying in a hotel. I should've seen the whole one-night-stand coming."

Nic watched Davis collect her clothes and put them on.

Keep your mouth shut. Let her go.

"I'll be back in town late Thursday night."

Davis stopped and turned to face her. She was in her jeans and her bra but hadn't found her shirt yet. She had a beautiful body, and her eyes were even more alluring. "You'll be back in town and…?"

"And if you don't mind giving your number to a perverted drug addict like me, I'll give you a call when I get in."

Davis smiled a little half smile that seemed to suggest she wanted to be happier but still held something back. "Why don't you give me your number, and I'll call you Thursday if I'm up for a late dinner in the park?"

Shit. Nic hadn't thought that through. She didn't need women calling her at home. "Uh, yeah, sure, but just to warn you, I'm terrible about remembering to carry my cell with me."

"Uh-huh." Davis pulled on her shirt. "I get it. If you 'forget to carry it with you' on Thursday, I'll get the message."

She was challenging her again, and Nic couldn't resist a challenge. She grabbed a pen and a hotel stationery pad off the nightstand. She scribbled her cell number on the paper, folded it in half, and held it out for Davis.

"All right, Nic McCoy." Davis took the paper. "We'll see what happens Thursday."

"You don't have to leave, you know? I've still got a few hours."

"Thanks, but I'm not ready for a sleep-over yet."

"I understand," Nic said with a mix of disappointment and relief. "Can I walk you home or at least get you a cab?"

Davis rolled her eyes. "I'm a big girl." She took two steps toward the door before turning around and walking back to Nic and placed one searing, open-mouth kiss on her lips. Nic cupped her face, their tongues sweeping and searching as she fought the urge to pull her back into bed. Before she could, Davis stood and said, "There's a little something to miss until Thursday."

Nic blew out a low whistle. "Yes, ma'am."

Davis walked away, and Nic let herself enjoy the view one last time before the door closed. She lay back on the bed with one hand behind her head and stared at the ceiling for a few minutes until her cell phone vibrated on the table signaling she had a new message. Smiling smugly, thinking Davis decided she couldn't wait until Thursday, she sat up and reached for the phone and readied herself for round two. Her heart thudded when the caller ID read *Belle*.

With shaky hands she pressed the button to check the message and read, "I hope you're sleeping soundly, but in case you're not, I wanted you to know somebody out here is thinking about you. I love you."

Nic dropped the phone on the bed and covered her face with her hands.

God. What have I done?

CHAPTER TWO

Annabelle had been awake since exactly five thirty in the morning. When she had nothing to do, why couldn't she sleep late? Probably because Nic wasn't there, or maybe she wasn't tired enough to need much sleep because she didn't do anything all day. She tried to stay busy with weekly tennis dates with her sister, Liz, and almost as frequent movie dates with her niece, Julie. She tended some flowering plants around the house and would have taken care of the yard if Nic hadn't hired landscapers and a lawn service. She sat on the board of the neighborhood association and remained active in her University of Georgia alumni circle. She would have happily taken on more, but there just wasn't much call for lesbian housewives in suburban Georgia. There was no real gay community to speak of, and even if there were, Nic preferred them to stay away from "political issues" for the sake of her career.

She'd spent an hour flipping through the one thousand channels Nic thought their television needed and couldn't find a single thing to hold her interest, so at seven thirty she'd walked around the subdivision and watched all her neighbors leave for work. On mornings like this she regretted having left her job as a first-grade teacher. They didn't need the money. Nic made more than enough to support them, so it seemed wrong to take a job away from someone dependent on the income. Nic had been proud to give her that kind of freedom, and at the time Annabelle had thought it would only be a matter of months before they'd start trying to get pregnant. Three years later and still no baby or wife at home to care for—had she made the right decision?

Now sitting at the country club hours later she thought she was just being silly. She had a beautiful home, a supportive family, financial security, and a thirteen-year relationship with a partner who spoiled her. She would spend the morning playing tennis at a top-tier country club, then have her pick of five-star meals. She could spend the afternoon sipping a mint julep, sleeping in the shade, or shopping until she couldn't walk.

Still…

A little voice in her head told her no matter what she did or how much she had, she'd sleep alone tonight. She told that little voice to hush.

"Hey, little sister." Liz's voice pulled her back into the moment. "You ready to play?"

"You bet."

"Be prepared for some aggression on my serve this morning. Jason blew off his night with the kids again. I missed my haircut appointment and can't get rescheduled for two weeks."

"I'm sorry, hon. You should've called me." Annabelle wasn't surprised. Her ex-brother-in-law had never been as fond of anyone as he was of himself. "How'd the kids take it?"

"Unfortunately they didn't seem to mind. They're used to him." Liz blew back a strand of her blond hair. "Part of me just wishes he'd disappear for good."

"If you mentioned that to Daddy, I'm sure it could be arranged."

Liz laughed. "Don't think I haven't thought about it, but Daddy's not the kind who'd let something like that go down quietly. We'd all end up in prison."

"True." Daddy was a powerful man in their part of the state. A third-generation horse rancher, he had both money and Southern heritage. Not the kind of man who minced words or held his temper, Buddy Taylor had a soft spot only for his little girls and his grandkids. "And, let's be honest. None of us look good in orange."

"It's my fault for marrying an artist," Liz said as they walked toward the courts. "I just loved his free spirit, thought he'd be so much more fun than one of these workaholic country-club types Mama always tried to set me up with."

"Oh, that type wouldn't have made you any happier, Liz."

"Easy for you to say. That's exactly the type you ended up with, and you're happy."

Mostly, Annabelle thought. "But Nic isn't exactly the type Mama had in mind." She rolled her eyes. "She like to have fainted the first time I brought her home."

Liz laughed. "That was one for the baby book. You could've told her ahead of time that Nic was short for Nicole and not Nicholas."

"I figured she'd give me an earful if I told her in advance, but she's too polite to actually be rude to a guest in her home."

"Well, you did peg that one right, but Daddy was a bigger risk. What were you thinking?"

"I didn't think. I was twenty and in love. I just didn't see how anyone could just not immediately fall for Nic."

Liz shook her head. "I'll never forget the vein popping out in Daddy's forehead while he grilled Nic. You could just see him getting madder and madder when Nic answered each question flawlessly."

Annabelle would never forget that day either. Each interaction was so very dramatic, like one of those great Southern plays where everything explodes in the third act. Ultimately her father's anger at the situation clashed with his inability to deny his baby girl anything.

"And when Daddy took her for that walk to the barn, you looked just green, but I knew Nic had won," Liz said. "Ever since then he's treated her like any of the boys we brought home."

"And Nic's the only one who continues to meet his standards even after all this time." Annabelle smiled proudly. "I really am blessed, aren't I?"

"I never thought I'd say this back when you told me you were gay, but yeah, I think you're the lucky one." Liz smiled wryly. "If I didn't love you so much, I'd be tempted to spare the tennis balls and just hit you with this racket."

"Okay, okay, give me a second while you get warmed up, and you can ace me all over the court."

"I'm going to hold you to that," Liz said, walking ahead while Annabelle fished through her purse and found her fancy cell phone, another extravagant gift from Nic.

She counted the rings before Nic's voice told her to leave a message. "Hey, baby, I know you're in meetings all day, but I just wanted to say thank you for being you. I don't tell you this enough, but I'm so proud of you. I love you."

The message didn't seem like nearly enough, but words would have to suffice for now. When Nic got home on Friday, she'd make sure to show her just how much she meant them.

❖

"I don't know, she's the kind of woman who could really sweep me off my feet if I let her," Davis said as she put a frozen loaf of garlic bread in the oven.

"From what you told me she already did knock you off your feet and right into her bed." Cass raised her glass of red wine in salute. "Have I mentioned yet how proud of you I am?"

"Yes, but that's not what I'm talking about. I could really fall for Nic if I'm not careful."

"Wait, that's a bad thing? You said you wanted more than a one-night stand."

"I did, but there's something about her. I can't think logically when she levels those intense blue eyes on me." Her heart fluttered in a mix of attraction and fear. "I can't believe I slept with her already. I probably shouldn't call her tonight."

"I'm confused," Cass said, sipping from her glass of red wine. "The woman looks like an ad for sex goddesses, and she apparently has the skills to back up her marketing. She can hold a coherent conversation, and you find her more than a little interesting, so... you're not going to call her?"

"She could hurt me, Cass."

"I thought you said she wasn't into anything kinky."

"Emotionally." Davis rolled her eyes. "She could hurt me emotionally, and I'm not sure I can go through another disappointment."

"And if you just blow her off, stay safe at home with your pasta out of a can and bread out of a bag, your life will be so much richer?"

"I've just learned if something seems too good to be true, it probably is."

"So you'll settle for something that doesn't seem very good in the first place?"

Davis sighed. "I hate it when you're the logical one in this friendship."

"Me, too." Cass polished off her wine. "You know you're going to call her. Do I have to sit here all night and talk you through each step?"

"No. I'm capable of dialing the phone, and as much as I want to pretend to be logical and guarded, the minute she walks in the door, all my planning will go out the window."

"Don't analyze this to death. Just take tonight for tonight, and don't let yourself think about happily ever after."

"You're right. I can do that," Davis said as convincingly as possible. "I'm going to call her. No, I'll sound too nervous and needy. I'll just text her my address."

"Good, play cool."

"Are you sure that won't seem too slutty? I don't want to be a booty call."

"You slept with her on your first date, so it's not like modesty is an option for you."

"Thanks." Davis pulled out her phone and typed a brief message saying Nic was welcome to join her for dinner at her place, then hit send. "Shit, I didn't say who it was from."

"You think she has more than one unidentified woman in Atlanta inviting her to dinner?"

"If so, then she's no longer invited here," Davis snapped. "Oh, but what if she thinks it's a wrong number? Maybe I should send another text saying the last text was from me, but that wouldn't seem very cool or casual or confident. Damn, why is this so hard?"

"Because you're making it hard."

Before she could come up with a clever retort, her phone buzzed. Davis glanced at the message on her screen and smiled.

Cass raised her eyebrows. "What'd she say?"

"See you soon."

"Uh-huh, I'm going. I don't want to see the gooey puddle of mush you turn into when she arrives."

"I'll be cool. I can do that," she said, trying to convince herself as much as Cass.

Cass laughed and hugged her. "No, you probably can't, but it doesn't hurt to try."

"I'll do that, and I'll call you tomorrow if I'm not too embarrassed by my behavior."

"No, please, give me the full recap, especially if you're embarrassed."

Davis opened the door and pointed to the stairwell down from her studio apartment. "Go."

She closed the door and scanned the room. There really wasn't much to see. The small kitchen was separated from the rest of the place by a bar. She had her couch set up to face the TV and provide a sort of barrier from the part of the room with her bed and dresser. The back of the space had a small enclosure with a bathroom. The whole place was tiny, even by Midtown standards, but since it was only her and she didn't have a car, location was paramount. Finding this place right out of college had been a coup. The rent was the right price, and it hadn't gone up since, even though the gays had gentrified the neighborhood. It had the added benefit of horrifying her family. They thought it was a dump and hated her living alone in the city. They thought everything about Atlanta was dangerous, and Davis loved that she thrived here.

Was Nic a city dyke or a country dyke? Her clothes, her hotel, and the fact that she jet-setted between Atlanta, Boston, and who knew how many other places suggested she probably didn't live in a six-hundred-square-foot efficiency above a pet-supply store.

A knock on the door roused her from her musings. She took a deep breath and checked her reflection in the window quickly to see that none of her short red hair was standing on end. *Just be cool.*

She opened the door. Nic grinned a sheepish little grin, her dimples sending a shot of affection-laced attraction right through Davis.

"Hi."

"Hi."

"How was your trip?"

"Fine. Cold." Nic shrugged. "Businessy."

Davis nodded, trying to maintain her resolve. *God, she's good looking.* "That's what you went for, right?"

"Yeah."

The silence stretched between them as Davis tried to decipher her conflicting urges to just shut the door in her face or rip Nic's clothes off.

"So…" Nic rocked on the heels of her shiny black loafers. "Do you want go somewhere, or do you want to, I don't know, not go somewhere?"

"I haven't decided yet," Davis replied honestly. She wanted this woman, and that terrified her.

"Okay," Nic said. "Is there something I could do to help you along? Submit to drug testing, a polygraph maybe."

"Sorry, no. I'm being silly." She stepped back to let Nic pass through. "Come in. Have you eaten?"

"No, I'd just gotten to the hotel when you texted."

"Help yourself to the liquor cabinet. I've got some pasta cooking."

Nic poured an amaretto and Coke, reminding Davis that they shared the same drink. It was such a little thing, nothing she would ever put her trust in, but right now she wanted any excuse to believe she wasn't making a big mistake.

Nic perched on one of the rickety bar stools and looked around like she was trying to find something to comment on.

"It's not much, but it's home."

"No, it's you. Great location."

"Yeah, I don't have a car, so it's handy. Close to public transit, and I can ride my bike almost anywhere I want to go."

"Aren't you worried about crime, riding alone after dark?"

Davis bit her lip. The comment sounded too much like her family. "I don't need a protector, if that's what you're asking."

"No, I didn't mean to imply that. I've just never met a woman who lives like this."

"It's not for everyone," Davis said, searching for something else to talk about. She'd had dates, and she'd had one-night stands, but their last encounter didn't really qualify as either, putting them in this weird realm of uncharted relationships.

Nic sighed. "Look, I'm sorry. I shouldn't have come over. We don't really know each other, but after the other night it didn't seem right to not show. Now I'm not sure. It doesn't seem like you really want me here."

"To be honest, I'm not sure I do, or I guess I want you here, but I'm not sure I should."

"Fair enough. I'm not sure I should be here, if that makes you feel any better."

"I'm not looking to get into a relationship right now." Davis didn't know why she'd said that. She did want a relationship, someone to share her life with. When had she gotten too bitter to admit that? Like somehow saying the wish out loud would mean she had to face how far she was from achieving it.

"That's good. My life is complicated." Nic seemed like she wanted to say more but struggled for the words, or maybe she struggled not to say too much. Could she have the same fears as Davis? "Yet here I am."

"You don't have to explain."

"I feel like I should." Nic looked guilty. "I don't want you to think I'm one more in your long line of bed-wetting pyromaniacs. You've obviously been through a lot, and like I said, my life is complicated." She paused. "But you're beautiful, and I wish I could get to know you a little better, so I keep getting the urge to justify myself."

"If you tell me some sad story about your life and your job and your ex-girlfriend or whatever, then I'll have to tell you mine, and then we'll feel a great responsibility to worry about wrecking each other, and I'm not sure I could handle any more worries."

"Wow. Okay then. So you didn't invite me over here for some big declaration about where our relationship is headed?"

"No," Davis said, even though she did want to hear the answer to that question, or maybe she didn't. She stirred the pasta and tried to keep her expectations low. "I'm barely convinced you're not a park pervert, much less relationship material."

"Good to know."

Davis whirled back around and pointed the pasta spoon at Nic. "But this isn't a booty call either, so don't get any ideas about popping over for a quickie anytime you're in town."

Nic held up her hands as her cheeks turned red, "No, ma'am, I wouldn't ever make assumptions like that. I won't make assumptions at all."

"Good." Davis plated two helpings of spaghetti and slid them onto the bar.

"So, no planning, no heavy talk about our pasts, no assumptions about our future? Just live in the moment?"

"Yep."

"I don't think I've ever tried that before."

Davis took the garlic bread out of the oven and plunked it right onto the bar between their plates. "I've never been a go-with-the-flow kind of girl before either, but it's not like planning has worked all that great for me. What do I have to lose?"

Nic waited until Davis sat down beside her, then raised her glass. "Here's to nothing to lose."

Davis echoed the toast but had to force herself to swallow the drink. Sitting there sharing a meal with a gorgeous, witty, understanding woman, she thought she actually had quite a bit to lose, namely her heart.

❖

Nic drove the speed limit. Once she got off the jam-packed fruit loop around Atlanta she always did at least ten miles an hour over, but tonight she limped along in the far right lane. She'd already texted Belle to say she'd be late since she couldn't bring herself to actually call. Nic had wrapped herself in a cocoon of denial while with Davis. She'd had every intention of breaking it off on Thursday night. She'd even planned what she needed to say. She'd started to tell Davis her life was too full, too complicated, and Davis deserved better, but somehow the speech didn't translate to a breakup. Instead, Davis had set her own parameters. She didn't want a commitment; she'd only wanted her company and, later in the night, her body.

They'd talked about books, movies, and food. They'd discussed their favorite spots in Atlanta, current events, and sports. Exploring someone emotionally and physically had excited her. They'd had their bumbling moments and awkward silences, but she'd found even those thrilling in the sense that nothing was a foregone conclusion. She'd spent at least a decade on autopilot, but during her time with Davis, Nic didn't have a past or responsibilities. She was free, and life was fun again. She'd never once felt guilty with Davis, but the closer she got to home, the more her conscience made up for lost time.

She didn't live in a fantasy world. Pretending to be a free woman didn't actually make her one. There had been a couple of other women over the years, but always during hazy nights in dark bars. None of them ever saw her the next morning, and none of them connected in a meaningful way. Most importantly, Nic had never felt unfaithful. She knew it was a weak justification, but she'd never shared anything that seemed more personal than a handshake with the others. Those encounters had been only physical, and even in that area they'd always fallen short of what she had with Belle. This time, though, she couldn't deny her betrayal. She talked to Davis in ways she used to talk to Belle, beautiful sweet Belle, who'd never done anything but be everything Nic asked of her.

She rubbed her face and her car hit the rumble strip. She had to pull herself together. Falling apart after the fact wouldn't undo what she'd done, and a teary confession of her sins wouldn't bring any peace to Belle. In fact, Belle didn't need any peace. As far as she knew, she had everything she wanted. Was it better to tell her the truth and shatter her happiness just to ease Nic's own guilt?

She drove off the interstate and turned into their subdivision. The yards were immaculately cared for, and the houses were grandiose. She'd lived here for years, but she was still hit with a bout of pride every time she pulled into her driveway. It wasn't a mansion, but it sure beat a one-room apartment down the back alley of some seedy city street. She'd done well for them, better than anyone expected from a piece of no-name trailer trash from a hick town in southern Georgia. She couldn't lose that now.

Belle stood waiting at the door wearing a calf-length denim skirt that showcased her hourglass frame, with a white V-neck shirt and brown boots. Her long blond locks were loosely braided and her smile as sweet as honey. She had been pretty in college, but over the years Belle had grown into the perfect picture of Southern beauty.

She threw her arms around Nic's neck and kissed her cheek. "Welcome home, baby. I missed you."

"Did you really?"

"You know I did. This house isn't a home without you."

"You say the sweetest things."

Belle laughed and took Nic's suitcase. "Come inside and I'll tell you some more of them."

Nic walked through her front door and was surrounded by the aroma of freshly fried chicken and baking cornbread. There had to be a full feast waiting just around the corner. "Belle, what have you done? It smells better than a restaurant in here. I thought I was taking you out to dinner."

"Oh, did you really want to go out? You've had to eat out all week, and I know none of the restaurants make chicken the way you like, so I just took care of it for you." She led her into the dining room to a fully set table with a white linen tablecloth, their good china loaded down with chicken, collard greens, mashed potatoes and gravy, and tall glasses of sweet tea, no doubt all made from scratch. It looked like a photograph out of *Southern Living*. "Besides, now I have leftover buttermilk to make you biscuits and gravy for breakfast in the morning."

"It looks like you've been cooking all afternoon. You didn't have to do this."

"I know I didn't have to, darling. I wanted to."

"Why?" Nic asked, honestly in awe of her wife's devotion.

Belle smiled a smile so sweet it implied she thought the question just a little silly. "Because I love you."

Emotion tightened Nic's throat, and she had to blink away her tears. She'd risked all this, everything she'd worked for, everything she'd been so blessed with, and for what? A few hours of carelessness, the illusion of freedom, the thrill of a chase? What an idiot, and so damn weak. Davis was an unknown, and Nic had gotten swept up in the excitement of her newness. But Belle was beautiful too, and more than that they shared a history. Their fears, their dreams. Belle had loved her when she'd had nothing. She'd seen her sick and weak. She'd held her when she'd cried and had faith in her even when she'd fallen. What kind of person would put her whims before the feelings of the woman she loved most in the world? Certainly someone unworthy of that kind of love.

"What is it, Nic?" Belle asked. "We can go out if you want to. The food will keep."

Nic pulled her in, holding her snugly to her chest. "No, it's perfect. You're too good to me, Belle. I don't deserve you."

"Hush now," Belle whispered. "None of that. You take such good care of me. It makes me feel good to take care of you, too. Why don't you sit down and tell me all about your week?"

"Okay." Nic nodded. She couldn't fall apart and alert Belle to anything out of the ordinary. Not now, not after she'd learned her lesson. She wanted to spend this weekend being grateful for what she had and living up to the faith Belle put in her. "On one condition."

"What's that?"

"You let me show you how much *I* love *you* later tonight."

Belle's cheeks flushed a delicate shade of pink, and Nic loved that even after thirteen years of sharing a bed together she could still make Belle blush with merely the hint of her desire. Yet another blessing she'd no longer take for granted.

CHAPTER THREE

Annabelle checked her reflection in the mirror. She still felt self-conscious trying to be sexy but couldn't pinpoint why. She worked hard to keep her body toned and her skin soft. She'd been blessed with naturally blond hair, so her few grays blended in well. She wasn't being immodest to think herself attractive, and her nightgown should have only added to her confidence. It was a beautiful piece of silk, tactfully tailored around her breasts and waist before flowing loosely to her knees. Nic had brought it home for her from San Francisco, and Annabelle could only imagine what she'd paid for it. She was so fortunate to have a woman who loved and appreciated her the way Nic did, and maybe that's why her stomach still fluttered with anticipation at the thought of joining her in their bed. And to think, she'd actually left the house frustrated with her life yesterday.

Annabelle opened the door to their bedroom and Nic glanced up from her book. She was propped on a pillow, her bare torso elongated and her boxer-clad legs stretched out on top of the sheets. Her dark hair, still damp from her shower, hung recklessly across her forehead. Everything about her was sexy. Belle's mouth went dry at the desire smoldering in Nic's eyes. The sensations Nic stirred in her were decidedly unladylike, but she doubted any of the ladies she knew had anything this alluring in their bed.

"Belle, you're a vision. Are you going to join me over here, or would you like me to come to you?"

Belle smiled and walked across the room. Turning back the covers, she slid beneath the sheet and propped herself on one elbow to face Nic. "I missed you."

Nic's eyes shifted from Annabelle's face to her body. She ran her fingers lightly down the length of her arm, gently pushing back the sheet as she went. "I missed you, too."

Nic scooted closer until Annabelle felt the heat of her body. Her touch grew firmer, and she worked her way back up Belle's side. She stopped to caress the curve of her hip through the silk of her nightgown. "I love this spot. This curve right here is just perfect. And so is this one." Nic slid her palm farther up to graze the side of Belle's breasts just once, but she didn't linger there. Instead she continued on her trajectory until she cupped Belle's cheek in her hand and ran her thumb softly across her lips.

Enshrouded in a cone of soft amber light from Nic's reading lamp, Annabelle thrilled at the emotions she saw reflected in Nic's eyes. She loved to watch Nic watch her. Love and lust mingled in her dark irises, stirring a similar fire in Belle. She shuddered under the power of Nic's gaze and finally had to close her eyes to the intensity of it. "Please kiss me, Nic."

She felt an exhale of breath on her skin, followed immediately by the press of Nic's lips to her own, lightly at first but deepening quickly. She opened herself to Nic's mouth, sliding onto her back, and offered access to the rest of her body. Nic eased herself over her and, without breaking the contact of their kiss, began to stroke the places that brought her body to life.

Belle had been a virgin when they'd met in college. Ever a good Southern lady in waiting, she'd thought she had been saving herself for a future husband, but it turned out she'd saved herself for Nic, though she made her wait a year's worth of wooing before she'd allowed her into her bed. She'd been nervous and so unsure of herself, but Nic had been no less patient with her prize than she'd been during her pursuit. She had been steady and gentle in her guidance, and Belle liked to think whatever she had lacked in experience, she'd more than made up for with her eagerness to please.

Nic, on the other hand, was no novice. Already a skilled lover by the first time they slept together, she hadn't been content with her accomplishments. Over the years she'd studied every inch of flesh, learning exactly how and where Belle liked to be touched, kissed, or caressed. She pulled down the straps of Belle's nightdress and lowered them until she could run her fingers in a delicate pass over each breast. She understood from over a decade of practice that Belle responded best when given proper time, and Nic reveled in taking her time. She placed kisses of varying length and pressure along Belle's neck and shoulders, down her chest, and to her stomach.

Reaching down with her free hand she glided her palm up Belle's legs, pushing up the flowing length of silk as she teased her way along her inner thigh, then slipped outward over her hip and left the fabric gathered around her waist. She eased Belle up just enough to push the nightgown over the top of her body and off, before cupping the back of her head in one hand and lowering her gently back to the bed. Belle loved it when Nic cradled her descent back to the pillow, as if she cherished her too much to let her fall even a short distance onto the softest of surfaces. She lifted her own hands to feel the muscles flex and contract along Nic's back and shoulders as Nic kissed her again.

In full concentration now, Nic did all the things that would bring Belle right to the edge of herself. She used knowledge of her body, the places where she needed a soft touch, the times when she needed a deep kiss, to recognize the moment she was ready to let go completely. She slipped slowly inside and waited for Belle to set the pace of their rhythm with the subtle movements of her hips.

Annabelle watched through a haze of arousal as Nic's dark pupils dilated until they almost consumed the blue around them, when she registered the signs of Belle's impending release. Annabelle always held Nic's eyes for as long as she could, marveling at the sight of her until the physical overwhelmed her and she lost control of herself. Nic seemed to share in the power of that connection, but tonight instead of reflecting the intensity of the gaze, she closed her eyes as she kissed Belle. The move wasn't unpleasant, just an unfamiliar departure from their usual script, and Belle took a moment to adjust to the change. But distraction could never hold her for long with Nic's lips on hers, and she easily surrendered to the waves of pleasure rolling through her.

Nic never stopped stroking her until every last shudder subsided. Then she withdrew slowly before lowering herself next to her on the bed. She placed a kiss lightly on her temple and whispered sweet words in her ear. It was a beautiful wind-down routine, and Annabelle soaked up their closeness tonight as much as she always did. She snuggled into the crook of Nic's arm, her head resting on her chest to hear the familiar rhythm of her heartbeat. "Have I mentioned yet how much I like having you home?"

Nic kissed her on the forehead. "You might have said something to that effect."

"With what you just did for me, can you blame me for wanting to chain you to the bed and keep you all for myself?"

Nic's laugh sounded a little strangled. "You're too generous."

"Not at all. You're the best lover a girl could ask for."

"Not that you have any experience to judge that on."

"I don't need to go to anyone else to know I've got everything I want right here." Other women might have felt cheated to have only had one lover, but Belle felt blessed to have found everything she'd ever wanted on the first try. She raised her head off the pillow so she could look Nic in the eyes when she made her next point. "And besides, I love that you're the only one who's ever touched me. I gave my most precious gift to you, and it's yours for as long as you want me."

Nic sighed heavily and extracted her arm from under Belle. She scooted to the edge of the bed and rubbed her face before standing.

"Did I say something wrong?" Belle asked, startled at the abrupt departure.

"No." Nic turned around with a smile. "You're the best. I just have to go to the bathroom."

"Okay." Annabelle lay back on the bed. "But hurry back. I'm not through with you."

"Don't worry, honey," Nic called from the bathroom. "I plan on sleeping in your arms all night long."

Belle smiled. That's exactly what she intended to do too, but only after she'd exhausted Nic enough to assure she slept soundly.

"We've only had two dates, if you can even call them dates, but I can't stop thinking about her," Davis said as soon as Cass took a seat next to her in the coffee shop.

"It's your lesbian urge to merge."

"No, I already told you, we're not renting the U-Haul. We're just going to take it how it comes."

Cass raised her eyebrows over the rim of her tall skim latte with a double shot of espresso.

"Really, we are. Would you believe I don't even know what she does for a living or where she lives?"

"Those do seem like basic get-to-know-you kinds of questions."

"I know, right?" Davis said as she adjusted the margins on a pamphlet she was editing. "She knows where I live, of course, but not much more in the way of basics."

"And be honest, the not knowing is eating you up inside."

"I won't lie." Davis grimaced. "There are moments when I feel insane. Who sleeps with a woman twice without knowing anything other than her name?"

"Well, me, of course. But did you actually sleep with her, or just fuck her brains out?"

"Actually we haven't really slept. She had to be up early both times, and it's pretty obvious that if we're together anywhere near a bed, neither of us will get any rest. I'm not usually like this. I have all my usual doubts in between dates, but as soon as I see her I can't remember any of them."

"It's probably hard to concentrate on details with her firm tits in your mouth."

"Geeze, Cass." Davis flushed and slouched lower behind her laptop screen. "Do you have to have a gutter mouth all the time?"

"Come on, like anyone here cares. The only person who can even hear us," she nodded to the barista behind the counter, "probably had a tit in her mouth last night too, or at least wishes she did."

Cass had a point. Outwrite Books in Midtown Atlanta, where Davis liked to set up her laptop on weekday mornings, wasn't generally frequented by squares or prudes. Their clientele was largely young and gay, with a dose of straight hipsters and fruit flies thrown in, but even in the friendliest of crowds Davis had more respect for herself and others than to share Cass's vocabulary or cavalier attitude. "It's not just the sex."

"Well, if you aren't talking to her and it's not the sex, what's it about?"

"We actually do talk to each other, just not about the boring stuff. We talked for hours on Thursday night." Davis felt herself slipping out of her casual façade just a little as she remembered the connection they'd shared. "We only discuss things we're passionate about. Politics, art, and the city are on that list of things that matter. Our jobs and pasts aren't. And in bed it's the same story. There's no holding back. We just go where we feel moved to go. It's refreshing."

"I bet." Cass grinned conspiratorially. "Casual is key. And not to say I told you so, but did I tell you so?"

"Hey, you're preaching to the converted, but I don't think I could be like this with just anyone. I feel connected to Nic. We're open with each other without the pretense of awkward first dates. I'm trying not to get ahead of myself, because part of our charm together isn't planning things out, but I could really see myself having a future with her."

Cass's expression turned serious, worried even. "Ah, there it is. Call the movers. Pick out a sperm donor. I should've known all your 'whatever will be will be' talk was just an elaborate cover for 'I'm already gone.'"

"I can't explain it. I just feel it. She's attentive and easygoing. She doesn't pressure me to be something I'm not, and without all the acting and posturing and game playing, I can really trust her. I'm not picking out wedding dresses or baby daddies. I love this relationship exactly how it is."

Davis understood how silly she sounded proclaiming not to have any plans one minute and then talking about their future together in the very next breath. She wished she was more centered, but she'd been bounced around so much she wasn't even sure what to want any more. Early on she'd loved the adventure of life in the big city, standing on her own two feet and proving her family wrong. She'd become an independent woman, and she worked hard to maintain that status, but independence didn't have to mean lonely, right? "Nic's not too much and not too little for this stage in my life. She's exactly what I've hoped to find. Who wouldn't see a future in that?"

"Wow." Cass sat back in her chair, concern crossing her refined features. "You've really got it bad for this one."

Davis sighed. So much for being reserved and cautious. "Yeah, I really do."

❖

"Let's call a painter, Belle," Nic said. "You don't need to worry yourself over the color of the guest bathroom."

"Honey, I'm not worried. I think it'll be fun to do something together. Come on, it's just a small room, and I've already bought the paint. We could do it in an hour."

"Okay. If you really want to do it ourselves, let me go get the edging tape."

Belle kissed her on the cheek. "Thank you."

Nic wandered into the garage. She didn't want to spend her weekend working on something they could pay someone else to do, but she owed Belle big-time, even if Belle didn't know. Still, she would've rather paid up in other ways, like roses, jewelry, a trip to the beach, even seeing chick flicks with her. Why did she want to paint? She would've thought with all the money Belle had growing up she'd be above jobs like painting or cleaning or yard work, but she'd been raised on a ranch. Her family fixed things and built things and got their jobs done right.

Nic, on the other hand, had been raised in a trailer down at the end of a pockmarked road. When something broke, it stayed that way or got jerry-rigged with duct tape. Their yard was always littered with car parts her father only pretended to know what to do with. He was a deadbeat in the worst sense because he was too lazy to walk out on them. At least then they would've saved the money he spent on beer and cigarettes, but no; he had to stick around to spend his days bitching at Nic.

She remembered one time in their gravel driveway, handing him parts to an old Pinto he'd won in a poker game. It was at least a hundred degrees during the tail end of a southern Georgia summer, with visible heat waves radiating off the elevated hood of the car. Nic was late for a student-council meeting. She needed to start walking if she had any hope of making it, but her father had it in his head that the car was just minutes from running. He slammed the hood and wiped his grease-stained hands on his filthy shorts, then climbed in the driver's side, a cigarette hanging out of his mouth. "Give it a push while I start 'er up, Nicky."

Even then she understood it was douchey for a grown man to sit in a car while his fifteen-year-old daughter pushed, but she knew better than to sass him, so she threw her weight behind the car as he popped the clutch. The engine coughed and sputtered, pushing hot, black smoke across her legs as the car started to roll. Her father cranked and cranked the starter, but the car's only movement was clearly powered by Nic pushing. Hot, sweaty, and dirty, she had to get going or she'd miss the meeting entirely, so she stopped and stood up. He father cussed a few more times before getting out to stare at her disapprovingly. "Well, you fucked that up. For someone who gets such good grades you'd think you could at least follow simple directions."

Nic didn't dare reply, but she couldn't resist rolling her eyes, and that was enough to set him off. "What? You think you're too good to work on cars?"

"No, sir. I just have to get to school."

"Bullshit." He spat, only nearly missing her shoe. "You don't have to go to school on a Saturday. You don't have to go to school at all. You're just trying to be better than where you came from, and I don't like it."

She kept quiet. The best thing she could do when he got like this was let him burn himself out.

"All school does is put big ideas in that thick skull of yours." He tapped a pudgy finger on her forehead for emphasis. "You're no better than anyone else. Hell, if you keep chasing those stupid Ivy League dreams of yours, you're actually dumber than most. You learn to cook, you learn to fix cars, you learn how to make babies, and maybe you'll be okay, but if you keep your nose stuck in schoolbooks or up the ass of some teacher, you're on your own. You ain't coming back here to beg at my door when you don't know how to do anything useful. You hear?"

"Yes, sir."

"No, you don't." He flicked his cigarette and waved her off. "You might be listening, but you're too stupid for any of it to sink in. Get out of here."

"Sir?" Nic asked.

"You're going to keep fucking up anyhow. Just go to your meeting."

Nic had shown up to school late and disheveled, only to have her teacher lecture her about the importance of keeping her commitments. Once again Nic held her tongue and opened her mouth only to politely apologize. Nothing would come from arguing with her father, and she wouldn't gain her teacher's respect by trying to pass blame, so she soldiered on, using each insult, each disapproving glare, each condemnation to fuel her fire. She'd kiss all the asses she needed to in order to make sure someday things worked the other way around. Not only was she going to have it all, but she'd also make sure she had other people to take care of it all. She'd never again have to get dirty or sweaty if she didn't want to, and she'd never kiss any ass she wasn't attracted to. But she was attracted to Annabelle, and more than that, she loved her.

She loved Belle because Belle had loved her before she'd become the woman she was now. Sure, she'd done well for herself at the University of Georgia. She'd maintained the grades to hold a full scholarship in business, but she had only begun to come into her own while Belle had already cultivated so much style, grace, and social status. A third-generation member of the most elite sorority on campus, she had been formally introduced to society and had the eye of every eligible young man of good breeding. Belle had eyes only for Nic. She'd been the first person who'd truly believed Nic would be as successful as Nic believed, and she'd risked all her family comfort and social status on a glorified trailer-trash lesbian. The unconditional love, the unfailing loyalty, and the unabashed pride Belle had shown in her were foreign concepts to Nic, but she'd quickly grown accustomed to them, and what's more, she'd used Belle's confidence to bolster her own.

Soon she'd landed a prime internship in advertising for the largest cable company in the region. Belle had set up a home for them, one she was proud to bring colleagues to, and they entertained often. Between her own drive and Belle's social acumen, they'd soon been welcomed into business and society circles that wouldn't generally be open to a lesbian of low degree. At times it all started to feel tedious or she wondered if any of the accolades held any real meaning, but she preferred them to the insults she'd faced in the early part of her life, and even in the most mundane tasks she saw herself accomplishing the things she'd set out to do.

Nic had rapidly moved up the corporate ladder, becoming a full-time sales rep, then making one of the quickest leaps into management any of her colleagues could remember. Now she stood on the brink of another rise in status, one most would find utterly disproportionate to both her age and upbringing. Sometimes she marveled at how quickly everything had happened, as if her life had simply taken on a life of its own.

She'd worked hard, put in long hours, and learned quickly, but she understood Belle played more than a supporting role in her ascension. Belle had opened doors and given her both the confidence and skills necessary to walk through them. She ran their home with military precision and angelic grace. Plus, she always managed to look stunning while doing so. Nic liked to think of herself as a sort of self-made mogul, but when completely honest, if not for Belle's faith and grace, she might be painting other people's houses instead of her own.

She grabbed the tape out of a shiny toolbox filled with supplies she rarely used but enjoyed the look of. Belle was already in the guest bathroom waiting for her, wearing a pair of sweat pants and one of Nic's old Georgia Bulldogs T-shirts. She'd pulled her hair into a ponytail that curled just at the very end, and her eyes shone with delight as she saw Nic. She nodded to a square patch of robin's-egg blue she'd painted in the middle of the largest wall. "Hey, handsome, you like what you see?"

Nic grinned. Despite all their complications and all the ways she'd rather spend her Sunday, she did still very much like what she saw.

Chapter Four

Annabelle ran the iron over Nic's charcoal-gray suit pants while Nic sat on their bed with her laptop balanced on her outstretched legs and checked e-mail. They were both preparing for her trip to Atlanta the next morning. "You know I tell you this every road trip, but it bears repeating. I can iron my own pants."

"I know you can, but as I tell you every road trip, I like to do it for you," Annabelle replied sweetly.

Nic shrugged and looked back at her computer. "Okay. I'm not complaining. You do it better anyway."

"It's my job to make you look good, and it's your job to make the company look good."

"Then we make a great team. With you taking care of my wardrobe, I should be vice president in no time."

"I hope so." Annabelle felt Nic's eyes on her the second the words were out, but she kept her own gaze focused on the crease she was working into the wool trousers.

"I thought you didn't care about my title or paycheck."

"You know I don't, but it's been so nice to have you home for six nights in a row. I get spoiled by having you all to myself."

"It sure is nice waking up to your beautiful face every morning."

"And when you get promoted to vice president—"

"*If* I get promoted to vice president."

"*When* you get promoted," Annabelle continued, glancing up just long enough to see the corners of Nic's mouth twitch upward, "you'll work from Athens more."

"I'll still have meetings in Atlanta."

"But not nearly as many in places like Boston and Cleveland. You'll have a team of people to handle those calls, and even the meetings in Atlanta will be cut way back since you'll only have to go to the corporate offices and not out on any actual sales calls."

"True," Nic said, not unhappily, but sounding decidedly less than thrilled. She was probably checking sports scores instead of e-mail now. She always got a little glazed over when any game anywhere hit its final minutes.

"You'll be home almost every night, and our lives will finally settle into a nice routine."

"Uh-huh."

"We can have dinner at the same time every night, and then play tennis or maybe even take up a new hobby together." Belle looked so forward to those days. She'd understood Nic's drive from the beginning, and she had so much faith in her ability to be whatever she wanted that it wasn't hard to play the role of supportive wife. She'd even enjoyed the business trips early on, especially in the summers when she could go along. They'd seen a lot of the country, and even when she couldn't travel with Nic she'd enjoyed hearing stories of far-off places. Over the years, though, she'd lost some of her wanderlust and had begun to plan for the days when Nic would climb into bed with her every night.

"You think I'm cut out for a nine-to-five office job?" Nic asked in a tone that made Annabelle suspect she'd been paying more attention than she'd initially let on.

"I don't know if the transition will be effortless, but you're good at everything you set your mind to. The work will still be challenging."

"I suppose so. I like the idea of not sleeping alone more than I have to, but I like the excitement of being on the go. I'd hate to get into a rut."

Annabelle smiled. She wasn't offended by Nic's suggestion that life here could get monotonous. She lived with that prospect every day. Never content to just be content, Nic needed a challenge, and Belle loved that, but she also knew excitement didn't always have to come from the business world. Once upon a time Belle had been the object of Nic's drive to be better, and she was certain starting a family would produce that same desire. "Well, it certainly won't get too predictable when we have the baby."

"Oh, yeah, dirty diapers, spit-up on my suit, and sleepless nights."

"And tea parties, and backyard campouts, football games, and sidewalk chalk."

"It'll be much harder to find time for tennis matches and nights out, but I suppose that's what we'll get a nanny for."

Belle stiffened. "Nanny?"

"Yeah, don't people with babies get nannies?"

"Nic, what makes you think a woman like me, a woman who won't let you hire a cleaning lady or a painter, will allow our child to be raised by a stranger?"

"Surely there's a difference between having a nanny and giving our child up to a stranger. We'll need some help and some time to ourselves every now and again."

Belle allowed herself a flash of worry at the comment, then tamped it down quickly. She didn't want to negate Nic's fears. It was completely natural for her to question whether she could handle the responsibilities of parenthood. Belle might've been more worried herself if she had other obligations, but she'd let all her other childhood dreams fall by the wayside. She'd married Nic when she was barely more than a child, leaving little time to grow into other aspirations of her own. Motherhood remained the only wish she ever expended energy on anymore, so she'd had ample time to consider things Nic thought of only occasionally. "Of course my mama and my sister will help babysit on occasion so we can make time for us, but raising a child is a full-time job. One I'm looking forward to."

Nic rubbed her face. "I've got a very demanding career, and I don't have experience with kids. You already do so much around here. I don't know why you don't choose an easier road when we can afford it. I worry about you taking on too much."

Annabelle smiled at the underlying sentiment. Whenever she worried Nic was stalling, she'd say something that revealed how truly selfless her fears were. She always put Belle's needs first. "My mother ran the biggest horse ranch in northern Georgia. She kept the books, kept the house, kept her husband happy, and still managed to raise two debutante daughters. I'll be fine with nothing to do but cook for you and watch a baby. Besides, it's not like I'll be alone. You'll be the most dedicated, doting parent our baby could ever ask for."

Nic shifted nervously on the bed, and Annabelle tried to act like she didn't notice her discomfort. She lifted the pants off the ironing board and threaded them through the hanger, then covered them with their matching suit coat and took care to hang them neatly in the closet for tomorrow. Nic had sworn from the beginning that she wanted kids. Early on she seemed even more serious about the prospect than Belle, but she'd also expressed a great deal of concern for her parenting ability. She feared her own upbringing skewed her understanding of parent-child relationships to the point that, even if she committed herself to good parenting, she wouldn't be capable.

"You'll be a great parent," Belle finally said as she climbed into bed with Nic.

"You don't know that."

"I know you. You've never been bad at something you wanted to be good at." Belle snuggled in and rested her head on Nic's shoulder. "Our little boy or girl will adore you. She or he will wait at the door for you every night and want you to coach her T-ball team, or want you to be the one to read his bedtime stories every night."

"I never did any of those things with my parents."

"That's why you'll be extra good at doing them with our baby. You'll want our child to have all the things you didn't."

"I do want that, Belle. I never want to disappoint you or our family, but I don't have the faith you have in me."

"Shh." Belle kissed her softly on her cheek. She hated that Nic still had such unfounded insecurities about her abilities as a partner. It was almost like she had some invisible life of phantom failures, because all Annabelle saw was utter perfection. "Don't worry, honey. I have enough faith for both of us."

❖

Davis tried to sound as casual as possible with a text message that simply read "R U in the ATL?"

Her emotions still warred with her logic. Emotional Davis wanted to say things like "I miss you," or "Why haven't you called me for a whole week?" or "Don't they have phones where you live? And by the way, where the hell do you live?" Maybe Emotional Davis wanted to mention that hours of great conversation plus mind-blowing sex might have equaled falling a little bit in love if Logical Davis wasn't beating her about the head and shoulders for thinking such romantic drivel.

Logical Davis told her they hadn't made plans and Nic hadn't said when she'd be back in town. Logical Davis also said fifteen minutes had passed since she sent the text and she hadn't heard back. How hard was it to type a simple yes or no? Logical Davis said she needed to let go. If Nic wanted her, she knew how to reach her. If not, why fool herself? Emotional Davis saw no harm in trying one more time.

As usual, Logical Davis lost and was reduced to rolling her eyes while Emotional Davis typed another text. "Got Roller Derby tickets tonight. Want to go?"

Her phone vibrated in her hand, causing her to jump. Nic's number popped up on her screen, and she did a happy little jig before composing herself and answering as calmly as possible. "Hey, pervert."

Nic laughed. "Hi, Davis."

She fought the urge to ask why the hell she hadn't called and forced herself to act cool. "So, do you want to go to the match tonight, or should I go troll the park for someone else?"

"Sounds tempting. I've never seen live Roller Derby before."

"Then come with me and cross it off your bucket list."

"Actually, I'm stuck at the office," Nic said.

"Which office? The one in Boston? Atlanta? Or the one in whatever mysterious place you're from?"

"Ah, corporate in Atlanta."

Davis noted she still hadn't said what corporation or where she lived, but she was too happy that Nic was in Atlanta to care about the other details. "Well, it doesn't start till eight. You can't work all night."

"I don't know. I've got enough work to keep me busy all night."

"Work or Roller Derby. Doesn't sound like a tough choice to me."

"It's not about what I want, Davis. I have responsibilities and people counting on me. I shouldn't let them down."

"Fine, be a tool." Davis kept her tone playful even through the disappointment sinking into her chest.

"A tool?"

"Sure, another cog in the machine, a yes man, stiff in a suit. No wonder you're a kinky park sex bastard in your free time. Corporate America is eating your soul."

"Wow, when you put it that way…"

"Meet you at the Wyndham at seven thirty?"

Nic sighed heavily, and Davis held her breath. Something inside told her this was good-bye, and she felt almost frantic at the possibility, but she wouldn't beg. She wanted a romance, a relationship, even to fall in love, and she thought Nic could give her those things, but she knew better than to put that kind of faith in anyone, especially herself. So she waited, suspended in the moment, quietly asking the fates to show their hand.

"All right. See you then, but you're a bad influence."

Davis closed her eyes and smiled in a mix of relief and anticipation. "Oh, yeah, somehow getting called a bad influence by a perv feels like a compliment. Don't be late." She clicked off the phone and flopped onto her couch. Nic had chosen her over work or whatever else had battled for her attention tonight. Maybe that didn't mean commitment, but at least it signified interest.

Stop getting ahead of yourself. Just enjoy the moment. She wasn't in love with Nic yet, not by a long shot, but she got a little flutter in her stomach at the thought of seeing her, and she missed her when she was away. She felt comfortable around her, and she didn't have to pretend to be someone she wasn't. Well, sometimes she pretended to be more casual, but she didn't have to pretend to be sweeter or smarter or classier. If anything, Nic seemed to like when she got surly. None of her other lovers had wanted to be challenged or sassed. Half of them didn't want her to talk at all.

No, that wasn't fair. She'd had a handful of meaningful relationships, one that even lasted two whole years. In that case they'd moved in together before the woman had told her she didn't really see them going anywhere permanent. Since then she'd fallen for a string of flunkies and lunatics to showcase her bad judgment. None of them had lasted more than a month. Davis couldn't decide if she preferred to be written off without ever getting a fair shot or to get a two-year trial and still be found lacking.

She pushed those thoughts from her mind. There was no sense mulling over her past failures when she was supposed to be getting ready for a date. She needed to remind herself to let this be what it would be instead of letting past nightmares or dreams of the future override her enjoyment of the present. Logical Davis commended her on her level-headedness, but Emotional Davis went skipping out the door to meet Nic.

Nic winced as a petite woman on skates torpedoed a woman twice her size, sending them both clattering to the floor. The crowd went wild, and more points appeared on the scoreboard. Davis had explained the points system on the way there, but everything happened so fast Nic couldn't always count how many people got passed in any given heat. She'd always been a football fan, but the clash of pads and helmets she'd previously considered brutal now seemed demure as bare flesh and barely protected bone connected with hard floors at blurring speeds.

"This is wicked," Nic shouted, to be heard over the other spectators.

"Yeah, fast, sweaty girls in short shorts beating the crap out of each other." Davis laughed. "See, I know what you like."

Nic eyed the infinitely sexy woman pressed against her. Davis was totally unreserved, her green eyes mischievous, and her smile making it clear what she wanted to do when they left. She wore skinny jeans and a maroon T-shirt with the sleeves cut off. Her short red hair had been tousled with a hand full of gel, and she didn't appear to be wearing a bra. Best of all, she'd tucked one of her expert hands in the back pocket of Nic's jeans and used the hold to keep her close.

Davis did seem to know what she liked, or at least what her life lacked. She'd played everything so perfectly tonight. Nic got to town yesterday but managed not to call her. She'd locked herself in corporate headquarters to avoid any hint of temptation. She'd been a model employee, showing up early and staying late. She'd made phone calls, taken meetings, and made appointments with possible clients in Savannah, Macon, Athens, and Chattanooga. She'd assured herself she'd be busy for weeks to come, and just before she'd crashed last night, she'd called Belle to remind herself why she worked so hard.

She'd even resisted the first text message, but it was like Davis had intuited Nic was sitting at her desk suffocating under the stifling press of monotony. Davis couldn't have known that Nic had begun to waver under the pressure to be perfect: the perfect employee, the perfect wife, and soon to be the perfect parent with everything all planned out. Really, she'd been doing fine at home last weekend until Belle mentioned their seemingly foregone future of full-time parenting.

It wasn't that she didn't want kids. She liked kids just fine in a hypothetical sense. The idea of having someone else to spoil rotten was a nice one, and her kid would have only the best. She'd go to the best prep schools Georgia had to offer. Maybe she'd love horses like Belle did. Then Nic could buy her a pony, or if they had a boy she could get him a dirt bike. She smiled at her own stereotyping; maybe she'd buy a pony for a son and a dirt bike for a daughter. She'd get a lot of satisfaction from proving to all the old anti-gay bullies that she could rear a little one even better than they could. She'd enjoy showing off videos of dance recitals or her kid's report card. Sometimes she even longed to have her desk cluttered with crayon drawings and T-ball photos like her colleagues did. She especially liked the idea of being one hundred times better at parenting than her old man.

But what about all the other stuff that came with babies? A baby would monopolize all of Belle's attention, and their social calendar would get overrun with playgroups. And babies didn't stay babies. It'd be eighteen years of no breaks, no change, no spontaneity, no more adventures, probably no more sex. Maybe she was being overly dramatic. She lived the American freaking dream. Why did she feel like she was drowning?

When Davis had texted her about Roller Derby, it had sounded so random, so unscripted, so exciting. Of course the way her heart had pulsed a little faster at the thought of seeing Davis again hadn't done anything to put a damper on the suggestion. Still, she'd tried to bow out gracefully. Maybe if she blamed work, then didn't call back for a while, Davis would get the hint. Maybe she'd break it off and save Nic the trouble of disappointing her. Then Davis had accused her of being the exact thing she feared she'd become— boring, predictable, a tool. Nic's natural defenses wouldn't allow her to be boxed in, not even into a box she'd chosen. She couldn't resist a challenge, especially one as sexy as Davis, so she'd caved.

Davis cheered for a play, then snuggled closer, and Nic wished she regretted her moment of weakness. She wanted to have a terrible time. She'd hoped memories of her life with Belle would surface continually and assure her she wasn't missing anything in their beautiful life together, but nothing here made her think of that other life. Nic was in a totally new world in this glorified gymnasium filled with rowdy, young, vibrant spectators. There was no use trying to draw comparisons. Belle gave her stability and a past, and so much faith, strength, and devotion. Davis gave her excitement, energy, and passion. Belle comforted her. Davis challenged her. She couldn't walk away from Belle any more than she could cut off her arm, but Davis's influence was like air or water. Without the kind of passion she inspired, Nic would cease to be herself.

The buzzer sounded, pulling Nic back into the moment as Davis tugged her toward the door. They walked into the cool night air, and Nic opened the passenger-side door of her car for Davis, who looked up and smiled brightly. "Where are you from?"

"What?"

"Come on. No lesbian I've ever known opens doors and pulls out chairs like you do. I know you're not from the city."

"No. I'm from a rinky-dink little town in southern Georgia, but I live in Athens."

"Ah, a UGA girl." Davis got in the car, and Nic closed the door. She hadn't been prepared to give up any kind of personal information, and she wasn't sure she liked having done so. She fired up the engine and shifted into traffic on Ponce De Leon Boulevard and headed toward Midtown.

"What are you thinking?" Davis asked after a long silence.

Nic quickly thought of something to say other than the truth. "I'm glad you let me drive."

Davis laughed. "Taking the bus isn't that bad."

"It's not great, either. I don't run on anyone else's schedule or set of directions." Nic admired Davis's stubborn self-reliance and the way she embraced all things urban, but she'd be damned if she'd take public transportation. She was independent too, and that meant going when and where she wanted to go on her own.

"Is that really what you were thinking?"

"Yeah, why?"

"I just thought maybe you were upset I'd asked a personal question, and you might not like me knowing where you live."

Damn. Nic couldn't cop to that, so she deflected with a question. "What makes you think that?"

"You just haven't mentioned anything personal before, and when I brought it up you got awfully quiet. You don't have to worry about me going all crazy-stalker on you. I know we're keeping things casual."

"It's not that I don't trust you. I'm not sure I trust me yet. I haven't shown the best judgment in the past and…" Shit. She wasn't showing good judgment now. She couldn't keep rehashing the same internal crisis. She wanted to be true to everyone involved, and yet she couldn't even be true to herself.

"It's fine. You don't have to tell me. I know I'm not your girlfriend or anything. We are what we are."

Nic grimaced at the harsh edge Davis tried to brush away from her voice and pulled the car into some random parking lot so she could look Davis in the eye. "I care about you a lot. You make me feel more alive than I have in a long time. I like being around you, and the sex feels so right I can hardly stand it."

"But?" Davis asked, setting her jaw.

Why did there have to be a but? Why did one of them have to get hurt? "I'm worried I'll screw up a good thing, or I'll get hurt or hurt someone else. You said yourself the night we met, no one ever really has everything."

"And you said that doesn't mean we ever stop chasing it."

"Is chasing a dream enough for you, Davis?"

"It's better than giving up."

"You deserve more than I can give you, but I'm not strong enough to let you go."

"Then don't." Davis took Nic's face in her hands. "Don't give up. No fear, no pressure, no regrets. No one has to get hurt. Let's just try to have it all."

Could she do it? Could she have stability and excitement? Why not? She'd never failed at anything in her life, but she didn't do anything halfway, either. She couldn't go back and forth between craving Davis and being wracked with guilt. She needed to make a decision right now. She was either in for it all, or she needed to quit. Her heart started to beat faster at the challenge. She wasn't a quitter. Why should she have to choose between roots and wings? She could be everything she needed, everything she wanted. No one had to get neglected. No one had to get hurt. God help her, she didn't really believe that, but she wanted to, and want was a powerful ally to denial.

A tiny part of her started to ask what would happen if she couldn't pull it off, but before it fully registered, Davis kissed her. The tension exploded between them, electric energy surging until they formed a single mass of heat and passion. Then just as quickly as they collided, Davis wrenched herself away. "Does that help you make whatever internal decision you're wrestling with?"

"Yes." Nic panted. "I'm all in."

CHAPTER FIVE

May

"Those are hot, honey." Annabelle laughed as Nic cussed around a piece of Andouille sausage she'd plucked out of a bowl of grits.

Nic hopped around and employed a Lamaze-type breathing pattern, trying to cool the meat in her mouth.

"Nic." Annabelle laughed harder. "Spit it out."

Nic chewed a few quick times and swallowed. "Whew, woman, you could've warned me."

"You saw me take it off the stove."

Nic grinned. "I can't be expected to process details when I smell your cooking. I revert to my more animal state, and after three days away I feel like a bear coming out of hibernation."

"Even a bear would let go of something that burned."

"Did you just suggest I'm not as smart as a big dumb animal?"

"Maybe." Belle smiled sweetly and carried two bowls of shrimp and grits toward the patio. "But then again I'm in love with you, so I suppose that analogy isn't any more flattering for me."

Nic opened their sliding glass door for her. A pitcher of iced sweet tea and a basket of cheddar biscuits awaited them. It was a beautiful spring night with a refreshing breeze carrying the subtle scent of magnolias fresh in bloom. "Well, all I can say is I'm one lucky bear, because I think I've just stumbled into heaven."

Belle tried to brush off the compliment, but it did feel heavenly to take the seat next to the love of her life. Nic was always over the top in her praise, but Belle loved to make her happy. While sometimes she would've liked more, she took pride in doing all the little things right. She didn't enjoy cleaning, but she had an eye for detail, and her progress gave her a sense of accomplishment. Her real thrill, though, came on the afternoons Nic arrived home. She loved to cook, so she planned big dinners for them on those nights. She had all the intrinsic rewards that came with creating something from scratch: watching it take shape, smelling its aromas fill the house, and sneaking a taste under the guise of making sure everything was right. Then a few hours later she got a bigger delight when she saw Nic enjoy her meal. It wasn't that she held her own happiness less dear than Nic's, but rather Nic's happiness magnified her own.

And Nic had been very happy lately, as well as loving, attentive, and affectionate. She worked in Atlanta a little more than usual, which was always hard on Belle, but she couldn't complain because when Nic came home, she was a model partner. Instead of arriving exhausted, she seemed recharged. She rarely locked herself in her home office, choosing instead to spend evenings on the couch with an arm around Belle's shoulder. When she was away, she sent flowers, bought presents, and called daily just to say I love you. Maybe Nic felt better about their future as things picked up at work, but whatever the reason, Belle liked the results. Over the last two months Nic was more like the passionate woman she'd fallen in love with than she'd been in years.

Nic had dug into her shrimp and grits with gusto by the time Belle even took her first bite. "Do you not eat at all when you're in the city?"

"Not like this. I've never met anyone who can hold a candle to your cooking."

"Well, I hope you're not holding auditions."

Nic swallowed a mouthful of biscuit. "No, that's not what I meant. I was mostly talking about restaurants."

"I know. I'm teasing. Poor thing, you probably eat nothing but fast food."

"I try not to, but I just work so late most nights it's the only thing open by the time I turn in."

"I should come with you sometime. I couldn't cook much in a hotel room, but I could do better than burgers and fries every night."

Nic frowned. "I wouldn't put you through that to be my personal chef."

"You talk about it like you'd be sending me to a prisoner-of-war camp."

"It might start to feel that way to you too after three days in a hotel room by yourself from seven in the morning to sometimes eleven at night."

Belle's annoyance flashed close to the surface. "I'm alone longer than that here."

"This is a four-bedroom house with family nearby, and tennis partners at the ready. It's not like Atlanta has anything all that more interesting than Athens."

"It has you three nights a week," Annabelle said, perturbed at Nic's resistance to something so silly.

"I don't get to enjoy the city much, and I wouldn't get much work done either if I worried about what you were doing all day."

"I'm not talking about moving in. I just meant maybe I could come with you every now and again."

"And I'm telling you I'd rather have you here," Nic said tersely.

Belle faltered at the sharpness in Nic's tone. Why was she so resistant to the idea of their spending more time together? Nic never refused her anything, and her agitation seemed disproportionate to the request. What could she be worried about? "I wouldn't be a bother, Nic, but I'd like to be in your bed when you came home."

"You *are* here for me when I get home, to our home." Nic grabbed her hand. "You anchor me, Belle. You know I can't deny you anything. If you want to go to Atlanta, that's your right, but for me the best place you can be is here. That other world is always shifting and changing, but no matter what happens there I know I've got you, my rock, right here in the safe haven we've worked so hard to build. That means more than any dinner you could make in a hotel room."

Shock flooded Belle's heart and mind. She knew Nic enjoyed coming home to a nice house, but she'd never put her reasons in such emotional terms. It hadn't occurred to her that Nic wanted to keep her worlds separate to preserve a safe place for herself. Nic carried scars from her upbringing—never having anything of her own, never able to hold onto something beautiful, always fearing what the next minute might bring. Belle immediately felt guilty for pushing her as if asking for a holiday abroad or some petty extravagance.

Her eyes brimmed with tears, and Nic must have misinterpreted them because she apologized all over herself. "I'm sorry, Belle. I didn't mean to upset you. You can come with me. We'll figure out a way to—"

"No, baby. You're right."

"No, I'm silly. I didn't mean to upset you."

"You didn't, really. I'm not upset." Belle wiped at her tears, her heart achingly full. "I wonder how I got so blessed to have such an amazing, caring, insightful partner."

"You deserve so much more. You deserve the whole world."

Belle took Nic's face in her hands. "Nic McCoy, you are the whole world to me. Don't you know that by now?"

Nic's pupils dilated with that unmistakable mix of love and attraction Belle had also seen a lot more lately, and she smiled a slow smile of acknowledgment, then kissed her quickly before sitting back in her chair. The storm had passed, but judging by the way her body responded under Nic's gaze, a new kind of electricity was stirring between them, one that wouldn't be settled with a quick kiss on the patio.

Davis's call went straight to voice mail like every other call she'd made over the weekend. She found it odd Nic got such terrible service outside Atlanta. Athens wasn't a huge city but more than big enough to warrant adequate cell coverage. Then again maybe the service wasn't the problem. Nic had a habit of forgetting to check her phone. She'd noticed a lot of times when they were together Nic left her phone in the car overnight or turned it off, only checking in before going to work in the morning, though on those occasions Davis loved the habit. Having Nic's undivided attention made her feel important, and she found the complete disconnect from the outside world romantically old fashioned. When apart she wished Nic were a little easier to connect with.

She glanced across her apartment and could still feel Nic there. The vase of tiger lilies she'd had delivered yesterday adorned her windowsill. No one had ever sent her flowers, and the fact that Nic had remembered her favorite variety and had chosen them instead of the more generic roses made the gesture all the more special. In the kitchen was a new picture magneted to the refrigerator. It was a self-portrait, taken at the Braves' home opener. They both wore jerseys with matching ball caps and looked totally smitten with each other. Nic had pulled Davis close, then held the camera at arm's length in front of them before snapping the shot.

The phone in her hand vibrated, startling her so much she dropped it. She chased it across her hardwood floor, stubbing her bare toe on the couch as she went. "Shit, shit, shit." She doubled over, grabbing her foot with one hand and the phone with the other. "Ouch, ouch, ouch. Hello, hey, I'm here."

"You okay?"

"Oh, hi, Cass." She sat down on the floor and rubbed her toe.

"Wow, don't sound so thrilled."

"No, sorry. I just stubbed my toe."

"Stubbed your toe diving for the phone because you thought it was Nic calling?"

"What? No. Maybe."

"Is she in town this weekend?"

"No, but she usually calls to chat." Maybe chat wasn't the right word. Nic checked in at least every other day, but the calls were usually short and focused on making plans for the next time they'd see each other. Sometimes she felt like Nic called more out of duty than desire. They never had the in-depth conversations or the passionate dialogue they shared in person. Sometimes she thought the woman on the phone was someone other than the woman who shared her bed. Maybe Nic just didn't care to talk on the phone. Some people were like that, but Davis continued to try.

"You sit around all day waiting for her to call and chat?"

"No. Geeze, you make me sound pathetic. I work, I go for bike rides, I went to see a movie with you last week."

"That was two weeks ago."

"What's your point?"

"Nothing." Cass's annoyance gave way to sincerity. "I miss you. Let's go out."

"I'm not really in the mood for a night out."

"Come on. You can take your cell with you in case Nic calls."

"No, it's not about that. I'm just not into the bar scene. Why don't you come over here and we'll order Chinese and veg out."

"How about we go out for Chinese and then go dancing?"

Davis sighed. "I just want a night at home."

"All you get anymore are nights at home."

"Not true. Nic and I went out three nights in a row this week. Dancing, the theater, Roller Derby, it's nonstop. I think she tries to cram a whole week's worth of fun into our few days together."

"I think she's trying to cram something else into you," Cass muttered

"God, you're smutty," Davis said disgustedly, then added, "but yes, she does plenty of that, too."

"At least she has that going for her."

"She has a lot going for her, Cass. She's smart and ambitious and passionate. I've never met anyone who makes love with the intensity she does."

"Sure." Cynicism crept back into Cass's tone. "She's got everything except a house in Atlanta, so while the cat's away, let's go play."

"I'm done with that kind of playing."

"Damn, I knew it. You're not going out with me because you're doing the chaste-woman-waiting-for-her-man-to-return-from-war bit."

"I'm not doing a bit," Davis explained. "I'm not interested in fending off horny fakes and posers when I've got the real deal."

"You don't have the real deal tonight. Do you really believe she's holding herself to the same code of conduct up there in her college town full of hot, young coeds?"

"Yes," Davis said, then faltered. "I think so."

"Just so you know, I'm rolling my eyes," Cass said. "Are you still pretending to go with the flow after all this time, even though you're clearly already designing your wedding dress in your mind?"

"No, we're definitely a couple now. She's my girlfriend." Davis liked saying that aloud. She'd lost a lot of her fear of being needy or moving too quickly. Nic had been more open in the months since their Roller Derby date. "We're not U-Hauling it, but I'm pretty sure we're way past the casual-sex stage."

"Pretty sure? You haven't talked about it?"

"We don't have to talk about it. She's not like that." She wasn't sure if she needed to defend her judgment or Nic's. "She's respectful and attentive and considerate. The way she talks about her dreams and her fantasies when she's with me tells me all I need to know about her commitment level."

"Well, if she's so perfect, why isn't she with you tonight?"

"She works in Athens."

"On Saturday night?"

"She's got a lot of odd hours. Even when she's in the city she has to stay late and take conference calls with people in different time zones, and she can't just live on the interstate all the time."

"Why not go to her?"

"I, just, well…" Davis didn't want to say she hadn't been invited.

Cass seemed to grow more suspicious with each question. "Do you know where she lives?"

"You make it sound so shady. It's not like she's hiding from me. I've just never asked." Cass clearly didn't understand how much she and Nic had grown together over the last few months. Nic didn't withhold anything from her anymore. She loved to be challenged, and she never balked at Davis's sarcastic side. She was completely open. Well, maybe not completely. She didn't like to talk about her life in Athens or her childhood, but those were the only off-limit topics, and Davis respected her boundaries. She didn't like to talk about her upbringing either, so they fit together perfectly in that area, too.

"I'm sorry. I'm probably just jealous."

"Aw, don't be jealous. You could have a relationship too if you'd just open up. Women would line up around the block for you."

"No, you cheeseball. I'm not jealous you have Nic. I'm jealous she stole my wingman, and while you're recovering from all the hot sex, I don't have anyone to go out with."

"Oh. Well, yes, there's that." Davis laughed. "But if you miss me so much, come hang out at my place."

"Thanks, but no thanks." Cass feigned depression. "I'll just go out all by myself, with no one to make snarky comments to or judge women inappropriately with."

"Oh, I'm sure you won't be alone for long."

"Well, that's true. I *am* insanely good-looking. I'll probably have you replaced within the hour, but if you change your mind, give me a call, okay?"

"Okay, have fun," Davis said, knowing Cass always found someone to have fun with, but that brand of fun wasn't enough for Davis anymore. In fact, she wasn't sure anything other than Nic would ever be enough for her again.

Nic flopped onto her plush couch and flipped on her big flat-screen TV to check the Braves' score. "Shit."

"What's the matter?" Belle called from the kitchen.

"We're losing to the flipping Marlins."

"I'm sorry, honey."

Nic smiled. Belle didn't care about baseball, but she cared about her, so she always managed to summon up some sympathy for her sports-related woes, which was the next best thing. "Why don't you come watch with me, or we can watch something else if you want."

"No, baseball is fine. I'll be in as soon as I finish packing your briefcase for tomorrow."

"Don't bother with work stuff. I'll pack in the morning."

"It's no bother."

Nic shrugged and turned up the sound on the game. She didn't understand what Belle got out of jobs like that, but she swore she enjoyed it, so after thirteen years Nic had learned to let her go. Besides, who complained about having amazing meals, an immaculate house, and never having to do her own laundry? If only the Braves would pull it together, she'd have it made.

"Honey, you have some missed calls on your cell phone," Annabelle called.

"It's after eight on my one night at home this week. I'm off the clock, and you should be, too."

Belle came and sat next to Nic. "Okay. I like having you all to myself. I just noticed someone named Davis called three times. I thought it might be important if he's trying to get ahold of you so bad."

Nic's breath caught in her chest, and she tried to sound casual. "I'm sure everything will be fine. I'm not going to let it interrupt our evening."

"I don't think I've met Davis."

"No, you haven't." Nic tried to sound casual, but her heart hammered in her throat. At least Belle assumed Davis was a man, which made things easier.

"Is he one of the new sales reps?"

"He's an intern. He probably wants the itinerary for our proposal meeting tomorrow." The lie rolled off Nic's tongue so quickly it shocked her. She'd never thought of herself as deceptive. Even in her relationship with Davis, she'd only lied by omission.

"Maybe you should call him back. It's not nice to torment the interns," Belle said playfully.

Eager to end this conversation, Nic took the offered opportunity. "Sure. Let me go in the office and pull up the paperwork."

"Go ahead. I'll be right here when you're done."

She grabbed her phone and walked into her home office. What kind of a person was she becoming? The last two months had been amazing. Every part of her life was better than it had ever been. At home she relished the comforts of Annabelle and their life together, and in Atlanta she thrived on the passion and adventure Davis provided. Hell, even at work she'd experienced an added boost of confidence, but she couldn't get careless. She didn't want to lose any of her newfound balance, and that meant keeping her worlds separate. This was her time with Belle, time to relax, recharge, and enjoy the woman who'd been her world for thirteen years. Whatever Davis needed had to be dealt with quickly.

She hit the redial button on her phone.

"Hey, babe," Davis answered. "You been hiding from me this weekend?"

"I could never stay away from you," Nic said truthfully.

"Good, because I miss you."

Nic was both flattered and frustrated that Davis risked blowing her cover just because she missed her. "Is that why you called?"

"Pretty much."

"Then I tell you what. You hold that thought just long enough for me to get my presentation done tomorrow, and I'll be all yours."

"That's a very smooth way of saying you're too busy for me right now."

Nic smiled. Davis always called her on her bullshit. "Smooth, but true. Why don't I pick you up at six and we'll go blow off some steam before we go home and…well blow off some more steam."

"I like the sound of that, but I'm sure there's a way I could help you blow off some steam right now over the phone."

Nic's face flamed. Was Davis offering what she thought she was offering? "Oh yeah?"

"Sure, baby. Just unzip your fly and think about my fingers slipping beneath the waistband of your jockey shorts."

The blood that had colored Nic's cheeks rushed to some place decidedly lower in her body. She had to stop this quickly before she lost every rational brain function. "Hey now, that's not fair. You know my imagination can't hold a candle to the real deal. Let's save that energy for a time when you can really use it."

"Oh, you're no fun, you old prude."

Nic gritted her teeth against the competitiveness rising within her. "You'll get your fun, but you'll have to wait for it. When I get to you tomorrow, I'll have you ready to beg."

"You're mighty sure of yourself."

"With good reason."

"Pick me up at six o'clock and we'll see who begs first."

"Deal."

"Good night, dear."

"Good night, Davis."

Nic sat back in her black leather desk chair, the cool surface doing little to soothe the residual heat from their conversation. God, who was she? She'd lied effortlessly to both Belle and Davis within the span of five minutes. If Belle had answered the phone when Davis had called, she could've lost both of them. She cared about Davis, and she cared about Belle. She wouldn't be able to live with herself if she shattered them. The best way to avoid a disaster was to stop putting herself in these positions, but she wouldn't give either of them up. Few thrills compared to having two beautiful women adore her, even if at times like this she didn't like herself very much. She had the good sense to feel bad about considering phone sex with Davis while Annabelle did her laundry down the hall, but these instances were rare.

She wouldn't give in to some crisis of confidence over one phone call. Moments when her two worlds collided disoriented her, but she simply had to remember where she was. She stared out her windows. Even in the fading light of dusk she saw the magnolia tree in full bloom, sprinkling white petals across her patio and perfectly maintained yard. Taking in deep breaths, she could still detect the scent of the fried okra Belle had cooked for dinner, and she barely made out the sounds from the ball game she'd left on the TV. She wasn't in Atlanta with Davis. She was at home, surrounded by the things that anchored her, kept her safe, and soothed her.

She strolled back to the living room and sat down, wrapping an arm around Belle's shoulder and pulling her close. Belle rested her head on Nic's chest, filling her senses with the scent of her shampoo and the feel of her body melding with her own. Everything was once again exactly how it should be. Everyone was happy, especially Nic. She intended to keep it that way.

CHAPTER SIX

W here's Nic working this week?" Liz asked over her filet of salmon in a balsamic reduction sauce. Their country club had long been known for its haute cuisine, and clearly their new chef upheld the tradition.

Annabelle didn't even try to temper her pride. "She's in Atlanta. The big suits are keeping her close these days. She's had lots of meetings with the corporate brass that she didn't used to get invited to, and they're introducing lower reps to her accounts in other cities. We suspect the promotion is imminent." She didn't like to brag about her perfect partner when Liz spent her time chasing a deadbeat dad, but they'd shared a bedroom for years and their DNA for life, so she couldn't keep anything from her sister.

"I can't believe how fast she's climbed the ladder. Did you ever think you'd be married to a vice president of anything?"

"Honestly, no. I just wanted her to do what made her happy, but I'm not surprised. She can do anything if she wants it bad enough."

"Well, I'm happy for both of you," Liz said. "Plenty of the uptight old biddies around here would have loved to see you fail, and Lord knows this country-club set wasn't the most enthusiastic about one of their blue bloods falling for a woman with no connections to speak of, but you've outlasted half of their marriages and added more money to the coffers than most of their native sons."

Belle smiled as she speared one last piece of her Cobb salad. She and Nic had raised more than a few eyebrows in their early days, but she'd known all along she was the lucky one. "You always had a harder time with their attitudes than I did. It's never been about the money or appearances for me, and I have no political agenda."

"Maybe not, but I bet you won't mind the big fat raise that comes with Nic's promotion."

"No, but not because I want to impress anyone in this room. If anything, our plans for that money will make them just as uncomfortable as they were the first time we showed up here."

Liz leaned forward conspiratorially. "Do tell."

"Just last night Nic said I could get pregnant this fall."

Liz's eyes widened. "What did you have to do to get her to agree to that?"

"Nothing." Annabelle could hear the surprise in her own voice. "I haven't talked about a baby at all lately because I didn't want to put any added pressure on her. We were cuddling on the couch and all of a sudden she said, 'I think our baby is really going to like it here with us.'"

Belle's heart ached at the sweetness of the memory. She'd tried not to get overly excited or make too much out of it, but her eyes had grown misty at the emotion behind the simple statement. "When I asked where that had come from, she said she's just been thinking about the perfect life we've built together. She said she feels safe and comfortable when she's at home with me, and a baby would, too."

"Wow. I'd started to think she meant to put you off indefinitely on the baby issue."

"We always said we wouldn't take those big steps until we were ready. Early on, I was just happy to have her, and then we had careers to build and a house to buy. Even when we got settled in, we wanted to accumulate a nest egg. It's really only been the last few years she's had to hold me off."

"Yes, but you're thirty-three. You'll be thirty-four before a baby is born, and if you want more than one…" Their waitress approached.

Belle intercepted the check and quickly wrote it off on their club account. "Don't think I haven't done the math, but while I was thinking about my age, Nic thought about all the things she wanted to provide for our family, all the things you and I take for granted but she never had. I see now that she wasn't stalling. She just wanted everything to be perfect."

"And I respect her for thinking things through." Liz's smile turned sad. "I sure didn't, which is why I have to go pick up your niece for a dental appointment her father isn't going to pay for."

"I'm sorry." Belle's joy faded as she rose to hug her sister.

"Don't be. I'm so happy you found your fairy-tale romance. You give me hope I'll find my own Nic someday."

"I hope you do, too."

Annabelle walked her to the lobby before saying good-bye and heading for the locker room. She needed to pick up her tennis bag before she ran to the grocery store. She didn't see anyone else as she strolled past several empty shower stalls, but she heard two women talking on the other side of a tall row of metal lockers. She thumbed the dial to enter her combination on the lock, largely oblivious to their conversation until the sound of Nic's name caused her to focus on their words.

"Yes, I'm sure it was Nic McCoy. How many women do you know who look like her? You can't miss those eyes."

Belle smiled. She'd heard plenty of times that even straight women found something alluring in Nic.

"Did you know the other woman?"

"No, but it's the same one we saw her having dinner with a few weeks ago."

Belle stopped turning the dial. Her heart beat faster. What were they implying? She didn't want to listen anymore, but she couldn't stop.

"Is it the same one you saw her leaving the hotel with in Savannah last year?"

"No, this one is a redhead. She looks spunky, and she's more brazen than the one we saw her with before. This time they were holding hands and stealing little kisses."

She sagged against the locker at the image of Nic kissing another woman.

"Gross. At least Annabelle has a sense of public decency."

She eased herself onto a bench and tried to control her breathing. They were wrong. They had to be wrong. Just a bunch of uptight biddies, that's what Liz had called them. Her breath came quick and shallow, but a wave of dizziness made her suspect the oxygen wasn't reaching her head.

"Poor Annabelle, but what did she think would happen with someone like that?"

"I suppose she didn't think. You know those Taylor girls. They see something they want and they get it."

Belle's natural defenses rose. It was hard enough to hear Nic talked about like that, and now they were dragging her whole family into this mess.

"So how many times have you seen her with this one?" The question killed what little defiance she'd mustered. There was more than one woman? More than one date?

"I've seen them twice—at a restaurant and a baseball game. Martha saw them once too, at the Roller Derby, of all places. She said the tramp couldn't keep her hands to herself." The woman speaking changed her tone from distaste to glee at the salaciousness of her story.

"Which tramp, Nic or her girl du jour?"

The woman giggled. "Neither of them, I suppose."

Belle's stomach roiled. These women were either spreading horrible lies or revealing the greatest heartbreak she could ever experience. How could they laugh while her whole world rattled and shook?

"Wait, why was Martha at a Roller Derby? Does she want to go slumming, too?"

"No." The speaker scoffed. "She was touring the location for some function the Ladies Auxiliary wants to host in Atlanta. She'd never even heard of a Roller Derby and found it horrifying such a thing existed. Apparently Nic's taste in company and entertainment isn't up to Martha's standards.

"Well, you can forgive the entertainment, but not the company." Their voices trailed off as they walked way, but Annabelle remained stone still and quiet long after she heard the door close behind them.

It couldn't be true. Nic wouldn't hurt her. She couldn't. There had to be some mistake. Or three mistakes, since they'd seen her with someone three times.

She frantically ran through her memories of Nic's contacts. She recalled a few women reps, but all of them older and no redheads. It could've been a sales contact they'd seen her with. It wasn't unusual for Nic to wine and dine a big client. At a Roller Derby? Stealing kisses?

"No, no, no," Belle finally muttered. She couldn't even form a complete thought, much less process details. There had to be an explanation.

Lies, all lies. That was the only possibility she would consider. Bitterness, jealousy, homophobia, or just plain boredom ruled too many women around here. Someone must have seen Nic on a business call and let the story spin out of control. Rumors distorted truth like a child's game of telephone, where the original message got distorted beyond recognition by the time it came around again.

She weakly got to her feet and took a few steps. Too shaken to go to the store now, she'd go home, to Nic's home. She needed physical reminders of Nic's love, dedication, and desire to have a family with her. But Nic wasn't there now, and the questions would be. The questions about long trips, late-night phone calls, all the times she couldn't get ahold of her. So many things she hadn't thought about before now seemed suspicious, even sinister. She dropped back onto the bench and covered her face with her hands. The blunt force of their gossip had ripped a hole in her confidence. Now the questions flooded her like water through the ruptured hull of a once-sturdy ship. How would she ever bail out all these doubts by herself?

"You brought me out to where God lost His shoes to ride go-karts?"

Nic grinned one of those grins that made her dimples appear and Davis melt. "These are some of the fastest karts in the world, and I have a need for speed."

"The drug? I had that pegged the moment I met you."

"Sure, but I was mostly talking about fast cars and fast women."

Davis smiled and headed for the track. Competition and metaphors for sex—suddenly this little field trip made sense. "Well, I'm probably the fastest woman you'll ever meet, so if you came here thinking you'd enhance your macho sense of self by blowing by me, you've got another think coming."

They continued trash talking as Nic paid and they changed into their racing jumpsuits. The facilities were insane, with one of the largest interactive arcades she'd ever seen, a black and neon rock-climbing wall, two go-kart tracks riddled with hairpin turns, and a high-ropes course that allowed patrons to scamper around in the rafters above it all.

As they took their place in line, Davis couldn't help but stare at Nic's lean, athletic body, so languid and delicious in the single-piece black racing suit that cinched at the waist, giving a tantalizing outline of her powerful form. Though it covered any bare skin from the neck down, she was almost certain she'd never seen a sexier piece of clothing.

Nic turned around and gave a cocky little smirk that turned Davis on in spite of herself. "I don't doubt you'll give it your best, but you don't even have a car, so just have fun out there and don't feel bad if I lap you."

"Okay, honey," Davis said in her best sickly sweet Southern drawl. "I won't mind if you pass me. I will, however, put you in the wall."

Nic threw back her head and laughed. "If you can catch me."

Davis pulled on her full helmet and flipped down the visor. She might not be much of a driver, but she was every bit as competitive as Nic.

She adjusted her seat and listened carefully as the employee talked about the throttle and brakes. She tightened her knuckles on the steering wheel and took deep breaths, but when the green light flashed, composure gave way to adrenaline, and she jammed the gas as if her muscles had acted on their own.

Several other karts were on the track, but she saw only the one with Nic at the wheel. She had to slow around the first sharp turn but flattened the pedal again as she rounded the corner. Her arms shook, and the tension tightened through her back and shoulders, but she didn't lift the pedal from the floor until she hit the next turn. She had to back off to keep from skidding, but Nic pulled farther ahead. "Damn," she muttered as sweat beaded between her forehead and the helmet. Nic clearly kept the kart floored through some of the turns, and she'd have to get a little reckless if she wanted to keep up.

Did she really care about keeping up? It was just a freaking go-kart, a child's toy being used by adults in grand "whose is bigger?" fashion. No, if that were all she had at stake, she'd settle for a leisurely joy ride, but she wasn't just chasing a go-kart. She was chasing Nic.

The muscles in her jaw twitched as she set her teeth and trained her eyes on Nic's bumper. She hammered hard through the next set of S-turns. For the first time she didn't lose ground through a challenging part of the course, but she didn't gain any either. Her real gut check approached quickly in the form of a wide but complete U-turn. Her senses heightened, and her skin prickled with the anticipation of danger. She had to fight her natural instinct to slow down. She rushed into the turn and jerked the wheel so hard the back end of the kart lost traction, sending her tires skittering across the concrete track and rattling her bones with each bounce. Miraculously, she didn't hit the wall. Her steering wheel righted itself, wrenching her arms back into place as she flew down a straightaway, now almost even with Nic.

The race seemed to go on forever as they looped around again, and Davis fought to hold her position as they traded places into the turns. With every corner Davis readied herself for a collision but never gave in to her internal warning to back off. After one more pass they got the signal they were on their final lap, and she bore into another turn. She was a mess of heat and sweat inside her suit, and the ache in her arms spread to her back and legs. The smell of gasoline seeped into her helmet, and the hum of the motor buzzed through her ears, but her concentration stayed clear.

She felt more than saw Nic beside her down the final stretch. Their karts went nose to nose with the finish line flying toward them.

Nic had a slight edge, and she was out of time. In an instantaneous decision, Davis gave one small twitch of her wrist, just a little movement really, but more than enough to brush metal against metal against concrete in a crushing squeal of rubber and chrome that ricocheted through her as both go-karts skidded to an abrupt stop inches shy of the finish line.

As her blurred vision stabilized, she sought Nic's eyes and found that deep-blue gaze filled with wonder and mirth. Even under Nic's helmet Davis could tell she was smiling a wicked smile of acknowledgment. The implications of her actions seeped through her rapidly evaporating haze of competitiveness.

She'd wrecked them both rather than let Nic pull away.

The race crew jogged over to untangle them and ease the go-karts across the finish line. Davis quietly stripped off her helmet and racing suit, all the while staring at Nic, while she did the same. After her behavior on the racetrack, she didn't trust herself to act according to the dictates of public decency.

They walked quietly to the car, and Nic pulled through an alley to a deserted warehouse parking lot. She put the car in park before turning to Davis. "You put me in the wall."

"I did," Davis said simply, not willing to admit how much that bothered her. How had she gone from being distrustful and avoiding intimacy to being so crazy about someone that she'd risk bodily harm to both of them?

"That's kind of crazy and sexy all at once."

"Well, I'm both crazy and sexy. That's why you love me." The words were out before Davis had a chance to think them through. She hadn't meant to use the L-word. Even if she was ready to make that leap herself, she didn't want to project something so major onto Nic. Maybe she could play it off as just another flippant remark, but one glance at Nic in the dimly lit car told her she hadn't missed the significance of the comment.

"You're absolutely right," Nic said. "I do love that you're sexy and crazy. I also love that you're tough and don't put up with any shit. I love that you never give me a free pass or take easy answers.

I love the way all your walls fall down when I get you in bed, and I love that you demand the same from me."

Davis was on top of Nic before she knew what she was doing. She'd never in her life had anyone say anything so damn perfect, and she couldn't tell her anything more clearly than she could show her. She straddled Nic's lap and pulled her into a searing kiss as they became a tangle of arms, hands, and seat belts. The adrenaline of their competition hadn't disappeared. It had transferred right into their relationship. Once again Davis's pulse raced and her body temperature rose. Oblivious to their surroundings her muscles ached too, only this time they didn't scream for rest. They begged for more. More of Nic's mouth, more of her breath hot on her neck, more of her touch on more of her skin. She ripped at Nic's shirt, popping a button so she could get her hand inside the bra.

Nic didn't waste time with their shirts. She went straight for the zipper of Davis's jeans. The tight fabric and her spread legs didn't make the task easy, but Nic never shrank from a challenge. Within seconds she shifted them both to the backseat. Somehow the bumbling urgency turned Davis on more than the comfort of any silk-sheeted bed ever could. Their new position afforded them just enough room to get their hands in each other's pants. Davis latched onto Nic's clit, and Nic, always the one to push a step further, slipped inside her.

Their bodies rocked in an awkwardly pounding rhythm, like two teenagers forcing their way through a cloud of lust, feeding off each other's need for a rapid escalation. "God, yes, fuck me," Davis growled, refusing to let go of Nic even as her own orgasm threatened. Like their earlier race to the finish, she was adamant they end together. "Come with me, Nic."

Nic's clit hardened beneath her fingers as her thrusting became more erratic. She was close, and the realization only pushed Davis further into incoherency. As Nic lurched forward, her muscles contracting beneath Davis, she spun out of control as well, shouting out a profanity-laced release.

"Fuck…yes, Nic, don't stop." She panted as flashes of white surged behind her eyelids. "I love you…Nic…fuck yes…I love you."

Davis's head lolled back onto the seat, and the rapid rise and fall of her chest settled into a more natural rhythm. "I haven't done that since high school. God, you make me so crazy for you."

"I love the way you want me." Nic was still panting.

Davis searched Nic's blue eyes through an evaporating gaze of lust.

"What?" Nic asked.

"You love what I do to you. You love so many things about me. You're using the word 'love' freely, but just not exactly toward me, so I'm trying to figure out if you're telling me something important or if you're dodging something important."

Nic looked her directly in the eyes. "I love you, Davis."

She smiled so fully her face ached, and relief stretched her chest. "Yeah?"

"Yes." Nic kissed her quickly. "But if you keep looking at me like that I'll have to prove it again, so let's cool it until I can show you in your bed."

"That sounds wonderful." Davis climbed back into the front seat, and Nic followed.

They cruised down I-85, both of them riding in the comfortable silence of their afterglow until Nic's cell phone rang. She made no move to pick it up.

"Aren't you going to get that?"

"I hadn't planned on it."

"Why?"

"I'm with you now," Nic said seriously. "I don't want anyone to take away from that."

"That's a lovely thought, but it makes me wonder who you're with when I call and you don't pick up."

Nic squeezed her hand. "Are you okay? You seem kind of, I don't know…insecure tonight."

Davis grimaced. *Needy, damn it. I'm getting needy.* Just because they'd said the big L to each other didn't mean she needed to start micromanaging Nic's life. "I'm fine. I just don't mind if you check your phone. Despite my behavior on the go-kart track, I'm not some possessive maniac. Maybe it's your parole officer, or the STD clinic calling with your test results."

"Well, yeah. I mean if you're eager to hear about that stuff, I'd be happy to check the message."

"Don't put yourself out on my account. I mean, you might feel embarrassed to show your total ineptitude at using voice mail in front of me."

"Not at all. I can even do it one-handed." Nic made a big show of pressing her voice-mail button and exaggeratedly listening as the message played, but halfway through, her expression darkened and her smile disappeared.

She turned the phone off and tossed it onto the dashboard, her face grim and ashen. "I'm sorry. I've got to cut this evening short."

"What?"

"Something's come up. I need to get back to my hotel."

"Listen, if your herpes report came back positive we can work through it." The joke wasn't funny, but neither was the sense of dread spreading through her.

Nic's forced smile wasn't convincing.

"Are you fucking with me because I made you check the message?"

"I wish. I really do hate to, but I've got to go."

Nic was serious, and that scared Davis. "Are you okay?"

"Yeah, but a, uh, friend, is having a hard time. I need to go check on her."

"A friend?"

"Yeah." Nic paled. "My best friend."

"In Athens?"

"She lives in Athens, but she's coming to the city tonight, and she sounded pretty upset." Nic looked more shaken than Davis had ever seen her, or maybe this was just the first time she'd ever seen Nic shaken at all. It was disconcerting to see such a normally self-assured woman look so lost.

"Do you want me to come with you? I'd love to help any way I can."

Nic shook her head. "Thanks, but I don't want her to feel overwhelmed any more than she already is. You understand, right?"

"Sure, of course." Or at least she tried to. She fought her selfish urge to tell Athens to get back in Athens. She already had to share Nic too much, and she didn't want that other part of her life to infiltrate their time in Atlanta, too. Instead she said, "If it were Cass in trouble, I'd go in a heartbeat."

"Thank you." Nic pulled off the interstate. As the distance to Davis's apartment lessened, the space between them grew. It was just one night and for a reason that had nothing to do with them as a couple. Why did it feel like Nic was pulling away?

When they parked outside Davis's place, Nic didn't get out to open the door for her. "I'll call you when I know what's going on. Maybe tomorrow sometime, okay?"

"Yeah, take all the time you need." Ugh, why had she said that? She wanted to say, "Hurry up and come back to me." Instead, she kissed Nic full on the mouth, hoping she could make her feel something, but as she got out of the car, she wasn't at all sure she'd succeeded.

❖

Nic tore through the parking lot of the Wyndham and whipped the car into the first open spot she found. Grabbing a suitcase and her garment bag, she rushed into the lobby and struggled to function like a sane person as she checked in. All she could process was pure, white-hot panic. She tapped her credit card incessantly on the counter while the desk clerk typed her information into the computer, her gaze set on a permanent swivel from her watch to the front door. How much time did she have? It had been at least half an hour since Belle had called, but she didn't know if she'd called from Athens or some other place along Highway 78. She could've already come and gone.

No, no, no. "Gone" wasn't a possibility she'd consider. She still had time.

The clerk gave her the key to room three-fifteen, and Nic sprinted up the stairs rather than stand fully exposed in the lobby for another second waiting for the elevator. She burst through the door and slammed it behind her.

Safe, she was safe. She had to slow her breathing. This was bad. Belle was clearly upset about something, but if someone were hurt she would've said so on the phone. All she'd really said was she needed to see her…right now. Maybe it was just her guilty conscience that made her suspect Belle knew about Davis. It could be anything. It could be nothing.

Well, obviously it wasn't nothing. Belle had sounded upset but also cold and distant, almost clinical in her summary of the facts. Maybe she'd just had a rough day. No, Belle wouldn't rush to Atlanta over something trivial. Still, the situation wasn't as out of control as she'd first imagined. Belle hadn't caught her with Davis, and now that she'd made it to the hotel first, she had the upper hand. She tried to force her heart to stop racing.

Everything would be okay. Belle would arrive to find her sitting in her hotel room, all alone and smelling like sex. *Shit*. She had the scent of another woman all over her clothes, her hands, her mouth. She wrenched off her shirt and jeans as she jumped into the shower before the water even warmed. She fumbled the soap while trying to strip off the wrapper and got shampoo in her eyes, but she managed to scrub away all reminders of Davis. Or at least she hoped so. Stepping out of the shower, she examined herself with all the calm detachment she could muster. Her eyes were still a little wide and frantic, but the rest of her body was clear of scratches or bruises, and her lips had long since lost their swollenness, leaving no outward signs anything was amiss.

As she turned her attention to the rest of the room, her more calculating business instincts kicked in. She'd run damage control on more than one corporate account over the years and could do the same here. She crafted a story in her head about having been at dinner with a client and being so wiped out she went right to the shower when she got to the hotel. Had Belle called the hotel? If so, what time? It didn't matter. She had to keep details to a minimum, say she hadn't checked in until after dinner and—

A knock on the door interrupted her planning. Nic grabbed her phone, threw open the door, and immediately began to lie. "Belle, oh, my Lord. I was just listening to your message. Are you okay?"

Belle looked inexplicably small in the doorway. She held a tiny carry-on suitcase. Her linen pants were creased and wrinkled, but she clearly wasn't the average traveler. Her eyes drilled straight past Nic into the hotel room, like she expected something sinister to materialize.

"Belle, honey, come here." She held out her arms, but Belle didn't move.

"Are you alone?" Belle's voice was hollow, and Nic grimaced at her words. What had happened, what did she suspect, or did she know?

"Of course I'm alone." She gestured to the hotel robe she'd thrown on seconds earlier. "I just got out of the shower. Please come in and tell me what's going on."

Belle sidestepped past her into the room. Nic followed her line of sight to her pile of clothes on the floor and her garment bag tossed on the bed. "Sorry the place is a bit of a mess. I never remember to hang things up when you're not around."

"You haven't unpacked."

"No, I went right to the office this morning, then to a dinner meeting that ran long. I only got checked in a little bit ago."

"A dinner meeting with a client?"

"Yeah, honey, who else?"

"Which client?" Belle's voice held only steel.

"Why? What happened?"

"Which client, Nic?"

Nic scrambled to think of a name, any name, and said the first one that came to mind. "Andretti Racing."

"A local client? I thought you were above that now."

"I am, in general, I suppose, but with a name like Andretti…" Nic was getting no response from Belle, and she didn't stand a chance of breaking through that icy exterior with business talk. She touched her lightly on the shoulder. "I can't believe you're here. I was so worried when I heard your message. I can't believe I get to touch you and hold you. Baby, I don't know what happened, but I'm just so glad you're okay."

She slipped her arms around Belle's waist, pulling her near. "Nic, I—"

She placed kisses along Belle's neck and shoulder. "You feel so good."

Belle began to soften in her arms. "You didn't answer your phone, and you weren't here or at the office."

"Oh, Belle, I'm sorry I worried you. I just hate to carry that damn thing, but I'm here now. I'm all yours."

Belle finally met her eyes, still searching for something. Then came the question Nic feared. "You *are* all mine, aren't you?"

The air left Nic's lungs. Belle did know something, or at least suspected, but how much? What should she admit to? How had she let things get so out of control? And more importantly, how could she turn her life back around?

Her panic rose again. Losing any ground was simply unacceptable. Belle wouldn't settle for less than all of her. Some primal survival instinct kicked in as the lies began to flow. "Of course I am, Belle. You're my heart and my anchor. How could you doubt that?"

Belle seemed to waver. "I needed you, Nic, and I couldn't find you. You've been gone so much, and people are starting to talk. I didn't want to listen, but rumor has it—"

"Shh, slow down. I'm here now. There's no one else in this room. No rumors. It's just me and you. No one else understands, but you know me. You've always known me."

The corner of Belle's mouth twitched up briefly, so Nic kept going. "I'm sorry I've been gone so much. I get tunnel vision at work, but it's only because of our goals. I want to give us the life we've dreamed of, the family we've dreamed of. It's so close I can feel it. Sometimes when I'm tired or run-down, I think of you with a baby in your arms, and it's just so beautiful I can't stand it." That was low, and Nic hated herself for using Belle's dreams against her, but not enough to stop. "You're what helps me survive the extra hours or nights away, not because of me, but because of us. Only us."

"Oh, Nic, I'm so sorry." Belle's resistance broke. "I just love you so much it makes me crazy."

"It's okay, baby."

"No, it's not. I let some jealous old biddies rattle me, and I barged in like a woman possessed. I let myself doubt you, Nic, only for a minute, but I shouldn't have. Can you forgive me?"

"Hush now. Of course I forgive you. I love you."

"I love you, too. So much it scares me sometimes." Belle started to place kisses along the bare skin between the lapels of Nic's robe.

She was torn between the overwhelming relief of having escaped a potentially relationship-ending conflict and disgust at herself both for how she got into this situation and the lies she'd told to get out of it. Who the hell was she becoming? She couldn't go on living two lives. Well, technically she could. She'd skirted this disaster nimbly enough, but at what cost? What kind of person lied to the two most important people in her life? And the lies had come so quickly, so effortlessly.

Belle slowly untied the knot in Nic's bathrobe and slipped her hands inside. She had to stop this. She couldn't make love to Belle less than two hours after fucking Davis. Then again, she'd told them both she loved them during that same time span. Wasn't that a bigger betrayal? At least saying she loved each of them wasn't a lie. If her feelings for them were a lie, she wouldn't be in conflict now. She'd just let one of them go.

Belle worked her way up Nic's body until she pushed the robe from her shoulders and let it fall to the floor. Nic finally met Belle's gaze, and a mix of love and lust overcame her guilt. Then Belle whispered, "Please, Nic, I need you." All other thoughts vanished.

She scooped Belle into her arms and carried her to the bed. Lowering her gently, she immediately began unbuttoning Belle's blouse and placing kisses on the skin under each one. They moved so well together, years of love and devotion driving every kiss. The familiarity of Belle's skin, her scent, the sounds of her breath as it grew shallow drew Nic into their past and showed her the most magnificent glimpses of her future. Nic's arousal overwhelmed her. Skin to skin, mouth to mouth, body against beautiful body, she pushed into Belle, tears stinging her eyes as emotion overtook her.

Belle reached for her as well, seeming as eager as Nic to strengthen the ties between them. They rocked in a steady motion, the energy between them grew to combustible levels. Nic worried she might disintegrate under the weight of their connection. She claimed Belle and gave herself up in the same moment as they clutched each other fiercely. Belle was home, Belle was happiness, Belle was everything that mattered.

They collapsed, and Nic untangled herself only enough to wrap the comforter around them, then pulled Belle close. She couldn't get enough of her, not now, not ever.

"Thank you, Nic, for being who you are. I don't know what I'd do without you."

The words hurt deep in her chest. "Shh, just sleep now, Belle. I've got you."

She wasn't the person Belle thought her to be, or Belle wouldn't be thanking her. But she wanted to be better. She wasn't sure when she'd turned into someone she couldn't even recognize, but she had to turn her life back around. Could she do it? She looked at the sleeping angel in her arms. For Belle she could do anything.

CHAPTER SEVEN

Belle woke in a tangle of sheets and Nic's arms. How strange that a hotel room felt more like home than the home she'd made for them. She was torn between the overwhelming sense of comfort and a wash of embarrassment about why she'd rushed to Atlanta in the first place. How unbelievably silly she'd been to let two snide gossipers shake her confidence in Nic. She should've known she'd find Nic right where she said she'd be, doing what she had always done, taking care of them.

She visually traced the lines on Nic's face in the early morning light. Flecks of gray were beginning to appear around her temples, and lines of laughter curled faintly around the corners of her mouth, but to Belle Nic was the perfect picture of the woman she'd fallen in love with, the woman she was still in love with. How could she have questioned her?

When she'd barged into the hotel, she'd honestly expected to find another woman in Nic's bed. She'd conjured visions of some faceless redhead wrapped in Nic's arms. Her mind had played the most awful trick on her; even when she saw Nic she couldn't believe her. Thankfully, Nic never wavered. She hadn't gotten angry with her for dropping in or defensive about her suspicions. How would *she* have reacted if the roles were reversed? She would've been hurt if Nic didn't trust her. Guilt surged through her. She didn't deserve Nic's devotion, but Nic gave it anyway.

Annabelle needed to show her she appreciated her and prove the faith she had in them. Nic was strong and unwavering and the most attentive provider, but lately Annabelle had done nothing but question and ask for more.

A shiver ran down the length of her body at the thought of what she'd done, and she snuggled closer to Nic for warmth.

"Hey, beautiful," Nic murmured, and kissed her forehead.

"I'm sorry. I didn't mean to wake you."

"No, it's nice. I'd much rather wake up to you than an alarm."

"I'm glad to hear that, but I shouldn't be here."

Nic rolled over to face her. "What are you talking about?"

"This is your world." Belle ran her fingers through a shock of dark hair that had fallen over Nic's eyes.

"You're my world."

The ache in her chest throbbed at the surge of love racing through her. "How do you manage to be so perfect all the time?"

Nic grimaced, then turned the expression into a smile. "I'm not perfect, Belle. Please don't think that."

"You're perfect for me." She kissed her lips. "We're perfect together. We've always been so effortless together that sometimes I forget how good we've got it, but you reminded me. I'm going to carry that feeling home with me."

"You don't have to go." Nic pulled her tighter to her chest.

"Yes, I do. You're here working so hard for us. I want to do my job for you too, and that means making sure you've got everything you want when you come home."

"At least stay for breakfast. We can call room service."

"No, if I stay in this bed the only thing I'll be hungry for is you. Why don't you get ready for work and we can get coffee and a bagel on your way out."

Nic looked less than enthused about the option. "We could have coffee and bagels in the room."

"I see right through you. You know if you keep me here you'll get to have your way with me."

"Can you blame me?"

Annabelle smiled sweetly, then threw back the covers. She did so enjoy being the object of Nic's desire. "Get up. It's a beautiful morning out there. Let me enjoy a little piece of Atlanta with you now, and then I'll be on my way."

Nic sat up and rubbed her face as if trying to force herself to agree. "You know I can't deny you anything, Belle."

In less than an hour they sat at an outside table in front of Caribou Coffee. Belle loved Atlanta in the springtime. The smells of freshly brewed coffee mingled with magnolias. The buzz of traffic and rush of pedestrians filled her senses. She loved to soak up the atmosphere. This particular intersection was one of her favorite spots. To one direction was the busy hub of Midtown and to the other lay the lush oasis of Piedmont Park. Just across the street sat the cutest little bookstore. They specialized in gay and lesbian books and kitsch. Nic called it tacky, but Belle found it amusing even if some of their things bordered on vulgar.

She turned her attention away from the city scene before her and noticed Nic didn't look as if she was enjoying the setting nearly as much as she was. Nic sneaked a peek at her watch, then glanced over her shoulder in the direction of the bookstore.

"What's the matter, Nic?"

Nic shook her head and smiled. "Nothing, I'm sorry. I'm already thinking about rush hour."

"We could've gotten the food to go."

"No, I'm being silly. I've got plenty of time. What are you thinking about?"

"I like this part of the city. It's busy without being congested, and it's close to so many fun spots. Wouldn't it be exciting to live in a place like this?"

Nic shrugged and seemed to look past Annabelle again. "It's not as quiet as home, and not nearly as much space. I'm not sure I could relax."

Nic certainly seemed high-strung this morning as she chewed her bagel quickly and swilled her coffee. What was the hurry, or was she always like this in work mode? Annabelle reminded herself again they weren't on a date. They were only having this breakfast together because she'd stormed into Nic's carefully planned schedule to accuse her of adultery. No wonder Nic seemed uncomfortable.

"Honey, do you really forgive me for last night?"

"What? Of course. It's my fault for leaving you alone so much. It's easier to forgive you than to forgive myself for making you doubt me. I need to do better."

Her chest ached again at the emotion stirring there. She couldn't let Nic take any amount of blame for her lack of faith. "Please, I don't want to hear any more of that. You're nothing short of wonderful. Don't change a thing."

"Then the same goes for you."

"Okay, I promise." Belle reached across the table to take Nic's hand.

Nic glanced over her shoulder again. The move was quick and easily dismissed as her stretching her neck, but it sparked a twinge of residual suspicion, and Annabelle scanned the buildings behind them, in the same swift flick of her gaze Nic had used. She saw nothing but a lone woman sitting by the front window of the bookstore. She wouldn't have been noticeable at all if not for her striking red hair.

This one is a redhead. The words rattled through her brain and shook her limbs, but Nic quieted the tremor by taking her hand.

"I love you, Belle."

She nodded. Nic did love her. Her mind was playing tricks on her again. She was paranoid. Nic was right here, with her. Would she have loved her so fiercely last night if she shared her bed with someone else? No. Nic couldn't, wouldn't do that.

She swallowed the last of her bagel, forcing it past the dryness in her throat until she could speak. "I need to get home."

"As much as I hate to, I should probably get to work, too." Nic stood and cleared the table quickly. Did she feel relieved or did it only appear that way?

This was absurd. When had she determined to find fault in Nic's every action? How did she still manage to feel suspicious when Nic continued to be perfect? She had no valid reason not to feel happier and more secure than ever, but the facts of the situation offered a bleak contrast to her inner turmoil. Her pulse quickened and her palms tingled. She'd heard of women having nervous breakdowns.

Did they include this racing stream of illogical thoughts? Should she make an appointment with her doctor? A therapist?

No. She just had to stop this train of thought right now. Mind over matter. She took Nic's hand. She couldn't resist one more look at the bookstore window. The woman watched them openly now, but with Nic holding Annabelle's hand, nothing seemed nearly as threatening. She was okay. Everything was okay.

❖

Davis's heart sank, her chest constricted, the corners of her mouth drooped. Hell, she probably even had puppy-dog eyes, and any other sappy, overly dramatic cliché people use when they experience a rush of sadness. Why had Nic walked away? They'd made eye contact, and even across the intersection she'd felt their connection. Then, inexplicably, she'd turned and left, holding the hand of the most perfect Barbie Doll Southern belle she'd ever seen.

"Damn it." She kicked the leg of the table, then mumbled an apology to the coffee-house employees, slipped outside onto the small patio, and shut the sliding-glass door behind her. Flipping open her cell, she dialed a number from memory.

"Cassandra Riggins Realty."

"Cass…"

"Uh-oh, what happened?"

"I just saw Nic, and she totally ignored me."

"And?"

"What do you mean 'and'?" Davis's voice went up a few notches. "She blew me off. She was right across the street, and she looked at me, then walked away."

"She just wandered off down the street by herself?"

"No, not by herself. She was holding some other woman's hand."

Cass sighed. "Why did you leave that part out in your first draft of this story?"

"Because it makes it sound worse than it is," Davis said without much confidence.

"How do you know how bad it is? You wouldn't have called me if there was some logical explanation."

"Well, I'm sure there is. I just can't think of one." Davis pouted.

"So you expected me to think of one? What in our many years of friendship suggests I'm the person to turn to for sweet, naive reassurances?"

She had a point, but she'd panicked. "I don't know. I mean, I don't expect you to know what's going on. I just needed to vent."

"Now that I get. You just saw your sometimes-sleepover buddy in the afterglow of knocking boots with someone else. That's always a little awkward."

"That's not what happened. There has to be some misunderstanding."

"Occam's razor, darling. The simplest answer is usually the correct one."

"Not in this case."

"How do you know?" Cass asked.

"I know." Davis spoke with a certainty she didn't feel.

"How?"

"She told me she loved me last night. We both said it." Emotion thickened her throat at the memory. "We made love and then we said we loved each other. It was a huge step for us."

There was silence on the other end of the line.

"Cass, are you still there?"

"Yes. I just don't know what to say." Cass's voice softened. "I hate to be the killjoy, but if she spent last night professing her love, why aren't you still ensconced in some lovers' nest somewhere?"

Confusion and disappointment surged through her again. Those questions had kept her up all night. Something about Nic's explanation hadn't felt right. "She got a phone call from a friend and had to leave in a hurry."

"Uh-huh."

"What's that supposed to mean?"

"What? I just said 'uh-huh.' It means nothing. It means I heard what you said and I'm still listening."

"It means you don't believe her story."

"Darling, I think your defensiveness indicates that *you* don't believe her story. The way you're trying so hard to prevent me from jumping to conclusions means you've already considered them and don't like what you found." Cass was completely and maddeningly logical. "I think you didn't believe her last night, and this morning she confirmed your suspicions, which is why you didn't go to her and why you're upset now."

"You don't know her, Cass."

"No, but you do, and you can't explain the situation either."

"I feel crazy. Nic's never given me any reason to distrust her."

"Of course she hasn't." Cass snorted. "If you don't count the fact that she disappears for days on end, you can't ever get ahold of her, she's never invited you to her place, she ditches you right after sex, and she ignores you when you see her with some other woman."

Davis closed her eyes and tried to focus on the image of Nic holding her tight, the echo of her voice saying, "I love you." It had all been so real. The beauty of it had shaken her cynicism, but now her hands shook from something else. Doubt surged through her like bile. It had been months since she'd tasted the bitterness that used to govern her every interaction. Jaded had been her default until Nic had walked into her life. She'd come so far from being the woman who automatically assumed the worst. She barely remembered why she'd been so guarded in the early stages of their relationship, but now those awful feelings came rushing back.

The skepticism felt like an icy hand at her throat. Where had she gone wrong? How had she slipped from cool and collected to passionate professions of love in four months? Had she ignored all the signs she'd sworn to be on guard for? She searched her memory: the unanswered calls, the lonely weekends, the lack of personal details. When examined with a critical eye, everything seemed dark and sinister. But nothing about their relationship had ever existed in a clinical sense. She couldn't explain their connection, but she could trust it. Couldn't she?

Did it make her a fool to believe in what she had with Nic instead of the phantom fears and shadowy suspicions choking her right now? Or would she be stupid to give in to residual cynicism over the connection she felt so strongly? Every option made her feel insane. Was she imagining things? Had she imagined things all along?

"Davis, are you still there?"

She startled at the voice on the phone. "Sorry, Cass. I just, I don't know what's going on with me this morning. I'm a little disoriented."

"Do you need me to come over?"

She shook her head and then remembered Cass couldn't see her. "No, I just need to pull it together."

"Are you sure?"

She took a deep breath and glanced around, trying to anchor herself to the here and now. She took in the traffic, people passing along the sidewalk, the restaurant across the street, anything tangible. Then she turned around and looked right into Nic's deep-blue eyes. She'd come back for her, and the depth of emotion that passed between them without a word evaporated the haze of doubt.

"Yes, I'm sure."

Nic watched relief flood Davis's features as she smiled wearily, but her initial reaction was only the first battle in a bigger war she shouldn't even fight. She needed to let Davis go. When she'd walked away with Belle, she should have kept on walking. That would've been the easiest path, the one she longed to take, but she couldn't. She owed Davis a good-bye, a formal end to what they'd done. And it did have to end. She couldn't hurt Belle the way she had last night, and she couldn't become the person who lied, cheated, and took what she wanted no matter whom she hurt.

She tried to find words to explain what had seemed so clear last night, but then Davis was in her arms. She didn't know how it happened. Maybe they were just drawn to each other in a way neither of them could control. Davis's warm breath fluttered over the sensitive skin of her neck, causing a thrill to course down her spine. She hugged her tighter, trying to imprint the press of their bodies on her memory while simultaneously forgetting why this was the last time she could hold her.

Oh, God, it's happening again. Nic had to pull away if she had any hope of being able to do what she'd come here to do. She summoned the image of Belle standing in the doorway of her hotel room last night, and her chest constricted. The pain wasn't as strong as the night before, but still enough to make her step back, and when she did Davis landed a sharp blow on her shoulder.

"Ouch." She hadn't expected Davis to hit her, but the thrill of the unexpected had always been part of the attraction. "What was that for?"

"For running out on me last night." Davis punched her in the other arm. "And that's for walking away this morning."

"Fair enough."

"No, not fair at all. You left me sitting here thinking all kinds of crazy things. Damn it, you've spent the last four months teaching me to trust you and have a little faith in my own instincts, and then you go and shake all of that."

"I'm sorry, Davis. I was stupid. I didn't think about how you'd feel." All true statements, but clearly the truth wasn't enough because Davis continued to wait for more. "I just, something happened last night…"

"Something blond and shapely who spent the night?"

"No." She shook her head. No more lying. "Yes, but it's not what you think."

"Really? You run out on me with some half-baked story, then stroll by hand-in-hand with some other woman, ignoring me completely, and all you can say is, it's not what I think?"

Nic cringed at the hard edge creeping back into Davis's voice. That doubt came from hurt deeply ingrained by years of disappointments, and everything she had to say would only make it worse. Her betrayal would confirm everything this stunning woman feared about love, honesty, and her own self-worth. *Damn it.*

"Was she the friend you mentioned last night?"

"Yes." Nic's stomach roiled at the thought of discussing Belle with Davis. "My best friend since college."

"Is she okay?"

"I think she will be."

"Why ignore me?"

"I didn't know what to do. She's going through a rough time. She thinks her partner is cheating on her. She's scared and suspicious." Each answer came easier than the one before. They weren't lies really, and they seemed to soothe Davis. They soothed her, too. When had these sorts of conversations become more comfortable than the truth?

"I know how she feels. It's like you're suffocating, or your brain isn't working, like you're losing your grasp on everything you know."

The ache in her chest returned in force, and her animal instinct to avoid pain took over. "I'm so sorry. I hate that I made you feel that way, but I didn't want to flaunt our happiness in her face."

Davis didn't give in, but her expression softened, and Nic kept talking. "I'd just been in your arms telling you how much I loved you, and then she was there and hurting, and I spent all night trying to reassure her. This morning when I saw you and her at the same time, I don't know, the contrast made me feel guilty."

"Baby, you shouldn't feel guilty for being happy."

Nic smiled the first real smile she'd smiled all morning. She'd needed to hear that and wanted to believe it. Should she put her happiness first? Wasn't that selfish?

Davis moved closer. "Sometimes you make things harder than you have to."

Her heart pounded. If only Davis understood how true her words were. She made everything harder than it should've been. She should've been happy with her life, but she had to complicate it. She had to hurt Belle and Davis. She'd made a mess out of what should've been perfection, and now here she was telling half-truths to a woman she wanted to cling to. But were they really only half true? She was happy, and she did feel guilty about that. She did love Davis, and Davis loved her. That was a truth larger than any detail. Didn't the great truths matter most?

It would've been different if Davis didn't want her anymore, if she had been mad instead of sad, if she'd yelled instead of pleaded for reassurance. No, Davis didn't want the truth. She wanted to hold her. Belle didn't want the truth either. She wanted to believe. Nic could give them what they wanted just like she had for months. Belle had left happy, and Davis stood on the verge of the same kind of joy. She could secure them both, make them both feel safe and loved, and wasn't that what all of them really wanted?

She wrapped her arms around Davis's waist and squeezed her. "You're right. About everything. I do make things harder than they have to be. Can you ever forgive me?"

"I more than forgive you. I love you."

Nic exhaled all of the tension she'd been carrying, either in relief or resignation. "I love you, too."

They held each other for a long moment before Davis finally whispered, "Take me home."

Her blood pumped quickly, reigniting the spark she'd tried to extinguish last night. She took Davis's hand as the familiar heat spread through her body, then turned toward the sidewalk.

Her heart went cold. The ice spread through her limbs and froze the very breath in her lungs. Rendered completely immobile by what she saw in front of her, Nic could only stare wordlessly at Belle.

CHAPTER EIGHT

No air, there was no air, not in her lungs, not anywhere around her. Annabelle's vision blurred at the peripherals, causing a tunnel of sight straight to Nic in some other woman's arms. Even if there could be a logical explanation for the press of their bodies, the look on Nic's face told her everything she needed to know about what she'd just witnessed. She knew what Nic looked like in love and in lust, and both emotions were clearly visible in her eyes. Thirteen years of life flashed through her mind, like dominos toppling one after another and scattering across the floor of her memory as she watched all the blood drain from Nic's face.

"Belle." Fear caused her voice to sound strangled.

"Nic?" the other woman asked, pleading raw in her voice.

"Davis." Nic sighed. "Oh, God."

Davis? The name rattled through her as another piece of the puzzle snapped into place. Not a man or an intern, but a woman. A lover. A red-haired lover who had called Nic at all hours for months.

Months.

A wave of nausea surged through her.

She'd gone back to the hotel with the intent of leaving, but the nagging voice inside her wouldn't let go. As much as she'd feared for her sanity, she gave in to the compulsion and walked the few blocks back to the bookstore, chastising herself the whole way. Why couldn't she trust Nic over some little whine of intuition? Now she had her confirmation. Her instincts had been right. She wasn't crazy, or at least she hadn't been before she saw everything she knew about her past and her future evaporate. Surely she'd be driven mad now with grief and pain.

"What's going on?" Davis asked, sounding very much like she already knew the answer, or at least had a strong suspicion.

Nic turned from one of them to the other, her eyes darting futilely for a way out before taking a step back away from both of them, like a frightened animal ready to run. She took another step before bumping against the rail of the porch. She didn't have anywhere left to go, physically or figuratively. The denials didn't flow the way they had the night before. Nic seemed to search for something, anything to get her out of this hell, but found nothing in her surroundings or herself that offered any of them an escape. Fear, anguish, hopelessness, and then resignation crossed her beautiful features in the instant before she hung her head. "I'm so sorry."

"You're sorry?" Davis lashed out. "For last night?"

Nic rubbed her hands over her eyes as she shook her head.

Davis turned to Annabelle. "Just last night?"

She doesn't know who I am.

She doesn't know anything.

Annabelle didn't know if that made things better or worse. It certainly made Davis look better in her eyes, but Nic so much more guilty. The woman she'd loved and trusted unconditionally had not only betrayed her, but she'd also clearly done the same to another woman. This…this affair, this deception, wasn't a one-time mistake, but a way of life.

Unable to speak in the face of her own grief, or Davis's, Annabelle stood mute and watched Davis turn on Nic. "How long have you known her?"

"Always."

How many times had Annabelle heard Nic say always in the regard to them? Always love her? Always be with her? Always and forever? The word had never sounded so horrible.

"Always what? Always known her, always slept with her? "

"Thirteen years," Nic choked out. "She's my wife."

Davis was on her in an instant. She had Nic by the scruff of her shirt. "You son of a bitch. How could you? All your talk about tearing down walls and chasing dreams, and you had a whole other life?"

"I didn't want to hurt you," Nic whimpered.

"Hurt me? Oh, I'll show you hurt."

Davis raised her hand and Nic's eyes widened in fear. Something protective rose in Annabelle. The love they'd built over the years might not have meant anything to Nic, but it still made up a huge part of herself. Even in her despair, Nic was hers. She'd been hers to love, hers to lose, hers to grieve, and she couldn't stand by and watch another woman strike her.

"Stop it," she said in a voice so low and commanding she barely recognized it as her own.

Both Nic and Davis froze and stared as though they'd forgotten she was there. She felt raw and exposed. What could she do or say to her partner and her partner's mistress?

Nic's *mistress*.

Another wave of dizziness assaulted her as she zeroed in on the way Nic's hands steadied Davis's hips, then moved her gaze up to see Nic's shirt clutched in Davis's grasp. Even in anger they had a familiarity with each other's bodies that made Annabelle's stomach roil. They would be explosive together, and obviously had been.

"I'm so sorry," Nic said, taking a step toward her but failing to break contact with Davis.

"Sorry for what? For cheating on her with *me*? For lying to me about *her*? Or are you just sorry you got caught?"

Davis relentlessly asked the questions that spun through Annabelle's mind but died, strangled in her pain before they reached her lips. The anguish and fury in the other woman's voice mirrored the emotions burning through Belle's chest. She stood, rooted in her anguish, hands fisted at her side.

"I…I tried." Nic practically sobbed back. "God, I tried to tell you."

"You tried to tell me you had a wife? Really? Was that before or after you fucked me? Or maybe after you fucked me, but before you told me you loved me?"

Too much.

Too far.

Belle would never be able to scrape that memory from her mind or silence the echo of those words from her ears. She swayed, her legs suddenly unable to support the weight crushing her now. The tunnel of her vision shrank to a pinpoint of light, then disappeared as her knees buckled. Everything became mercifully still, quiet and black as night. She welcomed the darkness and the accompanying nothingness, but it didn't last long enough. In an instant she was in Nic's arms.

God, she was so strong, so comforting, so familiar. Annabelle started to snuggle in against Nic's chest, the power of their past recognizing her arms as a place of safety, but as her mind and vision cleared, she remembered what had caused the trauma she sought to escape.

Nic.

Nic had done this. The same arms that supported her now had held another woman. The lips that whispered softly had kissed someone else. The hands steadying her had made love to—

"No!" Annabelle jumped away on two wobbly legs. "Don't touch me."

"Belle," Nic said in her most pacifying voice.

Belle shook her head almost frantically, trying to avoid the image of Nic's beautiful features contorted in desperation. Even in the face of her pain, even with Annabelle within reach, Nic kept glancing over her shoulder, and every time she did, Annabelle saw her own emotions reflected in the anger-laced agony of Davis's expression. Nic clearly saw it, too, and stood paralyzed between them.

She can't choose between us even when we're both here.

The realization shot another dizzying wave of hurt through her, and she blinked away her tears. She couldn't look at them a second more. She felt like she was choking, or suffocating, as every pore of her body seemed to close off. If she couldn't trust Nic, she couldn't trust the air, or the ground, or the sun. Every part of her life shook and threatened to crumble around her. Nic took a step toward her, but was too late. She was already running. Wildly, blindly, fueled by adrenaline and pain, she fled.

❖

Nic stood in shock as her wife ran from her. The look on Belle's beautiful face had been a heartbreaking mix of pain and disgust. She should go after her. She needed to chase her down, beg her for forgiveness, make whatever grand gesture she needed to or take whatever punishment Belle doled out. Instead she stood rooted in place, paralyzed by the understanding that she'd caused the agony she'd seen in Belle's eyes. If anyone else had hurt her like that, Nic would've killed them. What made her think she deserved anything less?

"Go after her." Davis's voice crashed through her indecision, reminding her Belle wasn't the only woman she'd shattered.

"Davis, I—"

"No. Davis nothing. She's your *wife*. Your wife! I don't ever want to hear you say my name again."

Nic shook from the ice in her voice. All the fire had gone from her eyes. The passionate woman who'd clung to her minutes ago had vanished, replaced by the jaded woman she'd met in the bar four months ago. No, even then she'd carried a spark in her eyes that was absent now. Davis had shut down emotionally, leaving nothing but a bland expression of disdain. Nic would've given anything to see a flash of the dangerous temper she'd caught the brunt of in the aftermath of Belle's arrival. "Please, Davis, listen to me."

"Go after her, or go fuck yourself. I don't care, but either way, get away from me." The line was delivered without any emotion. The walls Nic had carefully dismantled brick by brick over the last four months were rebuilt in one disastrous instant, and she wouldn't get the chance to knock them down again. The prospect of never again seeing past those defenses to the beautifully vibrant woman behind them caused an ache to throb deep in her chest.

She had only herself to blame. In one moment she'd destroyed the two people she loved most and ended every relationship that ever mattered to her. She'd lost. She'd never lost at anything in her life, and the gravity of her first failure being tied to Davis nearly strangled her. Between the weight of grief settling on her chest and the mass of emotions choking her throat, she fought to breathe. No wonder

Belle had fainted. The reminder that she'd not only brought this kind of pain on herself, but she'd also inflicted it on the two women she loved, only amplified her misery.

She couldn't take it. Defeat had never been an option for her, and she wouldn't accept hopelessness now either. She'd created this mess. She had to create a solution, if for no other reason than to stop the hemorrhaging of her own emotions. If she stayed still, she'd free-fall into the void of nothingness emanating from Davis until it consumed her.

She scanned Davis's face, frantically searching for any crack in her seemingly impenetrable façade, but found none. The woman who'd reminded her of what it felt like to experience passion again was clearly devoid of the emotions she'd inspired in Nic. There was no visible chink in her armor, and despite Nic's desire to keep searching, she had to cut her losses if she hoped to salvage the other half of her disaster.

"Davis, I'm so sorry. I don't expect you to understand, and I won't even begin to hope for your forgiveness, but someday when you're able look back on the last four months without just seeing this day, I hope you'll believe I really did love you."

Davis's fists clenched at her sides, and she ground her teeth so hard Nic could hear them scrape against each other. "Get out of my sight."

She raised her palms in surrender. "Okay. I'm sorry. God, I'm so sorry."

Nic turned and took one step, then another. She couldn't turn around. She wouldn't look back. What they'd shared was gone, probably forever. If this really was good-bye, she didn't want any more haunting images of Davis to her memory. She wanted to remember her as she'd seen her last night. She pulled a little solace from the hope that someday that's how Davis would remember them, too. Then she turned her focus to the part of this battle she needed to win.

Belle. The image of her dropping earlier sent another shot of pain strong enough to make Nic wince. If hell existed, it must feel like she had in that moment. Her steps faltered. She had caused

Belle's pain. All the justifications she'd used while creating this mess came up pitifully hollow when examined against the life she shared with Belle. Did someone who willingly took that risk deserve another chance? Could she be worthy of a second chance if she got one?

No, damn it. She was getting ahead of herself. She'd failed in her horrendously stupid attempt to have everything. Then she'd failed Davis. She wouldn't fail again. She couldn't lose Belle. She had to shut down the panic and doubt, the disappointment and pain. She had to think logically.

Where would Belle go? Back to the hotel? She had to get her car, but she wouldn't stick around there. And even if she did, Nic couldn't make a stand there. That room held nothing but lies and betrayal. She might go to her sister's house or, even worse, to her father's. She cringed at the thought of Buddy Taylor's legendary temper. She wouldn't be able to win Belle back in the shadow of his protectiveness.

Home was her only option. Would Belle return to the last place they'd been happy, or would she now question everything they'd built together? Nic couldn't let that happen. She had to use their past to paint the picture of a future they could both believe in. Belle would have to return to their house eventually, and when she did, Nic planned to offer her a reminder of everything they had been, and could be again.

Davis stood painfully still as she watched Nic walk away. She didn't trust herself not to chase her, and she wasn't sure what she'd do if she did. Half of her wanted to beg Nic to love her, to tell her she chose her, or to just give her back to the oblivion that came from all her lies. The other half of her thought she might kill Nic, or at least beat her senseless in the attempt to make her feel something resembling her own pain. She hated herself for both impulses, almost as much as she hated Nic for making her feel them.

How had Nic done this? How had Davis fallen for it? Last night she'd feared some other woman was coming between them, and it had nearly driven her crazy. Then she'd found out *she* was the other woman. How could she live with the fact that she'd offered the best parts of herself to a woman who wasn't even free to accept them? Everything she'd ever known about her, everything they'd shared, and every dream for a future had been an elaborate lie. Davis was nothing more than Nic's dirty little secret.

Davis felt something inside her had died, something crucial, something like her heart. But even that idea was too romantic for her now. Her heart was nothing more than an emotionless organ. Any figurative value it had once held as the seat for emotion, passions, or intuition was lost to her. If her heart had ever been any of those things, it was now either worthless or a traitor. Clearly, it wasn't safe to trust anyone, especially herself.

Lies, all lies.

None of what they'd shared had been real.

Nic had seen all her insecurities and she'd played them. She'd played her, and Davis had let her. How long would she have gone on if she'd hadn't gotten caught? Obviously far enough to profess her love, enough to suggest Davis had been acting crazy even when she'd seen her with the woman she'd spent thirteen years with. Was there no end to her deception?

Actually there was an end. It had ended today, their relationship, the memories of their past, and any hope for a shared future. So what now? She glanced around, becoming slowly aware that life went on. Cars buzzed by the intersection before her, pedestrians strolled leisurely toward Piedmont Park, bookstore patrons sipped coffee, unaware of the life-shattering encounter just outside. Amazingly, the world didn't stop for her broken heart. Life continued, and she'd have to figure out how to be a part of it again, but how?

Davis fought the void threatening to consume her. She struggled to summon her ability for logic or reason. She had a job. Could she just go back to work? No, of course she couldn't focus on designing a pamphlet on the benefits of Lasik eye surgery, but she couldn't just stand here all day trying not to cry. She could go home.

And do what? Fall apart? Wallow in a bed of tears and Kleenex?

That sounded like a more pathetically soothing option.

Trembling slightly, she moved off the bookstore patio and toward her apartment. The half of a city block felt like a mile, but she made it without stumbling, crying, or yelling at random strangers. Of course her keys had to be all the way at the bottom of her bag under her laptop and cell phone and God only knew what else.

"Damn it," she muttered, refusing to lose it over a set of fucking house keys. Fighting the urge to dump the whole bag onto the sidewalk, she closed her eyes, took a deep breath, then tried again until the sound of a sob drew her attention. Had it come from her? She felt like sobbing but hadn't actually done so yet. This sound came from the alley along the other side of her apartment.

She stood, arms up to her elbows in the backpack, head and heart pounding, and considered her options. She needed to go inside. She was in no shape to help anyone, certainly not someone on the kind of crying jag she'd overheard. If anything, she needed to join in. Unless the person wasn't sad. What if he or she was hurt? God, what if someone had been mugged? Not likely at ten in the morning, but right then, she didn't have much faith in human nature.

She slung her backpack over her shoulder and walked cautiously toward the alley. Why did her chance to play Good Samaritan come on the day she felt most like committing murder?

She edged around the corner and peered into the shadows, wondering how this morning could possibly get worse, but she didn't have to wonder long. Halfway down the alley stood her second least-favorite person in the world. Nic's perfect little Southern belle slouched over, shoulders slumped and shaking, head resting against a dirty concrete wall.

Even amid the filth she was striking, a living Barbie, all dolled up like something out of *Southern Living* with her light-turquoise blouse and calf-length black skirt. She had a classic hourglass frame, long hair so beautifully blond it had to be natural, and if that wasn't enough, she turned to level her big sky-blue eyes on Davis. Seriously, who looked like that? She didn't even seem real.

Belle didn't appear nearly as taken with the sight of Davis, because she let out another body-wracking sob, then threw up.

Davis cringed as Belle continued to lose the breakfast she'd watched her consume an hour earlier. "Now, that made you seem more real."

"I'm sorry?" Belle asked as she wiped her mouth with the back of her hand.

"I was just thinking you couldn't be real, but the vomit added a down-to-earth touch."

Belle stared at her like she'd lost her mind. "I don't really know what to say. Did you follow me?"

"No, that's my apartment." Davis pointed to a window above them. "I heard the crying and wanted to make sure no one got mugged."

"Oh, I'm sorry."

"For what? Not having been mugged?"

"For disturbing you."

"Well, yes." Davis rolled her eyes. "Your crying was kind of the least disturbing thing that's happened to me today."

"Are you always this sarcastic?"

"Pretty much." David shrugged. "Are you always so polite?"

"Generally, yes."

They stared at each other for a long minute. Davis couldn't stop studying her. This woman lived the life she'd dreamed of. She'd shared Nic's life, not just her bed. She'd made a home with her, watched her age, and celebrated milestones. And why wouldn't she? She was flawless, stylish, demure, well mannered, everything Davis wasn't. It struck home the old adage about the type of girls you dated and the type you married. Davis was clearly the former, while this woman had been the latter for Nic. The reminder that Nic had been married nauseated her, and she felt a little less superior about having seen *Southern Living* Barbie throw up.

God, why couldn't she have been ugly or bitchy? Why wasn't she telling Davis off? Or ripping her hair out? She had every right to go all cat-fight on her, and then maybe Davis could have understood why Nic had cheated on her, but instead of flipping out, she stood there with her baby blues scanning Davis up and down. Was she making the same comparisons about their appearance and temperaments? Had she come to the same conclusions?

"Are you wondering what she saw in me?" Davis asked, angry at the sadness her voice revealed.

"Excuse me?"

"When you look at me, do you wonder why Nic did what she did?"

"No, when I look at you, I know exactly what she saw. But I still can't believe she cheated on me."

"Well, that makes two of us."

The woman began to cry again, making Davis's emotions feel dangerously exposed, too. She couldn't leave her bawling in the alley. Well, she could, but she'd never get any peace, not that she foresaw peace in her near future anyway, but she deserved a chance to wallow in her turmoil without obsessing about having contributed to someone else's. Then again, was it possible to separate their respective traumas? Davis played a crucial, if unwitting, part in the destruction of this woman's life, and getting her out of sight would not get her out of mind.

Standing there listening to her sob wasn't a much better option, though. Aside from being completely unproductive, serving as a silent witness to the pain she'd helped cause only compounded her already overwhelming emotions, and she was quickly approaching her breaking point.

"Look, I can't do this. I can't stand here and watch you cry, and I can't leave you out here alone either."

"I'm sorry."

"I swear to God, if you apologize to me again, I might slit my wrists," she snapped.

Belle blinked her red-rimmed eyes. "You're right. I'll go."

"No. Shit," she muttered. "I didn't mean to yell at you. It's just, you know, there's no playbook for this situation." Davis felt even worse. She didn't want to make things harder than she already had. And now she wanted to kill Nic, not only for what she'd done to her, but for hurting this apparently sweet, sensitive, and emotionally frail woman. It didn't make any sense. "Why don't you come in and get cleaned up, rinse your mouth out or something, then you can go, and I'll feel one molecule less of guilt before I fall to pieces?"

"I don't know." She seemed skeptical.

"Fine. I get you not wanting to be in my place. Quite frankly, it'd be hard for me too, but I need to get off my feet and into a bottle of scotch."

"You're right. I can't stand out here all day," she said, then softly added, "but I really don't want to go back to the hotel, either."

"So we're both back to crying in the alley? 'Cause seriously, if I don't get out of here soon, that's what's going to happen."

"I'm sorr—I mean, okay. I'll just use your bathroom quickly, then find somewhere else to go."

Davis managed to unlock the door without melting down, but as she climbed the stairs her doubt and fear multiplied with each step. Why had she invited Nic's wife into her home? Did she feel responsible for this woman? Did she want something from her? Was she looking for answers or some kind of absolution? Intellectually she knew she wouldn't find either from her, or anyone else for that matter, but like it or not they were tied together in this horrible knot of pain and betrayal. She owed it to both of them to try to untangle whatever parts of it they could.

Annabelle fidgeted on the threshold of Davis's apartment. It wasn't that she didn't want to go inside so much as she didn't think she *should* want to go inside. What woman wanted to be faced with the personal side of her partner's mistress? Was she so shocked she'd lost her ability to process logically? Probably, but she'd also experienced some sort of morbid curiosity about Davis. Why her? Nic had met thousands of women over the last thirteen years. What about this one made her willing to risk everything they'd built together?

She was beautiful, but not in the refined sense Belle strove to cultivate. Davis's short, flame-red hair and hypnotic green eyes made her seem exotic, and her low-slung boyfriend jeans and tight black T-shirt offered a sharp contrast to the slim skirts and button-downs Belle wore. Did a little bit of novelty have the power to destroy the foundation they'd built their life on, or did Davis hold something deeper?

"Um, you can come in, if you want." Davis pulled Belle back into the moment.

"Thank you," she whispered. "I just don't know how to behave in this situation."

Davis snorted. "I guess that's a good thing. I mean, who wants to be well-practiced at this sort of thing?"

"I suppose there's that silver lining, but I'm still feeling very unsure of myself and, well, everything else."

"Then you're in good company. About the only thing I know for certain is I'm Davis and this is my apartment. Everything else is under examination."

"Davis," Belle repeated, the name heavy on her lips. "I knew that much from Nic's cell-phone contact list, but I thought you were a particularly needy sales intern."

"Needy maybe, but not an intern," Davis said. "And you're Belle?"

"Annabelle. The only one who's ever called me 'Belle' is Nic."

"Annabelle it is. You live in Athens?"

"The suburbs. Nic didn't want to make a home or raise kids in the city."

"Oh, my God, you have kids?"

"No, no kids," Belle quickly said as another piece of her heart broke at the realization they would never have children. "We'd been planning to try this fall."

Davis paled. "She's been planning to have a family with you while sleeping with me? I'm going to need that scotch now." Davis walked behind the bar separating the kitchen from the living room. "Care to join me?"

"It's only eleven o'clock in the morning."

"Eleven o'clock on the longest morning of my life."

"I take mine on the rocks. Should I get the ice?"

"Knock yourself out."

She took the four steps necessary to cross the tiny apartment and removed a tray of ice out of the nearly empty freezer, noting again the differences in the life they led. Back at home their freezer, fridge, and cabinets were always fully stocked, but when she closed the door all her thoughts of food vanished as she saw the picture of Davis and Nic together. They wore matching baseball jerseys and were clearly at the ballpark, but what really struck her was the comfortable way Davis snuggled into the crook of Nic's arm. They looked so natural, so happy. They'd been out sharing an afternoon in each other's company. Any remaining hope that their connection had been solely physical shattered.

She turned helplessly to Davis as if she could explain why the love of her life had looked at someone else the way she'd always looked only at Annabelle. "Does she love you?"

Davis examined the picture, tears welling up her eyes before she took a strong swallow of scotch. "I thought she did. She told me she did, but she lied." She pointed back to the photograph. "I guess all of it was a lie."

Belle turned from the picture to Davis, wanting to believe her, but none of it felt like a lie. She thought she understood Nic well enough to read her emotions. Yesterday she would've sworn she recognized what Nic looked like in love, but clearly she was wrong. She'd never known Nic like she was getting to know her now, with doubt and suspicion questioning every "truth." Had any of them ever been real? Which ones? When had the lies begun? And why?

She sipped the scotch, relishing the physical sensations that accompanied the drink. The slow burn of the liquid on her lips grounded her to the present. She welcomed anything tactile to anchor her to the real world as opposed to the sinister darkness of her imagination.

"It just felt so damn right. How do you fake that?" Davis seemed to be talking to her scotch. "But it had to be fake, because you don't do this to someone you love. You don't lie and two-time someone you really love."

"By that standard she didn't love me either."

"Oh, shit." Davis looked up as if she'd forgotten about Annabelle. "I didn't mean to drag you any deeper into this. I know nothing about your life. I didn't even know you existed until an hour ago."

Annabelle nodded, still too bewildered to process what that fact meant about either of them, or Nic.

Davis stared at the image on the fridge once more. "When I see that picture of us together, I can't figure out how we got from there to here."

"Actually, that picture got you from there to here." Annabelle took another sip of scotch to steel her for the recounting of her nightmare. "Some women from our country club saw you at the game. I overheard them yesterday, and rumor has it you two also enjoyed a Roller Derby together. It's the talk of our social circle, only I was the last one to know."

"Oh, God, I keep getting the urge to apologize to you, but damn it, I didn't know. I won't take responsibility for her emotional fuckery."

"I wish I had your attitude."

Davis took another drink and slouched onto a barstool. "I wish I could maintain it. Don't get me wrong, I'm mostly angry at her, but I feel so stupid, too. So duped and betrayed. What if it was my fault? Shouldn't I have known? Shouldn't I have seen the warning signs? She was never around on the weekends, never invited me to her place. I know nothing about her past or her friends. Why didn't that add up?"

"The same way the long business trips, her not wanting me to travel with her, or the Sunday phone calls from work didn't add up for me. I never questioned why she didn't answer her phone at night." She slumped onto the stool next to Davis, no longer certain her legs would support the weight of her sadness. "I never knew I had anything to question."

"She answered her phone last night," Davis mused. "I made her listen to a message. Was it from you?"

"Yes, I'd heard the women at the country club, and I had to see for myself. I was so afraid of what I'd find, but she was waiting for me just as calm and reassuring as she'd ever been."

"She rushed back in time to meet you only because I made her check the message. We'd just finished having sex in her car when—" Annabelle must have looked as awful as she felt because Davis stopped talking. "Are you okay?"

"No, not really. I just can't take everything you can. The thought of you two," she choked down another healthy sip of the scotch before continuing, "of you two together, that way, is a lot to handle anyway, but the fact that she made love to me an hour later…I just don't know if I can take this."

Davis downed the rest of her drink like she was doing a shot. "She made love to you last night? Okay, well, that does call for another drink, because she made me feel certifiably insane for suspecting that. I saw you two together this morning, and she still denied it to the point I'd started to question my own judgment rather than her."

"You?" Annabelle no longer sipped her alcohol, but instead took it in gulps, unsure whether she'd become inured to the alcohol or simply needed a larger dose to overpower the burn of her anger and embarrassment. "How do you think I felt bursting into a hotel room scared to find my partner in the arms of another woman only to see her calmly getting out of the shower? She acted surprised to see me. She was sweet and even a little condescending, talking about how being alone too much led me to doubt her. Good Lord, she graciously took the blame for the figments of my imagination. She let me think I'd made a fool of myself. I worried I'd had a psychotic break."

"So she's not just a petty liar and an adulterer, she's also a masterful manipulator. She played both of us perfectly. Do you think she ever thought about how it would end?"

Annabelle felt like they were talking about someone else, not Nic. Not the woman she'd trusted with her life. Nic couldn't be capable of deception or calculated exploitation of her insecurities, but the more they put their stories together, the more they painted a picture of someone beyond untrustworthy, someone controlling and self-serving to the point of disregard for everyone she claimed to love.

"I'd like to think it wasn't all a game. If not for what that says about her, then for my own sanity." Annabelle's stomach ached again. Her head did, too. She wanted to share Davis's anger, and part of her did, but she wished it were a bigger part of her. Disorientation and confusion abounded. What had she missed in Nic's makeup over all those years that made her capable of such betrayal?

Davis reached over with the bottle of scotch and topped off her glass. "Could you imagine doing what she did?"

"I can't even imagine sleeping with someone else, much less carrying on an affair. She's the only person I've ever been with."

"Ever?"

"Yes." Her cheeks flamed from embarrassment aided by alcohol. "She said she liked being the only one who'd ever touched me, but she lied about that, too."

"No, I'm sure she meant that."

"Are you? I'm not. I'm not sure about anything. And I'm not sure if I'll ever feel certain of anything again, especially that. What does it say about me that I gave everything I had—my career, my body, my whole life to a woman who found me so lacking she had to live a whole other life in order to find fulfillment?"

"Annabelle, that's not true."

"You don't know that. You don't know anything about me." Her voice rose in both pitch and volume as she neared hysteria, but it felt good to vent some of the pressure threatening to cripple her. "You don't even know what she wanted with you. How can you possibly know what she thought of me? I obviously wasn't enough for her."

"No, it's not you. This is about her." Davis scooted closer, her hard edges softening in compassion, and the fire in her green eyes overrun by sympathy. "You can't do this to yourself."

"How can I not? How can I think about our life together, all that time, all those memories, and not pick them apart one by one trying to figure out where I went wrong?"

"Women like her are too self-absorbed to be rationalized. Trust me, I've dated enough of them to know it's never really about you."

"How can you say it's not about me? It's my life she shattered." She pounded her fist on the counter. "It's my home she wrecked, my dreams she rejected, my future she threw away, and my body that didn't satisfy her."

Tears streamed down her face as she continued to hit the counter, but the outlet for her internal hell mattered more than any physical pain she inflicted on herself.

"Annabelle, come on," Davis pleaded, tears filling her eyes now.

"No, you come on. Tell me how this isn't about me." She drained her scotch glass before slamming it back down. There was no more burn when the drink hit her throat, and she craved it. She was losing her grip on the here and now, slipping further into desperation. Frantic to feel something other than heart-wrenching torture, she grabbed for the bottle, but Davis caught her hand.

"I think you need to stop."

She tried to jerk away, but Davis held her tight. "Let go."

"Not until you settle down. You can't let her do this to you."

"She already did, and damn it, you helped her." She swung wildly, but barely landed a glancing blow before Davis caught her free hand in her own. Still she thrashed to get away.

"I didn't know, Annabelle. Please, you have to stop. I didn't know. You couldn't have known either."

She tried to back away. She couldn't be held by the same woman who'd held Nic, but Davis was too strong and pulled her closer, her gentle pleading a stark contrast to the strength of her body.

"Please listen to me. It wasn't me, and it wasn't you."

"It was me. I wasn't enough for her, and you were."

"I wasn't." Davis's voice cracked only slightly. "She cheated me, too. God, if you couldn't keep her, I didn't stand a chance."

"No." She didn't need to hear any of this. She couldn't be logical. She was suffocating, drowning, in pain and doubt and the anguish she saw reflected in Davis's eyes. She tried helplessly to break away again, but Davis shook her, strong arms encircling her body.

"You did everything right. You're beautiful. You're better than her. You can't let her destroy you."

The alcohol, the heat of their bodies, the haze of confusion, the agony of her own pain, and the passion in Davis's overwhelmed her. She couldn't escape, but she couldn't stand the clawing need to lash out either. In an explosion of raw, almost animalistic impulse, she surged forward and captured Davis's mouth with her own.

Davis stiffened, immediately letting go of her wrists but not pulling away from the kiss. The shock of what she'd done hit Annabelle a second later, as if on some drunken time delay. She stepped back. Mouth open, eyes cloudy, she could barely move, much less process what had come over her. Even if she could've made sense of it, she had no time to act before Davis surged forward, kissing her, this time with purpose.

She reacted on instinct, soaking up the feel of lips, soft but insistent against her own, warming her in a way the alcohol had failed to do. The kiss was the first satisfying thing she'd felt in hours, and she clung to it like a life raft. For a moment, she wasn't in pain or turmoil. She wasn't broken or lacking. Davis snaked an arm around her waist, holding her up and keeping her close. Secure again, for just an instant, she'd found something that felt right.

She ran her hand up Davis's shoulders and cupped the back of her head, sliding her fingers along the soft nape of her neck and into her short hair. *Her too-short hair.* Too short to sink her fingers into, too short to latch on to, too short to be Nic's. For the first time in her life she was kissing a woman other than Nic. More than that, she was kissing the woman Nic had kissed. The blunt force of horror slammed back into her consciousness, and she wrenched herself free from Davis's embrace.

Immediately she regretted the separation. It felt like someone was wringing her heart out from the inside, but now without the physical comfort of Davis's body or the distraction of her lips, only the pain was left to consume her senses. She couldn't stand it. She wasn't strong. She'd never survive this torture on her own. Floundering, she reached out again, knowing fully this time that she sought a crutch. She didn't care. She needed something, anything to ease the crippling hurt. She caught a fistful of Davis's shirt and yanked it toward her so hard their bodies collided, sending them both stumbling.

It wasn't right. She knew it wasn't right as she unclasped her buttons. It wasn't the body she sought. It didn't offer the familiarity she craved. *She's not Nic. Nic didn't want you, not the way she should have.* Davis at least offered her something honest, something she needed. And God help her she did need it. She needed Davis's hands on her skin, the press of her body, the graze of teeth against her lower lip. Her breath came in shallow, heated bursts, and her heart raced.

She almost felt human again instead of the hollow shell she'd been since seeing Nic in Davis's arms. Damn it, how could she have done this to her?

Davis was skilled with both her hands and her mouth, and God knows she exuded passion, but how had Nic been able to find any peace? Even with her body on fire, Annabelle's mind refused to let her forget this wasn't the woman she'd sworn to share herself with forever. Even with her nerve endings set alight with need, her heart ached beyond what any physical touch could soothe. Davis backed her toward the bed, and she went along, frantically trying to recapture the oblivion she'd experienced in the first moments of the kiss. She went through the motions, even going so far as to cover Davis's hand with her own and guide it to her breast.

Under any other conditions this would be fantasy material. Without the emotional trauma, the physical sensations and the touch would have been perfect. Davis was sexy and talented, and threw herself into worshiping Annabelle's body with the ferocity of someone whose sanity depended on blocking out every other aspect of their circumstances. She was a dream in every aspect, except for the one that made what they were doing a nightmare.

She wasn't Nic.

Her tears flowed again, but this time she didn't have the strength or the inclination to stop them. She sagged against Davis's shoulder, sobs racking her body. Davis wrapped one arm around her waist and cradled her neck in the other before gently lowering her to the bed. Too lost in her suffering to complain, she continued to cry while Davis curled around her, holding her close and whispering soft shushing sounds in her ear. At one point she thought the tears on her cheek weren't all her own and suspected Davis was crying now, too. No longer capable of feeling anything but grief and exhaustion, she surrendered to darkness once again, this time falling into the emptiness of sleep.

CHAPTER NINE

Someone knocked on the door, or was the pounding in her head? Davis didn't want to get up. She wanted to snuggle in closer to Annabelle and wallow in their shared pain, but the knocking wouldn't stop, and her arms were no longer around a warm body but a cold pillow.

She sat up and glanced around. Afternoon sun slanted low through her windows, shadows stretched long across her hardwood floor, and the hot Southern air hung heavy and still around her. Most disorienting, though, was the realization that she was completely alone. Annabelle had somehow slipped out of her arms, out of the bed, and out of the apartment without making a sound. It was as if she'd never been there at all, and if not for the two empty glasses and bottle of scotch on the bar, Davis might've convinced herself the whole morning had just been one horrible nightmare.

Hurt welled up at the memory of that sickening moment when she'd realized Nic had slept with someone else, then multiplied as she remembered the horrible feeling of being told Annabelle wasn't the mistress, *she* was. Anger, embarrassment, anguish, dejection, and so many more emotions she couldn't begin to sort out, much less name, scratched raw against her nerves. She needed to shut the pain off, or shut it out. Trying to decide which method of escape offered more, she looked from the bed back to the scotch. Ultimately the pounding at her door shook her out of her indecision. At least she could unleash her rage on whoever kept knocking and then get back to nursing a purer version of her sadness.

"What the fuck is the matter with you?" she shouted as she opened the door.

"I could ask you the same thing," Cass said, a look of concern cracking her usually cool exterior.

"What's wrong with me? How about my character judgment is shit? How about I fell in love with a compulsive liar? How about I unwittingly helped destroy a thirteen-year relationship? How about I hurt so damn bad I can barely stand up? How about," her voice cracked as she neared hysterics, "Nic doesn't love me?"

"How about we step inside and you tell me everything?"

Davis didn't want to tell her anything, not when she remained so calm. Cass's sanity served as a distressing mirror to how far she'd slipped from emotional stability. She didn't want to have to replay what had happened, and she certainly didn't want to relive the torture with someone who couldn't begin to understand her pain. Hell, even if Cass didn't mock her, at least she'd apply her detached judgment to the situation, and Davis wasn't ready to think logically about anything. She wished Annabelle were still here. As fucked up as they were together, at least Annabelle's misery served as good company to her own.

Where had she gone? Would she return to the home she shared with Nic? Would she be okay to face her alone? Would she take Nic back? If only she'd left her number or some assurance she was all right.

"No, damn it, she's not my responsibility," Davis said aloud.

"Who's not your responsibility?" Cass asked, still standing in the doorway.

Davis stepped back and let Cass into the apartment. Maybe she did need the objective eye of her best friend. Her grief had fed off Annabelle's in scary proportions, and now she felt some sort of unnatural protective attachment to the woman whose very existence shattered her hopes of a future with the love of her life. "Annabelle isn't my responsibility."

Cass looked at her as though she'd spoken gibberish, then glanced at the half empty bottle of scotch. "Is Annabelle one of the voices in your head?"

"She's Nic's wife of thirteen years," Davis said, wincing at the words. How long would it be before she could say them without feeling like she'd been stabbed?

"Well, now that's a plot twist I wish I found more surprising."

"Really, Cass? I know you didn't fall for Nic or anything, but you really thought she led a double life, and I wasn't her girlfriend but her mistress?"

"No, I admit I didn't give her enough credit for something like that. She always seemed too impulsive to pull off deception on that big a scale. I'm sorry I underestimated the extent of her fuck-upery."

"But you really thought she had someone else?"

"Of course. Or I at least entertained the possibility."

Davis could only blink. "How? Why?"

"Please, honey, I'm not saying this in grand 'I told you so' fashion, but something didn't add up from the beginning. I said it several times, and honestly you suspected it, too, or you would have if you'd let yourself examine it for more than a few seconds."

She couldn't believe this. "Are you saying I had it coming?"

"Don't put words into my mouth," Cass said levelly. "I wanted you to have a little fun, but you wanted more, and you wanted it so badly you valued the rewards over the risks. You're a grown-up. You knew you were taking a chance. It didn't pan out, and I'm sorry." Cass paused. "But I'm not surprised."

"I think you need to leave."

"Don't do that, darling. I know you're hurt. I want to help."

"You're not helping," Davis said, reaching for the doorknob to throw her out.

"Of course I am." Cass waved her off. "I'm pointing out the realities of the situation. You want to lie in bed and sob while you remember the good times and mourn a dead dream, and I get that. But it won't move you forward. Taking a hard line and saying none of it was ever real might hurt, but it will help. You can't grieve her like the lost love of your life. She wasn't that person."

"I thought she was," Davis cried.

"I know you did, but she's really a calculating bastard. She's not worth wallowing over. She's worth a good bout of woman-scorned type anger, and if you want to go slash her tires, I'll eagerly help. I'd even be happy to bash in her windshield for you, but I won't have a pity party over a woman who didn't respect you enough to give you more than half of her love and affection and a pack of lies."

Cass always had a fresh take on the subject, and once she allowed a peek behind her detached exterior, it was impossible not to listen to her unique mix of caring and cool reasoning. "Thank you. I think I needed to hear that."

Cass rolled her eyes but smiled as she pulled her into a hug. "I only ever disliked her because I didn't think she was good enough for you."

"That might have actually been the nicest thing you've ever said to me."

"I speak the truth, even the mushy ones, and you really do deserve so much better than her, than this."

"It hurts so bad I can't process anything else right now." Davis sniffled. "But you might be right."

"I know I'm right. You're smart and feisty and sexy. You're way out of her league, and if she's too dumb to appreciate that, screw her. Do you really want to let some two-timing emotional clusterfuck destroy you?"

"Well, when you put it like that…"

"There's no other way to put it. She's hot, but not God's gift. I certainly don't see what drove you to double-fist scotch in the middle of the day."

"What?" Davis stood back and wiped her eyes.

"There are two glasses." She pointed to the bar. "You couldn't chug from just one?"

"Only one of them was mine. The other belonged to Annabelle."

Cass arched one of her perfectly curved eyebrows. "Now, there's a part of the story I didn't expect. Do tell."

"Don't make it more than it is."

"Sit and spill, sister."

Davis flopped onto the couch. "She was devastated, Cass. They'd been planning to have a baby. She fainted and then she threw up."

"Oh, gag me. What is this, eighteen-sixty? Did you tell her to loosen her corset?"

"No, she's not like that. She's like this perfect little Southern belle, I mean, long skirts, long hair. I think she's a housewife."

"There's no such thing as a lesbian housewife."

"I'm not kidding. They live in the suburbs." Davis shuddered. "She came to check on Nic because she overheard a rumor at her *country club*."

Cleary not impressed, Cass made a motion for her to continue. "How did she end up in your apartment?"

"I found her crying in the alley."

"And?"

"And what? I couldn't leave her there."

"Yes, you could. After what you'd just gone through, most women would have, or they would've jumped her, scratched her eyes, and pulled off her Dolly Parton wig."

"Stop it." Davis felt a disturbing surge of protectiveness for Annabelle that she didn't care to analyze. "She's painfully sweet and fragile, and none of this is her fault. If anything, she should've jumped me for sleeping with the woman she'd built her whole life around. I had to make sure she wasn't going to hurt herself."

"Really, you thought she might kill herself?"

"I don't know, maybe not, but she wasn't really functioning. She couldn't drive. I felt responsible, and maybe morbidly curious, too." She sighed. "I wanted to see the woman who shared Nic's life, and maybe see if there was anything to suggest why Nic felt the need to break away from her with me."

"And? Fake boobs? Fake personality? Passive-aggressive? Bitchy?"

"None of the above. She's polite to a fault. She kept apologizing to me. She put all the blame on herself. Instead of sizing me up against some silly Southern ideal of domesticity she's obviously mastered, she went on and on about all the ways Nic might have found her lacking."

"Oh Lord, I can't imagine the two of you together." Cass pointed to the scotch. "No wonder you had to get drunk. How did you get rid of her?"

"We fell asleep, and when I woke up, she'd left. I didn't even feel her get out of bed or hear her shut the door on her way out. I hope she's okay." Davis's concern rose again. "If anything happens to her, I'll never forgive myself for the role I played in this."

"Yeah. How about backing up to before you misplaced your sense of responsibility and explain how you ended up in bed with her."

"It's not like that. She had a breakdown. We both did. She cried herself to sleep in my arms."

"Fully clothed?"

"Yes."

Cass looked skeptical, and Davis worried she could read her mind. So maybe the events that led to ending up in bed with Annabelle weren't as innocent as she'd indicated, but how could she explain their kiss, while intense and powerful, was born not out of passion, but pain? She'd known what they were doing was wrong even as she clutched Annabelle close to her. Part of her understood that while their lips pressed perfectly against each other's, it was distance they sought.

"Neither one of us was ready to be alone yet, but I guess when she woke up she felt strong enough to face whatever she needed to do next. In any case, she left."

"And you?" Cass still didn't seem convinced that was the end of the story, but it had to be, at least for Davis. If she intended to move forward, break free from Nic and begin to rebuild her own sense of self, she couldn't obsess about the one person she had no claim to or control over. Annabelle's journey would be her own from here out.

"I guess I have to move on to whatever's next for me."

"Are you going to get back on the horse? Resume the search for Ms. Right?"

"No," she said quickly. "I'm coming around to your thinking. Ms. Right is a figment of my imagination, and trying to put that dream on a real person led to nothing but pain, anger, and embarrassment."

"Okay, then why don't you put on something sexy and we'll go hunt up a little Ms. Right Now."

Davis shook her head. "Sorry, I know you want me to just be over it all, and I wish I could be more like you, but I don't even know how to be me at the moment."

"Why do I get the feeling you're about to go on some major self-sufficiency kick?"

"Maybe I am." Davis shrugged. "I've always done best for myself when I focus on me. It worked with my parents and my career. I think it's time to give it a try with women, too. From now on, I'm just going to take care of number one."

Nic sat up in her chair when she heard a key in the door. She hopped to her feet and straightened her rumpled dress clothes. The sun had set completely outside the large picture window. It had to be nearly ten o'clock. She'd paced for hours, tried to pick up the already immaculate house, and done any other menial task she could to keep her mind off the fear threatening to consume her with every minute that Belle didn't return. She must have dozed off about an hour ago, as the desperation took hold and she worried Belle didn't intend to ever come home. Where had she been for the last twelve hours?

It didn't matter. She was here now. She was safe and close by, meaning she still felt some pull to the home they'd made together. Nic's relief was enough to buckle her knees, but the look on Belle's face when she opened the door and saw Nic broke her heart. Pure instinct made Nic rush toward her, but the pain in Belle's eyes stopped her cold. Her makeup was gone, her hair disheveled, and her clothes wrinkled. Her skin had lost most of its natural color, replaced by dark circles under her eyes. She looked like a ghost of herself, and Nic fought the urge to turn away from the stark picture of the damage she'd caused.

"Belle, I'm so sorry." Words were incapable of expressing how she truly felt and to what extent, but she had to try. "You can't know how sorry, but please give me a chance, and I swear I'll spend the rest of my life showing you."

Belle stared at her, emotionless, as if examining a stranger or a piece of furniture. Nic shifted nervously under her unsettlingly dispassionate gaze. "Honey, please, I know what I did was wrong. I understand if you hate me, but don't give up on me. On us."

"Us," Belle said coolly as she stepped past her and into the living room. Nic watched, frozen in fear, while she ran her fingertips across the back of the leather couch. She turned and studied the dining-room table, then the kitchen with its granite and stainless-steel surfaces before finally turning back to Nic. She scanned her up and down again, then met her eyes. "I'm trying to find something to hold onto. Something about 'us' I trust or even feel connected to, but I keep coming up empty."

A ragged breath escaped Nic as she reached to steady herself against the wall. "Oh, God, please don't say that. Don't give up on everything we've worked for. We can be so good together. Look at all we've built, our life together. We can have everything again."

"All this?" She looked around. "If you think the house, the status, the money mean anything to me, you don't know me any better than I know you."

"Please don't say that. You do know me. No one knows me like you. I'll do anything. If you don't like this house, we'll move. We can start over. I'll go to counseling. I can't lose you."

"Can't lose *me*, or just can't stand to lose? That's part of it, isn't it?"

Nic winced. Belle *did* know her. She'd always seen to the heart of her, but never before had she been so ashamed of what Belle saw. Sinking, she grasped frantically for the only truth she had left. "I love you."

"But you love Davis, too." The matter-of-fact statement turned her blood to ice. The way she'd said Davis's name, the familiarity, the ease, it wasn't right. Something was wrong, and not just the things she expected.

"She thinks it was all a lie." Belle continued calmly. "She thinks you were playing a game and we were the trophies. I think she's partly right, but she doesn't know you the way I do, and she's only seen part of the picture."

Nic shook, and she clenched her fists to steady her hands. Annabelle and Davis had talked? Had she been with Davis the whole time? Was Davis okay? Did she really believe what they'd shared had been nothing more than a game? No, she couldn't lose focus now or she'd lose Belle, but what had Davis told her? "I don't know what happened, or what she told you—"

"And that drives you crazy, doesn't it?" There was no malice in her voice. She delivered the words like she'd read a grocery list. Nic felt exposed and raw as Belle circled her slowly. "You're panicking, but not because of the lies you told us both. You know I could forgive a lie, an indiscretion. You're terrified I'll find out you really do love her."

"No, Belle. I love you. You have to believe that."

"I do believe that."

"Thank God." Nic reached for her, in her relief, but Belle stepped back.

"But you love her, too, and more importantly, you don't love either of us as much as you love yourself. I've been over and over it in my mind, trying to figure out what I could've done differently, but I worshipped you. I gave up big parts of myself to love you more completely. Maybe that was a mistake. Perhaps I should've been harder on you, more demanding, but I didn't have it in me to love you any less."

"Please don't." Her chest constricted at the reminder of what her actions had done to the woman she loved. This second-guessing, the doubt, the distrust, they wouldn't disappear even if she got another chance. The scars might fade, but they'd never disappear. She hated herself for wounding Belle and worked quickly to stop the bleeding now before it took any more out of her. "You're perfect. I'm a fool, but if you don't believe anything else, you have to believe you're everything I need, everything I want. I love you more than anything."

"That's not true. You love a contest, a fight, a chance to prove yourself to anyone, even yourself."

"Belle, please—"

She raised her hand and Nic fell silent.

"You also love your image, your drive, your aspirations, and I loved that about you too, until I understood I haven't just been sharing the number-one spot in your life."

"Belle, you are the most important thing in my life. You're my everything."

"No, there's something you love more, and not just another woman. If it was just a woman I could fight, and I could win, but I'm not really up against Davis. She and I shared second place to your ego or your ambition or something else inside of you that you can't let go of." She shook her head, and for the first time sadness seemed to overtake all her other emotions. "I can't win that war."

The doors were closing. Even the signs of her pain receded behind this wall Annabelle was building between them. Nic watched helplessly as another brick slid into place. She didn't know what to say. Maybe it was already too late and there was nothing she could say.

"You loved her because of what she told you about yourself, and I'm not even sure what that was." Annabelle stopped, and for a second she was somewhere else. Nic watched her detach, a slight blush rising in her previously ashen skin before she shook her head. "But I have my suspicions about what you found so hard to resist."

What did she suspect? The possibilities sickened her, but she had no right to ask what had transpired between them. She had to concentrate on what happened right now between her and Belle. "I don't know what you know about her, and I don't care. You're everything that matters to me."

"No, I might represent everything that matters to you, but I, me, not the image but the real person, didn't matter enough to keep you from doing what you did." She continued her slow circle, her eyes now an impenetrable shade of blue Nic had never seen before. "If you really loved me most of all, nothing in the world could've tempted you to risk what we had, and if you really loved her the way she thought you did, you would've chosen her over me and had the respect to say so."

"You're wrong, Belle. You're hurt and I understand, but don't do something out of pain that we can't undo." She turned on every ounce of charm she had left, but it was laced with fear and the fringes of desperation. Their past flashed though her mind, and she grabbed for anything that might anchor them together. "We're better than anyone else ever gave us credit for. I know it will take time, but we can get back to that. Please, please don't give up on us."

Belle sighed, her shoulders sagging. "I've tried so hard. For hours I've worked to envision a future for us, a way to move past this, to move forward. I want that, Nic. I think I probably want that even more than you do, but I just don't trust you. And if I can't trust you to do the right thing when so much is at stake, I don't know how I'd ever be able to trust you about anything ever again."

"No." Nic sobbed as she sank to her knees, frantic and pleading. She'd never begged for anything in her life, but she didn't hesitate now. "Please, Belle, I'll do anything. Please, just don't walk out the door."

"I promised I'd always love you, Nic, and I will. Until the day I die you'll have a piece of my heart, but I'll never again give you all of it. We both deserve better." Her voice cracked, for the first time revealing a hint at the same crush of emotion currently choking Nic. "I'll be back tomorrow to pack our things. We have a new set of challenges ahead. If you really do love me, you'll apply your trademark drive to helping us get through them as easily as possible.

She nodded, incapable of anything other than sobs. Belle had resigned herself to this decision, and she was asking Nic to do the same. They were finished. The best thing she'd ever had was walking away, and Nic couldn't stop her. She'd failed them both, and the weight of that realization crashed down on her. She waited for the sound of the door closing behind Belle before she collapsed completely. She sank all the way to the floor, curled into a ball, and surrendered to her desolation.

CHAPTER TEN

Nic hadn't slept more than a few minutes at a time. Mostly she'd spent the night wandering around the house, reliving the memories they'd made there. She'd turned the stove off and on several times to hear the soft whoosh of the gas flame ignite, even though there'd be no more meals for her and Belle to share. She'd climbed the stairs to the bedroom and looked around their room. It smelled like Belle, the subtle mix of jasmine and Dove soap. Her things were set out neatly on her dresser, diamond earrings she'd bought her when she got her first job next to a gold clip she loved to unfasten from her long, beautiful hair. Her chest ached, and tears stung her eyes. She'd never touch her again, never undress her, never feel Belle's body against her own, never lead her to the bed and gently lay her down. Belle would never again look at her with that awe-inspiring mix of love and trust that made her feel invincible.

She quickly closed the door and retreated down the hall before her grief overtook her again. She stopped briefly by the guest room, placing her hand against the doorknob, but she'd find no peace there. She knew the dreams Belle had held for that room. Dreams of a baby, of a family, had filled the space since the day they'd moved in. She'd robbed Belle of the future she'd promised. Those dreams were dead, and she had no right to mourn them. She'd been ambivalent at best, and at worst actually inhibiting, but still she ached for the unrealized possibilities between them. Even if she had been uncertain about her own desire or ability to parent, Belle would make the most beautifully amazing mother any child could ask for. Nic would've liked to see her in that role. Why did it take the death of that dream for her to realize how wonderful it might have been to see it fulfilled?

As the sun finally peeked over the horizon, she went ahead and started a large pot of coffee. She hadn't eaten anything for nearly twenty-four hours, and her stomach showed no sign of stabilizing, but she needed to fortify herself for the gut-wrenching task ahead. How did you divide up thirteen years' worth of memories? Would they sort through the mementos of their trips? What about photographs of their best days? Was she entitled to any of them after what she'd done? Would Belle want them anymore? Would she ever be able to remember anything about them beyond how it ended?

Oh, God, this is the end. Nic sank into a dining-room chair and rested her head against the cold oak table. She wanted to believe she still had a chance. Maybe she could court Belle again the way she had in college and slowly win her over. She would wait, gladly even if she thought she had a chance, but the resolve she'd witnessed in Belle last night seemed so hauntingly final. The cool detachment with which she'd studied her and the emotionless summation of her distrust offered nothing but a crushing finality.

Belle had never cut her off in the entire time they'd known each other. Even in their worst disagreements, she'd still melted into Nic's touch. The impenetrable resolve she'd witnessed last night was something she'd seen her use only on strangers. Was that how she saw Nic now? A stranger? The pain in her chest surged again, disrupting her lethargy. Every time she thought she'd hit the bottom of the hurt, she found another layer below it.

As if on cue, the doorbell rang. Nic rose to answer it, wondering if Belle really believed she had to announce her presence in their home, but as she swung open the door she was jarred out of her musing not by the sight of Belle, but of her father.

Nic was a tall woman who'd never stepped down from any man, any man other than Buddy Taylor. She respected him immensely, but that respect was laced with a healthy dose of fear. He was everything her own father had never been. Strong, powerful, and capable, he exuded confidence in himself and inspired it in everyone around him. He ran his business and his household with a heavy hand, a watchful eye, and a reputation for brutal honesty. He was the kind of man many were proud to call a friend, and even his adversaries had to admire him at least a little. His physique didn't hurt his almost mythical image either. Even in his mid-sixties he looked the part of a true cowboy with sharply creased jeans, a barrel chest, and deep-set blue eyes boring into her from under the brim of a brown Stetson. There had been a time when Nic had wanted nothing more than his approval. Today she would settle for anything other than his wrath.

"Nic," he practically growled, "we need to talk."

The blood drained from her face, but he wasn't holding a gun, and she was pretty sure he wouldn't strike a woman, even one he'd previously treated like one of the boys. "Yes, sir."

She held open the door and tried not to look shaken. She'd put herself in this situation, and she wouldn't win points by cowering. "Can I offer you any coffee?"

"No." He removed his Stetson and pointed it toward the couch. "You can take a seat."

Nic wordlessly did as told and looked up at him, awaiting her sentence.

He scanned her up and down, much the same way his daughter had the night before, but his gaze was neither cool nor detached. His eyes filled with a barely contained blaze of disappointment and disdain. She wondered which one he'd lead with, since even he seemed at a loss for words at the moment.

"I consider myself a good judge of character, but you made a fool of me. When I had to have this talk with Liz's husband, I hurt for her. But I'd expected it all along, so I felt relieved to get it off my chest. But you," he shook his head, "I don't know if I've ever felt as let down by another human being as I do right now."

Nic's chest constricted and she hung her head. Few people's opinions of her had ever mattered more than her own, and now she'd disappointed all of them.

"I trusted you with my daughter, and I thought you understood that responsibility. More importantly I thought you were up to the job, even though other people told me you weren't. Aside from the gay thing." The word "gay" seemed to stick in his throat. "I don't pretend to understand that aspect, never have, but I judged you just as a person. I did my research on you early on. Folks told me you came from white trash."

Nic winced. Would she never be free of her upbringing? Was failure in her DNA?

"I didn't listen," Buddy said. "Hell, I admired how you pulled yourself up by your bootstraps, and when you looked me in the eye and told me you loved and respected my daughter, I believed you. Do you have any idea how hard it is to trust someone with your baby girl?"

"Yes, sir."

"No, you don't," he snapped, anger breaking his restraint and coloring his cheeks, "or you wouldn't have abused that trust."

"I know I failed her, failed all of us, and I'm so sorry."

"Sorry doesn't cut it," he said, regaining a little bit of control. "Sorry doesn't comfort her or keep her from crying all night on her sister's shoulder. Sorry doesn't save her mama the heartbreak of watching her daughter fall apart."

Nic thought of Liz and Lila holding Belle, comforting her. Those strong, beautiful women she'd so proudly called her family would hate her now. People always said you didn't just marry a bride, you married her whole family, and apparently betrayal worked the same way. Would she ever see them again? If so, it wouldn't be around a holiday dinner table. She'd never watch the children she'd considered her niece and nephew grow up. None of their friends would ever look her in the eye again. They would close ranks around Belle and villainize her in the process. No, Nic had done this to herself.

"Yes, sir. You're absolutely right. There're no words to make up for what I did. I can't even explain it to myself." She remembered the passion with Davis, the pull of their desire, the way they burned each other up, but now her chest was on fire with a different kind of heat. The sting of shame singed every nerve ending. No amount of pleasure was worth the pain that consumed all of them now.

"I'm glad you recognize that. It'll make this next part easier."

She raised her eyebrows. Was this where he hit her? Part of her hoped he would. She'd prefer a physical punishment to the emotional beating she was taking.

"You're going to pack your things, and I mean only your things, and you're going to walk away. You're going to leave everything to Belle, and whatever she doesn't want, you're going to sell and give her the money. You're going to make sure she's taken care of until she gets back on her feet."

Nic didn't have to. Everything was in her name—the house, the cars, the bank accounts. Her salary paid for all of it. Georgia had no legal provisions for lesbian divorces, much less for galimony payments. They weren't talking about her legal responsibility, but her moral one. She deserved to pay, on every level, and she would. The money would be the easy part, and one night alone was enough to tell her she couldn't live with the memories this house held. "Of course, whatever she wants."

"You have a lawyer write up the paperwork, and I'll have mine look over it."

"Yes, sir." Lawyers. No more handshakes. Her word was worthless now. Even when she willingly gave up her claim to everything she'd worked for, they still wouldn't believe in her.

"And then, this is the big part, you're going to walk away and stay gone."

Nic froze. She'd agreed on every point up until the last one. She had done everything wrong, and she deserved to pay. She couldn't and wouldn't argue, but the idea of willingly walking out of Belle's life was too much. Maybe it was the right thing to do, but it would be like amputating her own arm or leg. She didn't think she was capable. If Belle threw her out that'd be one thing, but she couldn't be the one to let go.

"Nic." The warning in his voice was clear. "If you have a shred of respect for her, you won't hold her back."

"I only want the best for her." She sighed, remembering the sight of Belle fainting from the sheer pain she'd inflicted on her. If agony was all she had to offer, she would force herself to sever ties, even if it meant cutting off the best parts of herself in the process. She only hoped she was strong enough to survive that kind of torture.

She finally met his steel-blue eyes. "I promise I won't stand in her way, but if she contacts me I won't be strong enough to deny her anything."

A small muscle twitched at the side of his clenched jaw. "If you ever hurt her again, I will kill you."

Nic shook her head. One mistake like this was hard enough to bear. "No, sir. If I ever hurt her again, I'll do the job myself."

Annabelle sighed when she saw her father's pickup truck in her driveway. He'd left before she'd come downstairs that morning, and her mother would only say he had some chores to take care of. She'd had her suspicions what kind of chores and worried they involved a shotgun and a shovel.

She'd rushed Liz to get ready and even threatened to leave without her. She hadn't really wanted anyone to come along today, but her overprotective family wasn't comfortable with her going through this ordeal alone. She should have been grateful for their undying support, and maybe someday she would be, but right now she felt only pain. It clouded her vision, weighed on her limbs, and settled achingly in her chest. She wanted to lie down and let it swallow her, but not even sleep offered respite, because in the few hours she'd lain in bed, her dreams replayed an endless loop of both real and imagined images of Nic in Davis's arms.

She'd made the decision to leave Nic, and it was the right one. She'd never trust her again, and she couldn't build a relationship with someone she didn't trust. She didn't know how she'd face all the long, lonely nights ahead, so she tried not to think any further ahead than her next step.

If she let herself think about the dreams that wouldn't come true, all the holidays she'd spend alone, all the mornings she'd wake up by herself, she'd collapse. Her behavior yesterday at Davis's had frightened her. She'd been so overwhelmed she barely recognized herself. She simply couldn't become that irrational again. She had to focus only on things within her immediate control, and right now that meant she had to face the challenge of dividing up their things. She just wanted this part to be over, and breaking up a fight between Nic and her father wouldn't expedite the process or lessen the strain on her already frayed emotions.

"His Remington is still in the gun rack of the truck," Liz said as they pulled into the driveway.

"His truck shouldn't be here."

"Honey, you knew he'd have to exact his pound of flesh at some point. It's better to get it over with."

"I'm trying to get today over with. I don't need tempers boiling over or, even worse, to be put in a position where I feel the need to protect her."

"I wouldn't think that would be a problem after what you went through yesterday. Aren't you even a tiny bit hopeful he's making her hurt a little?"

"I'm angry with her, madder than I've ever been, but I've spent every day for over a decade trying to take care of her. I can't shut off those instincts overnight, even if she can." It had taken every ounce of fortitude she possessed not to crumple when Nic had collapsed last night. The woman she loved was hurting, and that pain nearly did her in. Even in the midst of her own turmoil, she couldn't stop worrying about how her actions would affect Nic. It was only the realization that Nic hadn't felt the same compassion for her that had enabled her to walk away.

She pushed open the door to her home, bracing herself for shouts or even an all-out brawl. She didn't think her father would actually hit Nic, but she'd seen his anger boil over before. If he was willing to overlook Nic's gender in their relationship, he might be capable of doing so in a fight.

Hearing nothing, she stepped farther into the house to see her father sitting at the kitchen table. "Daddy, where's Nic?"

"Hey, baby girl." He wrapped his arm around her shoulder and rested his chin on the top of her head. "You should've stayed with your mama. I took care of things here."

Annabelle stepped back. "Took care of it how? Did you kill her?"

The corners of his mouth twitched up in a humorless smile. "We came to an understanding. She'll be out of the house this morning."

Belle bristled at the comment and straightened her shoulders. "That wasn't for you to decide. Where is she?"

"Upstairs. Why don't you stay here until she's done? Better yet, you girls go get some breakfast, my treat."

"That's a great idea," Liz interjected. "Daddy can call us when Nic's gone."

"No," Annabelle said sadly. "I have to do this."

"And you will," Liz said. "But there's no sense making it harder than it has to be. Let us help you."

"I will. You'll have to help me a lot over the next few weeks, probably months, but only when I ask you to. I've had so much taken from me in the last twenty-four hours. I won't give up control of the last few things I actually do have a say in."

"I don't want you alone with her," her father said gruffly, but she understood he was trying to protect her. If only the trauma could be kept out of mind simply by keeping Nic out of sight.

"I need to do this." Belle lifted her chin in what little show of defiance she could muster. "This is my life, my home, and my chance to say good-bye. I'd appreciate you letting me do those things my way."

Her father didn't budge, but Liz's eyes softened, and she tugged on his arm. "We'll go get some coffee and be back in an hour."

"Thank you," she said, and then waited for the door to close behind them before she climbed the stairs to the bedroom she'd never again share with Nic.

Nic sat on the bed holding her head in one hand and a photograph of them in the other. The image of her sadness was one more to add to the mental scrapbook of things that would haunt Belle for months to come. Nic immediately jumped up and wiped her eyes.

"I'm sorry. I didn't mean to startle you."

"No, I'm sorry. I should've been gone by now. I've packed my clothes and toiletries." She motioned to the three suitcases on the bed, refusing to make eye contact. "I'm sorry to use so much of the luggage. I didn't have any boxes handy."

She looked like she'd hadn't slept, and she'd clearly been crying.

Annabelle clamped down on her instinct to soothe her. "It's okay. There are some boxes in the garage. I can go get some and start in your office."

"No, you don't have to. I'll do it. Or not. If you want to ship the stuff to me at work, you could. I won't come back."

"Nic, it's your house, too."

"Not anymore. I don't have any right to be here, and even if I did, I just can't."

She understood that. She didn't think she'd be able to survive the memories here either. "Where will you go?"

"I'll go to a hotel close to work, try to find an apartment maybe. Honestly, I haven't thought that far ahead."

Would she go to Davis? She wouldn't let her in, but the thought of Nic trying hurt. "I guess thinking ahead hasn't been your strong suit lately."

"No." Nic's shoulders sagged. "I'm so sorry."

"I'm sorry, too." She looked away and slid another wall up, this time to block her anger. "I didn't come here to fight with you."

"You're entitled to be angry. I deserve it."

"Oh, I am, and yes, you do, but that's not how I want to leave things."

"You're right. As always."

She shook her head. She didn't want the flattery. It felt so empty now. Had any of it been real? No, she couldn't do that either. No sympathy, no anger, nothing introspective or retrospective. She had to focus on the task ahead. "We need to divide up the furniture."

"I'll need my laptop and the stuff in the file cabinet in my office. That's all."

"What about your tools? Your recliner? The TV?"

"I don't need any of it. I'll have the paperwork drawn up to put the house in your name. Your car, too."

"Nic, I don't want all of it. It's just stuff. It's always ever been empty baubles to me." She balled her fist in frustration, then released it in a wave of sadness. It's never offered me any comfort without you."

"I just…please let me do something right. I know it won't make up for everything, or anything really." She sighed and swallowed forcefully, as if trying not to choke on her own emotions. "But you're going to get started in a new life, and I need to know you're taken care of."

Her heart twisted, ripping at her insides. If Nic had wanted to take care of her, why hadn't she been able to summon that sort of honor or dedication months ago? Or maybe she had, but not in any of the ways that had mattered. How had they let their priorities grow so far apart? "If it makes you feel better, then go ahead and soothe your conscience."

"It won't really, but thank you."

"I'll get the boxes and meet you in your office."

With nothing left for them to say, they spent the next half hour working in sad silence. One by one they carried boxes to Nic's car until she closed the door on the last of them. As she stood in the driveway, she couldn't help but notice what an absurdly beautiful day it was. Across the street the neighbors' children played catch in their front yard, oblivious to the two lives falling apart in front of them. Why wasn't it raining? The sun felt so wrong amid all the gloom she felt.

"Will you be okay?" Nic asked softly.

"I guess I'll have to be. The world clearly won't stop for my broken heart." Tears filled Nic's eyes again, but she did an admirable job of blinking them back. Annabelle didn't possess the same control over her emotions anymore. With the immediate job at hand completed, she let her own tears run freely. "What about you?"

"Yeah, don't worry about me."

She wished she could promise that, but she couldn't. Worry would keep her up at night, along with doubt and fear, anger, and, most of all, sadness, but there was no sense explaining that. "Take care of yourself."

She didn't know how much more of this she could take, and Nic didn't look to be faring much better, her breath coming shallow and quick as if to fight back a sob. They needed to make a clean break. Instead, they stood staring painfully at one another, as if trying to soak up one last memory, even an agonizing one, to put off the emptiness.

Then in an instant they were in each other's arms. They clung to one another shaking from sobs. The muscles of Nic's back rippled as she squeezed her to her chest. She breathed deeply to take in the scent of Nic's cologne and listened intently to imprint the sound of her rapid heartbeat.

"I'll always love you," Nic whispered.

"I'll always love you, too. I wish that could be enough."

Nic nodded, her tears running down and mingling with Annabelle's. "I'm so sorry."

"I know, but you have to go."

Nic inhaled deeply and stepped back, her strong hands steadying Belle as she withdrew from their embrace. "Good-bye, Belle."

"Good-bye, Nic."

She watched Nic drive out of view, then took one deliberate step after another until she was back inside. She made it to the couch before collapsing under the weight of her grief. She lay there in their big, empty house and wept. She cried until she couldn't see, until she could barely breathe. She cried even after she heard her father return and felt Liz's arms wrap around her. She cried for herself, for Nic, for their relationship, for all the tarnished memories, and for the future they'd never have.

Chapter Eleven

August

Davis typed furiously on her computer. Why did so many of her clients have to be idiots? If she could spend half the time she wasted putting out fires on doing her actual job, she'd be rich. Not that she was hurting for money. Business had become her life over the last few months. She had more word-of-mouth contacts than ever before, and she never turned them down. She rarely slept and had no desire to socialize, so she might as well work. She'd completed double the number of projects in the last three months that she had in the entire time she'd been with Nic

Nic. Why did it always come back to her? Fine. Whatever. Let everything remind her of the massive mistake she'd made. Those memories kept her focused on taking care of herself instead of daydreaming about something that didn't exist. The wretched feeling in the pit of her stomach every time her mind wandered back to what might have been served as the fuel to make sure she never put herself in that position again. If it also meant she occasionally shot off a slightly too terse e-mail to one of her idiot clients—oh, well. Collateral damage.

Closing her inbox, she finally opened an ad she was working on for the Margaret Mitchell house. "Oh, Maggie," she mumbled as she adjusted the font. "It's a good thing you didn't have e-mail, or you'd have never finished *Gone With The Wind*."

She stared at the ad, silently condemning the color scheme the tour company wanted. Who put sepia-tone photos on a Georgia Tech yellow background? She saved the document and copied her layout onto a new one. She'd claim artistic license and send him two different versions, one done his way and one done correctly. From there it was his own problem if he chose to print the crap version.

"Excuse me."

"What?" Davis asked not looking up.

"I wondered if you wanted a refill on your coffee."

Did I ask for a refill on my coffee? She glanced over the edge of her laptop screen. The young barista who'd taken her order earlier stood looking at her expectantly with a pot of the fully caffeinated stuff in one hand. "Sure, go ahead and top it off."

"Cool." She filled the cup. "I also brought you one cream, no sugar."

"Thanks." She took her coffee more on the bitter side these days.

Davis looked back to her work but couldn't ignore the young barista who lingered next to her small table. Did she want to hold the cup to her lips for her?

"So, what are you working on?"

Davis tried not to roll her eyes. "Work."

"Right. I guess that makes sense. Probably something very important and top secret since you're doing it in the middle of a coffeehouse and bookstore."

What a cheeky little chick. Davis almost smiled. "Can I help you with something?"

"That's my line."

"Well, I think you're good there." She tapped the rim of her coffee cup. "All filled up."

"Right. Actually there is something you might be able to help me with."

Here it comes. Davis sat back, crossed one leg over the other, and folded her arms across her chest. "What's that?"

"I thought maybe you'd do me the honor of letting me buy you dinner."

What a nice way to phrase that. It was certainly better than most of the come-ons she'd heard lately. It almost sounded sincere. The girl was actually cute, maybe in her mid-twenties with wispy chestnut hair and a line of small silver hoops pierced down her right ear. A slight blush tinted her neck a flattering shade of pink, suggesting she'd had to summon some courage to ask her out. Davis almost felt bad about what she was about to do. Almost.

"I prefer to eat alone."

"Always?"

"Always."

The girl's shoulders dropped, but she forged on. "Do you see movies alone, too?"

"Look," Davis said in a voice that sounded just enough like her mother's to disturb her, "you're cute and persistent without being intrusive, and you seem really sweet."

"But?"

"Not really a 'but' so much as a 'therefore,' because when I see qualities like that in a woman, I become very leery. My track record suggests either you're a deceptive master of manipulation, in which case I'd like to stop this thing now, or you're actually a good person, in which case you should want to stop right now, because you won't be any of those things after a date or two with someone as jaded as I am."

"Wow. So do you only date people who aren't sweet or good looking?"

"No." Davis sighed. "I don't date anyone."

"Okay, then." The girl shook her head, then as she walked away added, "I'm sorry about that."

Davis went back to her advertisement. She wasn't sorry about it. She wouldn't let herself feel anything other than cold resolve.

"That's the last box," Liz said, slamming closed the tailgate on her father's Dodge Ram. "It sure doesn't look like much."

"Thirteen years of my life, and all that's left fits into one pickup."

"I didn't mean that."

"I know." Annabelle shrugged. "In some ways it's better like this. A clean break and all that, but sometimes it still feels like such a waste."

"You can't do that to yourself, honey. You can't think about what you'd like to have back or what you could've done differently."

"I know." And she didn't think about those things most of the time. She'd become a master at not thinking about anything. At first it had taken all her energy to do the most basic tasks. She'd been so proud of herself the first time she'd eaten and showered in the same morning. As she'd grown a little stronger, she'd focused on getting the house ready to sell, then sorting through the belongings to decide what she wanted to keep, what should go to Nic, and what would stay with the house. The job had been emotionally exhausting, but in the end most items had fallen into the latter category.

It had been a full month before she could think about anything other than the most immediate problem at hand. Her parents wanted her to move back in with them, but a few nights on the ranch with her father hovering protectively and her mother chattering constantly to fill any shred of silence proved that wasn't the answer.

She'd also spent a week with Liz and her children, which was better. Her sister, niece, and nephew had been through this kind of trauma two years earlier, and they all seemed to understand the types of distractions she needed as well as how to handle her emotional outbursts when they couldn't be avoided. However, they'd all come out the other side of their ordeal and made peace with Liz's divorce. Annabelle worried that the presence of her very raw grief was too stark a reminder of the pain they'd only recently escaped. She was proud of herself that even in her anguish she refused to inflict any of the torture Nic had put her through on anyone else she loved.

In the end she needed a fresh start, but the prospect had been so overwhelming she'd spent another few weeks wallowing in uncertainty about how to start the long and arduous process.

"Are you sure you don't want to just commute for a while until you find a place to live in the city?" Liz asked once again, but without much hope in her tone. "I'd love to have a few more days with you before you go."

"I don't have much time before school starts, and I don't want to spend it wavering between my old life and my new one. I have to take things one manageable step at a time, and that means proving to myself I can handle Atlanta at least a little before I start to worry about whether or not I can still teach."

Liz took her hand, giving it a little squeeze. "I know you'll do great. I'm so proud of you and all the strength and grace you're showing, but I wish you could've found someplace closer."

"I do, too." Lord knows she'd tried to find a job in Athens or the surrounding areas. She'd even looked closer to her parents' home, but teaching jobs were hard to come by, especially since she'd had zero classroom experience in the last few years. In the end she was lucky to have found anything at all, even in Atlanta.

"I'll miss you so much," Liz said, her voice cracking.

Annabelle choked up, but by now she'd learned how and when to control her tears. She'd become a pro at compartmentalizing, and now was not the time for a breakdown. "I'd really like you to visit next weekend if Jason takes the kids."

"If he doesn't, I'll let them spend the weekend with Mama and Daddy. They're more reliable, and the kids enjoy the ranch more than their dad's shitty apartment."

"At least he has an apartment," Annabelle said wistfully, then rushed forward before she could feel any pity, "which is why I have to get going. I refuse to be outdone by your flunky of an ex-husband. Maybe I'll even be ready for you to help me decorate by the time you get there next weekend."

"If anyone can do it, you can."

Annabelle smiled at her sister's confidence. She would miss the daily support she offered and hoped she could survive without the safety net her family provided. Until two months ago she'd never lived alone, and tonight would be her first night in her entire life alone in the city. Insecurities threatened to cripple her every time she let herself wander down the treacherous slope that always ended with her dying alone. No, the fear of being alone was just another in a long line of things she'd learned to clamp down on. Those emotions never went away. Sadness was her constant companion. She kept from being consumed only by pushing toward whatever next step she needed to take. Happiness was a thing of the past, as were laughter, humor, and real enjoyment, but she had productivity and the shred of satisfaction that accompanied it.

With that in mind, she hugged her sister one last time and pulled out of her driveway. She felt no excitement at the start of her new adventure, and only a modicum of nervousness. This journey was just one more joyless step she had to take, whether she particularly wanted to or not. The emotions would overtake her eventually. She'd cry when she got to the hotel tonight, but she wouldn't give herself that luxury before then.

Nic threw another tie into her trashcan. It was too stained to salvage, at least by her sub-par laundry skills. She wasn't helpless. Growing up the way she had, she'd learned early to separate whites from colors and to tumble-dry delicates. When she'd started climbing the corporate ladder, she'd also learned to be friendly with a dry cleaner, but she couldn't beat the stains. Belle could take a white shirt dribbled in chili or khakis caked in grass stains, and within an hour she'd have them looking like something in the window of a designer boutique.

Belle.

God, she missed her.

She missed the security and the comfort, the unconditional love and steady support. She felt aimless, unmoored, and unsettled to the point that a silly stain left her almost morose. Not to mention frazzled by all the day-to-day details she was left to consider alone instead of simply handing them over like she used to.

Now the damaging mix of ketchup and grease she'd let leak from her cheeseburger had claimed her last lavender tie. She'd run out of baby-blue ones last week. She would have worn darker colors, but the men in her line of work often found it hard enough to handle a woman in a tie, so she stuck to more feminine colors. Maybe if she went without a tie and just left an extra button undone at her collar no one would notice.

She glanced at her reflection in the plate-glass window of her office, trying to decide whether a well-kept butch would be more pleasing than a disheveled femme. She could shed her suit coat, which was rumpled after she'd failed to hang it up the night before, but that revealed the way her shirt bunched up at the waist of her slacks. She'd put on a few pounds in the last couple months. She thought she'd get skinnier without Belle's Southern cooking, but apparently substituting Kentucky Fried Chicken for the homemade variety wasn't an even trade in either taste or fat content. She needed to get to the gym more, and by more she meant she should actually go instead of working until ten every night, then snuggling up with her fast food and ESPN until she fell asleep.

The absence of excitement was the price she paid for what she'd done to Davis. No more verbal sparring, no more spur-of-the-moment adventures, no passion, and no sex. In her attempt to chase both roots and wings, she'd ended up cutting off both. Not that she sulked. She rarely let herself feel any genuine emotion beyond remorse or regret. She didn't deserve sympathy or even sadness. She'd made her bed, and she'd sleep in it…alone.

"Hey, Nic." Wade Williams stuck his head in her office door. "You coming to this meeting?"

"Yeah, I'm on it." She grabbed a leather-bound portfolio off her desk and joined him as they walked through the massive office complex.

"What's your read on the Dillon contract?"

"Pretty standard. They've been advertising with us for almost a decade. Steady income, mid-level package, solid, but nothing to write home about."

"Have you talked to the old man recently?"

"Not in person, but we touched base about two weeks ago." She eyed him suspiciously. Wade reminded her of a young George W. Bush. He was puny, standing two or three inches shorter than she, and a bit skinnier, too. His expensive suit was wasted on his lesser frame. His frat-boy demeanor and goofy grin would've made him a joke at this level in business if not for his trust fund and his daddy's social connections. "Why? You got something going on?"

"Nah, like you said, nothing to write home about."

"Really? 'Cause I'm your senior regional manager and—"

"Hey, dude." Wade raised his hands and smiled without a hint of embarrassment about being ten years too old to call anyone dude. "You don't have to pull rank on me. I've just been shooting the breeze."

She stopped outside the door of the conference room. "I'm not pulling rank, but if you've been shooting the breeze with one of my clients, you have a responsibility to report it to me."

His smiled faded to a smirk, but he offered no further explanation as he held open the door and said, "Ladies first."

She scowled as she moved past him, and he at least had the good sense to look away from the daggers she shot him with her eyes as they took their seats. She nodded at her regional vice president. "Mr. Clarke."

"Hey, Joe, how's Tami?" Wade asked with a familiarity that made Nic want to slap him upside the head. She always addressed her bosses with their formal title to show respect for their position, even if she didn't carry any admiration for them as people. "Mom said she missed her at the gala this weekend."

"We spent last week in Athens." Joe Clarke was not a big talker. He did his job well with little fanfare, and he rarely missed a detail. He expected the same out of his subordinates.

Wade raised his eyebrows at Nic, no doubt noting that their boss and his trophy wife had been on Nic's home turf, or they would have been if Nic still lived in Athens, which she didn't, but no one at work needed to know that. Especially Wade.

A couple more sales reps took their seats before the meeting got under way. They went over each account, updating information, reviewing contracts, and making suggestions on how to pitch certain features to niche markets. Nic tried to stay focused, but she was bored and distracted by her lingering unease about her earlier conversation with Wade. That little snake was up to something, and she needed to figure out what before she got blindsided.

Suddenly it occurred to her that the room had gotten very quiet and everyone was looking at her. Damn, what had she missed?

"Dramatic pause before revealing the composite numbers, Nic? You're always the salesman, huh?" Vince Ruckle said. He was about thirty and the only African-American in the room, or their entire district for that matter. Nic had always liked his self-deprecating but steady approach, both in and out of the conference room. "I wish I had your flare for storytelling."

Nic smiled and tried to silently convey her thanks for not only cueing her into what she'd missed, but also offering a plausible explanation for her delay.

"All right, without further ado," she said, pulling the meeting back into her wheelhouse, "we're up six percent on the quarter."

Nods of approval came from all around the table, but most notably from her boss as he added, "Good work, everyone."

She sat back, relieved to have dodged that bullet and getting to deliver some good news in the process. She was about to give herself a metaphorical pat on the back when Wade cleared his throat.

"Well, I've got a little bit of good news to pile on top of that. Not sure if it'll go on this quarter's numbers or next, but I golfed in a foursome with the Dillons this weekend and talked the old man into bumping his package up to the next level. That'll be a thirteen-percent increase on our third-biggest district account. That's got to help the overall picture a bit too, right, Nic?"

"Those numbers will go on next quarter," Nic said, behind what she hoped was not a too-transparent smile, "after I confirm the details of the contract."

"It's all confirmed, Boss Lady," he said, just cheekily enough to hide his condescension. She wanted to choke him. "Contract is getting vetted by legal right now. Any idea how that will affect our projections?"

Nic flipped through her folio quickly, her panic rising along with her anger. She wanted to believe she wasn't seeing her projection spread sheet because she was simply too flustered with Wade to focus, but she might've forgotten to bring it to the meeting altogether. Unfortunately this sort of thing happened more frequently than she was comfortable with. "You know what, I don't want to jump the gun on anything. Why don't I review the numbers this afternoon, and you'll all have the adjusted figures in your in-boxes tomorrow morning."

She had another full night of work ahead. It wasn't like she had anything to rush home to, anyway. She didn't really feel like she had a home anymore. The cheap efficiency apartment she rented hardly qualified. Why did it feel like she was working harder to make less progress? Forgetting numbers, losing focus in a meeting, getting scooped by one of her own reps—none of it was acceptable. Work was all she had left. Wade had gone from being just a nuisance to a real problem, and she already had all the problems she could handle.

CHAPTER TWELVE

"Oh, for the love of all things holy, would it kill you to open your blinds occasionally?" Cass was barely through the front door before she started in on Davis.

"Good morning to you, too." Davis didn't try to keep the caustic edge out of her voice. She'd never been a morning person and was even less so now that she'd developed the habit of working until two or three am.

"Is it morning? How do you know if you can't see the sunlight, Vampire Queen?"

"I didn't want to see the sunlight. I wanted to sleep in this morning. Hence—" Davis nodded down at her pajama shorts and tank top.

Cass gestured to her own impeccably tailored pinstripe suit. "And here I am woefully overdressed, except for that fact that it's almost noon on a workday in the middle of a bustling city."

"Good point. I should let you get back to that high-powered job of yours." Davis started to close the door, but Cass caught it.

"Get dressed. I'm taking you to lunch."

"I'm not hungry."

"I know this bereavement diet of yours has you down a whole pants size, but I got stood up for a house showing, and my next one is right in your neighborhood. I refuse to spend the next hour bumming around Midtown like a hobo."

She rolled her eyes. No one anywhere could mistake a striking six-foot blonde in designer clothes and freshly manicured nails for a hobo, but Davis acquiesced, pulling on shorts and a clean T-shirt. She hadn't been outside in two days, and while she'd never admit it to Cass, part of her did worry about slipping into an oblivion she couldn't pull herself out of.

"Can you at least find it in your bitter little heart to put on khakis and something with a collar? I thought I might splurge for a restaurant where the flatware isn't plastic."

Davis shot Cass her best "don't push it" look.

"Okay, The Flying Biscuit it is."

They strolled down the street, the slow rhythmic smack of her flip-flops against the blazing hot concrete providing a lethargic baseline to the light click of Cass's two-inch heels. August in the middle of Atlanta brought temperatures a few degrees warmer than Hades. It was the only time of year she wished she had a car because the thought of riding a bike in this heat made her want to punch someone. This year had been better so far because she had zero desire to go anywhere or do anything anyway. If not for the coffeehouse on the corner or Cass dropping in uninvited, she could go weeks without talking to another human being.

They took their seats at a table near a window so they could see all the people passing by on the sidewalk and feel grateful to be in the air-conditioning.

Cass ordered a warm chicken salad and managed to refrain from making a snarky comment when Davis ordered eggs with both cheese grits and home fries. Comfort food had been the one traditional post-break-up luxury she allowed herself. She rarely had any desire to eat, so when the urge did arise, she felt entitled to a little bit of bad etiquette. Cass rarely tolerated any hint of wallowing, so her silence on the double helping of starch made Davis suspicious.

They shared an uncharacteristically polite conversation about the weather and exchanged some politically correct comments about the gay community's most recent attempts to gentrify a neighborhood adjacent to Midtown. The longer they went without bitching at one another, the more surreal it felt. They were nearing the end of a perfectly civil hour in a public place before Cass said, "Now, darling, doesn't that feel good?"

Davis glanced at her empty plate. "Are you asking if my lunch went down all right?"

"No, I was referring to being a social member of society. You know, fresh air, conversation, people passing by without you hurling insults at them."

"Is that why you brought me out? Was this some sort of a test of my social fitness?

Cass smiled. "If it was, you passed. You're fully capable of functioning outside your cave of pity. Let's do it more often, okay?"

"I really appreciate you trying to help me—"

"Help you? Oh, you know I'm more selfish than that, and I'm bored out of my skull without you."

"I've seen you work a women's bar too many times to believe you lack for company."

"Do you really think any of those women serve as a substitute for my best friend? Nic has had six months of your life, and I hate her for that, but mostly I miss you. I want the old Davis back."

Davis had no snappy remark for Cass's sudden bout of sincerity. "I'm not sure I'll ever be that person again. I don't think I'm grieving anymore. It doesn't feel temporary."

"So that's just it? No more nights on the town? No more trashy movies and martinis?" Cass looked deflated. Her shoulders slumped and she stared into her iced tea. "I'd even let you drag me to the park or to some hippie art festival or, God forbid, on a bike ride."

Davis felt her lips quirk into a near smile. Offering to do something outside was a major concession for Cass, and while she didn't feel like doing anything other than going back to her apartment and slipping on some sweat pants, she couldn't stand to see her cool and confident friend so dejected. "You'd really ride bikes in the park with me?"

Cass grimaced. "I'd ride a bike or go to the park, not both."

"Okay, look, I can't promise to be good company, but if you're willing to try that hard, I'll see what I can do."

"Much like my luck in the clubs these days. I'll take what I can get and make it work."

"That's the Cass I know and love."

"I'm also the Cass who needs to get back to work. I'm meeting a new client across the street in like two minutes. Walk with me?"

"Sure." They left the restaurant, but Davis took only two steps into the steamy afternoon sun before she went cold. She stopped and shook her head, trying to erase the vision before her. It had been months since she'd been overwhelmed by the image of Annabelle standing on the corner in front of the bookstore, but there she was. Davis dreaded the flashbacks of watching her crumple to the sidewalk or hearing her sobs, but she prayed that's what she was experiencing now. Surely this ghost would fade or vanish, slipping away silently like she did in her dreams, but Annabelle remained standing across the busy intersection staring blankly at the empty bookstore patio.

"Oh, that must be her. She's supposed to be an elementary-school teacher. Looks the part, doesn't she?" Cass's voice sounded far away over the hammering of Davis's heart. "You want me to just come by your place tomorrow night for our park trip?"

Davis couldn't process the question, much less answer. It took everything she had to breathe. The pain and confusion all rushed back, dragging her into that awful moment when she'd seen Annabelle in that spot for the first time. She wanted to run, and even started to back up, but Cass caught her with an arm around her waist. "What's wrong?"

She shook her head but couldn't say anything yet.

"Davis, good Lord, are you having a stroke?"

"No." She kept shaking her head, which only made her dizzier. "I just…God, I didn't think it could still hurt like this."

"What hurts? Where?"

"Seeing her. It hurts to see her."

"Who? My client?" Cass felt her forehead. "Or do you see something else?"

"Annabelle." Davis took a deep breath, steadying her nerves. "Your new client."

"Yes, Annabelle Taylor, I think."

"Nic's Annabelle."

"Oh, shit." Cass looked over again. "You were right. She looks like a modern Southern belle."

"Don't call her 'Belle.'"

"I'm not going to call her anything. I can't work with her."

"No." Davis found her voice again, and the blood slowly returned to the upper half of her body. "Don't be silly."

"Silly? You almost passed out at first sight, but I'm silly?"

Davis tried to steady her voice, both for her own sake and for Cass's. "I was surprised to see her standing in the same spot where it all happened. I'd just let down my guard—"

"Right, you finally let down those walls. I don't want them to go back up. She can find another realtor."

"No, Cass." Davis grabbed her wrist, maybe tighter than she meant to. "Please help her. None of what happened was her fault."

"It wasn't your fault, either. You don't have any responsibility to her."

"I know." And she did know, intellectually anyway, but memories of Annabelle's anguish had been almost as hard to escape as her own pain. There was something so fragile about her, something Davis had the urge to protect, maybe out of her own guilt or perhaps something deeper. "Please, just help her."

Cass regarded her skeptically. "Help her find an apartment? Or are you asking me for something else, 'cause it sounds like there's something more going on."

"Three months ago she had a perfect life with a house in the suburbs and spent her days at the country club. Now she's looking for an apartment in Midtown and teaching elementary school to support herself."

"Again, why is this our problem?"

"I know it isn't my fault, but I…" Davis sighed. She couldn't let herself feel guilty for something she hadn't known, but her connection to the destruction of another person's life upset her. Her own pain undid her, and knowing she'd played any part in inflicting hurt on the beautiful woman across the street could break her completely. She couldn't explain any of that to cool, logical Cass, so she simply said, "I know how she feels."

"Fine. I think there's more going on here than a kinship of grief, but I promise she'll have an apartment by the end of the day."

"Thank you."

"Do you want to go say hello?"

"I'm not sure that's a good idea."

"Maybe not, since last time she saw you she fainted then threw up."

And we shared the most intense kiss of my life, then held each other until we fell asleep. As much as she'd tried to forget that part, memories of Annabelle clutching her fiercely invaded her dreams as often as any other image from that awful day. She shivered at the reminder of how easily her emotions had transferred onto the one other person in the world who really understood them. "Maybe I should slip back inside until you get her out of here."

"Good call, 'cause if either one of you were to pass out, I'd pretend not to know you."

"Promise you'll be nice."

"I promise," Cass said grudgingly, then added more softly, "Will you be okay?"

"Fine." Davis lied, then forced her most convincing smile before retreating back into The Flying Biscuit. She tried to breathe normally and keep her hands from shaking. She looked at the posters and event flyers, anything to keep herself from glancing out the window. She didn't want to watch Cass greet Annabelle or see which direction they went. She'd spend the rest of the day fighting enough of their collective pasts. She didn't need to add speculations about the present or future as well.

❖

"Ms. Taylor?"

Annabelle looked away from the bookstore patio for the first time in she didn't know how long. She must have zoned out. When her realtor had suggested they meet here, she'd thought it might be a fitting test for her return to the city, but now she wished she'd started with a smaller step. She didn't want to spend the first day of her new life reliving the worst day of her old one, but it was too late. Her chest constricted, her stomach seized up, and tears threatened as all the memories rushed back. At least she hadn't fainted. That had to count as some sort of progress.

"Ms. Taylor, I'm Cassandra Riggins, your realtor." She extended her hand, flashing French-tipped nails.

"Right, hello." She tried to smile, but it was more important to breathe. "Sorry, I was just a little distracted."

"I bet."

"Excuse me?"

"It's hard to focus in this heat." The realtor smiled politely. She was attractively polished. Her pantsuit looked custom-made to show off her curves, and her blond hair was professionally highlighted a shade brassier than Annabelle's natural color. This woman clearly paid attention to fashion trends, and with great results, but instead of inspiring any genuine appeal, her appearance only made Annabelle feel more out of place in her cotton skirt and pink scoop-neck blouse. Since arriving yesterday she felt more like country-come-to-town than an independent woman.

"Right. The heat." The weather, such a perfectly normal excuse for being lost in thought. It sounded more reasonable than explaining her distraction stemmed from standing in the spot where the love of her life had shattered her hopes and dreams.

"Shall we go find you an apartment with an air-conditioner then?"

"Please."

As they walked down Market Street, she tried to orient herself to her surroundings. Outside of that one intersection, she had no ties to this or any other part of the city. She'd chosen the area only because it was close to the school where she'd be teaching. She wondered for about the hundredth time if she remembered how to teach but pushed the thought quickly from her mind. *One step at a time.*

"How many places do we have to look at today?"

"Unfortunately, only two. This is a popular neighborhood. There's not a lot in the price range you mentioned on the phone."

It had been a long time since she'd had to worry about finances, and in all honesty her nest egg was well padded after selling the house, but she didn't want to live off Nic's guilt money. She needed to see if she could really make it on her own, and that meant living within her means as a schoolteacher. At least it was a private-school salary, or she wouldn't bother looking in this neighborhood at all. "That's okay. I know it'll be hard. I'm getting used to that, but I do appreciate you meeting with me today."

"It's not every day I get a call from a Fortune 500 business consultant asking me to find an apartment for his goddaughter."

Annabelle's face flushed. She'd suspected that someone had pulled some strings for a professional of Cassandra's caliber to look at low-end rentals with her. She'd asked her father to stay out of the process, but apparently he hadn't listened or he felt having someone else do the work absolved him from direct involvement. "I'm sorry. A friend of the family gave me your number, but I didn't know he'd called. You don't owe me any favors. I won't tell him if you'd rather spend your time elsewhere."

"Don't be silly. Networking makes the world go round. I owed him a favor, and now he owes me one. Debts are currency around here," she said as she walked around the back of a condo complex. The place wasn't extravagant, a little dated, but it didn't look too bad. She could certainly do worse than one of the sand-colored units, but they walked right past them toward what looked like an old garage. "This is the first place."

"The shed?"

"It's got a bathroom, so technically it's an apartment."

"Okay." She tried to keep an open mind. Well, as open a mind as one can have in a shed.

"It's not much, but it's cheap and close to your school."

The space was small and dirty, but she could clean. She'd have room for her bed and a dresser, maybe a small table in one corner. Her eyes fell on the kitchen, or kitchenette. No, even that term was too generous. There was a sink and a glorified set of Bunsen burners with an "oven" smaller than her microwave.

Cassandra hadn't done more than step through the doorway, as if she couldn't bring herself to fully enter such a hovel. "It's probably not what you're used to."

"No." Annabelle shook her head. "But what I'm used to isn't what I need now. It's close enough to walk to work, which is important because I'm not used to driving in the city."

"It's awfully run-down," Cass said.

"I have time to clean."

"It's not very big."

"Maybe a smaller place could feel cozier, less lonely." She tried hard to talk herself into this place, but why did it feel like her realtor was trying to talk her out of it? Shouldn't it work the other way around? "I'm starting over again, or maybe for the first time. I've never lived alone. I'm not at all sure what I'll require. I would've liked a passable kitchen, but maybe this will inspire me to get creative."

"You like to cook?"

"I used to. I just—it's been a long couple of months." She smiled in a way she hoped didn't show the sadness she felt. "But I hope to get back to some sense of normalcy again someday, and that involves cooking."

Cassandra looked slightly embarrassed. Maybe she'd gotten too personal. "Sounds like someone put you through the wringer."

She clamped down on the emotions threatening to rise in her. "I…I don't want to go into it, really. I have to move on somehow, just for me now. As soon as I figure out who I am without her."

Cassandra looked her up and down one time. She exhaled forcefully, then muttered, "You two are killing me."

"I'm sorry?"

"Come on." She walked out of the shed and back up Tenth Street while Annabelle tried to keep up. Tension welled in her again as they neared the bookstore, but thankfully they turned down Myrtle a block before the intersection she dreaded. Mature trees lined the street, shading well-kept, single-family homes with pristine yards.

Clearly she couldn't afford this neighborhood, but Cassandra walked purposely up the driveway of an adorable bungalow and down a stepping-stone path. "It's another garage, but I think you'll find that's all it has in common with the last one."

She led her up a set of freshly painted wood stairs and let them into a loft above the two bay doors. Annabelle stopped in the doorway, almost afraid to go in. The studio was too beautiful for her price range. The space was small, probably no bigger than the shed, but the large windows and bamboo floors made it feel bigger. The kitchen space ran along the entire length of one side wall, with a full-size gas range, a built-in microwave, and a large, stainless-steel fridge and matching sink, reminding her of the only space in her old house she'd ever really loved. Well, she'd loved the bedroom at one point, too, but that wasn't because of the room as much as the love it'd once held. She forced her attention back to the task of this moment.

The space was sparse, but clean, and Annabelle began decorating in her mind. She'd put her small love seat against the front wall and a throw rug in front to create the sense of a living space, then a small table with two chairs. She'd only need one, of course, except for when Liz came to visit. She'd put her bed by the back window. She walked in to look out at the view. The immediate surroundings weren't impressive, just some more apartments and store rooftops, but beyond them the sun would set between city high-rises, providing a nice image in the evening, serving as a reminder that there was life out there beyond what she'd previously imagined for herself.

Cassandra stepped up beside her, seeming to look at something specific. Her brow furrowed as she inspected an apartment across the wooden fence a few doors down, but before Annabelle could examine it further, her professional demeanor returned. "So, what do you think of the apartment?"

"It's amazing." Annabelle stopped short of gushing because something still didn't feel right. "I'm not sure why you bothered to show me the other if this is the competition."

"To be honest, this isn't the one I intended to show you. The other place in your price range is considerably worse than the first."

Annabelle's hopes dropped what little distance she'd let them rise. "So this one isn't in my budget?" She supposed that was a good ploy. Show the customer what they were missing to make the contrast all the more clear, maybe push them out of their comfort zone.

"No, at its current price you couldn't afford it on your own."

"Thank you then, but if you're implying I pull from a little of my family's money, I guess I'll take the shed."

Cassandra flashed a genuine smile filled with a mix of amusement and admiration. "What I meant to say was, 'It's not in your price range now, but by the time I talk to the owner it will be.' She enjoys my…company, and it won't be unpleasant to even up the price if I also forgo my commission."

"Why would you do that?" Annabelle asked, guarded. "You don't know me, and surely you aren't that indebted to a business associate."

"No, but remember what I said about debts being currency here. I owe a big one to someone else."

"And now I'll owe you one, too?"

Cass smiled again, this time with more sympathy. "No, you've paid enough of yours. All I ask from you is to never tell anyone around here about this conversation."

"Who would I tell?"

She looked out the window again, back toward the same apartment, the same look of concern crossing her stunning features. She seemed more real when she let down her guard, and Annabelle actually worried she wasn't more attracted to her. Who wouldn't be turned on by the softer side of such a classically beautiful woman? Had her capacity for feeling those types of connections died completely?

"You never know where life in this city might lead you. It's a smaller community than you can imagine."

"I'll take your word, and I'll take the apartment if you'll accept my sincere gratitude in return."

Cass waved her off casually, her cool façade returning, but Annabelle sensed that under her flawless exterior she was pleased with the compliment. "I'll have a courier run the papers by your hotel. If you can pay first and last month's rent in cash, you can move in this weekend."

"Thank you," Annabelle said as she rushed to keep up as they exited the apartment.

"It's just business from here on out. Do you need a ride somewhere?"

"No, I walked from my hotel."

"Would you like me to walk you back?"

The request seemed odd from a woman who'd just asserted their relationship was purely business related, but as they neared the spot where they'd met, Annabelle considered taking her up on the offer. "Thank you, but I'll be fine."

Cassandra stopped and turned to offer her hand one more time, along with a smile. "I do believe you will be."

Annabelle liked this woman and her confidence. She pulled a little strength from her and used the positive energy to walk right past the bookstore without giving in to the crushing weight of emotions. She was moving forward, and she intended to keep doing so, no matter how hard she had to work.

Nic stood in her boss's doorway, quietly admiring his view of the expansive Atlanta skyline. Over a week had passed since their last meeting, and she had no idea why he'd summoned her today. Nothing on her schedule should require his direct attention, and as far as she knew, he had no idea about the changes in her personal life. She worked hard to keep her split from Belle and subsequent loneliness private, both out of sadness and embarrassment. She might be a mess on the inside, but on paper she continued to perform at her usual level. She hadn't missed an objective or muffed any other meetings, but Joe Clarke wasn't the kind of man who called someone in just to chat.

"Nic." He motioned for her to take a seat, then closed the door. "I'm sure you know there's a vice-president slot opening up out of the Athens office."

"Yes, sir," she said as evenly as possible, and tried to use her suit coat to cover the way her dress shirt gapped a little over her stomach now.

"You were in the running up until a few months ago."

Her heart sank at his use of the past tense, but she wouldn't let those emotions show. "I'm honored to have been considered."

"Yeah, that's the problem. When you first came up, you would've been livid you didn't get it."

"I'm sorry, sir?"

"You're getting by, Nic. You're one of my top salesmen, er, salespeople."

She wished he'd stuck to the male term rather than remind himself she was somehow different from the rest of his boys. Those little separations only kept her on the outside of an elite group.

"The thing is, when I hired you, you wanted to be the absolute best."

"I still do," she said, but instead of looking at him, she glanced down at the rich maroon carpet.

"I don't see that. You haven't dropped the ball, but more and more you're happy with a first down when you used to run for the end zone every play."

"I don't mean to give you that impression. It's certainly not how I feel."

"I know you and your lady friend had some issues." He adjusted his position in his big leather chair and straightened his Georgia Bulldog tie as if uncomfortable with the topic. "And I'm sorry. She seemed like a good girl."

Nic's face heated rapidly. What did he know, and how did he know it? Why did he care? Had she lost out on the promotion because of her personal life? Shame and anger rushed to the surface in frightening proportions. Suddenly she felt fifteen again and that she didn't measure up to her old man. She held her tongue now, just like she had then, but it was harder than ever before.

"We've all been there. Most of us are on marriage number two, and some of us on three." He twisted the gold band on his ring finger and sighed. "It's not something we're proud of, but it's par for the course, an occupational hazard."

At least he wasn't hypocritical, but she interlaced her fingers, knuckles turning white at the thought of the damage she'd done as something that just happens in this world. Failed relationships were one part of his boys' club she wasn't proud to share.

"You're better off than most since you don't have to worry about kids."

From his standpoint that was one less complication, but maybe parenthood would've helped her get her priorities in order. Then again, given how she'd failed Annabelle, she had no reason to think she could've done better with a baby. Only Belle had ever believed she'd make a good parent, but she'd also thought she made a good spouse.

"Anyway." He seemed to snap out of his pensiveness and started to sift through a stack of papers on his desk as he shifted back to business. "We're promoting Vince to VP out of Athens, but I want you to see the silver lining."

Her chest ached. The promotion was gone, along with Belle and Davis. The only upside she saw was the job hadn't gone to Wade.

"Athens is too complicated for you, and the next promotion will come out of the home office here in Atlanta. It's a better fit, and it'll give you time to try to get the fire back."

"I don't think I've lost the fire."

He grinned. "You can't shit a bullshitter, McCoy, but I admire you for trying. The other silver lining is you've got real competition now."

She raised her eyebrow.

"Wade will take Vince's old spot, and he's gunning for you."

"He hasn't been on the job very long."

"Nope. He just beat your record for quickest promotion." He didn't look any happier about that statement than Nic felt.

She clenched her jaw to hold in a smart remark.

"I know you don't like him, and honestly I don't care for him either. He's got all the breeding and none of the class. He feels like that job is rightfully his, and he intends to take it. You remember how that feels?"

"I'm starting to," she said through gritted teeth.

"Good." He stood to signal this discussion had ended.

The conversation was as close to a pep talk as she'd ever gotten from him, but he hadn't said he believed in her. He hoped she'd win, but he seemed to place the odds at fifty percent, and if she failed he already had her successor in place. If this meeting was supposed to jump-start her ambition, it had only partially succeeded. A fire burned inside her again, though not from drive so much as anger. She'd given up her dream home for an efficiency apartment and her country-club membership for burgers and late nights at the office. Now she had to fight against a man ten years younger who had no skills but all the connections. On top of everything, she was lonely in a way that weighed on her muscles and ached in her bones. It felt like the start of her career all over again, except this time she would have to face the challenge alone.

CHAPTER THIRTEEN

Davis paced at the top of her stairs. In the twenty-four hours since she'd seen Annabelle, she'd thought of little else. She'd had to fight hard to keep from calling Cass to ask about their meeting. She didn't want to seem obsessed. She wasn't obsessed. She had no reason to be. Curious, maybe, but if she spent all day and part of the night worrying about Annabelle and her life now, that would be unhealthy. Plus it would mean she still had some tie to Nic, and she absolutely wouldn't allow that. She had enough concerns of her own without piling someone else's grief on top. Misery might love company, but she wasn't miserable any more. Mostly she felt numb. Maybe that was the problem. Perhaps she could block all the awful emotions in herself, but she couldn't prevent Annabelle from feeling them. Was she using her as some sort of surrogate for all the issues she'd refused to deal with? Oh, God, she should probably call a life coach or something.

No, she needed to calm down. She wasn't obsessed or lost in some sort of psychological transference. She simply wanted a little assurance Annabelle was okay, and she hadn't sought her out or stalked her to get answers. She had an honest, coincidental connection to her. It would be weird not to inquire, and that's why she threw open her front door as soon as she heard Cass's approaching footsteps.

"Hello, darling. To what do I owe this eager and fully clothed welcome?"

"I'm just looking forward to going to the park with you."

"Really? The park? Me? Or are you hoping for word on a certain blue-eyed, blond-haired, domestic goddess?"

Damn, Cass knew her too well. Still, she didn't want to admit to herself how frantic she was for information, so she played it as cool as she could while still being honest. "I am intrigued about your meeting, but can we walk and talk because I really do want to get outside."

"Sure, it's only one hundred degrees now, so of course the Vampire Queen suddenly shows an interest in the outside world."

"Did you come over here to bitch or to go for a walk?" Davis snapped. She didn't want to answer these questions.

"Oh, honey, why choose? I can do both at the same time, but I applaud your little show of backbone."

Davis rolled her eyes, but it did feel good to be back out with her best friend of her own free will. She couldn't remember the last time she'd looked forward to something. So what if that something was a chat about her ex-lover's ex-wife?

"What brought about this little power surge of yours? Yesterday when I left, you were cowering in a doorway and talking about wanting to go back to bed."

"I don't know what you're talking about. It's not like I've had a personality change overnight." She wasn't exactly exuding positivity. As much as she wanted to hear about Annabelle, she also dreaded it. What if she was a wreck? What if she hated her? What if she was completely fine, proving herself stronger than Davis and making her feel inadequate for continuing to wallow in her jadedness?

"No, you're still surly, and judging by the shadows under your eyes, you're keeping horrendous hours, but there's something else there." Cass paused and regarded her closely. "It's interest."

"I'm not interested in Annabelle in the way you're implying."

"I didn't imply that at all, but your need to get defensive makes me wonder. I only meant you showed an interest in another person or thing or feeling outside the little shell you've been in. You've spent months glassy-eyed and walled off in your cave trying to avoid everything that might spark any real emotion in you."

"I have not." Davis didn't know why she bothered lying.

"You don't go any place you might run into someone you used to know. You don't watch TV or movies that might stir a memory. You haven't engaged in any task other than the ones absolutely necessary to your survival since everything fell apart."

"You're overly dramatic. And if you remember correctly, I agreed to come out with you tonight before we saw Annabelle."

"Yes, but you weren't looking forward to it. You agreed only to appease me."

She didn't answer. Instead she turned toward the park and picked up her pace slightly. Why did Cass have to be right all the time? Maybe she hadn't let herself take an interest in anything to protect herself, or maybe nothing had been interesting enough to reach her since Nic. Either way, what did it say about her that Annabelle had been the one to break that spell?

"She's okay, you know?" Cass said softly. "She's not happy or thriving, but she's all right."

Davis swallowed and nodded, slowing her pace so Cass could fall in easily beside her. Relief tinged her sadness to learn Annabelle had fared just about the way she had. Her life had gone on, another thing they had in common.

"She's stubborn, insisting on standing on her own two feet, but I think she's got what it takes."

Davis didn't find it hard to believe that Annabelle was stubborn or independent. If anything, the news strengthened Davis's connection to her since they'd chosen similar methods of coping. "Did she find a place to live?"

"Yes, a nice little efficiency on…" Cass paused for a second as if reconsidering. "On a nice street."

"Good." She didn't know what else to ask. She wasn't sure what she even wanted to know. Annabelle was stable. What had happened between Nic and Davis had changed her life but didn't destroy it. What more did she really need to know? "Thanks for helping her."

"It's business, darling. I don't know the woman from Eve."

"Right." Neither did Davis. Well, maybe she knew her a little better than Eve, what with their insanely passionate kiss, but that's where their association ended. What more could there be between them? She'd gotten the information she'd wanted. Annabelle was fine. She had a job, a place to live, and the drive to support herself. Davis could move on.

So why was she still thinking about her?

She had no reason to wonder if her blue eyes were clear of tears now, or if she was even more beautiful without the mask of anguish across her delicate features. She certainly had no right to think about how she'd greet her if they ran into each other.

"So are we going to the park?" Cass asked cautiously.

"What?" She pulled herself back into the moment and realized she'd stopped walking. Once again she stood on that fateful corner, thinking about the woman whose very existence had shattered her dreams, trying to convince herself to move on. "Sorry, yeah. Let's go."

"Really, because if you want to skip the park and go right to drinking a nice Riesling, I wouldn't argue."

She smiled and shook her head. "Not going to happen."

Cass slipped her arm around Davis's waist and gave her a little squeeze. "Good. I like a woman who makes me work for my fun."

"I'm sorry I haven't been that kind of girl lately. I've made you do plenty of work but never let you have any fun."

"If you expect me to say it's okay, you're woefully mistaken, but I expect you to snap out of this funk any day now, and when you do, I want to be around to see it."

She rested her head on Cass's shoulder as they strolled through the city. Maybe things would get better. With Annabelle settled, she did feel a modicum of relief. She could pack that part of the disaster into a neat little box of resolved issues. Perhaps the closure could jump-start her own recovery. She didn't have Cass's optimism, but at least now she was willing to consider the possibility.

Annabelle and Liz left the apartment and walked down Myrtle. The heat was still insane at seven in the evening, and the humid air didn't move nearly as well as it did in the suburbs. She'd put on capri pants and a peach-colored Polo shirt, but by the time they'd crossed the street she was already sweating. Liz looked cooler in her khaki shorts and baby-blue T-shirt. She would do better in the city. She'd always been more free-spirited, but as fate would have it, she was the one with a family and roots in the country, while Annabelle, ever the homebody, was off on her own far from home. Life could be as funny as it was unfair, and she'd stopped trying to make sense of it. She used to think things happened for a reason, but now she didn't think about greater plans or even anything beyond her immediate future. She could only afford to focus on setting up her apartment.

"I can't believe your realtor found you that place," Liz said about the apartment. "She's gay?"

She paused, trying to process the non sequitur. "My realtor?"

"Yeah."

"I think so. She never said so, but she made a reference to my landlord enjoying her company."

"Your landlord is gay, too? Is that why you got the place? Family discount?"

"I suppose it's possible, but this is Midtown Atlanta. Half the neighborhood is gay. I don't know why Cassandra went out of her way for me." She recalled the moment when she'd seen something sincere, something personal, under her impeccable business front. "I got the sense she felt a connection with me, but we weren't supposed to talk about it."

"Right, totally secret-handshake deal, but anyone who sees that place is immediately going to know you couldn't afford the rent on your own. They'll assume Daddy pays for it."

"Let them think what they want. I've had people think a lot worse about me lately. Even Mama had the nerve to suggest that if I found a nice young man I could avoid going through this again."

"Oh, yeah, like that worked so well for me." Liz rolled her eyes. "You find whoever trips your trigger."

"I need to find myself first, because no one is tripping anything for me now."

"Well, like you said, you're in a new world here. Gay landlord, gay realtor, gay bookstore on the corner. You never know who might spark your interest," Liz said. "You'll turn heads all over the gayborhood."

Annabelle smiled at her sister's confidence, wishing she could share it. She hadn't felt so much as a spark of attraction since Nic had left, and she didn't see herself inspiring something in anyone else if she couldn't even feel it herself. "You're good for my self-esteem."

"Good, but I'm serious," Liz said with a not-so-subtle nod to two women approaching them. "I think the blonde up there is checking you out right now."

She glanced ahead and noticed Cassandra walking toward them with her arm around a woman who focused her attention on her to the exclusion of everyone else around them. Cassandra, on the other hand, had noticed their approach and studied her with concern creasing her brow. "No, that's my realtor, and…" Suddenly the other woman looked up, sending a lancing shot of recognition through her. "And Davis."

"Nic's Davis?"

The label still sent a terrible stab of pain through her chest, but she nodded. Liz squeezed her hand in support, but the move couldn't compete with the emotion tightening around her throat. Fear, embarrassment, jealousy, and sadness filtered in through her initial shock. Sure, she knew Davis lived around here, but so did thousands of others. Why did they have to run into each other? And what was she doing with Cassandra?

Her vision blurred again, but she stood her ground. She wouldn't faint this time. She wouldn't run away either, the way she'd slipped out of Davis's bed. Blush burned her cheeks hotter than the summer sun as she remembered untangling herself from Davis's arms. She could feel the strength and caring of their embrace as she met her hypnotic green eyes once again.

"Do you want me to cut her?"

"What?"

"The home wrecker," Liz growled through clenched teeth. "Should I jump her?"

"Oh, my good Lord." She glanced away from Davis long enough to see her sister's eyes had narrowed with the dangerous focus usually witnessed in jungle cats. "Don't even think about it."

"But she—"

"She didn't know."

"But if she hadn't—"

"Then someone else would have."

"Damn it, you wouldn't let any of us kill Nic. Now you're protecting her *mistress*?"

"Yes, I am."

Liz sighed. "Why can't you act like a woman scorned for a few minutes?"

With her sister's claws retracted for the time being, Annabelle turned her attention back to Davis and Cassandra, who approached at a slower but steady pace, their arms wrapped around each other's waists. Were they a couple, or was Davis using her as an anchor to her own flight instinct? She hoped for the latter, but she couldn't pinpoint why. Davis was certainly entitled to move on. Just because losing Nic had shattered Annabelle's confidence didn't mean it had to wreck hers, too. Davis seemed like a strong, independent woman, the kind of woman she wanted to be, but she remembered too clearly the anguish she'd seen in her eyes. That kind of betrayal wasn't overcome lightly. Then again she also remembered the ferocity of Davis's kiss. Any woman capable of passion like that probably wouldn't remain single for long. She and Cassandra certainly shared a powerful aesthetic. Women like them probably gravitated toward each other.

"Hi," Davis said shyly, her voice revealing an uncertainty she didn't show.

"Hi."

"How are you?" She asked the question with genuine concern and a hint of self-consciousness, but none of the pity Annabelle had grown accustomed to.

"I'm doing all right." It was the simplest version of the truth, and she wouldn't go into the more complicated version, not here, not now, maybe not ever with Davis.

"Good."

The silence stretched while Annabelle searched for her manners. "How are you?"

"About the same."

"Good." They stood, suspended in each other's gaze, seemingly unable to think of anything else to say, but equally unable to move on. Liz and Cassandra had no such trouble and promptly introduced themselves to each other.

"I'm sorry. Davis, this is my sister, Liz. Liz, this is…Davis." She didn't dare try to explain their relationship to each other. She didn't have to. It hung over them all, and they all knew it. Another piece of the puzzle fell into place. Cassandra must have known who she was all along. Was Davis the friend she owed a favor? Did she know the whole story? None of them would ever know the whole story, but did she know about the kiss?

"Annabelle just showed me her new apartment."

"Oh, did you get the keys?"

"I take possession tomorrow, but they let me show it off tonight. Thank you again for rushing the paperwork."

"I'm glad it went to someone who will appreciate it," Cass said.

"Do you live around here?" Liz asked Davis, her voice falling short of suspicious, but not by much.

"I do. I'm just a block up."

"So you're neighbors?"

"Are we?" Davis sounded surprised. Maybe Cassandra hadn't told her everything.

"Her apartment faces west off Myrtle," Cassandra said, sounding about as pleased with that fact as Liz did. Was that what she'd been thinking when she'd stared out that window? Maybe the two of them were a couple. The thought turned her stomach. Right or wrong, she couldn't stand the thought of watching them recover happily while she struggled in her own loneliness. Life wasn't a race, but she didn't need that kind of mirror to her lack of progress.

"Wow, I guess I'll probably see you around."

"I guess so," Annabelle said, forcing a smile and wondering how Davis felt about their proximity. Would having Annabelle close by feel like rubbing salt in her wounds, or were they healed over now?

"Great, well, then we'll let you get back to your evening and just see you around," Cassandra said, nudging Davis, who looked like she might have more to say, but with a quick glance to their companions thought better of it.

"Right, we don't want to hold you up," Liz added. "Have a good evening."

Annabelle wanted to say something more, something meaningful, something to express a hint of the feelings splitting her open. Instead she mumbled, "It's good to see you."

She'd taken about two steps before she felt Davis's hand on her own. She stopped, her breath catching at the contact, and looked once again into her expressive eyes. A rush of questions passed unspoken between them.

"Do you mean that?"

Annabelle paused, giving the question its due. It was jolting and painful to see her again, but also a powerful reminder of how much had changed, a vision of how far she could go. Most of all, Davis served as a reminder that she wasn't alone in all her emotions. "Yes. I really do."

Davis smiled, a beautiful flash of genuine relief and pleasure. "Good. Me, too."

❖

Nic stared at a contract for her home—*their* home—in Athens. Her lawyer had handled everything by proxy. She simply had to sign and date it to finalize everything. The house was her last tie to Belle, and with its sale, everything they'd built together would be gone. Of course, she had a new place to live, but it still felt like signing the papers would make her homeless. As final as their emotional good-bye had felt, until this moment she and Belle were still a couple in the legal sense.

This was officially the end of them.

Well, signing the document was the end of her role anyway. She still had to mail the contract to Belle. She looked once again at Belle's name printed next to her own, wondering if she'd ever see them together again. The addresses were an afterthought until she saw Atlanta under Belle's name. She, blinked, read the address again and then a third time in disbelief. Nic knew Belle had vacated their house but assumed she'd gone to live with her family.

She tried to tamp down the hope rising in her, but could Belle's choice of a new home really be a coincidence? The logical part of her brain said yes, millions of people lived in Atlanta for a million different reasons, but her heart said for Belle the city held only memories tied to Nic. Maybe she wasn't so eager to cut ties after all. Even if she didn't want her back as a lover, she'd need a friend, wouldn't she? Someone to help her through the transition? Belle had always turned to her in difficult situations. Maybe she couldn't help but do the same now. If that were even a little true, Nic still stood a chance. If nothing else, she owed it to both of them to check up on her—or at least, that's what she told herself.

She was out the door and in her Lexus before she could process anything else. Belle was close, and Nic needed to see her. She thought fleetingly about the promises she'd made to Buddy Taylor, but she had no intention of holding Belle back. Her motives were pure. She wanted to help. She couldn't stand the thought of Belle alone in some Midtown apartment lost and overwhelmed by her surroundings with no one to lean on. Nic only wanted to offer some stability, some familiarity, some comfort.

An image of Belle's despair the last time they saw each other flashed in her mind, and she wondered if familiarity was exactly what Belle had fled back to in Athens. Nic slowed her car. She didn't want to hurt Belle any more than she already had. More importantly, she didn't want to face the pain she'd caused. She could take losing the promotion and her home, but the images of Belle's torment still kept her awake at night. Maybe showing up unannounced wasn't the best option.

In an unexpected show of conscience, or perhaps cowardice, she pulled out her phone and dialed the number she knew by heart, hoping Belle hadn't switched cell carriers. Nic's heart beat in her throat when the most soothing voice she'd ever known answered.

"Hi, Belle." Nic hoped the emotion wasn't evident in her voice.

"Nic?" Annabelle didn't sound nearly as happy.

"Yes, it's me. I, uh, I got the papers."

"Papers?"

"For our house." She paused. Nothing. "You know, the old one. The ones finalizing the sale." Damn, she had to pull it together. She held her breath through another long silence.

"Is there a problem with them?"

"No, no everything looks good." *Except for the finality of it all.*

"Okay...then—"

"It's just...I'm in the neighborhood, and I wanted to know if I could have you sign them right now."

"Now? You're in...my neighborhood?"

"I had some business in Midtown—"

"How did you know I live—"

"The address is on the forms," Nic said, swallowing through a tight throat. She hadn't figured on Belle's wariness.

"Oh."

"I thought I might kill two birds with one stone, since I'm... since I'm here." She hesitated, then, "I'll understand if you can't stand to see me," she lied. "It's just the contract is time-sensitive, and I thought we could get everything wrapped up faster if we cut out the courier. You know, so we can both move on."

"Of course. This whole thing has taken longer than I expected anyway."

The way Belle's hesitation dissipated at the prospect of being free of their past almost made Nic turn around. But surely Belle wouldn't dismiss their connection when she saw her in person. With the exception of the most horrendous twenty-four hours of her life, Belle had always melted for her. They needed each other.

By the time she pulled into Belle's driveway, she'd almost talked herself into believing they were destined for a happy reunion. Unfortunately, her visions of grandeur were tempered when Belle met her on the stairs. "You don't need to come up. I'll just sign the papers here."

She looked stunning, though dressed more casually than usual, in khakis and a turquoise top that deepened the blue in her eyes. Nic was momentarily overwhelmed by the desire to trace a line over the curve of her hip or brush against the softness of her lips. It was as if she'd lived the last months in black and white and only now saw life in color. Sadly, the color rising in Belle's cheeks hinted at embarrassment or frustration, signaling she wasn't enjoying this reunion as much as Nic was. "I'm sorry, what?"

"The papers." Belle extended her hand.

Nic handed them over.

"Do you have a pen?"

Nic had one in her pocket, but everything was moving too fast. They hadn't even made small talk. She didn't want to lie, but she didn't want the moment to end before she'd had a chance to realize its full potential. "Sorry, I don't have one on me."

Belle glanced over her shoulder, then frowned. "I'll be right back."

"I'm sorry if I implied I was in a rush. I can come in for a minute."

Belle opened her mouth, then closed it before Nic realized she hadn't been invited in. She felt like someone had hit her. "Or if you don't want me in your new place—"

"No, it's fine." Belle covered quickly, but clearly only out of social responsibility. "You can come up, but I haven't unpacked everything. It's a bit of a mess."

"You should see my place."

Belle didn't acknowledge the comment as she turned and went inside. She crossed straight to a school bag to find a pen. Nic took the chance to glance around the apartment. The space had an undeniably homey feel, or maybe any space with Belle in it felt like home. Still, it seemed impossibly small, less than half the size of Nic's one-bedroom rental. Belle deserved better. She should live like a queen in a castle, and she had until Nic had destroyed everything.

"Won't you need more room than this?"

Belle looked up as if the words jarred her. "Why? It's just me."

"I know." Nic shook off the reminder that she didn't belong here. "But what about when your sister and the kids come? Or your parents? Your mama can't sleep on the couch, and there's no place to put a table big enough for everyone."

"This is all I can afford on my new salary."

Salary, what salary? Nic thought she'd live off the money from the house.

"Plus I can walk to work," Belle said.

"You…work around here?"

"I'm teaching again. This is the only place I could find a job after so many years off. I didn't have a lot of options in schools or apartments."

"I could've helped. I know people. I have money."

"I don't want your help, Nic. I can do this on my own."

Nic felt her chances slipping away and fought to keep from lashing out. Belle was giving her no *in* here. "You're entitled to half of everything that's mine. If I were a man, you'd get alimony, enough to buy a real place, not a rented room. I'll have my lawyer write up the papers. I'll have a portion of my paycheck put in your account."

Why hadn't she thought of this sooner? She could help Belle and stay connected to her. They'd have to stay in touch at least through other people, plus if part of her pay supported Belle, she'd have a reason to care about her job.

"Absolutely not," Belle said with a finality that chilled Nic's blood. "I don't want your money. I never have. I got enough from the sale of the house to fill my savings, and I'm looking forward to living off my own wages for the first time in my life."

What could she say to that? Belle didn't seem happy, and she certainly wasn't living the high life, but she didn't appear to be floundering either. A job of her own, a place of her own. A life of her own. Belle's budding sense of independence was somehow terrifying and sexy. "I admire you, Belle. Most women would make me pay through the nose, especially since I wouldn't fight you."

"I don't want that."

What do you want? Surely she had something to offer. "Okay, I'm sure you'll do great here, but I'd be happy to show you around." Nic's hopes rose once again. "Maybe recommend some good restaurants. You're close to the park, too. There's a spot I love right down—"

"Thank you, but no," Annabelle said, then turned quickly and signed the papers. "I've got plenty to keep me occupied, and I'm sure you do, too. With these papers out of the way, we're both off on new adventures."

Separate adventures. Annabelle had politely dismissed any opportunity for them to spend time together, no matter how well-meaning or innocent. Her chance to earn her way back into Belle's good graces was evaporating. "Well…if you need anything…"

"Thank you, but this…my freedom…was the best thing you could've given me." She handed the papers back to Nic. "It's a relief to be out from under the constant reminders of what we left behind. Now I can move on." She lifted her chin. "You should, too."

Nic nodded, unable to speak around the lump in her throat. Belle even handled a brush-off with her trademark grace and class.

She managed to mutter a good-bye and climb back into her car before letting any tears fall. On her way over she'd worried about facing Belle's anguish. Turned out her indifference hurt just as badly, if not more. Belle had always needed her. How could need just disappear, unless maybe it hadn't ever really been there to begin with. Maybe she'd been the one who'd needed Belle all along.

She couldn't go on with this emptiness inside her. As she drove around the block, she glanced at Davis's apartment building. She wouldn't even let her mind go there, but not for lack of desire. If she couldn't get through to Annabelle, she stood no chance with Davis. She couldn't go back, and she had no idea how to go forward alone. Maybe she needed to stay put for a while.

CHAPTER FOURTEEN

Annabelle sat up in bed and immediately slipped her pillow sideways so Nic could curl around it instead of her. The move was purely psychological, like an amputee scratching a phantom limb, and every time she did it, grief flooded her. She hated the daily reminder of how much she'd lost, and every night she swore the next day would be different. But each morning, she woke herself by reaching for a woman who wasn't there. She tried to remember that even when Nic had been in her life she wasn't always in her bed, and while she'd spent those mornings counting down to her return, Nic had been spending them with someone else. She glanced across her backyard fence to a window two buildings down, another disturbing habit she couldn't shake.

She didn't want to feel like some obsessed stalker, and mostly she didn't. Throughout the day she stayed busy and kept her mind on her to-do list, but the first thing in the morning and the last thing at night, when the loneliness of her empty bed and empty heart crept from the shadows into the forefront of her mind, she couldn't help but wonder about Davis. Did she stare at the ceiling and wonder where she'd gone wrong? Had she managed to sustain her anger at Nic? Or did she long to hold her, blissfully oblivious one more time? Had she moved on? Her lights weren't on now. Was she sleeping peacefully? Sleeping alone? Cassandra was a beautiful woman, and she seemed more than a little protective of Davis.

Belle threw back the covers and put her feet on the cool wood floors, soaking up the physical, the solid, the tangible. She'd spent the last two weeks wondering about her realtor and her ex-wife's mistress. It felt strange to think of them that way, but that's all they really were to her. She didn't know either of them. There was no logical reason why their relationship status should consume her thoughts, yet it did. She wavered several times a day between hoping Davis had moved on, because it would give her hope for life after Nic, and praying she hadn't, because if someone else out there felt like she did—someone who could understand the pain and brokenness she couldn't pull herself out of—maybe she wouldn't feel quite so alone all the time.

She dressed quickly and mentally chastised herself for being so melodramatic. Lots of people had failed relationships. Her own sister had been cheated on, had grieved, and had moved on. Why couldn't she gauge her progress by Liz's standards? Simply because she hadn't lost Nic? That made no sense, but deep down in her heart she worried it was true. It had taken every ounce of energy she'd had not to fall apart after seeing Nic a week earlier. Even knowing much of what she'd believed about Nic had been a lie, she still feared Nic was a once-in-a-lifetime kind of woman. The only other person in the world who could confirm or disprove that theory lived in her line of sight. How could Annabelle not be curious?

She pulled on the clothes she'd laid out after her shower last night and bypassed her coffeemaker. The thought of making a single cup of coffee was too depressing, so she'd get some at school. She grabbed her lunchbox from the refrigerator and a granola bar she'd set out the night before. She'd perfected her morning routine after just a short time. In the evenings, she prepared for the next day to keep herself busy until she crashed, and then she was ready to go so quickly each morning she didn't have time to be alone with her thoughts. She was out the door in half an hour, even though the short walk to her school would put her at work an hour earlier than she needed to be.

She entered the Midtown Children's Academy and turned down the hall to her classroom, but before she could open the door, someone called to her from the office area.

"Good morning, Annabelle." Her principal, Ailene Werner, was the only person who ever seemed to arrive before seven. "Can you come in here for a second?"

"Sure." She rounded the corner and was greeted with a warm smile. "How are you?"

"I'm well. How are you settling into the school year?"

"I think I'm getting the hang of it," she said truthfully. While her concerns about getting back into teaching weren't totally unfounded, she enjoyed the challenge of updating lesson plans and learning a new curriculum. Each day her students served as a breath of fresh air in her otherwise oppressive existence. She couldn't feel lonely or morose in a room with sixteen first-graders who saw the world through wide, excited eyes. "I love the kids."

"And they love you. Jeffery Moore is smitten with you."

She smiled, thinking of the little cutie who followed her around like a puppy. "He's a doll. I just want to snuggle the stuffing out of him."

"I'm glad the feeling is mutual." Ailene laughed. "And I'm glad to hear you're happy."

Happy? She didn't have it in her to think about the last time she felt truly happy. That had been a lie. What she felt now wasn't even close to genuine happiness, but at least it was real. "Did you need help with something?"

Ailene raised her eyebrows at the sudden shift, but she'd never pried into Annabelle's personal life, and she apparently wouldn't start now. "Actually, yes. We're doing new promotional materials for the school, and I've got a meeting with a graphic designer this morning. I'd like your opinion on the early drafts she sent me."

Annabelle leaned over Ailene's shoulder and scanned a PDF document on her screen. She immediately noticed the school colors, navy and maroon, had been offset with light print, brightening up a potentially dark palette. The school's academic credentials were bulleted for an official feel, while quotes from students were scattered throughout in a font resembling a child's handwriting. "The designer did an impressive job of balancing the official with the playful. I think that's one of the key elements we strive for in our classrooms."

"I agree. I love the feel, and she worked in everything I asked her to, but something's still missing," Ailene said.

"The kids."

"What?"

"You've got pictures of state-of-the-art classrooms, but there are no children in them," Annabelle explained.

Ailene studied the screen, then sat back. "You're right. I thought showcasing the updates we made last year would be appealing, but progress feels empty until you share it with someone."

Annabelle grimaced at the parallel to her own life, but Ailene continued. "We're not a school in theory. We're a school that practices for the sake of our students. We need to showcase them."

"Excellent." Annabelle straightened up and moved toward the door. "Glad I could help."

"Me, too. Here comes our designer now. Maybe she could get some pictures of your class as they arrive this morning."

"I don't know if I'm the right person for that."

"Let's ask her." Ailene rose and went to unlock the front door while Annabelle waited in the office. She didn't want to see anyone right now, much less be photographed. The comment about empty progress stung, and if she let herself dwell on it, she could easily slip into the depression that always hovered on the edge of her consciousness. She had to get out of her head and into her class. If she could lose herself in her work, in her students, she wouldn't have time to think about anything else.

"I was just showing your first draft to our newest teacher," Ailene said, opening the door.

Annabelle turned to face their guest, plastering a fake smile on her face, but it faltered the minute her eyes met the hypnotic green ones of their graphic designer. She gasped. "Davis, you're a graphic designer?"

"I am." Davis rubbed her forehead. "You teach here?"

"I do."

The silence stretched between them as Ailene peered from one to the other. "You two know each other?"

Heat immediately spread up Annabelle's neck and into her cheeks. She had no intention of explaining to her boss how they'd met, but she didn't know how to keep dodging the cloud over them. Thankfully Davis was quicker in her response. "We're kind of... neighbors."

The explanation seemed to appease Ailene. "That's nice, and convenient for our suggestion for the brochure."

"How's that?" Davis seemed distracted because, even when she addressed Ailene, she kept darting glances at Annabelle, her eyes seeming to search for more than could be revealed in a business meeting. She appeared both weary and wary. She'd lost weight, her once-lean figure appearing almost gaunt.

"We love everything about it except the photos we selected."

"That shouldn't be hard to fix. You can certainly send me others to try."

"That's the thing. The pictures we took after our summer renovations don't have the students in them, so we need you to take some new ones."

"New ones," Davis repeated. "Sure."

"I thought maybe you could just hang around Ms. Taylor's class this morning as the kids arrive and see what you think would work best."

Davis shrugged. "Okay, but I'm not really a photographer, and I didn't bring my camera with me."

"You can use the school's new one. It's high-definition and has all the fancy bells and whistles."

"Wouldn't you rather have a professional come in?" Davis offered diplomatically.

"Or maybe we could get the art teacher to just stop in and take them," Annabelle said, trying to let Davis off the hook. She certainly didn't seem too excited about spending any more time with her, and who could blame her?

Ailene waved them both off. "We've never used professionals before. Besides, we've got cute kids, and I can't imagine Ms. Taylor ever having taken a bad picture."

"No, I'm sure she'll photograph beautifully," Davis murmured.

Annabelle's face flamed again, this time less from embarrassment and more from pleasure. She'd gone from being complimented almost daily to wondering if she was worthy of love and devotion. Praise from Davis, of all people, caught her off guard.

"Great. The kids will arrive soon. Why don't you show her to your classroom?"

"Do you even have time this morning?" Annabelle offered Davis one more out, trying not to make more out of her sweet but surely passing comment.

Ailene answered for her. "I'm sure it won't take any time at all. Then you can just pick your favorites to put in the brochure."

Davis shrugged. "It's okay with me, as long as it's okay with you. I don't want to invade your world. The world of your classroom, that is," she rushed to add.

Annabelle smiled. Davis was trying to protect her by respecting her personal space. Suddenly her own defensiveness over her sanctuary didn't seem quite so important. Funny how receiving someone else's concern could make her want to be more open. "I've got a lot going on right now, but we can work something out."

"I'll try not to get in your way or hold you back."

Were they still talking about taking pictures or something bigger? Either way it didn't change her feelings about this situation or her response to Davis. "I trust you," she said. And strangely, she meant it.

Davis followed Annabelle down the brightly lit hallway. On one side, a beautifully detailed mural covered the wall, featuring children at play near The Carter Center, The Martin Luther King Memorial, and other famous Atlanta landmarks. The other wall displayed student artwork and poems in splashes of color, scribbled with a mix of joy and concentration by tiny hands and big imaginations. The space held an exuberance that would've been contagious if not for the tension radiating from the woman in front of her.

Annabelle hadn't wanted Davis in her classroom, she didn't want her behind the camera lens, maybe she didn't even want to be in the same airspace as Davis, and who could blame her? Davis respected her so much for the strength she'd displayed in rebuilding her life. She wasn't wallowing in remorse and anger. She seemed tired and cautious, but appeared to have escaped the weariness holding Davis captive. Annabelle didn't need to be pulled back into the fire. Then again it wasn't as if Davis loved bumping into a life-size reminder of her biggest failure either, but somehow she couldn't relegate Annabelle to the "to be avoided at all cost" category of her life, especially with the spark of connection that'd shot through her when Annabelle had looked into her eyes and said, "I trust you."

Trust wasn't something she thought herself capable of anymore, and by most standards Annabelle had even more reason to feel that way. How could she look at anyone, especially Davis, and utter those words? But she'd said them, and Davis had believed her. She seemed nervous, sometimes awkward, but never hostile, never angry or resentful. Davis once again found herself in awe of Annabelle's grace.

Trust—check. Belief—check. Respect—check. And neither one of them seemed to hold the other responsible for what'd happened. So why did seeing her make Davis's chest ache? Was it because, when she looked at Annabelle, she saw every way in which she fell short?

Annabelle entered her classroom and glanced nervously around. "So this is it."

"Nice."

"Thanks. It's a good school. I'm lucky to have access to such wonderful resources."

"Yes. Not many of the city schools are stocked like this one, but they're lucky to have someone like you to put them to good use."

Annabelle turned away at the compliment. "I've still got a lot to learn."

Was she really the most self-deprecating woman in Atlanta, or had Nic's betrayal shaken her self-esteem so completely that she doubted her ability to shine even in other areas of her life? A wave of anger surged through Davis, but she tamped it down. She hadn't known Annabelle before, so she couldn't make assumptions about how the last few months had changed her. Maybe she'd always blushed easily or shaken off compliments. Maybe she'd never understood how beautiful or strong she was. It wasn't hard to see how she'd held Nic's heart. Still, Davis had a hard time believing the sadness in Annabelle's eyes had always existed or that her smile had never shone brighter than the politely distant line it formed now. What had she looked like when truly happy? Davis wished she could have known her before that awful morning.

"Are you okay?" The gentle brush of Annabelle's hand against her shoulder was so light she could've convinced herself it wasn't real, if not for the tremor it caused. She couldn't remember the last time someone had touched her with such tenderness. No, that wasn't true. She remembered but she didn't want to.

"Sorry. I zoned out. I'm not much of a morning person."

"I wasn't only talking about right now." She shrugged. "I meant, in general."

"Oh." Now it was her turn to look away from the concern in Annabelle's eyes. "Sure, I mean, life continues, right?"

Annabelle nodded. "It does."

"What can you do but walk on?"

"I honestly don't know, but I like that you said 'walk on' and not 'move on.'"

"Yeah, well, I'm pushing through, but I can't say I've gotten anywhere yet."

Annabelle looked curious. "Really?"

"I work, I eat, I sleep…sometimes. What else is there?"

"I don't know. I just, I thought maybe when I saw you and Cassandra…"

"Cass?" She paused for a moment. "Wait. You thought Cass and I were a couple?"

"I'm sorry. It's none of my business."

"No, no." She rushed to calm Annabelle's embarrassment and correct the misconception that would've been funny if not for how sad it seemed to make her. "Cass is a friend, my best friend since college, so I guess that makes her my longest relationship, but never romantically. She doesn't have a romantic bone in her body."

"And that's important to you?"

"I, um…" She turned away again, staring out the window as she considered the question. With anyone else she would've given a flippant remark to avoid examining her fear of being alone, but Annabelle deserved the same kind of genuineness she'd offered of herself. "I don't know. I used to dream of finding someone passionate, and I even let myself believe I had, but now I can't imagine letting my guard down enough to enjoy anything like that. How can I ever trust my emotions again after where they left me? God, I don't mean to be maudlin, it's just—"

"No, people keep telling me 'next time you'll know when something is off,' like that's some sort of comfort. I thought we were happy right up until I overheard someone else. My intuition didn't save me, but even if it had, it's like…if I ever let myself fall in love again, I'll have to wait for the other shoe to drop. For years, decades even." She seemed to suddenly realize her voice had risen and immediately pulled her tone back to the level expected from an elementary-school teacher. "I just meant, I understand what you're saying."

Davis finally met Annabelle's deep-blue gaze again, this time searching for the connection she'd avoided. So, she did understand the pain, the grief, the loneliness, the doubt. Relief overwhelmed her, clogging her throat and stinging her eyes. So many people nodded sympathetically or offered clichés of encouragement, but they couldn't really feel the kind of heartbreak she saw reflected in Annabelle's expression. Emotion exploded in her chest, stretching mental muscles she hadn't used in a long time. Compassion, sorrow, and reassurance mingled within her to create a sensation she'd both avoided and longed for: connection with another human being.

As quickly as the connection had been forged, it was severed at the sound of children racing toward the classroom door. Annabelle looked away as three boys careened around the corner, crashing into each other in a mass of arms, legs, and superhero backpacks.

Davis stepped backward to steady herself from the shift of energy in the room. The emotional ties between Annabelle and herself had been all-consuming for those heavy seconds, but now the children captivated Annabelle's attention. Davis felt cold and empty outside her focus and struggled to remember why she was there.

She glanced to the camera clutched in her hands. Pictures. Right. She hit the power button and flipped up the flash even though she probably didn't need it, given the classroom's abundance of natural light. Each little motion moved her one step closer to her professional self, her controlled self, her detached self.

She switched off the viewing screen on the back of the camera and lifted it to her eye instead. She liked the protective barrier the lens offered, allowing her to zoom in on people around her while keeping her most expressive features hidden. Focusing on the boys as they hung their backpacks on tiny hooks, she snapped a couple shots, then directed her aim toward the door where Annabelle greeted a little girl. The child clung to the folds in her mother's skirt so that it tented out in front of her, revealing only two big brown eyes and a set of dark pigtails. The mother attempted to shoo the girl into the classroom while talking in a stern tone about the fact that they were in the second week of school and should be past the shy stage.

Annabelle, on the other hand, crouched down to the child's level and spoke in a gentle tone. Davis couldn't make out what she said, but it was clear that instead of shaming the little one, she tried to ease her with praise and reassurances.

She snapped one picture and then another, and with each shot she saw the child slip farther from her mother's side. If the frames played back in rapid succession, they'd serve as a how-to movie on soothing children, with the final frame beautifully displaying the girl snuggled safely and happily in Annabelle's arms.

The exchange was so comforting to watch, Davis almost felt as though she were the one receiving the embrace. When Annabelle rested her chin on the child's head, looked directly into the camera, and smiled sweetly, Davis's finger snapped another photo seemingly of its own will. The picture would never be in a brochure, but it deserved to be framed and displayed proudly on someone's bedside table.

Davis shook her head and lowered the camera. She didn't know where that thought had come from, and she didn't like the accompanying surge of warmth. Annabelle was a beautiful woman, and she exuded all sorts of amazing qualities that would make some very lucky woman happy someday, but Davis wasn't that person. She wasn't capable of that kind of openness or genuine caring, nor could she afford to give someone else the power to hurt her. Annabelle didn't seem adept at deception, or to even possess a devious impulse, but Davis had been devastatingly wrong before. No way in hell would she put herself in the position to make a mistake like that again.

❖

Annabelle turned back to face the class after adding the roots to the tree she'd drawn across her chalkboard. The sight of Davis in the back row still startled her. She'd been so unobtrusive, at times Annabelle had forgotten she was there, but every time she caught sight of her bright-red hair, it disconcerted her all over again. At least she wasn't forced to confront the sadness in Davis's eyes, since she'd mostly hidden behind the camera. Surely she had enough photographs by now. She'd been shooting for almost two hours. It wasn't that she minded Davis staying. She didn't mind at all. That's what bothered her.

Shouldn't she hate her?

And even if she didn't hate her personally, shouldn't she hate everything she represented? The thought of Nic in someone else's arms still hurt so badly she thought she might be physically sick, but for some reason she didn't associate those feelings with Davis—at least not all the time. She certainly didn't feel that way about her now as she smiled and glanced up from her viewfinder politely, almost expectantly.

Expectantly.

Right.

She's waiting for me to go on with my lesson.

Annabelle flushed at having been caught daydreaming in front of her class. She often spaced out while doing menial tasks, but she'd never slipped in front of her students.

"And those roots suck up water that soaks into the ground and carries it up to the leaves," she said, quickly finishing her lesson and glancing at the clock. Two minutes till ten o'clock. She must not have spaced out too long since they were still on time for their next activity. "All right, if I see pencils and books put away neatly, bottoms in chairs, and mouths closed, we'll line up for recess."

The children snapped to order quickly under the promise of playtime, and within a minute she had them all out the door.

Davis walked beside her to the fenced-in playground. She took one shot from a wide angle, then zoomed in on various children using the slides or swings stationed around them. In the classroom, Annabelle had avoided looking at her for fear of feeling exposed, but out here she allowed herself the luxury of watching her work.

Davis's face was so expressive, even with her eyes largely covered. Her forehead furrowed and her eyebrows arched as she lined up the lens with her subject. Then her lips would either curl upward or purse together, making it immediately clear whether she got the shot she wanted.

Annabelle caught herself watching those lips. They were full and beautiful without a hint of embellishment, their natural pale pink a complement to Davis's fair skin tone and strong jawline. Those lips…soft and confident, fit her personality as well. Annabelle realized she'd moved past her current observation to knowledge she wished she didn't have, and her cheeks flamed at the memory of Davis's mouth crushed against her own.

"Are you all right?"

The words sounded far away beyond the rushing of her own pulse, but she knew the voice belonged to Davis, which only heightened her embarrassment about where her mind had wandered.

"I'm fine."

"Are you sure? You look, I don't know, flushed."

"It's the heat," she said quickly, drawing from her now-familiar excuse. "I'm still not used to being out in it all the time."

Davis didn't look convinced.

Annabelle had to change the subject quickly. "Are you getting the photographs you need?"

"I've filled the memory card. I'll sort them tonight, but in addition to the brochure, I think they might want to frame some of these for around the school or use them as stock photos for things like the website or press releases."

"Well, you certainly went above and beyond."

She smiled almost sheepishly. "I've had fun. Ailene was right about the cute kids. Not to mention your photogenic qualities."

Thankfully, the blush the compliment inspired paled in comparison to the one she'd been recovering from, so it probably wasn't noticeable. "That's very sweet of you."

"It's the truth. I mostly do boring corporate stuff. Lots of old white guys along with charts and graphs. Being around you and the kids is rejuvenating."

"Well…I know what you mean about the kids. They're a breath of fresh air in what could easily be a very stagnant existence."

"They're so excited about the whole world. Who would've thought root systems could be mind-blowing, but when you see it through their eyes, it's like, 'oh yeah, those things I never see until I hit them with my bike actually sustain everything growing above ground.'" Davis's smile burned brightly for a few seconds before it faded back to sadness. "It was a refreshing change from my current outlook on life. I just wanted to stay in their world as long as I could."

"That, I understand."

"I hope I didn't wear out my welcome."

"Not at all." She touched Davis's shoulder, both to comfort her and to try to reestablish the connection she'd felt listening to her talk about the kids. It was so affirming to have someone to share those kinds of feelings with. "You can stay all day if you want, and I hope you have fun when you have to review all the photos tonight."

"I appreciate it, but I should go."

"That's fine, too."

"And thanks, about tonight. It'll be a lot to sort through, but I hope I captured a little piece of what drew me to them in the first place."

"Me, too."

They stood there, staring at each other for a long, heavy moment. Annabelle felt like she should say something more. There had to be more, didn't there? After sharing the things they'd shared, the understanding that passed between them, the first genuine connection she'd felt in months, could they just walk away? They should. They'd been thrown together by uncontrollable circumstances, both this morning and in months past. They weren't friends. They didn't really know each other, in fact.

Why did she have to keep reminding herself of that?

"Well, I guess I'll see you around the neighborhood," Davis said.

Bumping into each other around Midtown was becoming a habit for them. Aside from glancing at Davis's apartment every morning, Annabelle would have to leave future meetings to chance. "Enjoy the rest of your day."

Davis's smile seemed strained, as if she had to work to make herself believe that possible. "I'll try. You, too."

They hesitated another few seconds before Davis finally turned to go. Annabelle's loneliness returned before she was even through the door. Was she really that bad off? It was hard enough to live with missing Nic every day, but at least that made sense. Missing Davis was beyond illogical, even dysfunctional, but for the first time in a long time, she was certain what she wanted. The instinct to call Davis back gripped her so completely she didn't have time to question the fact that her instincts had only betrayed her in the past. "Davis?"

"Yes?" She turned around so quickly she startled Annabelle

"If you'd like some help, with all that sorting through…" She hadn't *actually* formulated that thought until the words tripped off her tongue, but she always fell back on work these days.

Davis's lips parted silently.

"I mean, not that you need help," Annabelle rushed to explain, "but I know the kids and the school, and I thought—"

"I'd like your input."

"Really?"

"Really." Davis's sweet smile reassured her. "Do you want to come over this weekend?"

"To your apartment?" The thought immediately reminded her why hanging out with Davis was a bad idea. Davis's apartment held only bad memories. Maybe bad wasn't the right word. The kiss wasn't bad, but the circumstances surrounding it tinted everything in a nightmarish light.

"Or we could meet somewhere else, if you're uncomfortable," Davis said, candidly. "There's a lot of baggage there. Trust me. I know."

Baggage. Yes, there was. Baggage Davis lived with every day and night. Surely Annabelle could survive for a few hours. She forced a smile. "No, your place is fine."

"You sure?"

"No." She laughed. She wasn't sure of anything. "But let's find out."

❖

"Damn," Nic muttered, and rubbed her eyes in an attempt to make them focus on the television. She was drunk. There was no use lying to herself even if she didn't want to think about how regularly she put herself in this position these days. She'd had her first hard drink her first night away from Belle, just to numb the pain. Later, when she'd gotten used to the constant companions of disappointment and sadness, she'd used a little whiskey to fall asleep. She didn't need much since she usually worked herself to the point of exhaustion. One glass on the rocks kept her from thinking about everything she'd lost. If she'd forgo the ice she could also avoid thinking about how she'd played into Davis's fears about her ability to love. Making the drink a double assured she'd drop off to sleep without wondering how Davis and Belle were doing. At least it used to be enough.

She glanced at the half-empty bottle of Glenlivet she'd bought three days ago, or had it been only two? After three months her tolerance had risen, and her ability to induce sleep seemed to have decreased exponentially. Her limbs felt heavy and her thoughts slowed, but now she could have three or four drinks and still not slumber. Instead she squinted at the ESPN ticker running across the bottom of her TV screen, completely unable to make out the score of the Braves game or even decipher which team they were currently playing. She was also alone, painfully alone, which according to common sense was a bad time to drink, but if she followed that rule she'd never drink again.

Then again, drinking with someone else was just one item on a long list of things she might never do again, like eat a home-cooked meal, fall asleep in someone's arms, or have an orgasm that wasn't self-induced.

She flipped off the TV and walked to the bathroom, running her hand along the wall as she went just in case she lost her physical balance. Her mental and emotional states spun constantly. She went from self-hate to regret and remorse to resignation in a matter of minutes. She hadn't just devastated the two most important women in her life; she'd destroyed her self-image in the process. Even if she met someone she wanted to have sex with, she feared what it might lead to. What kind of person let her libido run that far out of control? Then again, what she'd done with Davis had never been about libido, but she'd rather blame an out-of-control sex drive than consider the possibility that maybe she was her father's daughter after all.

Splashing cold water on her face, she stared at her reflection in the mirror. Her cheeks looked fuller, her hair shaggier, her eyes glossed over. Her forehead creased with concern. God, she even looked like him, sitting alone in a lifeless room unable to pull herself out of a stupor. She walked back toward her bed, taking one last swallow of scotch along the way, but it didn't even burn, much less carry the power to erase lingering questions about her genetic predisposition toward failure.

Could she turn into the man she'd spent her life trying to prove wrong? Did she have that little control over herself? She flopped on the bed and tried to think of all the ways they weren't alike. She hadn't seen him in fifteen years, but when she'd left, he'd been sitting in a recliner in a run-down trailer, cussing at a football game. She fought desperately to think about something else, anything else, but the alcohol numbing her mind also allowed it to wander freely. He'd lost every job he'd ever had, he'd lost her mother, and then basically he'd lost his will to live. He was overweight, out of work, and once she walked out of the door, completely alone. Fear settled in her chest as she looked around the little room devoid of any personal touches. The comparisons flowed unbidden through her mind's eye.

Panic tightened her chest and constricted her throat. She hadn't thought she could feel any worse, but with each realization she sank deeper into despair until finally she thrashed upright, gasping for air.

"No," she said aloud. "I'm not him."

She had a job, she had money, and while she was single by choice, she could have a woman anytime she wanted. Maybe not either of the women she wanted, but there were others. She could even have more than one of them. Isn't that what had started all this? Her father had nothing. She could have everything. She needed to remember that. She needed to feel it at her very core. She wasn't finished living. She would prove herself to all of them.

She lay back down and closed her eyes, trying not to question who all she intended to prove herself to, since no one was left who cared. Maybe her first step should be finding someone new to impress.

❖

Davis glanced at the clock when she heard footsteps on the stairs outside her door. Three o'clock? Shit. Where had the day gone? She'd just meant to rest her eyes for a little bit, but she must have fallen asleep hours ago. Sleep was such a fickle impulse these days. When she wanted to, she couldn't, and when she really shouldn't, she absolutely had to. Naps in the middle of the day virtually guaranteed she'd be awake all night.

A knock formally announced Annabelle's arrival as Davis kicked yesterday's clothes under her bed. "Just a second."

She glanced around the apartment. The place wasn't a total disaster zone, but it was probably messier than Annabelle was used to. Then again, she didn't know what she was used to for sure. Just because she looked like *Southern Living* Barbie didn't mean she actually lived like one. Maybe her apartment had empty food cartons and old newspapers stacked all over the place, too. Not bloody likely, but she didn't need to impress Annabelle. If anything, Annabelle might be the one person who understood how cleaning could take a backseat to things like showering, sleeping, and other baser functions.

Davis gathered a stack of paper plates and dumped them in the trash before mumbling, "Fuck it. That's as clean as this place gets."

She opened the door, trying to look casual. "Hi, Annabelle, come on in."

"Thank you." She stepped in and held out a loaf of bread. "I would've brought some wine, but I don't really drink anymore."

"Oh?" She took the bread and examined it, confused.

"Well, after things…happened that day, I didn't really trust myself around alcohol."

Davis's memory flooded with images of things that had occurred between them over a bottle of scotch. Come to think of it, the bottle was still in the cabinet above her sink, untouched since that day for the exact same reason. "That's understandable, but why the bread?"

She smiled and shrugged. "I may have traded one possible addiction for another. I can't stop baking, and if I eat all those carbs myself I won't fit into my new school clothes much longer."

"Wait, you baked this yourself?"

"Yes, last night."

"Like you went to the store and bought a box or a can of dough and put it in the oven?" Davis asked.

Annabelle raised her eyebrows. "Yes, but without the box or the can part."

"How do you do it without the box or the can part?"

"You know, you mix yeast and flour, a little sugar. It's not rocket science." Annabelle frowned. "You don't have to eat it."

"No, no. I didn't mean that. I've just never met anyone who baked their own bread."

"No one? Not even your mama or your grandma?"

"Especially not them." Davis walked over to the counter and grabbed a serrated knife. "My mother is a dental hygienist, and her mother sold furniture. My father's mother is a paralegal. They bought their bread at the store on the way home from work like everyone else I know."

She took a bite of the bread and immediately started talking with her mouth full. "Amazing."

"It's just regular old country bread."

"No, it's light and fluffy and perfect. You could sell this. I'd pay twice what I pay for the store bakery stuff."

Annabelle seemed pleased with the praise even as she shook it off. "Well, you don't have to. I bake at least two loaves a week and barely manage to eat one of them."

"What do you do with the others?"

"I usually give them to neighbors or friends. Last week I gave some to my landlord. She seemed to like it, but I think she liked the brownies better."

"You make brownies, too?" Davis asked. "Are those from a box?"

Annabelle clucked her disapproval. "Nothing I make comes from a box."

"What else can you make?"

"Cookies, cakes, scones, pastas. I can make anything I have a recipe for. If you can read, you can cook."

This woman couldn't be real. No one really had it all the way Annabelle seemed to, a classic beauty with a sweet disposition who just happened to also be a domestic goddess and a great kisser. Davis's stomach clenched.

"What's wrong? You look like something hurt you. Are you getting sick?"

"No, I just—" Davis shook her head trying to stop the words, but she'd fallen out of the practice of holding her tongue. "I just wondered why the hell anyone would ever cheat on you with me."

Annabelle gasped and stepped back.

Davis reached out, instinctually trying to steady her as she sank onto the couch. "I'm sorry. What a shitty thing to say."

"No, it's not that. I'm getting used to talking about what happened, but that's a terrible thing to think about yourself."

"It's the truth, though." Davis shrugged, her dispassionate façade slipping comfortably back into place. "You're everything a person could want in a wife: graceful, generous, sexy, and talented. What could she have possibly seen in me to hold her attention?"

"I see what she saw in you," Annabelle said sadly, her eyes glazing over. "You're beautiful and passionate, fiery even. I bored her."

She thinks I'm beautiful?

Davis shook her head, but Annabelle kept talking. "While I cooked and cleaned for her, you took her to the Roller Derby and go-kart racing. How could she not be pulled away by someone as exciting and full of life as you?"

"I didn't pull her away. She didn't choose me. When you called she ran to you." Davis could hear the detachment in her own voice. The anger was gone, and the hurt throbbed at a manageable level. All that remained was the haunting whisper of unanswerable questions and truths she couldn't avoid. "We shared a few nights a week, but she shared her whole life with you. I'm the kind of woman people like her screw, but women like you always win out in the end."

"I didn't, though. I lost, too." Annabelle sighed. "And I guess that's the ultimate commonality between women like you and women like me. We both ended up in the exact same spot."

❖

Annabelle sat back and rubbed her eyes. They'd settled into a nice rhythm of eliminating pictures they didn't love, then sorting the remainders into one pile of possibilities for the brochure and another group to keep for future use. Despite the heavy tone they'd established early—or maybe because of it—they managed to work smoothly together. Several hours had passed without so much as an allusion to Nic or their shared grief.

"Wow, it's six thirty already."

Davis's stomach growled loudly. "We should think about getting dinner. Do you want to order takeout, or are you opposed to food prepared by other people?"

"Why would I be opposed?"

"Because you can probably cook them all under the table."

She laughed, but it felt nice to have Davis compliment her culinary prowess. Cooking for herself wasn't nearly as much fun as sharing her creations with someone else, especially someone so easily impressed. "No, takeout would be great. I want to see what the neighborhood has to offer."

"Well, then, you came to the right place." Davis opened her desk drawer and unloaded a stack of restaurant menus. "We've got Chinese, Japanese, Thai, pizza, Mediterranean, wings, bar-b-que, tacos, soul food, and much more. Name your poison."

She scanned all the menus but couldn't begin to process so many options. "I've never seen so many restaurants in my whole life."

"Surely they have all these things in Athens."

"Yes, in Athens, but we lived in the suburbs. We never went into the city to eat, only to the country club."

"Right, suburbs and country clubs." The edge of bitterness returned to Davis's voice. "I'm sorry, but you're not in Kansas anymore."

"I'm not." Annabelle touched her lightly on the arm, hoping to reach past whatever wall Davis was trying to build between them. "I've been wanting to try sushi."

"You've never had sushi?"

"There was some at a bar we went to in San Francisco once, and I tried one kind, but Nic didn't care for it, so we never ordered any again. She mostly stuck to American food."

Davis started to say something, then seemed to catch herself, and Annabelle felt the hair on the back of her neck stand up. "What?"

"It's nothing important."

"Please, Davis, don't lie to me." She'd had enough lies. She'd had enough of people trying to spare her feelings. "You of all people understand what that leads to."

"It's just that…Nic and I ate out a lot, at a lot of different places." Davis rushed to soften the blow. "She probably did it because my cooking was so bad compared to yours."

"She ate at all these places with you?" Annabelle picked up the menu for the Mediterranean restaurant and tried to imagine Nic eating lamb over couscous. Then she moved to the Thai food and tried to find anything Nic would choose to order. There was no steak, no baked potatoes, no grits, no banana-cream pie. Were they talking about the same person? "She enjoyed these kinds of food?"

Davis nodded apologetically. "She seemed to. Maybe she was lying, though."

"She lied to one of us about her tastes, but why?" She covered her face with her hand. "God, I'll never stop asking that question. Why? I would've gone out with her. I would've loved to come to the city and try new food. If she wanted an adventure, we could've taken one together."

"And I would've stayed home. I would've cherished movie nights curled up on the couch or Saturday strolls through a farmers' market. I would've even gone to the suburbs for her, and you don't know me well enough to know this, but that's a big deal. I would've planted a vegetable garden or flowers or whatever homeowners grow."

"No, she wouldn't have let you."

"What do you mean she wouldn't let me? Like I'd need her permission to plant some fucking peas in our own hypothetical yard?"

Annabelle tried not to show her surprise at Davis using the F-word. She didn't know any women who talked like that, and the men never said it in front of her. She liked the way it sounded—strong, jarring, and more powerful than politeness. "Nic took pride in being a provider, a caretaker. She had people to mow the lawn so I didn't have to."

"I guess that's nice of her. You just strike me as someone who'd like to grow some tomatoes or something."

She smiled in spite of the heavy topic. Davis had noticed something about her that Nic somehow managed to miss for thirteen years. "I actually would like a garden."

"Then why not do it?"

She sighed. "It sounds stupid now, but I thought she wanted to provide for me. I didn't want to take that away from her, so instead I took those things away from me."

"Wow." Davis, for all her bluster, didn't seem to know what to say, which only made Annabelle feel worse.

"It didn't happen all at once, you know?"

"You don't have to explain."

"No, I kind of feel like I do, for me."

Instead of arguing or trying to change the subject, Davis hunkered down into the corner of the couch, crisscrossed her legs, and rested her hands in her lap the way Annabelle's students sat when she needed them to pay close attention. Her focus made it easier for Annabelle to continue, knowing she wouldn't rush to judgment.

"At first we were both working toward the same things: the house, some money in savings, a family. It wasn't until Nic's career took off that we got more focused on the work than what we were working toward. I quit my job to support hers in the hopes it would move us toward a family faster, and she seemed so happy to be able to support me. I thought it was because she loved me and because it proved she could take care of us when we had children. Now I see it was never really about *us* so much as *her*. A stay-at-home wife was a status symbol, not much different from the manicured lawn or big house."

Davis didn't rush to correct her or offer quick condolences. She turned pensive. "Do you think she lied about wanting kids to string you along?"

Annabelle pondered that. "I don't think she lied purposefully. A baby was always my dream more than hers, but she liked the idea of a picture-perfect family. I think she hung on to the possibility because she wanted to think she gave me everything I wanted, but every time we got close and she had to face the practicalities of what a baby would mean for her life, she'd find an excuse to put me off."

"Are you glad now that she did?"

"You want the truth?"

"Yes." Davis answered quickly. "Always."

"Even knowing I couldn't trust her to be a good parent or a good partner, sometimes I still wish we'd had a baby." She shrugged. "It wouldn't have changed how we ended. It might have even sped up the process, but I worry I missed my only chance to be a mom."

"You won't try again with someone else?"

"I can't imagine dating right now, and even if I met someone tomorrow, it'd take years before I could trust someone enough to share something so important. I'm thirty-three. My window for starting over is shrinking."

"Shit, don't say that. I'm thirty-one and I'm in the same boat trust-wise."

"Do you want kids?"

"I don't know. I kind of thought I might someday, but now you've got me looking at my biological clock." Davis shifted uncomfortably on the couch. "I've been so mad at her for breaking the final strand of faith I had in human nature, but my anger mostly stayed in the present. I hadn't stopped to think about what she did to my future."

"I didn't mean to upset you again." She tried to force a smile and nudge them back into lighter topics. "All this because I haven't had sushi in ten years."

"Right," Davis said resolutely. "She took that away from you, too."

Annabelle didn't want this to turn into a pity party about what Nic had taken from her. She had to move past that stage of grief. "Only because I let her, and I won't do that ever again."

"So, tonight is sushi night?"

"Yes." She grabbed the menu, feeling a tingle of excitement. "Only I have no idea what any of these words mean. Why don't you order your favorites?"

Davis hesitated. "I don't want to do that."

"Why?"

"You spent years doing what Nic liked, or said she liked. I don't want you to just start doing what I like because we're friends. You need to learn what you like."

Annabelle thought about her logic. It made sense, but it was also overwhelming, and not just because most of the menu was in Japanese. She'd been with Nic since college. Trying to undo thirteen years of basing her likes and dislikes on someone else's wouldn't change easily. Where would she even start?

"What's wrong?"

She looked up from the menu to meet Davis's beautiful eyes. "It's so much more than dinner, you know."

"Why don't we just get one of everything?"

"Can we do that?"

"Sure, why not? And if you don't like anything, we'll try again tomorrow with the Thai, and then the Mediterranean until you find something you love."

The allusion to more nights spent together should have bothered her, but instead she found it strangely comforting. "You'd do that for me?"

"Trust me, eating is never a hardship for me," Davis said, then caught herself. "Honestly, eating has been a hardship over the past few months. I haven't had much of an appetite. This is the first time I've been excited about a meal since Nic left."

"Then maybe we *should* order everything on the menu."

"As long as you promise to take the lead. I don't want this to become the all-Davis-and-no-Anna show."

"Okay, as long you're honest about what you like, because I'm just getting started and—did you just call me 'Anna'?"

Davis blushed. "Sorry. I know not to call you Belle, but shortening your name came naturally. I won't do it again if—"

"No, I like it. I used to go by Annie when I was younger."

"Do you like Annie better?"

"Either one is fine." Davis arched her eyebrows, and Annabelle realized she'd settled for whatever someone else wanted rather than state her own opinion. "Actually, say them again."

"Annie or Anna?"

"I was Annie before Nic, and I don't think I can or even want to go back, and you're right, I'll never be Belle to anyone else. I think I like Anna."

Davis grinned. "I like Anna, too. It's like you've put the first part of you first."

She wasn't sure she'd go that far, but she liked the little surge of confidence she felt every time Davis said the name. "Yes. Anna. It's a start."

CHAPTER FIFTEEN

Nic slapped on an extra dose of cologne before getting out of the Lexus. She didn't want to smell of the stale air and old fast-food containers that filled her car. She didn't have any real desire to be all the way out in Decatur, entering a lesbian dance club at nine o'clock on Thursday night. She'd already put in a twelve-hour day at the office, but if she was going to do this, she intended to do it right.

The woman at the door didn't card her. She barely even looked up as Nic pushed through the door. The whole building reverberated from a dance beat, and she waited for her eyes to adjust to the darkened room. She didn't feel any sort of affinity to this place. She'd never come here with Annabelle or Davis, which is why she'd chosen it tonight. Still, she'd expected a bit of a thrill to be back among other lesbians. Instead of seeking out the press of bodies against her own, she carefully threaded her way between women on the dance floor until she claimed an empty bar stool. The woman next to her was smoking and waved her beer wildly as she shouted about some woman who'd stood her up. She hadn't missed dyke drama. Then again, she'd created enough of her own to last a lifetime.

No, she wouldn't wallow. Not tonight. She gave herself an internal pep talk about getting back on the horse and how meeting women was like riding a bike, but even she found her lack of originality disappointing. She caught the eye of a bartender, who headed her way without the enthusiasm she'd once inspired in women.

That wasn't true.

She'd never had women falling into her lap every day, and there was absolutely nothing wrong with the way this woman took her order of a scotch on the rocks. Nothing had changed except Nic's own outlook on life. She had to stop her downward spiral. Tonight she needed to feel the press of a warm body against her, even if that's all it ever amounted to.

In the past she would've gone slowly, waited for a woman to come to her. She wasn't a pressure salesman at work, and she didn't intend to be one in a bar either, but she had more at stake than ever. She scanned the room, looking for a worthy companion, and thankfully she didn't have to look far. At the end of the bar, three women occupied a tall table, but only two of them seemed involved in the conversation. The petite brunette with them looked more like a third wheel. She stared at her brightly painted toenails, swirled her red wine idly, and sighed so hard it caused a little wisp of hair to flutter over her forehead. Nic smiled. This woman was cute and alone and clearly bored, making her an easy target.

She grimaced. Women weren't targets. Even with something to prove, she wouldn't let herself become a person who callously used another human being. She knew that's probably what others thought about her. Belle and Davis, their families and friends likely all believed she'd maliciously played them, but that wasn't true. She'd made mistakes, serious ones bordering on self-absorption, but she'd never willfully hurt anyone. If anything, she'd gotten in so far over her head by constantly trying not to disappoint—*damn it, why did she keep reliving this?*

She wasn't here to justify or redeem herself. She needed to move forward or prove she could move on if she decided to. Standing up and checking her reflection in the mirror behind the bar, she straightened her shirt, ran her hand through her shaggy hair, then headed toward the brunette before her mind could wander back to subjects she needed to avoid.

"Hi, I'm Nic."

The woman looked her up and down, the corner of her mouth twitching upward, but she couldn't discern if the move stemmed from amusement or approval. "Hello, Nic. I'm Tyra."

"Hi, Tyra, it's a pleasure to meet you."

"Is it?"

"Well, it's more pleasurable than sitting at the bar by myself all night."

"Really? Because sitting here with company isn't all it's cracked up to be, either." She nodded to her friends, who'd yet to acknowledge someone else had joined them.

"I noticed your rapt expression from across the room and thought that might be the case."

"So you decided to swoop in and save me?"

Nic winced. She might have played the role of hero once upon a time, but these days she was more suitably cast as the villain. Tonight she wasn't interested in playing either of those parts, and she wouldn't offer anything she couldn't honestly give. "If you're looking for a knight in shining armor, I'll take my leave now. The only thing I might be able to save you from is drinking alone tonight."

Tyra scanned her again, this time meeting her eyes instead of focusing only on her body. Nic waited nervously, a hint of anticipation stirring somewhere deep in the pit of her stomach. She relished the urge to hold her breath while she got sized up. She didn't feel any spark of heat or rush of excitement, but she did detect a possibility, a challenge, an opportunity to feel something other than dejection. For the first time in months, she actually cared what someone thought of her enough to stand a little straighter and turn on a bit of charm.

Tyra, for her part, didn't give in easily. She drew out the moment, allowing Nic to savor a sliver of the hunt she'd once enjoyed. She was far from her old form, but excitement built with each passing second. Finally Tyra nodded, her eyes softening in a way that broadcast her answer even before she said, "All right, Nic. If the first drink is on you. Then you've got yourself some company."

Relief flooded her, followed quickly by a wash of confidence. She'd done something right. She hadn't failed. She tried not to get ahead of herself as Tyra said good-bye to her friends and followed her to the bar. It wasn't as though Tyra had begged her to take her home, but for the first time in months, a woman had responded to her.

Nic took care of the first round, then the second as they talked about the unbearable Atlanta heat, the awful techno beat in the bar, and their utter boredom with their day jobs. Tyra was average height, average build, generally average looking, and she seemed to be of average intelligence. Nic couldn't find a single outstanding feature to bolster her attraction, but then again she didn't find any real turnoffs either. More importantly, Tyra seemed interested. Not too long ago, Nic had thrived on being adored by two amazing women. Now, plain old interest might suffice.

At no single moment did she think she'd like to sleep with Tyra, but she felt bolstered by the growing awareness that she could. She hadn't been swept up in emotions. If anything, she had to work to keep her mind away from the vague feeling that she was betraying the memories of two women who'd stirred something genuine in her. When those thoughts arose, she silenced them with a hard swallow of whiskey.

She had something to prove. She wasn't washed up, and she didn't have to be alone. Tyra wasn't beautiful, but she was real and here, and while she hadn't thrown herself at Nic yet, when the drinks and the conversation wound down, she agreed to let Nic drive her home.

❖

Tyra hooked a finger into one of Nic's belt loops and tugged her through the door. They'd kissed for several minutes on her front porch, and Nic hadn't hurried them along. She took intellectual satisfaction in the knowledge of where they were headed, but she felt no sense of urgency. She was content to enjoy the sense of triumph in making it this far until Tyra decided she was ready to go further.

"Where's the bedroom?" Nic whispered as she ran her mouth lightly down the curve of Tyra's neck.

"This way." Tyra grasped her shirt collar and walked backward down a hallway, then pushed open a door.

Nic didn't look any farther than the bed. She didn't want to see how the room was decorated or take notice of any photos on the bedside table. She didn't want to know Tyra in any sense but the Biblical, and if she were completely honest, she didn't even want that very badly. However, she wasn't being completely honest. She'd tell herself anything in order to get to the point where her body would shut out her mind completely.

Thankfully, Tyra sped up the process by pulling her own shirt over her head, then unclasping her bra. She let it dangle from her finger for a second, then dropped it to the floor. The room suddenly felt hotter, and Nic was all too willing to shed her own clothes in order to adjust. She kicked off her shoes first, then set to work unfastening her belt while Tyra stared at her, a flicker of hunger flashing through her dark eyes.

"Need some help?"

Nic grinned and pushed the pants to the ground. "No, but I need help with something else."

Tyra stepped closer and ran her hand teasingly along the waistband of Nic's boxers before slipping her hand inside.

Nic groaned and tried not to let her eyes roll back in her head at the feel of a woman's touch. Her breathing increased as Tyra cupped her and squeezed lightly. It wouldn't take much. It had been too long, but she wasn't so hard up that she'd turn pillow queen on some stranger. Sucking a sharp breath through her clenched teeth, she clutched Tyra's wrist and extracted her hand. "Easy, baby. That thing's loaded."

Oh, God, who talks like that? Just because she wasn't genuinely interested in Tyra didn't mean she had to treat their time together like a B-grade porno.

She tried again. "Tell me what you like." That approach lacked originality, but at least it wasn't so cheesy, and she did want to give Tyra what she liked. This whole evening hung on her ability to perform, to please, to live up to her standards, especially since she'd set the bar low. If she couldn't live up to the demands of a stranger for a few hours, what hope did she have of sustaining any sort of meaningful relationship again? God, why was she thinking about a relationship? She didn't need that kind of pressure or the reminder of how far she'd fallen. All she needed was to feel good for a few freaking hours. No wonder she couldn't think of anything original to say. Thankfully, Tyra wasn't grading her on creativity as she lay down on the bed and beckoned for her to join.

Nic stripped off her shirt and undershirt, then climbed onto the bed, propping herself over Tyra and lowering her head for a kiss. The position was wonderfully familiar. Memories tried to come rushing back. Images of Annabelle looking up at her lovingly, trustingly, pushed at the back of her eyelids, but she blocked them out, slipping deeper into the physical. The sound of her own pulse mingled with the rasp of the breaths they stole between kisses. Tyra cupped her ass and pulled their bodies firmly together. A flashback of Davis's form crushing passionately against her own threatened to overtake her, but she held her eyes open, forcing herself to stay present in this moment.

"Fuck me," Tyra moaned.

Nic didn't usually go for profanity during sex, but here it seemed a raw and brutally accurate description of her intent. She slid inside of Tyra quickly and with enough force to make her intentions clear. Tyra's fingernails raked across the skin of her back, clawing for more.

"Oh, God, yes, like that."

She felt a power surge that dizzied her mind and sent a shot of excitement right to her clit. This woman wanted her, and she was living up to her requests. Hell, from the way Tyra panted after a few quick thrusts, Nic exceeded her expectations.

She thumbed Tyra's clit each time she pushed inside, and her confidence grew as Tyra's control disintegrated. The sounds of sex filled her ears, overwhelming her senses until her mind went mercifully blank. There was no emotion, no fear, no doubt, nothing but the physical. Overcome by lust and greed, she reached for more, slipping her free hand between her own legs. The crash was inevitable, and they both rode every ounce of pleasure, refusing to separate until the last wave of aftershocks subsided.

Nic rolled over and stared at the ceiling without trying to temper her satisfied smile. She'd done something right. She'd given a woman everything she wanted, she'd done it well, and she'd claimed her own reward in the process. She now had one person in her life she hadn't let down. A little part of her whispered that the person in question had only known her for two hours, but that's all she planned to know her for. They'd go their separate ways, both sated, and the only memories they'd have of each other would be good ones.

"Damn," Tyra said, rolling onto her side to face Nic.

"Yeah."

"I gotta ask one thing, though." She ran a fingernail down Nic's chest. "How's a woman like you still single?"

Her stomach tightened like someone had punched it, and she had to forcibly tamp down her sudden urge to run. The memories she'd held at bay washed over her now, clouding her visions and suffocating her airways.

"You're good-looking, easy to talk to, and fantastic in bed. Why hasn't some woman snatched you up?"

What could she say? Not the truth. Not that she was incapable of being faithful and she'd disappointed everyone who'd ever showed any faith in her. Not that her successes only existed on the surface. She couldn't even speak at all, much less explain something like that.

Her thoughts spun back into the endless downward spiral she'd tried to escape tonight, only this time the darkness felt starker in contrast to the high she'd experienced minutes earlier. Like a junkie jonesing for another fix, her body and her brain screamed out in withdrawal.

"Hey," Tyra said. When Nic didn't respond, she shook her shoulder. "Nic, it's okay. You don't have to tell me."

"What?" Nic fought to focus through the haze.

"I didn't mean to pry."

"No, I'm sorry. I'm just not good." Her voice sounded hollow in her own ears. She was probably scaring the crap out of Tyra. *So much for not being a disappointment.*

"Not true. I can say with absolute certainty that you're very good."

"Thanks." Nic sat up and pushed her hands through her hair. Tyra was offering her an out. She had to pull herself together long enough to take it. Maybe she could still extract herself from the situation before she had a meltdown.

"No, I mean it. You were *very* good at making me be very bad." Tyra kissed her shoulder, then lingered long enough to leave a little mark. Nic relished the sting of her impending hickey. She'd preferred physical pain over her emotional torment. The thought probably would've scared her if Tyra's mouth wasn't so damn hot.

She took a deep breath and let her head roll back as she exhaled. Tyra dragged her lips up her neck until she nipped at her earlobe. The press of a woman's mouth against her skin stabilized the tremors in her clenched fists, and the darkness faded, burned away by the heat spreading through her. It felt intoxicating to be desired again.

Her breath grew shallow and quick. Tyra still wanted her. She hadn't given her an answer to her question, honest or otherwise, and she apparently didn't care.

An arm snaked around the front of her as long slender fingers worked their way south along the plane of her stomach. Tyra wanted something Nic could and would gladly give her. She could make the pain go away again, or at least override it. Of course the fix was temporary, like the liquor she'd consumed earlier, but unlike the drink, sex didn't numb her senses. It set them on fire.

Acting on almost animal instinct, Nic turned on Tyra, not even seeing her now, but taking her nonetheless. She was a body, a vessel, a drug, or, more accurately, the syringe that delivered the drug she sought. She consumed what she craved again and again, until, as the sun rose, she quietly slipped away.

By the time she pulled out of the driveway, she'd already begun to count the hours until she could chase that high again.

Davis hadn't grown accustomed to Annabelle's beauty and was struck by it once again when she opened the door to her apartment. After a month in the city she'd begun to trade some of her skirts for more casual attire, but even in the olive-green capri pants and light-blue baby-doll T-shirt, she still managed to look glamorous enough to make Davis momentarily speechless.

"Hi, Davis," Anna said, as though she was used to being stared at.

"I don't want to barge in, but I got the pictures back from the printer and thought you'd like to see them."

"Of course I do. Come in." They'd hung out several times in the last two weeks but never without planning ahead, and always at Davis's apartment or on neutral territory. She hadn't wanted to crowd Anna's personal space, but the last time they'd talked, she said she should stop by her place sometime. When Davis saw how perfectly the pictures had turned out, the moment seemed right. Now she wasn't so sure. It somehow felt so personal, almost intimate to witness Anna in full domestic glory.

"Are you okay?"

"Yes. I'm just really impressed with your apartment."

"Really?"

"Yeah, you moved just a few weeks ago, and already it's looking like a home."

Anna blushed at the compliment. "That's sweet. I've still got a lot of finishing touches to add."

"It's already beautiful."

Anna looked at her questioningly. "You're not just saying that to make me feel better, are you?"

"Of course not. Why? You don't like it?"

"No, I do, but when Nic stopped by, she implied I could do better."

Red flashed hot and disorienting behind her eyes at the thought of Nic in Anna's apartment. "Nic was here? When? Why?" Anna took a step back, making Davis realize how accusatory she'd sounded. "I'm sorry. I'm surprised you still hang out with her."

"I don't hang out with her. She had to drop off the final paperwork for the sale of our house in Athens."

"Hasn't she heard of the postal service?" She didn't mean to sound so bitchy, but how could Anna stand to be in the same room with Nic, much less have her in her home? She thought they were on the same page about Nic, but maybe not, and the questions rising in her now threatened to plunge her back into the awful thoughts of them together.

"We both wanted the sale finalized."

"Are you sure she didn't want to weasel her way into your life here?"

Annabelle gave the comment some thought. "She did offer to pay for a new place."

Davis almost choked. How could Anna say something like that so casually? "She offered to buy you a house?"

"Not with the condition of me coming back," Anna quickly said. "She said I deserved alimony after all our years together."

Right, they'd been married. They'd shared a home and bank accounts. Women in that situation deserved to be cared for, and mistresses didn't. "You do deserve it. I just couldn't stand to ever see her again after the way things ended. I got the feeling you felt the same way."

"I do. It killed me to see her and feel that hurt all over again. It took everything I had to stay calm when I wanted to cry or scream about how far we'd fallen. I'd love to pretend she never existed, but I don't have that luxury. Thirteen years of life together doesn't just go away," Annabelle explained. "It's been months of lawyers and realtors and so much paperwork, so you'll have to forgive me for wanting it over badly enough to let her within a three-hundred-foot radius of me."

Davis hung her head. She hadn't meant to judge. It wasn't Anna's fault Nic had left her with a house and financial ties she couldn't simply escape. She had no idea what she'd do in her situation. She might've killed someone if she had to live with constant physical reminders of Nic to accompany her emotional ones. Perhaps that's another reason Anna had been the wife and she'd been the dirty little secret. Maybe that's all she was capable of. "Well, for what it's worth, your apartment is nicer than mine, but your standards are probably higher than mine."

"I wouldn't go that far." Anger seemed to fade to sadness. "The apartment isn't what I'm used to, but not because of my standards as much as Nic's. She picked out our old house. I never really cared for all those extra rooms."

"She picked your house, your job, the kinds of food you ate. Did you get to pick your own clothes?"

Annabelle's face flushed again. "You make her sound abusive. Nic never told me no. She never demanded anything from me. If anything, she gave me too much, more than I wanted."

"But she didn't let you make your own decisions."

"It wasn't a matter of letting me or giving permission. Her opinions were always so much stronger than mine, like she saw some bigger picture for us. I had everything a woman could ask for, or at least I thought I did. Why argue over things like sushi or an additional bedroom? Over time, her opinions became my opinions." She sighed heavily. "Maybe that's the root of the problem. If I'd challenged her more or had even challenged myself to be something more than her shadow, I wouldn't be in this mess."

Davis felt guilty for questioning Annabelle's resolve and making her question herself in the process. Clearly this amazing woman was struggling to find herself. Who was Davis to criticize how she did so? "I can't imagine having to relearn who you are after so much time. Do you feel any connection to who you were before Nic? Surely you had your own interests when you dated other people or lived on your own."

"I've never had any other partners or lived on my own. I lived with my parents, then in a sorority house at college until I moved in with Nic. Before her I only dated men, or boys really, and never seriously."

Davis didn't know what to say. She knew Belle had never slept with anyone else, but how could a grown woman have lived under someone else's care for every minute of her life? How did someone begin to learn such basic things about herself in her mid-thirties, especially after giving herself over to such a commanding personality for so long? Hell, how did she even know for sure she was gay? What if Nic's magnetism had simply convinced her of that, too?

Davis felt for her. She really did, but she couldn't relate to Anna's conflict. She'd lived alone for so long she couldn't imagine any other way, and she wondered if Anna could understand her life. Then again, why would Anna even want to learn Davis's way of life? She didn't have to. She had other options. People would want to take care of her the way Nic had. Sure, people like that didn't offer freedom, but Anna hadn't minded before. Why start now? She could go back to her parents. Cass had said they had money. Or she could become someone else's trophy wife. Hell, she could go back to Nic.

Her stomach twisted at the thought, but they'd been happy together once upon a time and clearly still had ties. If she was willing to talk to Nic now, maybe in a few months she'd consider forgiving her. Nic could return her to the life she felt comfortable with. She wouldn't have to struggle to get by or learn a new way of living or worry about her biological clock. Anna had happily put her own emotions aside before. Why not do so again?

"Davis, please say something."

"What?"

"Is it so awful to have been with only one person?"

She flashed back to Annabelle's anguish about her inadequacies on their first day together. "No. God, no. I was just thinking how different our lives have been."

"You probably don't have a very high opinion of the choices I made." Tears filled Anna's eyes. "I understand how people see me."

Davis looked at her again, seeing the insecurities and the fear, but also her potential, her beauty, her talent, her grace. No, Anna had no idea how she really saw her. Anna was so far above the life Davis had led, the life she chose for herself now. She could do better, and some day she would, but until then Davis refused to be one more judgmental voice telling her how to live.

"I see you as a very brave, strong, sweet woman who has so many amazing adventures in front of her."

Anna's smile shone so gloriously brilliant that Davis's stomach flip-flopped. "I thought I'd make fried chicken for dinner. Do you want to join me?"

Davis grinned in spite of her misgivings about the differences between them. So what if Anna's destiny led toward better things? She was here now, and for some reason that made Davis feel a little happier than she had in months.

CHAPTER SIXTEEN

November

Nic popped four Advil and washed them down with a big swig of her espresso-fortified coffee. She had to look alert for this meeting, even if she didn't feel focused after another in a long line of all-nighters. She probably shouldn't have gone out the night before an early meeting with her boss, but she didn't get any sleep when she stayed home either. Insomnia had taken over her solitary nights, keeping her awake with vague fears and haunting whispers of her shortcomings. Lonely nights were dangerous nights, so she spent fewer and fewer of them in her apartment, instead opting for a quick stay in somebody else's bed. Lately she'd found quite a lot of willing somebodies.

"Nic." Joe Clarke startled her out of her stupor, and she jumped out of her seat. He looked her up and down, then shook his head as he turned to go. "Walk with me."

"Yes, sir." She followed him down the hallway and to a conference room.

"Were you aware we had a meeting this morning?"

"Yes, sir."

"Were you aware that meeting was supposed to start five minutes ago?"

She glanced at her watch. *Shit.* "I'm sorry, sir. I was answering some e-mail, and I must have lost track of time."

"You lose track of a lot of things lately."

She didn't deny the accusation. "It's been a rough few months, but I think I've turned it back around."

"I don't think you have, and I'm beginning to think you might not ever get it back together."

"I beg to differ." She straightened her shoulders and turned to face him, but she was only going through the motions. She used to be able to summon all her fortitude for even the slightest challenge. Now facing the prospect of being fired by her mentor, she barely mustered fear, much less defiance. He no longer held the key to anything she craved.

"I've always liked you, Nic." She fought the urge to roll her eyes. He had a funny way of showing it. "You're a hell of a salesperson, and you're better in a boardroom than any of the boys I handpicked. Businesswise, I thought you had what it took to go all the way, and I stand by that assessment, but I'm no longer sure about your personal mettle."

Personal mettle? What the hell did that mean? Thankfully he was on a roll now, and maybe if she just kept her mouth shut, she could get out of this unscathed.

"I think losing that gal of yours hit you harder than either of us realized."

A flash of pain at the mention of Belle finally sparked a genuine emotion in her. She found it strange the only thing she felt any urge to fight for was something she'd already lost. "My personal life is—"

"Your personal life affects my bottom line." He cut her off, his tone hardening enough to make it clear this wasn't a debate. "I'd hoped to promote you next month. I never thought I'd be faced with the prospect of firing you."

"You're firing me?" She tried to drum up some indignation but wasn't sure she could. She felt only a mild panic about how she'd continue to pay for her nightly trips to the bar.

"No, I know you probably don't believe me, but I meant what I said. I still think you've got what it takes, but you need to get your ducks in a row, which is why you're going to take some time to yourself."

"Time to myself?" That's not what she wanted at all. Time to herself meant time to think, to feel, to suffocate in her own failures. "I want to keep working."

"You haven't been working for months." He shook his head. "Now you're on a thirty-day leave. You've got one month to pull yourself together. Go to therapy, go home, go to the beach, I don't care, but deal with whatever you need to deal with. You'll be paid and you'll keep your insurance, but you won't have access to any of your work accounts or company e-mail until the leave is up."

"Then what?"

"Then you come back motivated, clear-eyed, and sober." He put an emphasis on the last word, and she lowered her head like a child who'd been caught in her daddy's liquor cabinet. "When you've done that, I want you to bring me a plan, in writing, about how you're going to get your business accounts back on track."

She rubbed her face with both hands. She should be grateful. He'd fired others for a lot less. A paid leave was damn near unprecedented, and she didn't deserve it. Perhaps he worried about the human-resources backlash for firing the only woman at her level, or maybe he was concerned about her. Either way, she couldn't bring herself to give a damn, much less feel any gratitude. Honestly, the only thing she managed to feel concerned about was her lack of concern. Why didn't anything bother her anymore? Had losing Belle, the only thing she'd every managed to care for more than herself, somehow voided her ability to find meaning in anything else?

"We all face challenges, Nic." Joe's voice shifted into what must have been his best attempt at pep-talk mode. "There's no shame in getting knocked down. The shame comes in not doing what you have to do to get back up."

"Yes, sir." She didn't want to hear anything else from him. He didn't know anything about her shame. She reverted to her childhood skills in going along to get along. Arguing would only prolong this meeting.

"I know you have it in you to rise to this challenge."

"Thank you, sir," she said, only because it seemed socially appropriate. She didn't care about his faith in her, and she sure didn't feel challenged. She worked hard almost every night to manufacture a sense of urgency with the women she went to bed with. They held the key to her release, to her escape. Joe Clarke held none of those things. No one had legitimately challenged her or stirred any passion in her to succeed since Davis. She'd lost her foundation and her impetus for growth months ago, and this old man wouldn't return either of them. He could offer more meaningless drivel, more stress, more judgment, and for what?

A chance to sell commercials?

She didn't even like commercials.

All they were good for was interrupting her baseball games. She used to take pride when a spot she'd sold came on TV. Now they annoyed her. Sure, she experienced a momentary feeling of satisfaction when she inked a deal, but that kind of winning took a lot of work for a little reward. At least with sex the work was pleasurable and the reward personal, if short-lived.

"I'll see you in thirty days, Nic. Good luck to you."

Oh, was he still there? She'd already moved on mentally. Several months ago, in fact. She had nothing left to say, so she simply nodded.

Eventually she'd have to find a way to either keep her job or get a new one, but right now she could think only about how little she wanted to do either of those things. She had thirty days to figure out her next step, but the only unknown she could manage to worry about even a little was getting laid again.

"Hey, you." Davis answered her phone immediately after the caller ID showed Cass's number.

"Hey, you? Seriously, I haven't heard from you in weeks, and I get a 'Hey, you'?"

"Um, sorry?"

"How about, 'Cass, darling, I'm so sorry I've been away from you. I'd offer an excuse, but I don't have one. I'm a terrible friend who makes you spend all your nights alone.'"

"Alone? Really? Have you spent all your nights alone?"

"Well, not completely alone, but you know it's not the same without you."

She smiled. Cass must really miss her. Maybe she was a terrible friend. Ever since she and Anna had begun spending more time together, she hadn't seen much of Cass. "You're right. We need to get together."

"That was too easy. What's the catch? Do you need help cleaning or moving something heavy?"

Davis laughed. She'd been doing a little more of that lately, too. "No, you're right. I miss you, and for what it's worth I haven't been in my cave as much lately. I'm actually outside right now. You should try it sometime." She sat down on a bench to soak up the autumn sun and cool breeze while they talked.

"Let's not get crazy. I never said anything about the out-of-doors. I was thinking dinner and drinks, or maybe drinks and dinner. You choose."

"Wow." Davis laughed. "So many options. Are you sure you really want to leave a decision of that magnitude up to me?"

"Seriously? First you agree to go out with me, and now you sass me? Where are you? I'll pick you up right now."

"I can't right now. I'm on the way to the school for a meeting."

"The school?" Cass's tone turned suspicious. "Would this happen to be the school where your ex-paramour's ex-wife works?"

She winced. "Why do you keep doing that? Call her Annabelle, or Anna. She's got an identity outside of what Nic did to her, and frankly, so do I."

"Do you?"

"What's that supposed to mean?" Damn, her good mood slipped away.

"You seem to spend a lot of time wallowing in your incestuous little pity party with her. When are you going to break the cycle and let some fresh air in?"

"Incestuous?" The word hurt to repeat. "That's unreasonably harsh, even for you."

"Is it? If you were Kevin Bacon, this would be the easiest game ever. You both slept with, and were devastated by, the same woman. Now you spend all your free time sitting around morbidly gabbing about how it hurts."

Davis sighed. Maybe it'd felt that way at first, but somewhere along the way they'd transitioned from trying to undo Nic's damage to building something better, some kind of friendship of their own. Of course sometimes when she looked at Anna she remembered Nic, but those times were fewer and further between. "I know, on the surface, it probably doesn't seem like the healthiest friendship, and I'd be lying if I said Nic never came up. We don't dance around the subject, but we don't dwell on it either."

"Sure, you don't always talk about Nic. Maybe sometimes you talk about how lonely you are, or how you don't trust anyone, or perhaps you reminisce about your pinkie swear pledge never to date again."

"Well, yes, of course we had to pinkie swear and spit on each other's shoes before she'd let me braid her hair. What the hell, Cass?"

"How am I supposed to know? You're with her all the time, and I can't see a single thing you have in common with a suburban, Southern-belle housewife, except you both got screwed by the same jerk."

"We aren't together all the time. We see each other once or twice a week." Come to think of it, she wasn't completely sure how that'd happened either. At first, it had been about work, then food, and proving to both of them that there was more to life than Nic, but some time during the last two months, they'd stopped making excuses to see each other. More often than not Davis would pick up the phone or drop by Anna's house simply because she wanted to. It really wasn't different than the evolution of any other friendship, except for the events that had initiated it.

"Second, she's not a housewife anymore." Davis continued to defend both Anna and the connection they shared. "She's a single woman trying to learn how to thrive on her own, and she's doing a damn good job, which is what we have in common."

"Great, you're both Mary Tyler Moore. Do you meet on the street corner and toss your hats up in the air?"

"Sometimes." She chuckled at that image. "Mostly we order ethnic food and go for walks around different parts of the city. We've been to some outdoor concerts and the farmers' market. I helped her pick out a bike, she taught me how to fry chicken, and don't act like you've never been invited along."

"I know you've tried to drag me on all your little hipster adventures—wait a second, did you say you can fry chicken?"

Davis laughed outright. She should've known the way to get to Cass was through her stomach. "Well, in theory I know how, but it's a lot of work and even more time. I don't know how Anna does all her cooking. She leaves for work before seven in the morning, comes home at five, and still makes a full dinner every night. Never anything from a box or a tray."

"Uh-huh. What else does she do?"

"She reads, like, everything, and plays tennis. She's got a competitive streak that's really kind of shocking. I think that's why she's doing so well. She refuses to surrender. I see how scared she gets, and it's not like she doesn't have resources to fall back on, but she's determined to take care of herself."

"Sounds like someone else I know," Cass said softly.

Davis warmed to the compliment. "Yeah, sometimes. But she's not really like me in any other ways. She sees good in people, despite Nic's betrayal. She carries extra change to give to homeless people at the bus station. And she sees every new experience with such excitement. No matter how sarcastic I get, she never snaps back. She's got a quiet way of disarming any situation."

"So now you're in love with her?"

"What?" The words hit her like an unexpected slap, catching her so off guard that she dropped her phone. It clattered to the sidewalk, bouncing once with a sickening scrape of plastic against concrete. "Shit, shit, shit."

"Hello? What happened? Did you faint?" Cass's voice called out as Davis wiped the screen, trying to determine if it was scratched or simply dirty.

"No, I didn't faint. The phone just slipped."

"Convenient."

"No, inconvenient. I think I dented the touch screen."

"Which allowed you to dodge my question." Cass wouldn't let go.

"There's nothing to dodge. I am not in love with Anna." The very idea was absurd, so absurd it sent her heartbeat skipping around her chest.

"Good, 'cause you *know* that's unhealthy, right?"

"Yes." She answered with a certainty she didn't feel. Of course if a friend or acquaintance had asked if she should fall in love with her ex-girlfriend's ex-wife, she would've said no. Their combined baggage would likely be enough to suffocate any new relationship. Still, two months ago she would've said the same thing about forging a friendship under the same circumstances, and yet they'd done so successfully.

"Do you think maybe it's time to go out with someone else?" Cass asked.

"Sure." Davis agreed, ready to change the subject. "I'd love to go to dinner with you. How about tomorrow?"

"Tomorrow's fine, but I meant actually go out with someone else, as in a date."

"Come on, Cass, why does it always have to come back to that?" Wasn't it enough to be happy with single life? Okay, maybe she wasn't deliriously happy, but she wasn't unhappy.

"You said yourself, you're a young single woman, trying to thrive in Hotlanta, and if you're not in love with Annabelle…"

"The logical end to the sentence isn't 'so you should screw anything that moves.'"

"I said nothing about screwing. I said date, though, really, without the screwing, what's the point?"

Davis sighed. "I'm not interested in either, and that has nothing to do with falling for Anna. For me to date or even sleep with someone casually, I'd have to trust her and my own judgment. I'm not there yet, and for what it's worth, neither is Anna. It's been less than six months. We've both got a lot of growing to do, but for the first time I feel like I might be able to do it."

"I know you can do it."

"Thanks, Cass. You've had faith in me all along." She hoped her voice conveyed the sincerity of her gratitude. "But it's only been in the past few weeks that I've let go of some anger and started to enjoy my life a little."

"Because of her?"

"She's been a huge part of it, but that doesn't mean I'm in love with her. If anything, it's the biggest reason why I can't fall in love with her. I need this friendship, and so does she. I won't do anything to mess things up."

"Fine." Cass sighed dramatically. "I have to admit you're making progress, even if it's not as quick or as slutty as I'd like."

"I love you, too."

"Yeah, yeah." Cass brushed off the sentimentality. "Dinner at Six Feet Under tomorrow?"

"See you then."

She hung up her now-dented cell phone. She did love Cass and needed to show that more, but she wouldn't doubt the newfound friendship she shared with Anna. Their connection might be unconventional, but it was genuine and meaningful, and most importantly, it helped her put her life back together. She couldn't let go of something valuable just because someone else didn't understand how it worked. Equally important, though, she couldn't let anyone, herself included, confuse friendship with something more complicated and a lot scarier.

Annabelle hugged her last student good-bye for the day, then stood in the doorway of her classroom to make sure he actually met his mom in the lobby. She was tired. How could she not be after six hours with sixteen six-year-olds, but a part of her still hated to see them go. For every ounce of energy their supervision took out of her, they gave it right back with their enthusiasm and joy.

"Hey, Annabelle," a voice called from the principal's office. "You coming to the meeting with Davis?"

"Sure, I'll be right there."

Ever since she'd helped pick the brochure photos, Ailene had included her in meetings and decisions regarding promotions for the school. Actually, she included her in a lot of things, from early morning coffee chats to strategic-planning sessions with other teachers. She'd even invited Annabelle to have dinner with her husband and children at their home on occasion. Ailene had helped make the transition back to teaching smoother than she'd anticipated, and she loved their free-and-easy exchange of ideas. It had been a long time since her opinions had mattered this much.

Nic might have listened to her or made her feel valued, but she'd put her on a pedestal to be cherished. Here her thoughts and ideas got put into action, and she saw the results every single day.

She missed the overall satisfaction of keeping a home and caring for a partner, but she didn't miss the day-to-day life of a housewife. She didn't miss her tedious committee meetings or empty social obligations. She certainly didn't miss their big cookie-cutter house or country club. She actually preferred sandwiches in the teachers' lounge to the five-star restaurants she used to frequent, and the company at work was better as well. Annabelle admired her colleagues' dedication and passion. She especially looked up to Ailene, who had shown her that she could have a family, and a home, *and* a meaningful job.

She'd given up so many of her own dreams to chase Nic's ideal life. Maybe that wasn't fair. She'd thought they were also working toward her dream of a family, but why had she felt she'd had to choose one over the other? Every now and then she caught herself thinking about how she'd do things differently the next time around, but she always suffered a wave of sadness at the realization that there might never be a next time for her, at least not in the way she'd hoped.

When she started to dwell on what she might never have, she forced herself back into the here and now. She had a good job, colleagues who valued her input, and a meeting with a friend. She hurried to the main office, leaving thoughts of "what might have been" behind.

"Hey, there." Ailene greeted her warmly. "You survived another week. Only one more to go until Thanksgiving break."

She forced a smile. All the other teachers were counting down to the holiday, but she didn't look forward to the time off. She did best when she could focus on work. The weekends with their freedom and time to kill were harder to compartmentalize. A five-day weekend would be challenging enough without adding the emotional baggage of her first holiday in thirteen years without Nic by her side.

"We're going to the in-laws," Ailene said. "Or I'd schedule a teacher in-service workshop day, because Lord knows I am not going to try to cook a full-scale meal like that."

"I know you'd do fine if you had to," Annabelle answered halfheartedly.

"You know no such thing. You strike me as the kind of person who knows how to bake a turkey, though."

"I can, yes, but I don't have to. My mama cooks the turkey in our family. I'm in charge of side dishes while my younger sister is relegated to setting the table."

"Really? Will you spend the whole week with them?"

"I don't know."

Ailene arched an eyebrow, which was about as close as she ever came to prying into Annabelle's personal life. For as close as they had become professionally, she still knew nothing about what had happened with Nic, or that she even existed, and Annabelle loved that. Ailene never asked about her past or even her present love life, thus providing her with the only relationship that wasn't tainted by Nic's memory. Annabelle cherished having a portion of her life where Nic and her betrayal were irrelevant. At school she was insulated from the memories that haunted her when she was alone. She could almost make believe that had all happened in a different life, if not for little things like not sharing everyone's excitement about the holiday break.

A knock on the open door interrupted her thoughts just before Davis stepped into view. She wore low-slung jeans and a square-cut denim jacket over a black T-shirt with the only shock of color coming from the copper of her hair. The look was chic and sexy to the point it might've been intimidating if not for the sweet smile she gave her. "Hey, Anna."

Her mood lightened immediately at the sound of Davis saying her name. Her new name. Davis was really the only one who called her Anna, though some of the other teachers were starting to pick up on it. The name served as a strong reminder she wasn't the woman she used to be, the woman who'd put everyone else before herself, the woman who'd let herself be lied to and cheated on. Anna had a job and outside interests. She ate Thai food and took the bus to Whole Foods. She rode a bike to art fairs and sat in on meetings with graphic designers. And she had Davis to thank for much of her transition.

She watched Davis present her new designs to Ailene. She was so cool and confident, with such a beautiful eye for detail. She had beautiful eyes, period, but Anna enjoyed it most when Davis looked at a piece of art or one of her own layouts. There was an intensity there, a determination, and a passion that made her whole body come alive.

"Do you agree?" Ailene asked, glancing up from the T-shirts Davis spread out on the table between them.

"I'm sorry, what?" She blushed at the realization she'd been so distracted by Davis she'd missed their conversation.

Davis's forehead creased in concern, but she said nothing. These momentary lapses were something they'd dealt with a lot early on, and they always called each other on them, consistent with their promise to always be honest and up-front, but that was harder to do with other people around. Davis probably thought she'd sparked a memory or unpleasant thought, when in reality the opposite was true.

"Ailene liked them both and thought we might do some in the lighter color with the darker logo for summer, and the darker color with light lettering for winter sessions."

"Then I do agree." Anna smiled and let her hand rest lightly on Davis's to indicate she wasn't upset. On the contrary, she was happy to see her. She wasn't sure when that'd happened either. When had Davis's presence gone from being a cause for heartache to being a catalyst for joy? "I like the way you didn't just enlarge the logo from the children's shirts as they get bigger, but also adjusted the details, so it grows along with the kids."

"Yes, it's beautiful and a much higher quality than anything we've ever used," Ailene interjected, "but for no extra charge, which tells me Davis also gave us a handy little discount on her own fee to keep us within our budget."

"Lies, all lies." Davis laughed, but her cheeks colored with a hint of pink, suggesting she'd been caught.

"It'll be our secret, but don't think it's unappreciated." Ailene signed an order form and handed it back to Davis. "I promise not to drag you back here until after the holidays."

"It's no problem. I'm glad to do it."

"I'm sure you and Ms. Taylor have better things to do with your Friday evening."

Annabelle felt a jolt. Why had she assumed they had plans? Did she mean together?

Davis looked sheepish, probably wondering the same thing. "Do we?"

"Not that I know of."

"Then go find something to do. I'm the principal, and I don't want to hear about either of you working late tonight."

"Yes, ma'am. Wow," Davis said, and held the door open for Anna. "Do they teach you that tone of voice in teacher school? The one that sends chills up the spine of children everywhere?"

Annabelle smiled. "Maybe."

She headed toward her classroom, and Davis followed, waiting patiently while she gathered her things. Annabelle wondered again how they'd developed a level of comfort that allowed them to move so casually in each other's spaces. Less than six months ago Davis's mere existence had shattered everything she had loved about her life. Two months ago her presence in this room had shaken her stability and her sense of accomplishment. Now, as Davis peeked into the fish tanks or flipped through a children's book in the corner, Annabelle couldn't summon the sheer panic that used to consume her. Of course, the thought of how they'd met could still summon a dull ache in her chest, and the thought of her touching Nic made her stomach roil, but those thoughts were no longer the first ones that sprang to mind. Now, she was mostly consumed with amusement as Davis compared the size of her own hand to the little handprint turkey paintings lining one wall of the classroom.

Davis turned and caught her watching. "Oh, ready to go?"

"I guess so. If I've forgotten anything, I can come back tomorrow."

"You've got orders to have fun this weekend, or else you'll get called to the principal's office on Monday."

"She said no work tonight, not all weekend."

"Come on." Davis prodded her. "If you can't survive one weekend of free time, how will you handle a whole week off?"

She sighed, maybe heavier than she'd meant to. Perhaps her facial expression gave too much away too, but whatever the cue, Davis picked up on it quickly.

"Damn, I'm sorry. I didn't mean for it to come out like that."

"No, you're right." She closed and locked her classroom door behind her.

"I know the holiday will be hard for you," Davis said as she stepped into the beautiful Georgia autumn.

"And you?"

"I don't know. I don't have holiday memories with her. I guess part of me will want to mourn what might've been, but it was a stupid fantasy. She was never going to spend those days with me. I just didn't know enough not to hope for it." The shell was back up over Davis's emotions, her voice cold and hollow, and her eyes more cloudy than clear. Anna understood now that she often tried to pretend her pain wasn't as bad as hers, like somehow comparing it to the betrayal Annabelle had suffered would lessen the impact of what she'd been through.

"It's okay, you know?" She brushed her hand against Davis's. "You're allowed to be upset. She stole different things from us, but she hurt you as much as she hurt me."

"She shouldn't have. I should've never let her. I shouldn't have gotten in so deep without knowing her. I should've realized things didn't add up."

"And what about me? I shared every part of her life for over a decade, and I couldn't see it."

"I didn't mean to compare our situations," Davis said.

"Good, because neither of us is entitled to less grief than the other."

"A lovely sentiment to start off the holiday"

She smiled in spite of herself. "Happy Thanksgiving. Would you like grief with your mashed potatoes?"

Davis laughed. "Okay, now *that* I would love to see in one of your cookbooks."

"You never know. I am in charge of making the gravy. I may have to try a new recipe."

"So you'll go to your parents'?"

"I think I have to. They'll worry if I don't, and I can't put it off forever. If I don't do it now, it'll be Christmas or my birthday or Easter, and I don't want to miss special occasions with my niece and nephew. They're growing up too fast, and I don't see them as much as I'd like."

"But?"

"I'm not sure I'll stay all weekend. I don't even want to stay the night."

"Is that different from the past?"

"Yes. Even though we lived only an hour away, we used to get there the night before and stay until Saturday. We were one big, happy family."

"To each her own." Davis shuddered. "You can still have that, you know?"

"I could try, but at the end of the day I'll go to bed alone. Here, I have a nice routine of my work, the house chores, hanging out with you. I go whole days without thinking of Nic, but there will be so many memories back home."

Davis nodded but didn't cut in. For as much as she could be a smart aleck to distract from her pain or produce a witty retort for just about any awkward situation, she also seemed to understand when to let Annabelle feel the emotions underneath it all.

"It will be such a contrast to all those happy times with her. I always worked hard to make holidays special for us. Now I dread special occasions, and not just because I'll miss her, but because I feel like even the memories are tainted. When I look at her empty place at the table, I won't just wish for the old times back. I'll wonder if they were ever real to begin with."

"That's the shittiest part of the whole thing, isn't it?" Davis said emphatically. "Wondering if the greatest moments of your life ever really happened or if you just imagined those feelings so much you projected them onto her."

Annabelle frowned at how accurately Davis had summed up her feelings. "I don't want to spend my holiday with doubts swirling around my head. If that's what I have to look forward to on special occasions, I wish I could just ignore them completely."

"That's what I do."

"What?"

"I put up with my family on Christmas," Davis admitted with a grimace, "but for every other holiday I sleep in, then Cass comes over and we order takeout and watch movies all afternoon. No drama, no large groups, no slaving over hot food or making small talk."

"A year ago I would've considered you almost sacrilegious, but this year it sounds pretty nice."

"You're welcome to join us."

Her father would have a fit, and her mother would worry herself sick if she didn't come home. Plus her absence would put an undue burden on Liz. She had to go home. Part of her even wanted to, but a bigger part of her wished she could spend the day in her pajamas on Davis's couch. What did that say about the person she'd become? She loved her family, she loved holidays, she loved a busy kitchen and a full house. Why would she consider giving that up to spend time with Davis?

She didn't have the answer by the time they arrived at her driveway. She wasn't even sure she'd asked herself the right questions, but that didn't stop her from inviting Davis to stay for dinner or from being pleased when she accepted.

❖

Every time Davis visited Anna's apartment, the place felt less like a studio rental and more like a home, from the hand-sewn curtains to stacks of books by the worn reading chair to the framed pictures of family members scattered throughout the space. She'd lived in her own apartment for ten years and it still didn't feel this homey. It also didn't hurt that Anna kept her space tidy. She'd yet to see the bed unmade, even when she stopped by on a whim, and really, who made their bed when they weren't expecting company? She would've thought a house that always looked so perfect would feel intimidating, as if she should fear touching anything lest she leave it out of place, but here she'd always felt comfortable.

Something about Anna's perfection didn't make her feel bad about her own shortcomings. She was gracious and genuine, the perfect hostess. If someone had described Anna like that before she knew her, Davis would've made plenty of snarky comments, but getting to know her had neutralized even her most suspicious impulses. All the *Southern Living* Barbie comparisons were gone. Anna might seem too good to be real, but she was the most real thing Davis had had in her life in a long time.

Anna poured them each a glass of sweet tea and slid one across the small table before Davis had a chance to sit down. They chatted easily with the heavy subject of the holidays behind them. They'd become pros at letting the emotion flow, then letting it go. She never got stuck in a funk with Anna around. She loved to hear stories from her classroom. In just a few short weeks of listening to Anna talk about her students, she'd learned that kids really did say the darndest things. She'd even caught herself wishing she had more children in her life because they seemed to work wonders on Anna's temperament and self-esteem. She was no longer the shell of a woman she'd met in front of the bookstore six months ago. She wasn't even lost in the ways she'd been when she'd arrived in the city. Davis wished she could take some credit for that, but she suspected Anna was simply and beautifully resilient, which unfortunately made her wonder when she'd move on. While Davis was content with single life, Anna was the marrying kind, a fact someone was bound to notice soon.

She watched Anna move around the small kitchen with confidence. This was clearly her domain. Her hands moved quickly and gracefully as she zested a lemon, and her long, slender fingers never faltered as she easily fileted two sides of salmon. She seemed so focused on the task at hand, her blue eyes never once wandering to the cookbook she'd left open on the counter. She also held up her end of the conversation, something she did a lot more lately. She seemed to speak more freely with each visit, and not just small talk. She opened up about her thoughts and opinions, stating her preferences just as often as she deferred to others around her. She didn't shrink from disagreements either, though they'd yet to actually argue about anything more important than the merits of various movies or types of music. She couldn't be made to feel anything less than sheer pleasure at even the corniest country crooner, and while Davis would rather poke herself in the ear with a sharp stick than listen to George Strait's greatest hits, she did like the way Anna hummed along as she swayed to the radio.

Anna turned around and flashed her a sweet smile. Come to think of it, she did that more often these days, too, and she never failed to impress. At times she could see a sadness deep in her soft blue eyes, the kind that couldn't be traced back to a single source but rather flowed throughout someone's awareness, but even that disappeared when she smiled.

"What are you thinking about?"

"Hmm?" The non-verbal response was her attempt to prevent herself from admitting she was actually thinking about how beautiful Anna was.

"You just looked like you had a nice thought."

"Did I?" She played off the remark, not because it wasn't important, but because of its truth. She'd been caught admiring her, and she didn't want to admit that to either of them. Cass's accusations rushed back. Was some part of her falling a little bit in love with Anna?

That didn't make any sense.

Well, it made some sense.

Who wouldn't fall in love with a beautiful, caring, talented, easy-to-talk-to, great cook? Still, it'd be an epically bad idea to let things go any further. Admiration she could live with, but falling in love or even developing a crush would complicate not only their friendship, but her own tentative emotional progress. Women like Anna didn't fall for women like her. They occupied opposite ends of the relationship spectrum. Hadn't Nic taught them that?

"Why don't you spend your holidays with your family?" Anna asked.

"I've never fit into their life. Everything's so neat and organized and mapped out. They're safe and predictable and cheery, but I've never been any of those things."

"Don't they love you anyway?"

Davis paused and thought about the question. She'd never had this conversation with anyone. People rarely pressed past the basics, and when they did she always dodged them with a sarcastic comment. A few seconds of faltering in her defenses had her dissecting family relationships. "Yes, I suppose they love me in their own way."

"Of course they do. What's not to love?" Anna smiled again, easing some of the tension the mention of her family always brought to her chest.

"We just don't understand each other very well."

"How so?"

"They live a very suburban existence. They all have nine-to-five jobs. They mow their lawn every Saturday and vacation on the Gulf of Mexico."

"Yes, I can see what you mean. They sound like monsters."

"I know, right?" Davis laughed in spite of her frustration. "This is why I don't bring it up a lot. It's silly to complain when you think about parents who beat their kids or disown them for being gay. My family never did a single terrible thing to me."

"But you don't connect with them?"

"No, not at all. I kind of hate their life."

Anna raised her eyebrows as she set a plate of fried okra on the table. The smell of cooking oil and season salt mingled with the undertones of the fresh vegetable below.

"Okay, so here's an example. My mom's into Paris. She's got a bunch of little Eiffel Tower statues, and she's wallpapered her bathroom in French café scenes, and she's got a silly beret she wears around, but when my dad offered to actually take her there, she said no."

"Why?"

"Oh, a million reasons. She's afraid to fly, she's afraid of terrorists, she doesn't speak French, she might get lost, she doesn't have a passport. Who wants to decorate their house like every day is Bastille Day but doesn't want to actually go to Paris?"

"I don't know."

"People who are afraid of their own shadow, that's who."

"Ah, I see."

"Do you?" Davis asked, surprised.

"Sure. I see why you wouldn't want to live like that. You're too vibrant, too passionate to conform."

She shook off the compliment, trying not to be absurdly pleased Anna saw her as vibrant and passionate. "I don't see why anyone would choose that existence. Who would willingly wear a tie to work or actually want a subdivision lot with two point five kids in a playpen while you burn antibiotic-soaked beef patties on the grill? No worldview, nothing to challenge you, and no sense of the bigger picture."

Anna frowned as she transferred the fish to their plates and took a seat. "The way you put it doesn't sound too appealing, but I don't imagine that's how they see it."

"What do you mean?"

"I lived in the suburbs, I like to cook, I have a steady job, I want kids, but I also think I've held up decently when challenged."

"I didn't mean to imply—" She struggled to backtrack, but she couldn't summon much of the anger that usually accompanied this subject with Anna looking so sweet and sincere. "It's not the trappings that bother me, you know. It's the ideas behind them. You're not like them at all. You're living your own life with a job you love."

"Do your parents hate their jobs?"

She thought about her father's office with his little awards and certificates. "No, they actually seem pretty proud of them."

"And do they resent having kids?"

"They're natural parents. They loved the endless T-ball games and helping with homework," she said with certainty, as Anna's motive became clear. "I see what you're doing, and it's all well and good. They chose what they wanted, and that's fine for them, really, but I don't see any reason why I should spend my holidays wrapped up in their life when I spend the rest of my year trying to escape it."

"I never said you should."

"You're going to do that with your family."

"Yes." Annabelle nodded thoughtfully. "But I'm not trying to escape my parents' life. I enjoy our holiday celebrations, or I always have in the past."

"But you like your life in the city, too. You said so yourself."

"I spent years with Nic boxing me into this ideal she had for my life, and I'm realizing there's so much more out there for me. I could easily be swept up in this new life." She reached across the table and covered Davis's hand. "But I had things I loved about my old life, too—my family, traditions, cooking. Isn't there any part of your parents' life you didn't want to escape?"

She sat back, trying to focus on her words through the distracting shot of affection Anna's touch inspired. She'd never let anyone tell her what to do, and if they even tried, she'd made damn sure she did the opposite. She was jaded and stubborn. She looked at things objectively, and that's why she'd survived alone in the city, but had she taken the attitude too far? Had she inadvertently thrown out some piece of her parents' life that might have enriched her own? As soon as she allowed herself to consider the question, her answer was immediate. "I kind of like kids, I guess."

"Really?" Annabelle smiled. "Apropos of nothing, you decide you like kids?"

"It's not out of nowhere. I actually thought about that earlier. With all the things we've tried together since you got to the city, I could start to feel a little superior about being the one to help you see what you'd been missing, but you've made me see I've missed things, too."

"And you miss kids?"

"Yeah, maybe." Davis chewed a piece of okra and mulled over her words. "I mean, I have two nieces and a nephew I don't really know. When I hear you talk about yours and see the kids in your classroom making turkey handprints, I wonder if my sister's kids would like that. But then I think that's silly because I won't see them until Christmas, and I'm supposed to be happy about that, but I'm also kind of jealous of your attempts to have it all." She was blabbering now, as if simply opening the door to those emotions had let them all come rushing out at once. Had she really kept herself from experiencing things she wanted all in the name of her cynicism?

"But I'm not going to have it all on one day," Anna said, picking at her food. "I've chosen to go with my family, you've chosen to stay in the city, and we both still only get to celebrate one part of ourselves. Unless…"

"Yes?" Her heart beat a little faster at the way the corners of Anna's mouth quirked up like she'd just had a mischievous thought.

"What if we didn't choose one over the other?

"Can we do that?"

"Why not? We're both tired of living halfway."

Davis's hope rose, but cynicism didn't let go easily. "There are some physical challenges to being two places at once."

Anna rolled her eyes playfully. "We could go visit our parents the night before Thanksgiving, spend time with the family, have the big sit-down meal in the afternoon, then head back to the city for an evening filled with junk food and trashy movies."

Her first instinct was to say no. A whole night with her family? It couldn't work. It'd be awkward. What would they talk about? Could she suddenly decide to have a relationship with her siblings' children?

Davis laughed.

"What? I thought it was a good idea."

"It is. It's a great idea, but all I could think of was the reasons it wouldn't work, until I realized the loop in my head sounded just like my mother listing all the reasons she couldn't go to Paris." She shook her head, not sure if she should be terrified at the realization or thrilled she'd been able to stop it. "I think I've gotten fixated on what I didn't want, that 'no' became my default response to everything."

"I never made a decision for myself," Anna mused, "and every decision you make is a 'no.'"

"Which is kind of like never making a real decision. We make quite a couple."

Anna tilted her head to the side and regarded her seriously. Had she gone too far? Davis hadn't meant to refer to them as a couple, but thankfully Anna seemed more pensive than offended. "I've started making my own decisions now. I've decided to learn to tell the difference between what I really want and what's old baggage."

"Do you think I can do that, too?"

Anna smiled in an adoring way that made Davis's chest swell. "I don't know. Do you want to say yes?"

"To you?" Davis asked.

"To yourself."

She smiled right back. "Yes."

CHAPTER SEVENTEEN

"Hey, sweetie, how you holding up?" Liz said, bringing another stack of dishes into the kitchen.

Annabelle hated her sister's tone, the one that said everyone expected today to be hard on her. Her whole family had used that tone on her at least once over the last twenty-four hours, and each time she hated it more. She hated being an object of concern or pity. She hated them spending their holiday thinking about her pain. She hated being expected to break down. Mostly, though, she hated them being right. Everything about this day had hurt, which also meant she'd started to hate herself for missing Nic.

She didn't actually miss Nic, the person she no longer trusted, so much as she missed the way things used to be. She missed having someone's hand to hold under the table. She missed making eye contact across the room and smiling. She missed stealing little kisses when no one was looking. Most of all, she missed reliving those moments in her mind. Holidays were a time for reflection, to mark the progression of time and think about things to come. While she tried to remember all her accomplishments, she couldn't help but examine memories from years past. Had Nic reached for her hand, or had it been the other way around? And were her kisses real or a decoy? Did Nic love someone else then, too? And when they'd gone to bed at night, had Nic wanted to hold her, or was she biding her time until she could get away?

"Honey? Are you all right?" Liz asked again.

"Yes." She shook her head. How long had she zoned out for? No wonder her whole family worried. "I'm fine. I mean, I don't really have a choice, do I?"

Liz eyed her sympathetically. "I hate her all over again for ruining your holiday."

"She's ruined more than just one of them. All the holidays we ever spent together are tarnished now, and it makes me so angry."

"Good. Anger's good. Anger's productive."

"I don't know. I don't like the person I am when I get mad. I actually find myself wishing she'd died."

"I'm sure Daddy could arrange that."

"No, I don't mean I want someone to kill her. I just mean that if she'd died, I would've gotten to keep all our memories. I could've grieved her in peace without ever doubting how much she loved me."

Liz opened her arms and pulled her into a hug. "I wish I could undo everything."

"I don't even know what I wish," she said, her voice muffled against her sister's shoulder. "I used to wish I could go back and somehow unknow the things I learned about her. Now I don't want to live that way. It might've been easier, but not better. I like my life now. My home, my job, my new friends are all better than my old ones. I don't even miss *her* per se. But I miss being sure of things, knowing what I wanted. I miss being happy without feeling guilty or suspicious."

"I know it doesn't help to hear, but it will get easier."

"I believe you. In some ways it already has. Like I said, I don't want to go back. I'm done wishing she was still here." She didn't add that the only person she'd really wished she had beside her when she sat down to dinner earlier was Davis.

She wanted to tell Liz about her strengthening connection to Davis to prove she wasn't completely fixated on Nic anymore, but Liz wasn't thrilled about the friendship, and she'd said so on her last few visits to Atlanta. She didn't have anything against Davis personally. She hadn't taken time to get to know her, and she didn't want to. But she still saw Davis only as the other woman and worried she'd keep Annabelle from moving forward.

Annabelle couldn't argue with her underlying logic. If she could see Davis only as Nic's mistress, she wouldn't be able to get around the dysfunctional aspects of their friendship, but then again, if that's all Davis was, they wouldn't have built a friendship in the first place. She could've never opened up to her or trusted her if she was only the other woman. Instead, she'd become a confidante, a shopping buddy, a colleague, and an inspiration for personal growth. Davis was self-sufficient, smart, resourceful, and approached every challenge head-on. She had a wicked wit and didn't roll over for anyone. She could be so tenacious, but she never failed to listen to Annabelle's thoughts or opinions, even when they conflicted with her own. The thing she admired most about Davis was how she made Annabelle feel like she could be all those things, too.

"Are you sure you won't stay tonight?" Liz asked.

"I'm sure." She took in a deep breath, inhaling the scent of her sister's perfume and the smell of her mother's kitchen. This house had been home for so long, but the familiar connections didn't satisfy her the way they had in the past. The more she thought about all the things she'd shared with Davis, the less she wanted to remain surrounded by broken memories. She wanted to make new ones with the only person she could be truly open and honest with right now.

"I hate to think of you running back to that empty apartment."

"I actually have plans with friends."

"Really?" Liz seemed skeptical, but Anna didn't intend to give any details. She loved her family, but she couldn't explain her feelings to them yet. She couldn't even explain them to herself. She didn't want to arouse their concern, any more than she wanted to analyze her rush of emotions at the thought of driving back to the city. Most of all, she didn't want to postpone her evening with Davis any longer.

❖

"I'm going to put the movie in," Cass said impatiently.

"I just got a text from Anna. She'll be here in fifteen minutes."

"Seriously? You made me wait all damn day for you to get home, and now I have to wait for her, too?" Cass was as close to whining as Davis had ever heard her.

"I was home at three o'clock. That's only a little bit later than we usually start."

"I still don't see why we had to rearrange the schedule at all. You've never gone to your parents' house before."

She didn't want to admit that Anna had sparked her transition. "It was just a little experiment."

"Like a science project?"

"More like a sociology project. I wanted to see if my own biases skewed my earlier interactions with the foreign species known as suburbanites."

Cass regarded her suspiciously. She knew her too well to dismiss a voluntary interaction with her family as the result of mere curiosity. "And what did you find?"

"The food is still pretty bland, and I still don't get the obsession with lawn care."

"Why does it sound like there's a 'but' coming here?"

Davis turned to her cabinets and pretended to rifle around for the microwave popcorn that was right in front of her. She didn't want Cass to see her smile for fear it would give too much away. "They love each other, and they trust each other, and there's something refreshing about that."

"Refreshing," Cass repeated, but didn't elaborate or question further.

Maybe refreshing wasn't the right word, but when she'd looked closer at her parents, they hadn't seemed unhappy or even bored. Her mother did kind of wait on her father, always filling his glass before it was empty and bringing him his reading glasses without being asked, but Davis now saw how little of that came from obligation and how many of her gestures were borne out of love. He, too, seemed to enjoy his role, proudly pointing out the new remote starter he'd gotten for her car so she wouldn't have to go outside to turn on the heat in the mornings, even though it didn't get that cold in central

Georgia. The petty things would've annoyed her in the past, but now for some reason she saw they stemmed from love.

Her siblings, too, moved easily, comfortably around each other. She found herself almost envious at times. They didn't watch what they said around each other and instead joked and teased constantly. They didn't keep to their personal space, either. Her brother had yanked playfully on her sister's ponytail, and she had poked him in the side with her fork. They still behaved in the carefree manner of childhood around each other. She used to think they'd failed to grow up, but now she saw their simple camaraderie as a sign of how safe they felt together.

"So is this little experiment over now?" She finally turned around to see Cass standing a few feet behind her with her arms folded across her chest. Even dressed down, she was imposing. It didn't help that even her sweat suit was Tommy Hilfiger. Most telling, though, was the way her eyes scanned Davis's face, clearly trying to discern what she wasn't saying.

"I'm not going back until Christmas," she said, then sheepishly added, "but my mom and sister are bringing my nieces up in a couple weeks for me to take them Christmas shopping."

Cass's eyes went from being narrowed in suspicion to wide in surprise. "All right, who are you and what have you done with my best friend?"

She laughed nervously and put the popcorn in the microwave. "They just wanted to have a girls' day."

"And what about you? Do you want to join them?"

She didn't particularly love the idea of going to a mall, but she did want to be part of their outing. She wanted to share in their connections. She wanted to know what it felt like to accept something simply for what it was instead of what she thought it should be. "I wanted to be invited. I can't explain why it mattered, but it did, and when they did invite me, I just said yes."

"You just said yes." Cass parroted the words back to her, likely in an attempt to make it clear how odd they sounded, especially coming from her.

"It's something new I'm trying."

"Another experiment?"

"Maybe," Davis said, trying to dodge further introspection.

"Am I correct in assuming these new projects of yours stem from the influence of the lovely and talented Annabelle?"

"I don't know what you mean."

"Why are you lying to me?" Cass sounded more hurt than angry. "You *do* know what I mean, and I'm sure this was her idea. You've never had the slightest interest in hanging out with your nieces until now."

"I have, actually. I like kids. I've just never known how to reconcile them with my hipster city-girl side."

"And now suddenly Anna shows up and you're a Renaissance woman?"

"Is that so wrong?"

"No, of course not. I just worry about you getting hurt again. I wish we could go back to the way things were before Nic showed up."

"Here's a news flash for both of us. I was hurt then, too," she snapped, then softened. "Even before Nic came along, I'd been cheated and lied to and made a fool of so many times, I'd shut down. I'd stopped putting myself in a position to feel the distrust and the disappointment until Nic cracked through my defenses. I pretended to go slow and keep it casual, but I didn't because I didn't really want to."

"I tried to tell you." Cass's tone held no satisfaction.

"I know, and I appreciate it. It's my fault. I missed the warning signs. I got hurt."

"You've got to learn to keep your heart out of things."

"I tried to ignore my heart in a relationship, and I can't. I've tried to shut everyone else out completely, but honestly that doesn't feel much better."

"So we're back to Annabelle."

The buzzer on the microwave saved Davis from having to answer, but she considered the question while she filled two popcorn bowls and carried them to the couch. Maybe she did keep coming back to Anna. She seemed to be the only one who understood her.

She never had to be anyone other than herself around her, whether she was sad or angry or silly or joyful about something totally unusual for her, like a kid. She loved and trusted Cass, but her connection with Anna held something more, something she couldn't explain yet, and that worried her.

Had she felt the same way about Nic?

Had she kept Cass out of their relationship for the same reasons?

Did she worry Cass wouldn't understand or that she'd see the situation more clearly than she did? Ultimately Cass had been right about Nic, and Davis had simply been unwilling to hear it. She couldn't bring herself to doubt anything about Anna, but could she put the same faith in her own judgment? She searched her memory for something, anything to suggest she should be suspicious of their newfound friendship.

"Are we going to start the movie or keep arguing?" Cass asked as she took her seat on the couch. "Really, the choice is yours, darling, but I'd rather watch the movie."

"Why don't you like her?"

"Excuse me?"

"What don't you like about Anna?" Davis had to hear the answer even if it hurt her.

Cass rolled her eyes. "Okay, I'll take that as 'no' to the movie, then."

"I'm serious. I need you to tell me the truth because I can't see anything to dislike, and it scares me that you do."

"Oh, Davis, I don't mean to scare you. I'm sorry I didn't say something sooner about Nic. Really, I feel so guilty, and you know I don't do guilt."

"Nic doesn't matter. I wouldn't have listened if you'd tried, but I don't want to repeat my mistake, so I'm listening now. Tell me what bothers you about Anna."

"Nothing."

"Come on, you've never liked me being around her."

"I'm serious. There's nothing wrong with Annabelle. I like her a lot. I told you as much the first time I met her. She's like a reverse M&M, all sweet and smooth on the outside with a tough shell inside. She's graceful and strong, and she's got a determination that impresses me."

"So what then? You think she's too good to be real?" Davis needed the other shoe to drop, and fast. To hear calm, objective Cass list all Anna's good qualities only made her feel more drawn to the woman she was supposedly warning her away from.

"No, she's almost absurdly genuine, and while she's entirely too Stepford for my tastes, if you'd met under other circumstances, I would've immediately pegged her as the perfect match for you."

Her heart pounded. Every one of Cass's statements affirmed the subtle stirring of hope she'd tried to tamp down for weeks. Could Anna be happily-ever-after material? Did she even believe in it anymore? "You really think so?"

"Damn it, the glassy look in your eyes tells me you only heard the last part of what I said." She snapped her fingers in front of Davis's eyes. "I said '*if* you'd met under other circumstances,' but you met under the most fucked-up conditions possible. You can't escape the fact that you're the other woman. No matter how many memories you build, no matter how much joy you find together, your relationship will always be founded on mutual pain."

"That's not true." Her rebuttal sounded as weak as her voice, but she didn't know what else to say. She'd gone from feeling like everything was right for the first time in six months to a hopelessness she hadn't experienced in almost as long.

"It *is* true." Cass slid closer and offered a hug. "And I hate it, but you'll never have a time when it's just you and Anna. Nic will always be between you. Even when she's not there, you'll still feel her ghost, and you both deserve better."

Davis rested her head on Cass's shoulder. She didn't know if she agreed with her assertion that they'd never be free of Nic, but she did agree that neither of them deserved that kind of a cloud hanging over them. "I don't want to hurt her."

"I know. I don't think you would if you'd just keep things casual, but I also know you don't do casual well, and I don't think she does either, which is why it's not a good idea for you to spend so much time together."

"She'll be here any minute. She left her family dinner to spend the evening with me. What should I do?"

"Just relax. Enjoy the evening for what it is, and then say goodbye."

❖

Annabelle laughed so hard throughout *Bridesmaids* her side hurt. The ache in her stomach more likely stemmed from the entire box of Whoppers she ate mixed with a bag of Fritos, another culinary creation Davis had introduced her to. "This is not my usual Thanksgiving fare."

"And?" Davis asked. "How does it compare?"

"You can't really compare the two. It's Monet to Picasso."

"One's only coherent from afar, and the other doesn't even offer the pretense of sanity?" Cass asked.

"Now that you mention it, yes." She laughed. Cass was funny and smart with a wickedly dry wit, and the more she got used to her often-abrasive sarcasm, the more she found herself enjoying their time together. She'd never had many girlfriends, much less lesbian friends. The girls in her sorority had been so cliquey and focused on boys, and then she'd become a housewife and all the women she'd met were partners of Nic's business associates. It was refreshing to be around intelligent, self-possessed women.

"You didn't strike me as the raunchy-comedy type of woman," Davis said.

"I wouldn't have thought so either. I guess that's something else to add to the list of things I'm still learning about myself, thanks to you."

Davis smiled one of her brilliant smiles. Annabelle still remembered the first time she'd seen such an unguarded look of pleasure on her face. They'd been spending time together for a couple weeks when Annabelle had offered to teach her how to bake bread. Davis had battled the dough as though it were some mutant foe, but when the time had come to braid it, she'd easily and artfully threaded each strand through the others. After several minutes of teasing and prodding, she'd admitted she used to have long hair as a child and had braided it before bed each night. Without thinking, Anna had run her fingers up the short copper stubble at the back of Davis's head, casually remarking that the utility cut suited her no-nonsense personality, but she imagined many a woman would kill to be shrouded in long, beautiful locks of red.

She'd been embarrassed when she'd realized how flirty the compliment had sounded, but Davis's smile was bright and full, almost in the way a child smiles when complimented, albeit tempered by a grown woman's understanding. Anna'd found herself wondering many times since then if Davis really knew the extent of her own beauty, especially when she didn't know or care that someone else was watching. She suspected other women told her she was sexy or alluring, and those things were true, but she wondered if any of them ever made Davis feel beautiful. Then again, she also got the sense Davis didn't let just anyone see her smile in that unreserved way. The thought only made her feel luckier every time she had one of those smiles directed at her.

"Well, the 'continuing education' aspect of our friendship goes both ways, you know? Thanks to your prompting, I sat down and talked to my nieces and nephews today, only to find out I'm the cool aunt."

"Of course you are."

"You say that with such certainty, but it shocked me," Davis said. "I thought they considered me a spinster they worried about supporting in her old age."

"I doubt anyone worries about you not being able to take care of yourself."

"I think my parents do," Davis admitted. "They're obviously still perplexed about my choice to live alone in the city when I could work from anywhere, but this time I also felt like maybe they're a little proud, too."

"How could they not be impressed with the way you've carved your own path?" Annabelle was certainly impressed with the life Davis lived. The people who loved her had to at least admire her determination.

"The kids are. They didn't question me about my sudden appearance in their life." She shook her head like she found that a little unbelievable. "They didn't treat me with suspicion or hold me at arm's length. They hugged me and asked a bunch of questions about life in the city. I think they may envision it as more glamorous than it is in reality, but I like them believing I'm some sort of rock star."

"You kind of are, compared to their parents."

Davis laughed. "Right, which is why they all want to come visit without their parents. They have a city bucket list full of items like concerts and sporting events and riding the metro."

"Fun," Annabelle said, immediately beginning to plan group outings in her mind. "Maybe we could find them some bikes to ride with us in the park."

"I'd love to. We could look for some next time we're out."

Cass stood suddenly. "I hate to cut this short, but I think I better call it a night."

"What? Why?" Davis asked. "It's only nine o'clock. We've got two more movies."

"I have a full morning of showings tomorrow. You know how it is. When normal humans get a day off, I have to work twice as hard."

Davis seemed skeptical, which in turn made Anna suspicious of the otherwise benign explanation. Cass had been uncharacteristically quiet for the last few minutes. Now, she looked like a woman with a purpose as she gathered her things and hugged Davis. She seemed like she might hug Anna, too, then caught herself, saying, "I'm glad you're doing well in your bold new world."

The comment struck her as oddly formal and yet oddly sentimental all at once, catching her off guard and leaving her to reply with a simple, "Thank you."

"Call me tomorrow?" Davis asked.

"No, you call me later tonight," Cass said, rather pointedly.

Davis nodded seriously as she closed the door.

"We didn't run her off, did we?"

"Who knows with Cass?" Davis said flippantly, but Anna got the feeling she did know. She would've pushed harder, but Davis had never lied to her. If there was something she wasn't saying now, she needed time to think it over herself. Davis didn't rush to judgment, almost as if she didn't trust herself to make decisions based on intuition, but with time she always came around.

"What are you thinking about?"

"You," she answered honestly. While Davis was deliberate, Anna felt freer in her company than anywhere else and rarely held back anymore.

"What about me?"

"I'm getting to know your patterns, the way you process information. I don't mind when you get silent or pensive. I don't rush to please you or make up for your down moments. You'll talk when you're ready."

"And I know you'll listen when that time comes." Davis sat on the couch, curling one leg underneath her. "I'm comfortable with you. I never had that with Nic."

"I like how you don't dance around her memory. I spent over twenty-four hours with my parents, and they never once said her name. They acted like she never existed, which only made me feel crazy, because they all look at me with pity, but none of us can mention why."

"Cass thinks we'll never be free of Nic."

Annabelle sighed. "Liz all but said the same thing, and I get why they think that, but honestly, the only time I truly feel like I'm moving on is when I'm with you."

Davis readjusted herself on the couch as if she'd wanted to jump up but forced herself to stay put. "Really?"

"Yes. Don't get me wrong. I like my job, and I'm doing fine living on my own, but that's just getting by. When we're together, I actually enjoy myself. With you I like who I am, or at least who I'm becoming." Annabelle hoped she sounded calm even as her body temperature rose. "You're the only person who knows everything about Nic but doesn't treat me like I'm broken."

"You're not broken. You're amazing. You're inspiring." Davis sighed. "Which of course is why Cass is right. You deserve better."

Deserved better than what? Better than Nic? The comment seemed out of context. Did it have something to do with why Cass left, or whatever Davis had held back earlier? She felt like she'd missed half of the conversation. Why did Cass care about how Nic's memory affected Anna's friendship with Davis? Unless it wasn't friendship they'd discussed.

Her mouth suddenly felt very dry, but she didn't dare reach for her drink for fear her hands would tremble.

"Anna? Are you okay?"

She nodded slowly. She was overreacting. Davis hadn't said anything that warranted her current line of thought. She'd merely paid her a very sweet and genuine compliment. Annabelle had turned the sentiments into something romantic. Her entire overreaction was probably only wishful thinking.

Did she wish Davis had feelings for her? And if she did, could she even return them? Six months ago she thought she'd never feel this way again. Even earlier today she'd thought she didn't want to be anything other than stable, but now her body told her something altogether different.

"Did I say something wrong?" Davis asked nervously, moving closer.

"No, of course, not." She swallowed her emotions. She'd made Davis uncomfortable, and she hated the doubt rising in those beautiful green eyes. She never wanted to make this strong, beautiful woman question herself. "You're wonderfully sweet, and I want you to always be open and honest with me."

"And you know I am, right?" Davis asked, a hint of shyness creeping into her tone. "You know I'd never lie to you?"

"I know. I trust you completely, and I never thought I'd say that again to anyone."

Davis smiled, seeming relieved. "Good, and I know what you mean. I didn't think I'd even want to trust anyone again, much less be able to."

"And now?" She tried not to hold her breath, but so much hinged on Davis's answer.

"Today with my family I watched them laugh and joke and talk about their hopes and fears, and I felt jealous. They were completely themselves with each other, and I wanted to feel that kind of comfort, but as much as I enjoyed being around them, I realized you're the only person I trust enough to let see all of me." Davis shivered like the reality of what she'd said was enough to shake something at her core.

The urge to reach out to her was too powerful to resist. Annabelle tentatively ran the back of her fingers down Davis's cheek. Her skin was so soft, so warm, stirring an ache in her chest she either hadn't felt or hadn't let herself acknowledge until it grew too strong to ignore.

Davis closed her eyes and leaned into the caress. *God, she's beautiful.* And she suddenly seemed vulnerable in a way she hadn't before. Annabelle had never been the initiator in anything, always the careful one, eager to please and content to follow, but the pull she felt to Davis now was stronger than anything she'd ever experienced. Doubt evaporated as she drew nearer, replacing the gentle touch of her hand with her lips. She ran her mouth lightly against Davis's smooth skin, slowly inhaling the scent of her, a delicate mix of soap and honeysuckle. She placed feather-light kisses along her cheekbone and down her jaw until Davis turned her head, seeking more.

Their lips met, and Annabelle was torn between the urge to run from the overwhelming honesty of their connection and the desire to immerse herself completely in it. Ultimately she gave in to the latter. The kiss felt nothing like the one they'd shared in pain and desperation. They came together now, slowly, intimately, and with a depth of feeling that would've terrified her with anyone else.

Davis was skillful at matching Anna's pace, accepting everything offered without pushing for more, even though she could have. The thought should've terrified Annabelle. Davis could have what she wanted. Annabelle wouldn't deny her anything, even the power to hurt her, and yet she felt safe.

No, she felt better than safe.

She felt free.

There was no fear or distrust, but there was no hurry, no pressure, only desire.

Davis took Anna's hand, intertwining their fingers. Anna's body temperature rose as the quiet spark between them grew slowly, not like a flash of lightning, but more like the way a single flame catches kindling and crawls along, spreading with every ounce of fuel it consumes. She savored each moment, each subtle shift of their bodies, the heated flush of Davis's breath, the brush of skin. The unbelievable rightness of their connection urged her forward, her tongue sweeping against Davis's. She couldn't remember the last time her mind, heart, and body were in sync like this, and she wasn't sure anything had ever felt so all-consuming.

She ran her hand up Davis's arm, relishing the ability to want something, someone, in a way that superseded reason. Annabelle grew dizzy with power that came from touching, craving, taking. She could've cried out, but she didn't want to stop. She didn't want this moment to end.

"Anna," Davis whispered, cupping her face in her hands. "God, Anna, you're amazing."

"No, it's you," she murmured against her neck. "You make me…you make me…feel."

"You make me need." Davis rested her forehead against Anna's and stared into her eyes, causing her to catch her breath. "I need you."

They pressed their mouths together again, their pace increasing with the heat between them. Davis threaded her arms around Anna's back, urging her closer, and she eagerly obliged until she was practically on her lap. Each touch bolder than the one before, they stroked and kissed, then reached for more. The caring didn't merely give way to passion. It fed it, giving them freedom to surrender. She didn't think about practicalities or all the ways this could go wrong. Instead, she gave in completely. They had plenty of time, and for the first time in months, time felt like a blessing instead of a curse.

CHAPTER EIGHTEEN

Nic tried not to look around the modular home. It reminded her too much of the trailer she'd grown up in, and not just because of its size. Hell, her apartment wasn't any bigger, but it was much cleaner. Here, dirty laundry littered the floor, and the smell of stale smoke hung heavy in the air. She would've sat down on the couch, but the torn, sagging cushion didn't look any more comfortable than the entertainment center she currently leaned up against. She never invited women back to her own place, but maybe this time she should've made an exception. It wasn't too late. Her date, Cindi, was just changing clothes. Then again, maybe Cindi couldn't find any clean clothes with all her laundry out here on the floor.

"Everything okay in there?" Nic called. She would've gone back to check on her if she wasn't terrified of what kind of mess she'd find in the bedroom. It was probably safer to stay in a well-lit area.

"I'll be done in a minute. I gotta take a piss," Cindi called. "Just make yourself comfy, sweet cheeks."

She winced at the vulgarity. Most of the women she went home with were classier. Her first clue that her current company might be more trouble than she was worth came when Cindi mentioned her license had been revoked for too many DUIs, so Nic would have to drive. She might've also questioned the fact that Cindi was alone in a bar at seven o'clock on Thanksgiving, if she hadn't been in the same position.

It was the first holiday she'd spent alone in thirteen years, and if she'd stayed in her apartment, she would've climbed the wall with regret and self-doubt. At least Cindi, with her too-loud laugh and her too-crude humor, seemed an improvement on solitude. It wasn't as if Nic intended to make friends with her, and they certainly weren't about to *make love*. This was more of a business transaction than anything else, and despite her current administrative leave, she was still very good at business.

Business. Thinking about women as things to be used and traded would've horrified her months ago. Even in the midst of an affair, she'd believed an emotional connection was essential for good sex. She still felt a little uncomfortable with the realities of these liaisons, just not uncomfortable enough to stop having them. She only felt awkward or guilty at transition times. In the bar she enjoyed the chase, and in bed she relished the oblivion of pure physicality. If she had to deal with a little discomfort to bridge the two experiences, she would. Then again, if she could talk Cindi into going somewhere else, she might not have to deal with quite so much discomfort.

Finally, the bathroom door swung wide, hitting the thin wall and casting a sepia shot of light into the narrow hallway. Nic opened her mouth to suggest a change of venue, but before she got the words out, Cindi stepped into view, holding a bottle of tequila in one hand, a strap-on in the other, and wearing absolutely nothing.

"You ready to rock?"

Nic stood in awe, her heartbeat sending a steady pulse all the way from her chest straight to her clit. What had she been thinking about wanting to leave? She cleared her throat. "Yes. Yes, I am."

Cindi strutted into the living room, allowing Nic to admire her. She was thin and taut, the belly-button ring glistening at her navel the only adornment on her slick, shaven body. Cindi walked a circle around her before pushing a stack of papers off the coffee table and onto the floor. Nic couldn't see the mess anymore, and all memories of her childhood home vanished as Cindy lay back on the table and smiled slyly up at her.

"You look thirsty, baby," Cindi purred. "Want a drink?"

Nic nodded. Now that she mentioned it, her mouth did feel awfully dry.

Cindi lifted the bottle over her chest and tipped it until a narrow stream of liquor ran down between her breasts and pooled at her stomach. Like a pilgrim before an altar, Nic knelt and closed her eyes, breathing in the harsh scent of the alcohol with a subtle undercurrent of strawberry body lotion. Leaning forward, she licked broad strokes across smooth skin, pulling more tequila into her mouth with each pass. The sensation of slick skin against her tongue was sheer gluttony, and she wanted to drown in it. Cindi arched her chest and tipped the bottle a little more, flooding Nic's mouth, covering her face and soaking her shirt, but Nic didn't care. She couldn't even bring herself to lift her head while she tugged at her own buttons, roughly yanking the fabric off her body and slinging it to the floor.

Her head spun from the combination of sexual arousal and the first effects of the alcohol hitting her system. Even though she'd built up quite a tolerance over the past few months, she usually sipped whiskey. Now she lapped at the tequila like an animal, running her tongue in a variety of strokes from short and fast to long sweeping loops around Cindi's breasts and back down again.

"Suck my tits." Cindi panted, splashing more tequila across her chest before bringing the bottle to her own mouth. Nic climbed onto the table so she could take one nipple in her mouth, licking and sucking it clean before moving to the other. She had no idea how much alcohol she'd consumed by now. Three shots' worth, four? It must have been more than she realized, because every time she moved her head to worship another body part, the edges of her vision blurred.

She didn't need to see, though. She could do this with her eyes closed. In fact, she almost preferred not to look too closely at the women she had sex with. If she looked too hard, she'd make comparisons to women she couldn't have, women she probably should've never had. No, sex was a purely tactile experience these days, a way to shut out the world, not embrace it. The woman below her differentiated herself from the others only by offering both of Nic's drugs of choice instead of just one.

"God, baby." Cindi pushed her fingers through Nic's hair and down her back, scratching with enough pressure to leave a mark. At least Nic thought it was hard enough, based on the pressure crushing her to Cindi's chest, but she couldn't actually feel any pain, the edges of her senses numb now. She walked a tricky tightrope between getting drunk enough to let go and losing her grip so far she wouldn't perform up to her usual standards. As amazing as the physical world could be, her need to prove herself capable provided as much pleasure as any orgasm.

Reaching out to anchor herself to the physical, she worked her hand between Mindi's legs. Or was her name Cindi? *Shit*. She had a fleeting awareness that she should've felt disgusted, but really, what did it matter once she was inside her?

"Fuck me hard."

Nic might not have known her name, but she knew what she wanted. She pulled back to give it to her, but lost her balance. Falling forward onto the woman below, she thought she heard something come unlatched. Had they broken the coffee table? Who cared about that piece of crap? She reared back again, but this time she kept going until she hit the wall.

Everything exploded as her head cracked against wood paneling, and she almost laughed, thankful for the questionable workmanship that meant the walls weren't cinderblock. She might've even said so if not for the feeling she'd been hit in the stomach. Another blow landed against her ribs, and she realized she hadn't fallen. Her feet weren't even touching the ground. Everything blurred, but pain burned through the cloud as she tried to open her eyes and steady her vision.

Somewhere in the distance Cindi/Mindi screamed. So did someone else, who sounded much closer. She took another punch to the side, and this time she was certain she'd been punched. Red flashed behind her eyelids, making it impossible to focus, but amid the yelling she heard the phrase, "fuck my wife."

The pieces, no matter how disjointed, began to form a picture she didn't want to see. They obviously weren't alone, and what's-her-name wasn't single.

"I didn't know." She coughed and sputtered. "I didn't know." If the Mack truck of a woman holding her against the wall heard her, she didn't care.

"Let her go!" Cindi or Mindi shouted. "You're going to kill her."

"Damn right," the other woman shouted. "She deserves it."

Did she? Nic tried to think of one good reason why she should live. Surely there had to be something?

Anything.

Shouldn't she have thought of a reason by now?

Her memory filled with images of the hurt in Davis's eyes, Annabelle's tears, Davis shutting off her emotions, Belle sinking to the ground. She couldn't remember anyone else's face, not even Cindi's. Oh, God, what if she did deserve to die?

Suddenly the woman let go, and Nic crashed to the ground. "You piece of trash," the other voice shouted. "Worthless, stupid whore."

Who was she talking to? Nic? She squinted up at the figure towering over her. Her father? The person was big like him, with dark hair, too, but all the details were foggy. The voice shouting obscenities sounded like him, or maybe not the voice, but the words. Was he right?

He was. She couldn't face him. She summoned her last ounce of strength and scrambled to her knees. She focused long enough to see the door. Adrenaline coursed through her as she zeroed in on her escape. She'd run before, and she could do it now, too. Leaving her shirt and her shoes, she bolted. In a flash of short-lived clarity, she made it to her car and slammed the locks from the inside while she fumbled for her keys.

She could still hear the shouting, but she couldn't tell if she'd been followed or if the voices existed solely in her head now. She didn't intend to find out. Turning the ignition, she slammed the gas, spinning her tires in the gravel driveway until she found enough traction to shoot off into the night.

She didn't dare slow down as she raced back toward the center of the city. At least she thought she was nearing the city, but the roads seemed so dark. Her mind processed her surroundings slowly, alcohol and fear making everything harder to examine logically. Why were there no lights? An idea burned deliberately through the haze. Lights. She needed lights. Her headlights weren't on. She clutched a knob near the dashboard and turned on the wipers.

"Damn it," she shouted. She couldn't do more than one thing at a time, but she wouldn't pull over. The voices still chased her. Fumbling with the controls, she tried again. This time she found the light switch and flipped it. The white of the headlamps blinded her as they bounced off a small reflective strip on a telephone pole.

Too bright. Telephone pole. Too fast. Too close. The stream of thoughts flashed through her consciousness in an instant. Then mercifully everything went dark until even the voices that chased her fell completely silent.

Davis was lost in the press of Annabelle's lips against her own. In the past she'd felt drunk on another's kiss, but this was altogether different. It wasn't frantic or delirious. It was better. She remained completely aware of every scent, every touch, every spark of electricity running through her. Anna's body against her own made her burn in a way she hadn't wanted, but couldn't imagine ever wanting to stop. Running her hands up over the bare skin of Anna's arms, she thrilled at the feel of a woman's body, and not just any woman, but Anna. Somewhere in the recesses of her mind she knew she wasn't supposed to crave her like this, but how could she not? Sweet, strong, determined, and so very beautiful, Anna was too much to resist even just on the surface, but beyond that, Davis trusted her. Until recently she wouldn't have thought of trust as sexy, but here, within the safety to surrender, she couldn't think of anything more attractive than the freedom to let go without fear.

Anna broke the kiss only long enough to inhale a deep breath, but Davis hated the lapse in contact. She pressed her lips to Anna's neck until she tilted her head back, shaking out her long, beautiful hair and exposing the slender curve of her throat.

"Davis, you feel so good."

"You," she murmured against her skin. "You feel so right."

Anna sank her hands into Davis's hair, holding her close. "How it that possible?"

"Hmm?"

"How did we miss this?" Anna pulled her up again, kissing her deeply, sensually, before pulling away. "How did we miss that?"

She shook her head. "You're beautiful. I never missed that. Not from the very first day, not in my pain or doubt. I always saw how stunning you are."

"I find that hard to believe. I'm so plain compared to you. You're stylish, and your eyes, there's something hypnotic about them. Even if you hadn't kissed me that first day, I would've known how passionate you were."

"You kissed me that first day," Davis corrected her, "and you kissed me tonight."

"Did I?" Anna asked, then kissed her again, this time more quickly. "See what I mean? You make me forget things."

"I hope I make you forget bad things."

Anna shrugged. "I don't know if you make me forget the bad things so much as you make them less important. When I'm with you, I feel safe, and when you touch me, I know you could hurt me, but it seems worth the risk somehow."

Now it was Davis's turn to initiate another series of quick kisses. "I don't ever want to hurt you."

"I know, but we both have so much baggage." Anna smiled sadly. "Matching baggage maybe, but there's a lot of it."

"Right, I know." All the reasons they shouldn't go down this road rushed up to meet her.

Anna deserved better.

She was better than Davis.

She craved security and stability, not the volatility and insecurity Davis brought to the table. Not painful memories either, memories most people thought they'd never break free of. "Not a single person in our lives would say making out on my couch is a good idea."

"True. When you look at the facts on paper, we're a very bad investment." Anna cradled Davis's face gently in her hands and pulled her close. "But this isn't happening on paper."

She sealed her comments with a searing kiss, pushing the temperature in the room up several more degrees. How did she take all the caution, the warnings, the well-reasoned rebuttals, and incinerate them?

"I didn't think I could ever feel this way," Anna whispered.

"I didn't think I wanted to."

"But you want to now. I can feel it." She placed her hand over Davis's rapidly beating heart.

"I do. I want you."

Anna's cell phone rang, causing them both to jump, then laugh.

"Do you want to see who it is?"

"Not really." Anna exhaled. "But if someone's calling so late, something might be wrong."

Davis glanced at the clock. It was nearly midnight. How long had they been making out? She couldn't remember the last time she'd felt so amazing just kissing someone. She'd always been quick to reach for more, but somehow everything about Anna filled her needs in a way she'd never experienced.

"I don't recognize the number," Anna said, coming back to the couch, and immediately reached for Davis. "Let it go to voice mail."

"You sure?"

"Very sure." Anna's tone sent a shiver through Davis's limbs. She'd been so impressed with how Anna had learned to state her desires more confidently as of late, but she'd never realized how sexy the trait could be until she had those desires directed at her.

They collided again. Davis groaned at the feel of Anna's hands on her body. She hadn't let herself miss this. She hadn't even let herself think about the need to be touched, to be wanted, to feel alive. This wasn't a performance space. She was weak and vulnerable, and in admitting that, she found the strength to allow Anna behind the walls she'd spent so much time building.

At first she couldn't tell if the buzzing in her ears was a result of sensory overload or something external. Then Anna pulled away, leaving a void she felt almost desperate to fill.

"That's your phone," Anna said with a wry smile.

Davis reached behind her to grab her still-vibrating cell phone and checked the caller ID. "Another wrong number."

She tossed the phone onto the couch between them. "Where were we?"

"Two wrong numbers at midnight." Anna glanced at the phone, her smile fading. "It's the same number."

"What?"

"That's the same number that called me."

Davis couldn't process that information, not with Anna's lips so close. "No one knows both of us except Cass, and that's not her."

Anna's face went white. "Answer it, please."

"Yeah. Okay." Her hand shook as the possibilities raced through her mind. Two calls on two different phones late at night from an unknown number didn't add up to good news. "Hello?"

"Is this Davis?" an official but unfamiliar female voice asked.

"Maybe. Who's calling?"

"I'm Janice Roberts calling from Emory University Hospital. We've had a patient admitted unconscious on arrival, and we're trying to reach next of kin for—"

"Oh, my God, is it Cass?"

"I'm sorry, I don't have a conclusive ID, but the car was registered to a Nicole McCoy. Do you know anyone by that name?"

Davis sagged against the couch. Cass was fine. All she could process for the moment was her relief, but the woman had asked a question. Nicole? McCoy. Nic. "Shit."

"Is it Cass? Has something happened?" Anna asked, fear plainly written across her beautiful features.

"It's Nic," Davis said to her, then into the phone added, "I do know her, but I'm not her next of kin."

"Is she hurt?" Annabelle whispered.

"She's unconscious." Davis answered over the sound of the woman on the phone trying to talk over her. "I'm sorry, what?"

"We need to get ahold of someone authorized to make medical decisions."

"Yeah, well, I'm not that person. Trust me."

"Do you know who that person might be?"

"No. Honestly I don't know if she has any family." God, she wanted to slap her forehead at the reminder of how little she knew about Nic's life. Anger welled up again at Nic for being so callous, and at herself for being so stupid. This little predicament might be her just reward.

"The only other person in the cell phone not listed under her work contacts is someone named Belle. Do you know her?" the woman asked.

Davis glanced at Anna with her tousled hair and her swollen lips. She looked more beautiful than ever. Davis should tell the woman on the phone to leave them alone. They didn't owe Nic anything. She certainly wasn't worth dragging Anna back into the fire she'd worked so hard to escape.

"Davis." Anna touched her hand. "What does she want?"

Rage flared in her, bitterness biting hard at her heart, and she fought to keep from lashing out about how little she cared about Nic's health or safety. Fear mingled with an overwhelming urge to protect Anna. She'd known all along that someone would pull Anna away from her, but why Nic? Why now? Terror and fury fed off each other, threatening to consume her, but she tamped them down. Anna had asked her a question, and she wouldn't lie to her. "She wants to talk to you."

"Okay." Anna nodded and took a deep breath before taking the phone.

"This is Annabelle."

Davis couldn't hear the woman from the hospital now, so she had to infer what she was saying from Anna's responses and her body language.

"Yes, I know her…No, she doesn't have any family she's in touch with…No drug allergies, blood type A positive…She didn't have any chronic health problems as of six months ago, but I haven't seen her for a while."

Davis felt a stab of jealousy, but of what she wasn't quite sure. That Anna knew more about Nic than she did? That was silly. No, maybe it was that Anna knew more about Nic than she did about *Davis*. Of course she'd only known her for half a year, but still. Nic was her past. Both of their pasts. Why should they focus on something they both wanted to leave behind? Davis wanted to be part of Anna's future, and she needed her to be a part of her own.

Anna's hands shook. "I was her last known power of attorney, but surely she's changed that by now."

Her what? Had Anna just admitted to a hospital official that she had the legal ability to make medical decisions for Nic? Why would she do that? Surely she wouldn't rush to her side. Not tonight.

"No, I can't think of who else she would grant those powers to." Anna rubbed her forehead as if trying to relieve a headache. "No, I didn't receive any notification of that being revoked. What kind of decisions are you talking about?" Anna's eyes grew wide, and she covered her mouth with her free hand.

"What?" Davis's curiosity got the better of her, and she cursed herself for caring even a little bit. She didn't wish her dead. Maybe hurt a little bit, but not dead.

No, she couldn't let herself care at all, or at least not any more than she'd care about a stranger on the street.

Surely they weren't talking life and death...?

They were at the hospital already. Couldn't the doctors take it from there?

"Right, I understand. Of course I'll sign the paperwork. I'll be right down."

"What?" Davis asked, a little louder than she intended. "Why do you have to go down there?"

Anna held out her hand, asking her to wait. "Yes, okay. I've got the number of our lawyer. Surely he has the papers on file."

How was she so stoic, so efficient? She'd volunteered to care for someone awful, someone who'd hurt them, and she didn't even look conflicted as she hung up the phone.

"Is she going to die?"

"She's critical but stable. She's going to need surgery, though. I have to go. Will you come with me?"

"No," Davis said forcefully, but when she saw the flash of hurt in Anna's beautiful blue eyes she softened her tone. "You don't have to go. Let the doctors take care of her."

"She's bleeding internally, Davis."

"You said yourself it's not life and death. The doctors have it under control. They don't need you." Davis argued when she really wanted to add, "I need you."

"I can help. I have access to her medical records. I can make this easier."

"Easier? On Nic?" She jumped off the couch and began pacing. "Damn it, why does she get it easier after the hell she put us through?"

"Davis, listen to me. She's hurt. She's got a long road ahead, and I'll never be able to live with myself if I leave her to face this alone."

"A long road? What are you talking about here?"

"Davis. Please—"

"You're not just going to sign paperwork, are you? You're going to stay with her." She finally spoke the fear that had gripped her chest from the moment she'd answered the phone. "You're going to leave me for her."

"No." Anna reached for her, but she stepped back.

"Don't touch me. Don't you dare touch me then go to her. You can't kiss me and then run when she calls. I've been through this before, and I can't do it again."

"Davis, please. I'm not leaving you for her. I want you to come with me."

"I won't go back." She shook her head frantically. This wasn't rational. Like a frightened child or a hurt animal, she felt the impulse to escape threaten to overpower her. Everything she'd feared had happened. "I just broke free. I just let myself breathe again. I won't throw myself back into that darkness. Not for her, Anna. Not even for you."

Tear's filled Anna's eyes, and she bit her bottom lip as she nodded. "Okay. I'm sorry you're in pain. It breaks my heart, but you're not the only one hurting here."

Davis couldn't bring herself to reply. She stood stone still in her resolve as Anna walked out the door and long after her footsteps had faded into the night.

Chapter Nineteen

Everything hurt. Nic tried to shift her body to relieve some of the pressure, but she couldn't. She couldn't move at all. Was she paralyzed? No, if she were paralyzed she wouldn't be able to feel anything, certainly not the kind of pain she experienced now. Something held her down. Ropes? Or straps? A rock, maybe? That didn't make sense. What had happened?

She searched the darkness of her memory but saw only black. There was no light anywhere, which in itself seemed like a sort of memory. Darkness, disorientation, but not stillness. Something had chased her through the dark. She ran.

No, she drove.

Now she remembered.

The car, the voices, but then it wasn't dark. There had been a white light. Not the proverbial kind, though. Blinding white, jarring and painful. Where did it go? Was it still there? The darkness was lifting now, a gray haze, then shades of pink followed by the low hum of machines or fans. A soft beep, a subtle click.

Was she still in the car? She wasn't moving, but maybe a seat belt held her down. Voices whispered to her side. She wasn't alone. Was someone else in the car? The voice? No, she'd outrun them. This someone didn't yell. Someone gentle, caring. That made even less sense than being stuck under a rock.

No one cared about her.

She had to see through the fog. She had to open her eyes. Her lids felt heavy and covered in sand. She wished she could wipe them, but her hands wouldn't move. The effort exhausted her, but she had to see who it was.

Suddenly the white light returned, burning through her slowly opening eyes, bright and sterile. She turned her head to the side what little bit she could, but refused to slip back into the gray haze that offered relief.

A figure rose beside her. "Nic."

The voice was so soft, so soothing, so familiar it burned away the clouds.

"Nic, it's Anna. Can you hear me?"

Anna? Opening her eyes wider, she fought to pull the blurry image into focus.

"Nic, it's okay. You had a car accident. We're at the hospital, but you're okay."

The hospital? She'd wrecked her car. The pain, the lights, the sounds made sense now, but the caring in that voice didn't.

"Can you hear me?"

Nic fought to nod and blinked again, trying to clear her vision.

Fingers tenderly ran across her forehead, sweeping her hair back and leaving no doubt as to who'd bestowed the touch. "Belle."

The name came out rough against her throat, scraping raw against her dry lips and her frayed emotions. Belle was there. Belle had touched her. Belle cared.

The crush of realizations sent the fog rushing up to consume her again. Relief sprang fast, but unworthiness soon overtook it. She wanted Belle there, she wanted so badly to matter, to mean something to someone, but she didn't deserve to. The guilt churned like bile in her stomach. She didn't deserve Belle's consideration, much less her compassion. The two emotions fought within her, dragging her back into the depths of darkness and pain. She couldn't even enjoy the soft touch of someone who cared without guilt choking out the light.

How long had she felt that way? When was the last time she'd experienced joy without remorse? Not in her one-night stands, not at work, not since she'd hurt Annabelle and Davis. Certainly not during the months she strung them both along. She struggled to remember a time before that. Had she been at peace then? The drive, the push to prove herself to her boss, to her naysayers, to Belle. She'd felt victorious, she'd felt needed and strong, even superior, but had she felt pure joy?

She tried to think of something that brought her joy, something that made her unabashedly happy, something that didn't carry a hint of insecurity or guilt or responsibility, something she did without expecting anything else from anyone else.

Maybe the fog or the pain blocked her mind, but she remembered so many times, so many emotions. She hadn't been miserable or even unhappy, but even the moments she'd cherished held an undercurrent of restlessness. Something in her had always reached for more until she couldn't think of anything in her life that made her happy.

Not one thing.

The thought terrified her, like the realization she couldn't give any reason why her life mattered. Did she really have nothing to live for? She opened her mouth to tell Belle she was scared, that she felt helpless and worthless, but the words wouldn't come. She'd slipped too far down until the pain and the haze covered her, choking her emotions and smothering her voice. She had to sit up, she had to crawl or push her way out, but when she tried, a gentle hand on her forehead eased her back.

"Hush now," Belle whispered. "Stop fighting and let yourself rest."

The words seeped through the cloud until they surrounded her, wrapping her in their meaning like a blanket swaddles a child, soothing in its confinement. *Stop fighting and let yourself rest.*

She closed her eyes, and for perhaps the first time in her life, she surrendered.

Davis still sat on the couch with her head in her hands when the sunlight streaked clean and painfully bright through her windows. She needed to move, but she didn't dare for fear that if she gave in even one inch, she wouldn't be able to stop herself from chasing Annabelle. She wanted to go after her so badly she had to clench

RACHEL SPANGLER

her fists to keep from reaching for the doorknob. She wasn't sure which betrayal was worse, Anna's for leaving or her own heart's for wanting to go with her. Either way, the ache in her chest only served as a reminder of how little she could trust her own judgment.

She wouldn't be a made a fool of again. She wouldn't run back into Nic's life. She had to stay strong. She couldn't get pulled back in, and if Anna didn't have the same kind of fortitude in the face of the past, everyone was right and they really had nothing between them but Nic.

The phone rang and she lunged for it, answering in a rush of hope that Anna had called to apologize.

"Good morning," Cass said, causing Davis to curse herself, both for hanging onto the hope of Anna's return to her and for not checking her caller ID.

"Hey, Cass, now's not a good time."

"So when you answered the phone on the first ring, you were expecting someone else? The lovely and charming Annabelle, perhaps? Did you not manage to say good-bye last night?"

Her throat thickened with emotion she didn't want to feel. "No, we definitely ended things."

"Why doesn't that sound good?"

Her voice cracked. "She went back to Nic."

"What?" Cass practically screeched.

"Don't act so surprised. You all but said she'd do it eventually."

"I said no such thing, and I don't believe you. She's too strong, too smart to take her back."

Davis hesitated. She didn't want to go into the details. "Well, maybe she hasn't taken her back yet."

"Uh-huh." Cass's skepticism was clear even through the phone. "What aren't you telling me?"

"She kissed me. And I kissed her. I trusted her, Cass. I wanted her, needed her, but when the hospital called and said Nic was in a car accident—"

"What?"

"She left," Davis said. "She left *me* to go to *her*."

A pause.

• 282 •

"And did you go after her?"

"Did you hear what I said?" Davis snapped. "I opened up to her. I let myself need someone. I practically begged her not to go, and she left. Why should I chase her?"

"Oh, I don't know, maybe for all those reasons you listed. You trust her, you want her, you need her, yadda yadda yadda."

"Cass, I felt like my heart had been hung out to bleed dry. I can't subject myself to that."

"Okay, but—"

"Every time Nic calls, Anna will run to her."

Cass remained silent for a long moment. "Ah…don't you think there are extenuating circumstances here?"

"Nic wasn't dying, and Anna all but said she'd stay by her side for the recovery."

"*All but* said?"

"She's said before that thirteen years of marriage don't just disappear."

"Which they don't."

"Right!"

"Right…how?"

Davis blew out a frustrated sigh. "Obviously they have something I can't compete with, Cass. And as long as Nic's between us we're just going to keep hurting each other."

"Davis, listen to me a second," Cass said, her voice forceful. "I don't want to say 'I told you so,' but—"

"Then don't." Davis practically whimpered. This was exactly why she hadn't wanted to talk to Cass. "It doesn't make me feel any better to know Nic's robbed me of hope and trust and a belief in forever all over again."

"That's a little dramatic, don't you think? And you're not hearing me." Cass paused, as if challenging her to argue. When she spoke again, her tone was low, serious. "No one has a lower opinion of what Nic did than I do. But destroying your future—twice—is a lot of power to give her, wouldn't you say?"

"You don't understand."

"Make me understand."

"You don't know what it felt like to open up to Anna, to touch her, to kiss her." Davis felt light-headed at the memory. "The part of me I thought was dead came back to life."

"Well, obviously Anna didn't feel good enough to override your hatred of Nic—"

"What are you talking a—?"

"Or," Cass demanded, "or you would've gone with her."

Time stopped. Davis couldn't believe she was hearing this.

"Wait. You're the one who told me how stupid I'd be to pursue Anna."

"Of course it would be stupid to chase Anna when you're still hung up on Nic."

"Anna's hung up on Nic, not me."

"Really? Annabelle's touch raised you from the metaphorical dead, and you *let her go* just to spite your ex? That sounds like a pretty big hang-up to me."

"Y-you're not making any sense."

"No, darling. I'm making perfect sense, and I'm saying the same thing I've said all along, even from your first night with Nic." Cass sounded exasperated, patient, and coolly logical all at once. "You'll never have a future with Anna, or anyone else for that matter, until you cut her and me and every one of your sob stories out of the equation completely. Make your own damn decisions for once."

Suddenly Anna's words about how she was done letting other people make decisions for her came rushing back. Anna'd stood up for herself and tried to hold onto her, too. She'd asked her to go along. Anna had held on.

Davis was the one who'd let go.

The sense of loss, of damage, of error crushed her.

❖

Annabelle slept fitfully in a chair for a few hours. Nic hadn't stirred since opening her eyes earlier. The doctors said she might not be fully awake for days, but her vital signs were as strong as could be expected. She had a row of stitches across her right eyebrow, and her nose and cheek were black with bruises. Internally she hadn't fared any better. The surgeons had had to place a metal rod in her leg and remove her spleen, but they'd finally stopped the bleeding, at least in the literal sense. Figuratively, Anna feared there would be open wounds for a long time, and not just for Nic.

God, what had she been doing? Lab work showed her blood-alcohol levels were more than twice the legal limit, and one of the doctors mentioned Nic didn't appear to have any solid food in her system. Clearly she had been eating, though, because she'd gained twenty pounds since Annabelle had last seen her. She looked again at the outline of Nic's body under the thin white sheet. It would be easy to focus on the signs of trauma. The bruises and scrapes, or the wires to monitors and IVs, served as a map to all the ways things had gone wrong. However, Annabelle wasn't squeamish, and she wasn't naive enough to think a single trauma could so transform the strong, proud, beautiful woman she'd once loved into this shell of a human being.

The dark circles under pallid skin, the strands of gray in her too-long hair, and the ring of extra weight indicated bad food and inactivity. Maybe a stranger would have missed the signs, and she wished she could ignore them, too, but she knew that body too well not to realize Nic had been slowly killing herself for months.

The thought hurt.

Maybe it shouldn't.

The idea of Nic destroying herself didn't bother Davis. Perhaps it shouldn't tear Annabelle up either, but she couldn't help what she felt. She couldn't pretend thirteen years of her life hadn't happened, and even if she could, she couldn't stand to see another human being—any other human being—suffer. If she'd come across a crash on her way home, she would've taken the victim to the hospital and made sure she received treatment. She'd wonder about her and worry and check in with her. Maybe she wouldn't spend the night by her bedside, but why would Davis expect her to feel less for Nic than she would a stranger?

Actually, she knew why. Davis was hurt and scared. Annabelle's heart broke at the memory of those green eyes clouded with tears. Davis was so strong, so stoic and independent. What must it have cost her to say she needed Anna? And so soon after she'd allowed herself to trust. If anyone understood what a tenuous balance trust could be, it was Annabelle. Maybe Davis was right. Annabelle never could be free of Nic, but not in the way Davis suspected. She didn't want to erase her past or forget the lessons she'd learned about herself. If only Davis would give her a chance to explain, but the more she tried, the more she hurt her. Maybe the others were right. Maybe they were destined to hurt each other.

She couldn't rehash her decisions any more. She'd always end up in the same place, and she'd decided to stop going in circles months ago. She had to move forward. She had to focus on things she could control. She had to fall back on the numbness and emptiness, survival skills she'd learned to depend on, but she couldn't shut out the memory of Davis's mouth against her skin, or the heartbreak in her voice when she'd begged her to stay.

She'd been able to compartmentalize thirteen years of memories but couldn't forget two hours in the embrace of a woman she'd known only a few months. It made no sense. Was it all too fresh? Had she been lonelier than she'd let herself admit? Had Davis's touch awakened something powerful in her body, or was it in her heart?

Sadness overtook her. She hung her head in her hands and took deep breaths, but the tears came anyway. She hadn't cried in months, and now sitting in an intensive-care unit, she wasn't crying for the broken woman in the bed beside her. The tears she shed were for Davis, whose wounds weren't visible but would likely take longer to heal. She cried for herself and the loss of a hope that had only begun to blossom.

"Belle?"

The voice was so soft she wasn't sure she'd actually heard it.

"Belle, are you crying?"

She wiped her eyes as she scooted closer to the bed. "Yes, but don't worry yourself about that."

Nic focused in on her face as if searching for something. "Are you crying over me?"

"It's complicated." She forced a smile. "How are you feeling?"

"Bad."

"I can get the nurse. Maybe they can give you something for the pain."

"I don't think they have anything that will work on this kind of pain, and even if they did, I don't know if I'd take it."

"What do you mean?"

"I've been running from this pain for a while now," Nic said, between heavy breaths. "Running isn't getting me anywhere. I deserve to feel it."

Annabelle was afraid to admit Nic's assessment might be true for more than one of them. "No one deserves pain, Nic, not even you."

"Maybe I need it, though. I thought being numb was better than pain, but numbness is painful, too."

"I know what you mean."

Nic's blue eyes weren't as clear as in the past, but they could still pierce her defenses. "I think you do understand. I'm sorry, Belle. So sorry."

"Hush." She sat back. "What's done is done."

"Is it?"

Annabelle watched her silently. Where had this reflective side of Nic come from? She didn't like it. She had no answers to these kinds of questions.

"Why are you here, Belle?"

"I'm still your power of attorney. The hospital needed someone to sign paperwork."

"You could have refused."

"Davis said the same thing." Anger rebounded, pushing some of the sadness out of her chest, and she sat up. "You know, fine. Maybe I should have."

"I didn't mean to sound ungrateful. I just didn't give you any reason to care about what happens to me." Nic shook her head, then grimaced. "I didn't even care what happened to me."

"Well, Nic, I know you might find this hard to believe, but sometimes it's not about you."

Nic stared at her for a long minute before she smiled. "Wow."

"I signed your paperwork. Deal with it." Anna flopped back into her chair and continued more calmly. "I'm a grown woman. I can make my own decisions."

"Okay."

"No, it's not just okay. It's better than okay. I've got my own interests and instincts, and I really don't need anyone else in my life to tell me where or how or what I should care about." Annabelle was on a roll. Nic could have lost consciousness and she would have kept right on. "Sure, I could've left you alone. I could've stayed when Davis asked me to. I could've walked out on both of you for trying to control me, but that's not who I am. And despite what either of you say, I like who I am. I like making my own choices. I trust my judgment."

"I'm envious of you."

"Let's not get ahead of yourself." She didn't feel like someone to envy. Her heart ached. She missed Davis's presence, her touch, her strength, and try as she might, she couldn't stop herself from wondering if any woman would love her if she didn't bow to their will. Was it possible to be herself while being with someone else?

"No, really. You know your own mind. I'm jealous."

"Really? I've never known you to be indecisive or apologetic about what you want."

Nic stared at the ceiling and sighed. "Maybe not indecisive. But I've begun to wonder if I've made my life decisions for the wrong reasons."

"What do you mean?" This wasn't the smooth, calculated Nic she knew. Her conflict was disarming in a completely different way than her confidence had been, which made Annabelle skeptical.

Nic seemed to wrestle with her thoughts before saying, "I can't remember a time when I wasn't proving myself to someone else. I never stopped to think about what I really wanted to do."

"I'm sorry if I contributed to that," Annabelle said sincerely. "I didn't mean to pressure you into a life you didn't want or make you feel responsible for my happiness."

"No. I'm sorry for wrapping you up in all of my issues. They started long before you." Nic frowned. "I did love you, but I've started to realize I never really saw you. You're clearly better off without me."

Certainly she lived a fuller, more self-directed life, but a lonelier one. Or at least it had been lonely except for the few hours she'd spent holding Davis. "It's all subjective, Nic, but if you're looking for absolution from me, if that's what you need, you've got it."

"I'm not sure what I'm looking for. I'm tired of running and not knowing what I'm running toward."

"Maybe it's easier that way, but running toward things didn't lead either of us to anything worth holding onto."

"But you do feel better now, right?"

She didn't feel very good at the moment. "I like myself a lot more than I did a year ago."

"Good." Nic hesitated, as though she wanted to say something else.

"If you have something to say, I suggest you do so." Annabelle shook her head. "I've learned a hard truth is better than a pretty lie."

Nic stared at her in wonder. "I'm so impressed with you, but I'm confused, too." She seemed almost sheepish. "Is it the pain or medicines, or did you mention Davis earlier?"

Now it was Annabelle's turn to look at the ceiling. She no longer felt the need to soothe Nic's fears or ego, but how could she put into words something she couldn't even label yet? "We've…spent some time together lately."

"I don't know what to say." Nic cleared her throat nervously. "I would say I don't believe it. But after hearing you talk, I guess it makes sense."

Annabelle rolled her eyes. "Maybe you need another CAT scan, because most people can't think of anything that makes less sense than me spending time with your ex-mistress."

Both of them winced at the term. She didn't know why she'd even said it. She didn't think of Davis as belonging to Nic at all, certainly not in such reductive terms. The distance she tried to force between them didn't feel right, not in the way Davis's lips had felt right. Somehow Davis had taken a powerful place in her heart, but her heart was a traitor, and for some reason this betrayal hurt more than all the others.

Tears stung her eyes, and she covered them with her hands.

"God," Nic whispered, the sound filtered through wonder. "Belle, are…are you…in love with Davis?"

Annabelle's face flamed, and her pulse accelerated so quickly she got light-headed. The overwhelmingly visceral response transported her back to the heated press of Davis's lips against her own. "I…I'm not ready."

"Not ready?"

"I mean, it's only been six months. You hurt me. And trust, Nic, how can I?"

"So no?"

No?

She didn't love Davis?

She needed more time to process, to heal. She needed to wait. She needed space and perspective. No, there had to be some other reason she felt so at ease in Davis's presence, and another explanation for the abiding trust they shared. Then there was the small issue of her powerful attraction to Davis…and the passion she stirred in parts of Annabelle that she'd tried to bury after the emotional wreckage of Nic's betrayal.

And what about the way she ached to hold Davis, touch her, to soothe her pain?

"Belle?"

"It's too soon. I'm not ready to say it."

"Oh." Nic looked at her with a mix of disbelief and humor. "I suppose you get to decide when you say something, but don't have much control over when you feel it."

Her heart swelled in her chest until each breath hurt. How had she not realized? Had she deliberately tried to force her heart to remain closed? Last night when everything had become too much to ignore, had she purposefully pushed Davis away? And now that she had slammed the door, could she reopen it? Did she even want to?

"What about Davis?" Nic asked. "Does she love you?"

Annabelle began to cry again, and this time she didn't try to stop or hide the tears running down her cheeks. Maybe Davis could have loved her if Anna had given her the chance instead of betraying her in a way that reaffirmed her deepest insecurities. Her shoulders shook with the onset of jagged sobs.

"I'm so sorry, Belle," Nic said. "Maybe with time she could feel the same way you do."

"Or maybe I already do," Davis said, causing Nic and Annabelle to jump.

"Davis." Anna gasped and tried to blink away the image, unwilling to believe she was really there. Davis's copper hair stood out at odd angles. Her eyes were red-rimmed and puffy, and her shoulder pressed against the doorframe as if supporting the weight she didn't have the energy to bear. She looked terrible, but Annabelle couldn't imagine a more beautiful sight. "What are you doing here?"

Davis shrugged. "Maybe I'm not ready to say it either, but that doesn't mean I don't feel it."

Annabelle was in her arms in an instant—delirious, giddy, and so painfully relieved. She didn't need a formal declaration of love or a fairy-tale ride into the sunset. She only needed Davis.

Davis surrendered to the rightness of the woman in her arms, oblivious to her surroundings or her audience. Pressing her lips to Anna's, she let go of everything else and clung to the connection between them. Tasting the salt of their mingled tears, she marveled how quickly they'd transitioned from cries of sadness to ones of joy. She cupped Anna's face in her hands, running her thumbs along her perfectly smooth skin, clearing away any reminder of the pain she'd caused. It wouldn't be as easy to erase the doubts and insecurities between them, but she felt an overpowering sense of gratitude about having the opportunity to try. Hope, promise, and potential were words she feared would never apply to her, but in Anna's kiss she experienced them all.

Nic coughed behind them, pulling them back into the moment. If Davis wasn't so happy, she might've strangled her for interrupting. Instead she said, "Hello, Nic."

"Hi, Davis. I'm glad to see you."

Davis scanned her battered form, finding little resemblance to the woman she'd fallen for, and even less appeal when she compared her to the woman she held now. Still, something akin to compassion stirred in her when she met the haunted blue of Nic's eyes. "I suppose I'm glad you didn't die."

Nic nodded. "Fair enough."

"Will you give us a minute?" Davis nodded to the doorway.

"Please," Nic said, sounding more exhausted with every exchange.

Not wanting to break the contact between them, she took both of Anna's hands in her own and backed out the door.

In the hallway, Anna jumped back into her arms. "What made you come?"

"I realized I didn't really want to be anywhere else."

"But Nic—"

"This isn't about Nic anymore. It hasn't been for a long time, and I'm sorry for not seeing that sooner." She lifted Anna's hand to her lips and kissed each of her fingertips. "I was so afraid she still had a hold on you and that's why you left. I wanted to go after you, but I made myself crazy thinking that if I caved now I'd never be free of her. If it hadn't involved *her*, I would've followed you anywhere."

Annabelle's eyes glistened with fresh tears. "What changed your mind?"

"You did. I remembered what you said about how living your life in opposition to someone gives them just as much control as living for them. It wasn't easy, but when I cut Nic out of the equation, there was no question about what I wanted. It's you, Annabelle."

"Do you really mean that? Do you really think we can have a life without her?"

"I don't know. I'm still afraid sometimes, and insecure, and I can't unlearn all my defenses in one night. I wish I could promise you a picture-perfect life, the life you deserve, but I'm a mess."

"Maybe I need a little more mess in my life." Anna laughed.

"Really?"

"I've already tried the picture-perfect life. Look where it got me." She nodded over her shoulder to Nic's hospital room. "All the pretty trappings were empty, and so was I. If we're going to take a chance on each other, I'd rather try something real."

"Something real. I want that, too." Davis barely finished the phrase before Anna was back in her arms, oblivious to anyone who might be watching, making it clear once again that all that mattered was them.

EPILOGUE

February

"Hey, Nic, I thought you had to catch the five o'clock bus," one of her colleagues, a young woman with dark eyes and a pretty smile, said.

She'd seen her around a few times in her first two weeks at work, though she'd yet to learn her name. She was cute and seemed genuinely interested in getting to know Nic, which would've been enough a few months ago, and maybe someday Nic would feel up for that kind of interest again. Right now she was content to steal one more look at the expanse of Turner Field laid out before her. "Yeah, I gotta get going. I just haven't gotten used to this view."

"Wait until you see your own work up on the Jumbotron. You'll never want to go home then." The woman clasped her on the shoulder and then walked away. Nic did look forward to that day, but not out of any sense of pride in her own sales prowess. Her work now held more appeal than personal accomplishment and more importance than the joy she got from working in a ballpark, even though baseball had been one of the first things she'd learned she really enjoyed. She liked coming to work in the mornings now because her work had meaning. She was still in sales, but instead of making money for a multinational corporation, she solicited sponsors for the Braves' charitable foundation. Her first assignment was to find businesses to pledge a specific amount for every double play the Braves would make over the course of the upcoming season.

She smiled even as she jogged through the rain-soaked parking lot to catch her bus. She was running late, but it wouldn't do any good to hurry. Speeding wasn't an option when someone else was driving. No more Lexus. She didn't even have a driver's license since she'd pled guilty to a DUI, and yet instead of feeling embarrassed or dependent, she felt incredibly grateful to be alive.

Of course the fear and the doubt could still overwhelm her, especially alone late at night. She awoke sometimes in a cold sweat, running from some phantom pressure to perform, to push harder, to succeed, but with the help of her therapist she was learning to work through the urge to produce answers out of the darkness. She had a second chance to decide who she was, and she wouldn't rush into the same mistakes. Patience was a big step. Admitting she was lost helped, too, and learning to ask for help was probably the most important yet.

She wouldn't learn any of those lessons overnight, but for once in her life she felt proud of the process and not just the results.

Stepping off the bus downtown, she splashed through a frigid puddle and gritted her teeth against the bite of cold that soaked through her shoes and socks. So maybe everything about her new life wasn't perfect. She would've rather been warm and dry back at work, or even at her new apartment closer to the ballpark, instead of tromping around the back of a church to the basement entrance. Her stomach rumbled as she passed a tray of pastries and a pot of coffee near the door, too, but she kept walking. This was an important meeting, one she needed to be at her best for, and she wasn't going to fill her body with caffeine or sugar to get through it.

Nic nodded to the few people around the long conference-style table, but she didn't talk. She didn't need to schmooze or fill the space with empty chatter. She tried not to tap her toe or fidget nervously as she watched the clock hand tick closer to starting time. It wasn't a boardroom, but she felt like this might be the most important meeting she'd ever attended.

At six o'clock sharp, a woman called the meeting to order. As they went around the table to introduce themselves, Nic tried to remain present, but she couldn't stop herself from glancing toward the door. She tried to tamp down her disappointment when her turn to speak rolled around. She'd hoped she wouldn't have to do this alone.

"Nic, do you have something you want to say tonight?"

"Yeah, um, I mean yes, I do. I'm Nic McCoy." The next words stuck in her throat, so she paused and stuffed her hands into her pockets, trying to hide their trembling. She looked up to try again just as the door opened and Annabelle pushed through, shaking the rain from her long blond hair. Davis followed closely behind, muttering an apology for being late and tracking mud onto the clean linoleum.

"It's okay. I'm glad you made it," Nic said with a broad smile, her joy tempered only by a twinge of sadness at the look of tenderness Annabelle directed toward Davis as she took her coat. She was happy for them and proud of them too, but the reminder of what she'd lost only underscored the gravity of what she had to say.

She looked into Annabelle's blue eyes full of sympathy and Davis's stoic expression for strength. These women had been through fire by no choice of their own, and she had no right to ask their forgiveness, but their growth and courage had inspired her to try.

"I was saying that I'm Nic McCoy, and I'm an addict."

Davis listened closely as Nic stated she'd been sober and had abstained from sex for ninety-three days before Nic began to share the story of her downward spiral.

She hadn't yet fully warmed to the idea of playing any sort of role in Nic's recovery. She wanted to move forward, and with a woman like Anna by her side, who wouldn't? She understood helping Nic get the medical treatment she needed, but once she could walk again, the legal trouble had started. She had been slightly impressed when Nic had taken full responsibility for her actions and had pled guilty to the slew of charges against her. Davis grudgingly admitted the Nic she'd known would've tried and probably succeeded in talking her way out of trouble. Anna had gone to the court date, but Davis had stayed away. She'd also stayed home the night Nic cleared out her office at her old job and the day she'd moved into her new apartment.

Annabelle, on the other hand, marked each occasion with a helping hand and a kind word. It wasn't easy at first to watch her go or to hear the pride in her voice when she told of Nic's latest accomplishment. At times the only thing that had kept her from dissolving into a brooding mass of insecurities was the way Anna always seemed to know when she needed to be reassured with a kiss or a touch. As if on cue, Anna took her hand as Nic approached the portion of her story when she and Davis had met.

"I spent so much time telling myself both women needed me and I could make them happy, even that I loved them both." Nic sighed, and her voice quavered. "The more I lied, the more I believed myself. I feel sick now because I think, in a way, I did love them both, but not the way either of them deserved. I loved them for what they offered me, which wasn't really loving them. It was always about me. I had to prove myself. I couldn't stand to lose, even something that made me happy. Hell, I didn't even know what happiness really was."

Davis squeezed Anna's hand. The story wasn't hers, but it carried enough similarities to make her shiver. She'd built her own barriers to happiness. She'd let fear and self-preservation rule her life. She'd defined her life against her family, against Nic, against vulnerability, and in doing so she'd almost lost her chance at genuine fulfillment.

"It'd be easy to blame the sex addiction for the affair, but honestly that didn't come until later, when I'd already lost everything that mattered. Sex was an easier high than maintaining a relationship, and drinking saved me from having to think about what I was doing, but they were temporary fixes, and soon a little bit wasn't enough. I needed more, and I chased it to the detriment of my job, my health, and ultimately my safety." Nic shuddered as sweat began to bead on her forehead. "You can cut yourself off from purpose, meaning, and basic personal connections only for so long before you start to devolve into something almost less than human."

Davis had a hard time watching her like this. Her voice shook, and her hands did, too. Her skin wasn't as pale as it had been in the hospital, but close. Davis couldn't muster any sympathy for her actions, but Nic's willingness to put herself through the torture of reliving her darkest moments in order to start to heal took courage and fortitude. It would be impossible not to be a little moved by Nic's attempt to clean her slate.

"The bigger the void got, the more it took to fill it, until one day I couldn't fill it anymore. I was drunk and hurting and running from everything I'd done and everything I couldn't do. I wrapped my car around a telephone pole, and all I could think of as I blacked out was, 'Thank God, it's over now.'"

Davis's heart beat a little faster, and she glanced at Anna to see her wipe a tear from her cheek. The night of the accident had been hard for all of them, and reliving it from Nic's perspective exhumed Davis's own guilt and regret over her willingness to abandon her. Nic hadn't been the only one consumed by fear, and it wasn't impossible to see how quickly things could spin out of control.

"When I came to, I was so embarrassed to see the two women I'd hurt most. They shouldn't have been there. I didn't deserve their concern any more than they deserved what I'd put them through. The physical pain didn't compare to how much it hurt to watch them struggle toward some sort of peace with themselves and each other. I'd been sorry before that point, at least on some surface level, but that morning in the hospital was the first time I really understood remorse." Nic hung her head. "I can't ever undo the damage I caused. I'll live with that for the rest of my life."

She looked up and made eye contact with Anna and then Davis. "When I look at your strength and your grace and how far you've come in your own lives, I believe I might make it, too. I wouldn't dare ask for your forgiveness, but I promise to live every day trying to be worthy of this second chance."

Davis blinked away her own tears, moved by Nic's emotion and her apparent sincerity. It would ultimately take actions to soften her heart completely, but for the first time she found herself pulling for Nic. She wanted to believe she could change, and she was encouraged by what she'd seen here tonight. Maybe she should say that. The room was disturbingly quiet, the gravity of what they'd all heard weighing heavily in the air between them. She was torn by her need for time and space to process her own emotions and the urge to fill the silence.

Nic wasn't the only one facing her demons tonight.

"Nic," Annabelle finally said quietly, "I'm proud of what you're doing here. This wasn't easy for any of us. I didn't want to relive everything tonight or ever. It still hurts, and I'm not sure the pain will ever go away completely. I struggle with distrust and sadness. No matter how far we move forward from this point, I'll never forget your betrayal, but I do forgive you whether you ask me to or not."

Nic closed her eyes, and her shoulders sagged with relief, "Thank you, Annabelle."

"You're welcome, but letting go means as much to me as it does to you. I'll never thank you or be grateful for what you did to me, to Davis, to yourself, but I honestly believe I'm better off now than a year ago. I believe you are, too."

"I am, too," Davis interjected. She wasn't ready to forgive. She wasn't even ready to outwardly applaud Nic's steps toward recovery, but it would be unfair to all of them for her not to acknowledge she was a better person with a better life and a shot at a better future than before she'd met Nic. "I'm not as sweet or as full of grace as Anna, but without you and all the fucked-up things you did, I wouldn't have her in my life. I like to think there was a better way to get us to this point, but ultimately I'm glad we're here. I hope someday you can say the same."

Nic nodded. "Thank you, Davis. I do, too."

A few people came up to shake Nic's hand after the meeting, and Anna spoke with the facilitator about the possibility of baking cookies for the future meetings, but Davis leaned against the wall, lost in her own thoughts. She should've been happier, but melancholy hung over her even as Anna looped her arm around her waist and said, "Let's go home."

They climbed the basement stairs back into the rain-soaked parking lot. As she opened the door to Annabelle's car, footsteps fell behind them, and she turned to see Nic on her way out as well. Her tall frame didn't seem nearly as commanding, huddled against the cold drizzle on her way toward the bus stop. The wave of compassion flowed so quickly she didn't have to second-guess herself before calling out, "Nic, you want a ride?"

Nic turned and squinted through the rain before her smile burst broad and bright across her face. "Thank you, Davis, but you go on home. You've got warmer places to be tonight."

She glanced at Annabelle. That was true, but she was finally making peace with the fact that Anna would be there, even if Nic was, too. "Are you sure?"

"Yes." Nic nodded. "The bus suits me just fine these days."

Davis chuckled and got in the car. "Maybe she is changing."

"Did you know she goes to church, too?"

"Really? And lightning hasn't struck the building?"

"Come on, I'm proud of her," Anna chided gently, then took her hand. "But I'm proud of you too, you know?"

"Yeah?" She could hardly believe the thought. They'd taken things slowly, resisting the urge to rush toward each other. Instead they'd shared dinners and movies and a few holiday traditions in a genuine attempt to get to know each other not just for who they'd been, but for who they could become. Still, it was impossible not to get swept up in Anna sometimes. She was so beautiful and caring, so sexy and so strong. Silk covering iron. The idea of Davis having anything to offer a woman like her, much less make her proud, was still difficult to comprehend.

"I know coming here tonight was hard for you, too," Anna said. "She hurt you. A lesser woman would be consumed by that, but you've worked so hard to not let her control you."

"I thought of that when she talked tonight. It scared me because I realized that could have been me."

"No," Annabelle said, "don't be silly. You'd never hurt anyone."

"I hope not. I'd hate to drag someone else down with me, but I lived in fear and closed myself off. I craved the numbness she talked about. I ran from honest relationships because I didn't trust my own judgment. Solitude was my drug of choice and anger my fallback emotion, but who's to say I couldn't have done the same thing with alcohol? You saved me from myself."

"You made those decisions for yourself."

"Maybe, but you made me want to try, and you showed me how. I might not have wanted to die, but I wasn't truly living until I felt your lips against mine."

Anna pulled into her driveway and turned to face Davis. "You know that goes both ways, right? You taught me who I could be, and it's so much more than I thought. You gave me the freedom to become someone I actually like, and I know I haven't always made it easy on you, but I couldn't have survived the last year without you by my side."

"I want to be by your side. Always." She smiled, realizing what she'd just said. "I couldn't imagine saying this even a few months ago, but you're in my heart so deep I can't not say it. I love you."

Annabelle kissed her soulfully, then, cupping her face in her hands, she pulled them apart just enough to look into her eyes. "Davis—"

"You don't have to say it if you're not ready."

"Ready or not, I love you, Davis." She laughed. "God, that feels good to say."

Davis grinned like the love-struck fool she'd finally admitted to being. "Really?"

"Yes. So many people will tell us it's too soon, but now that it's out, all I can think is why did we wait so long?"

She kissed Anna again. "I'll say it every day for the rest of our lives if you'll let me."

"I'd like that, but I don't want you to just tell me. I want you to show me."

"I'll do that, too, every day."

"No." Anna's smile turned sultry. "Show me now."

Davis's breath caught painfully in her chest as all the blood in her body suddenly rushed downward. "I, um, do you mean, you want…?"

Annabelle pressed a finger to her lips. "I love you. I want you. I want to make love to you."

There were no words and no fear. Awe mixed with a strong dose of desire carried them up the stairs. Davis closed the door to the apartment, leaving all the thoughts of how far they'd come on the outside. Tonight she'd revel in the luxury of marveling at where they were headed, together.

❖

Annabelle watched Davis's eyes darken with desire and felt the same flame spark in her. She'd invited Davis into her bed because she'd first claimed a place in her heart, but once she opened the door to those emotions her body quickly demanded for its own needs to be acknowledged.

Davis seemed tentative, almost reverent as she crossed the tiny apartment and stood a few inches away from the bed. Annabelle slipped off her jacket and slowly unbuttoned her blouse, letting it hang loosely from her shoulders while Davis watched, her chest rising and falling noticeably with each breath she took. Her awe-filled expression only endeared her further to Annabelle, but she wasn't a piece of fine china, fragile and cold. The strength of her need made her burn for Davis in a way that overwhelmed her. Her days of following had long passed, and she thrilled at the power surging through her as she caught her finger in a belt loop of Davis's jeans. Tugging her so close their bodies pressed together and her lips brushed against Davis's ear, she whispered, "Touch me."

That seemed all the inspiration Davis needed to shed her reserve. Wrapping her arms around Annabelle's waist, she backed her to the bed. Falling, tumbling, clutching one another, they were immediately intertwined. Every touch singed a trail of heat across her skin, and she tugged Davis's shirt over her head in a near-frenzied attempt to gain better access to her body. She pressed her mouth to every part of Davis she could reach—lips, neck, shoulders. The more she consumed, the more hunger consumed her.

Davis tasted delicious, her unique scent filling her senses and pulling her in for more. She felt greedy, but that didn't stop her from unapologetically rolling Davis onto her back and unclasping her belt. She didn't know what affected her more, the reaction of Davis's body to her touch or the way her own nerve endings buzzed with excitement. Davis didn't give her time to ponder the question as she sat up, pulling her close once again so Annabelle knelt over her lap. She pushed her blouse off her shoulders and kissed a line just above the lace trim of Annabelle's bra.

"Take it off," Annabelle rasped in a voice so low it barely registered as her own.

If the command or the tone in which it was delivered surprised Davis, she didn't show it. She quickly unclasped the bra and slid the straps down Annabelle's shoulders, taking a moment to look at her breasts. Anna blushed under the lustful gaze, but out of arousal rather than shyness. She loved the way Davis looked at her. Running her fingers around Davis's neck and into her hair, she pulled her head back until their eyes locked. "I want you so much it makes me crazy."

They kissed feverishly, giving their hands freedom to explore each other, caressing backs, sides, and breasts. She'd never been like this—voracious, ravenous—and she didn't want to stop. With Davis she was safe, free, loved, and desired. Rolling them back onto the mattress, Annabelle pushed Davis's jeans and underwear down to her ankles. She kissed a line between her breasts and down her stomach, breathing deeply dizzying breaths filled with Davis's scent.

"Anna, God, I won't last long," Davis panted through clenched teeth. "Please, let me see you."

The tenderness behind the plea melted her rapidly beating heart. Reversing her path she crawled back up Davis's body, kissing every inch of skin she could reach along the way. The fire built steadily without any barriers between them, but now the passion burned with a purpose. The rightness of their bodies pressed against the length of one another, curve to hollow, and the depth of emotion that passed between them with each glance and lingering look reaffirmed that what they shared went deeper than the all-consuming physical need of the moment.

Annabelle straddled Davis's legs and slipped a hand between them. She groaned as Davis opened to her, revealing her willingness to surrender to Annabelle's desire.

"You feel so good."

"No, it's you. I want more of you. All of you." Davis arched her back, allowing Annabelle to slip fully inside her. A gasp, an exhale, or maybe a groan escaped both of their lips as they became a part of one another. Annabelle fought the urge to close her eyes and submerge herself fully in the sensations surrounding her. Davis was too stunning to miss a moment of her.

"You're so beautiful." Annabelle ran her free hand across the plane of Davis's stomach. "I wish you could see yourself right now."

"I don't have to. I can see how you see me."

Davis arched herself into a sitting position, kissing Anna as she clung to her back. Red light flashed behind her eyelids as Davis licked and sucked her way across her chest, then worked a hand between their bodies. Her hips rocked forward, seemingly of their own accord, as Davis stroked closer to the center of her need.

"I don't want to let go of you," Annabelle mumbled as her movements became more erratic.

"Don't. Please don't."

They kissed until they had to gasp for air, and even then they broke apart only the distance of a shared breath. Riding the heat of their passion, they moved together, one seamless rhythm of pleasure. Every time Anna reached for more, Davis met her need, giving her everything she craved, then begging for more. Pressure built in her chest and radiated through her body. She clung to Davis, pushing everything from her heart into the connection that exploded between them.

Calling out, she threw her head back and pushed into Davis one more time to feel her muscles contract in a chain of release. Thunder reverberated through her in waves until she collapsed onto Davis's still-heaving chest.

"I love you."

Davis kissed her forehead. "I love you, too."

Annabelle snuggled into the crook of Davis arm, basking in the perfection of the moment and marveling at how words that had seemed so momentous earlier now felt almost inadequate in the aftermath of such a powerful affirmation of their truth. They did love each other, they trusted each other, they were right for each other, but no amount of saying those things could compare to the prospect of a lifetime spent living them.

About the Author

Rachel Spangler never set out to be an award-winning author. She was just so poor and easily bored during her college years that she had to come up with creative ways to entertain herself, and her first novel, *Learning Curve,* was born out of one such attempt. She was sincerely surprised when it was accepted for publication and even more shocked when it won the Golden Crown Literary Award for Debut Author. She also won a Goldie for her second novel, *Trails Merge.* Since writing is more fun than a real job and so much cheaper than therapy, Rachel continued to type away, leading to the publication of *The Long Way Home, LoveLife, Spanish Heart,* and *Does She Love You?* She plans to continue writing as long as anyone anywhere will keep reading.

Rachel and her partner, Susan, are raising their young son in western New York, where during the winter they make the most of the lake effect snow on local ski slopes. In the summer, they love to travel and watch their beloved St. Louis Cardinals. Regardless of the season, she always makes time for a good romance, whether she's reading it, writing it, or living it.

For more information visit Rachel online at www.rachelspangler .com or on Facebook.

Books Available from Bold Strokes Books

The Rarest Rose by I. Beacham. After a decade of living in her beloved house, Ele disturbs its past and finds her life being haunted by the presence of a ghost who will show her that true love never dies. (978-1-60282-884-1)

Code of Honor by Radclyffe. The face of terror is hard to recognize—especially when it's homegrown. The next book in the Honor series. (978-1-60282-885-8)

Does She Love You? by Rachel Spangler. When Annabelle and Davis find out they are both in a relationship with the same woman, it leaves them facing life-altering questions about trust, redemption, and the possibility of finding love in the wake of betrayal. (978-1-60282-886-5)

The Road to Her by KE Payne. Sparks fly when actress Holly Croft, star of UK soap Portobello Road, meets her new on-screen love interest, the enigmatic and sexy Elise Manford. (978-1-60282-887-2)

Shadows of Something Real by Sophia Kell Hagin. Trying to escape flashbacks and nightmares, ex-POW Jamie Gwynmorgan stumbles into the heart of former Red Cross worker Adele Sabellius and uncovers a deadly conspiracy against everything and everyone she loves. (978-1-60282-889-6)

Date with Destiny by Mason Dixon. When sophisticated bank executive Rashida Ivey meets unemployed blue collar worker Destiny Jackson, will her life ever be the same? (978-1-60282-878-0)

The Devil's Orchard by Ali Vali. Cain and Emma plan a wedding before the birth of their third child while Juan Luis is still lurking, and as Cain plans for his death, an unexpected visitor arrives and challenges her belief in her father, Dalton Casey. (978-1-60282-879-7)

Secrets and Shadows by L.T. Marie. A bodyguard and the woman she protects run from a madman and into each other's arms. (978-1-60282-880-3)

Change Horizon: Three Novellas by Gun Brooke. Three stories of courageous women who dare to love as they fight to claim a future in a hostile universe. (978-1-60282-881-0)

Scarlet Thirst by Crin Claxton. When hot, feisty Rani meets cool, vampire Rob, one lifetime isn't enough, and the road from human to vampire is shorter than you think... (978-1-60282-856-8)

Battle Axe by Carsen Taite. How close is too close? Bounty hunter Luca Bennett will soon find out. (978-1-60282-871-1)

Improvisation by Karis Walsh. High school geometry teacher Jan Carroll thinks she's figured out the shape of her life and her future, until graphic artist and fiddle player Tina Nelson comes along and teaches her to improvise. (978-1-60282-872-8)

For Want of a Fiend by Barbara Ann Wright. Without her Fiendish power, can Princess Katya and her consort Starbride stop a magic-wielding madman from sparking an uprising in the kingdom of Farraday? (978-1-60282-873-5)

Broken in Soft Places by Fiona Zedde. The instant Sara Chambers meets the seductive and sinful Merille Thompson, she falls hard, but knowing the difference between love and a dangerous, all-consuming desire is just one of the lessons Sara must learn before it's too late. (978-1-60282-876-6)

Healing Hearts by Donna K. Ford. Running from tragedy, the women of Willow Springs find that with friendship, there is hope, and with love, there is everything. (978-1-60282-877-3)

Desolation Point by Cari Hunter. When a storm strands Sarah Kent in the North Cascades, Alex Pascal is determined to find her. Neither imagines the dangers they will face when a ruthless criminal begins to hunt them down. (978-1-60282-865-0)

I Remember by Julie Cannon. What happens when you can never forget the first kiss, the first touch, the first taste of lips on skin? What happens when you know you will remember every single detail of a mysterious woman? (978-1-60282-866-7)

The Gemini Deception by Kim Baldwin and Xenia Alexiou. The truth, the whole truth, and nothing but lies. Book six in the Elite Operatives series. (978-1-60282-867-4)

Scarlet Revenge by Sheri Lewis Wohl. When faith alone isn't enough, will the love of one woman be strong enough to save a vampire from damnation? (978-1-60282-868-1)

Ghost Trio by Lillian Q. Irwin. When Lee Howe hears the voice of her dead lover singing to her, is it a hallucination, a ghost, or something more sinister? (978-1-60282-869-8)

The Princess Affair by Nell Stark. Rhodes Scholar Kerry Donovan arrives at Oxford ready to focus on her studies, but her life and her priorities are thrown into chaos when she catches the eye of Her Royal Highness Princess Sasha. (978-1-60282-858-2)

The Chase by Jesse J. Thoma. When Isabelle Rochat's life is threatened, she receives the unwelcome protection and attention of bounty hunter Holt Lasher who vows to keep Isabelle safe at all costs. (978-1-60282-859-9)

The Lone Hunt by L.L. Raand. In a world where humans and praeterns conspire for the ultimate power, violence is a way of life... and death. A Midnight Hunters novel. (978-1-60282-860-5)

The Supernatural Detective by Crin Claxton. Tony Carson sees dead people. With a drag queen for a spirit guide and a devastatingly attractive herbalist for a client, she's about to discover the spirit world can be a very dangerous world indeed. (978-1-60282-861-2)

Beloved Gomorrah by Justine Saracen. Undersea artists creating their own City on the Plain uncover the truth about Sodom and Gomorrah, whose "one righteous man" is a murderer, rapist, and conspirator in genocide. (978-1-60282-862-9)

Cut to the Chase by Lisa Girolami. Careful and methodical author Paige Cornish falls for brash and wild Hollywood actress Avalon Randolph, but can these opposites find a happy middle ground in a town that never lives in the middle? (978-1-60282-783-7)

More Than Friends by Erin Dutton. Evelyn Fisher thinks she has the perfect role model for a long-term relationship, until her best friends, Kendall and Melanie, split up and all three women must reevaluate their lives and their relationships. (978-1-60282-784-4)

Every Second Counts by D. Jackson Leigh. Every second counts in Bridgette LeRoy's desperate mission to protect her heart and stop Marc Ryder's suicidal return to riding rodeo bulls. (978-1-60282-785-1)

Dirty Money by Ashley Bartlett. Vivian Cooper and Reese DiGiovanni just found out that falling in love is hard. It's even harder when you're running for your life. (978-1-60282-786-8)

Sea Glass Inn by Karis Walsh. When Melinda Andrews commissions a series of mosaics by Pamela Whitford for her new inn, she doesn't expect to be more captivated by the artist than by the paintings. (978-1-60282-771-4)

The Awakening: A Sisters of Spirits novel by Yvonne Heidt. Sunny Skye has interacted with spirits her entire life, but when she runs into Officer Jordan Lawson during a ghost investigation, she discovers more than just facts in a missing girl's cold case file. (978-1-60282-772-1)

Murphy's Law by Yolanda Wallace. No matter how high you climb, you can't escape your past. (978-1-60282-773-8)

Blacker Than Blue by Rebekah Weatherspoon. Threatened with losing her first love to a powerful demon, vampire Cleo Jones is willing to break the ultimate law of the undead to rebuild the family she has lost. (978-1-60282-774-5)

Silver Collar by Gill McKnight. Werewolf Luc Garoul is outlawed and out of control, but can her family track her down before a sinister predator gets there first? Fourth in the Garoul series. (978-1-60282-764-6)

The Dragon Tree Legacy by Ali Vali. For Aubrey Tarver time hasn't dulled the pain of losing her first love Wiley Gremillion, but she has to set that aside when her choices put her life and her family's lives in real danger. (978-1-60282-765-3)